THE
VIRTUOSO

Her life is her cadenza

Virginia Burges

ISBN: 0993077714
ISBN 13: 9780993077715

THE VIRTUOSO

"Music is the mediator between spiritual and sensual life."
~Ludwig van Beethoven

DEDICATION

Completion of *The Virtuoso* has marked the end of a seven year journey for me. Conceived and written whilst I was pregnant with my third baby (my eldest daughter), the first draft manuscript was then left gathering dust in a drawer until after the birth of baby number four, (my youngest daughter), two years later.

For some inexplicable reason, although I was exhausted and struggling to cope with my expanded family, I thought I'd give myself the challenge of finishing what I started.

After I decided to potentially publish it, I worked on improving each subsequent draft, and I couldn't have finished it without the help of many people during the sometimes arduous process of refinement.

Firstly, I'd like to thank Gary Smailes of Bubblecow, the editor who had the unenviable task of setting eyes on my less than polished work. His insights and advice have been invaluable on my quest to become a published author.

Having the feedback of friends and acquaintances who did me the honour of reading my various drafts has been no less valuable. I appreciated everyone's honest feedback. It would be remiss of me not to mention my supporters by name, so here goes: Sophie Shaw, Megan Beynon, Linda Grierson, Michael P. Ker, and of course my mum and my dear family, for putting up with me during my writing odyssey...

I'd like to acknowledge my editor at Satin Paperbacks, Nicky Fitzmaurice, who has done a sterling job on the final edit, ironing out those last few grammar niggles and formatting the manuscript for Kindle and paperback.

Graphic designer Matthew Parish created the original artwork for the cover, but it has since been re-designed for the Kindle market by the talented Caroline Jaques at Media Tribe.

As my protagonist is a concert violinist I knew I wanted to have a musical narrative to accompany the book. That vision has now been realised thanks to my collaboration with two very special and talented people: violinist Adelia Myslov and film composer Tim Johnson. A unique and exquisite contemporary classical theme for The Virtuoso has been recorded and is now available as an MP3 download on Amazon.

I am very grateful to everyone who has helped and supported me on my journey, and lastly, I hope you enjoy reading *The Virtuoso* as much as I've enjoyed writing it...

PUBLISHER LINKS:

SatinPaperbacks:
http://www.satinpaperbacks.com/
http://www.satinpublishing.co.uk
https://twitter.com/SatinPaperbacks
https://www.facebook.com/Satinpaperbackscom
Email: nicky.fitzmaurice@satinpaperbacks.com

Author Links:
Virginia Burges
http://rhapsodyinwords.com/the-virtuoso/
https://www.facebook.com/profile.php?id=10000
8618194206
https://twitter.com/Ginsterbabe

TABLE OF CONTENTS

PART I –
FATE KNOCKING AT
THE DOOR

1

A frisson of fear ran through Isabelle as she crouched down to place her violin carefully into its red velvet lined case. She stood, straightened her back and turned to see shiny, eager eyes trained on her. She didn't regard her talent as an inspiration to others, not even musicians. She did, however, think of herself as very fortunate to have made a stellar career out of doing something she loved; playing the violin.

Now it was time to give something back.

'Do you remember your first time?'

The question came from the grinning face of a young male student. His lopsided smile and intense stare hinted at how awestruck he was by the presence of the violin virtuoso, Isabelle Bryant.

'My first time?' Isabelle gave a nervous laugh. 'I presume you mean my first solo performance,' she said, hoping the class wouldn't notice her blushing. *Stupid! I'm the virtuoso...can't believe I'm acting like a shy debutante.*

She had reluctantly agreed to run her first Violin Masterclass; having once been a former student at the Royal Academy of Music herself.

She longed for the Masterclass Q & A session to end. She was in her element performing in front of an audience, and even coaching the students, but transformed into a bundle of nerves and quirky gestures when she was alone talking to groups of people. In fact, Isabelle loathed public speaking of any kind.

Heart racing, she took a deep breath and delved into the recesses of her memory. It was an intoxicating visit.

'No artist ever forgets their first major professional performance, and I'm no different. It was at The Royal Albert Hall, playing Beethoven's Violin Concerto, and it was a huge success for me because it was the launch pad of my career as a soloist.'

Seemingly unsatisfied with her answer the young man pursed his lips and proceeded to quiz her over the event. How had she remembered the music score? Was she nervous? What was it like playing at that venue with the London Symphony Orchestra?

Isabelle offered them her heartfelt thoughts;

'Every player gets nervous before a performance. The self-doubts can creep in, and that inner voice that lets you know that you played it less than perfectly last time is only too keen to point out where you made mistakes before. But the really great virtuosi use their awareness to overcome these self-inflicted obstacles to the music. You have to master the mental monsters to reach your peak. If I can do it you can do it too.'

The questioner looked bewildered, while the other students watched her with interest, hanging onto her every word. She cleared her throat.

'You may have noticed at certain times when you are playing that destructive thoughts can pop into your head. As a result maybe you've fumbled your fingering, or perhaps your intonation was off, or your vibrato was askew - or the phrasing, say. The key is not to let these disruptions take you away from your "flow state". I'm sure you've all experienced this state of mind, it's when you are in deep concentration but your action is almost effortless. When you begin to try to play, it just doesn't give you the same results. The less mental interference you experience the better your performance will be.'

Her mind drifted briefly to Paris. She could hear Jean-Christophe's authoritative voice, shrill and thick with accent over her music.

'Isabelle, ma cherie – sentez-vous la musique, ne pense pas!' She'd heard the command many a time while studying at the Conservatoire. *Feel the music.*

The young man noticed her eyes glazing over and quizzed her. 'How do you block it out?' He looked almost annoyed as if she was giving him the greatest secret in the world, but he couldn't fathom its meaning.

Isabelle took a deep breath. *I must keep calm under their scrutiny.*

'Apart from all the technique you've learned and the many hours of practise you've all undoubtedly put in to your development as musicians, there is yet another aspect of yourself you can use to reach your full potential.' Isabelle tried to remember what she had written in her preparation notes.

'You can use your awareness, the part of you that does not judge, but simply notices. If you've ever meditated, you will have experienced alpha brain waves. That's the optimum state to play in. For me personally, I like to clear my mind of thoughts and that helps me to practise with a relaxed concentration.'

The students were silent, their expectant faces turned towards hers. *Don't falter now Isabelle.*

'There are many facets to awareness, but the main thing to remember is to just observe. If you can remove yourself from your thoughts, and witness your experience of the music each time you perform, that will massively boost your learning ability each time you play. Also, by focussing on certain aspects of the score it can help you to divert the destructive dialogue in your head. So to recap; getting deeper into an aspect of the musical experience will help you to avoid those thoughts.'

The auditorium remained quiet as the students absorbed her words.

An unwelcome thought popped into her head as she paused to take a sip from her water bottle. *Why don't you practise what you preach Isabelle Bryant? If you are so good at using these techniques for playing your violin, then why can't you use them effectively for public speaking?*

There was something about playing her violin that transformed her like nothing else. Over the years she had learnt to throw herself into the music and dismiss her anxieties about playing in front of others, but take away her violin and she felt bare – vulnerable even. Such was her confidence with her music that people often were surprised at her reluctance to speak. It was the paradox of her personality. Knowing she would have to give Masterclasses at some point in her career, Isabelle had diligently worked on articulating the many facets of her success so that she could help students.

She forced her attention out again onto the students gathered before her, acutely aware of her every movement being watched, and her every word analysed. She remembered the young man asking her about her first professional performance. *I've gotten off-track a little.*

'On the night in question I recall feeling hot under the lights. They were so bright I couldn't really see in to the auditorium. The orchestra were right behind me, and the conductor actually winked at me. The Royal Albert Hall has such a grand ambience and interior setting; I couldn't help but feel a little intimidated. I mean here I was, barely out of my teens, standing on a stage that had hosted so many historic performances. I had big shoes to fill! I was terrified one of my strings would suddenly snap, or that my nervousness would make me break wind inappropriately.' Stifled giggles escaped into the air.

That has broken the ice a bit more.

'And then there would be the reviews to read afterwards. I kept tuning my violin excessively beforehand. I experienced a whole gamut of emotions, but underpinning all that was the desire to just play. Once that first note was out my fear began to dissipate. The important thing is that I gave myself permission to be scared. To make mistakes even. If I had gotten hung up on them then I would have allowed my nerves to interfere with my playing.'

Some of the students were scribbling in notebooks, and the young man was still staring at her, then he was asking her another question. 'How long did it take you to learn the Beethoven violin concerto?'

'All my life I guess...every time I played it was preparation for that moment. Obviously I learnt the notes over many, many practice sessions. It was the concerto I played when I won the Young Musician of the Year competition. It's burnt into my brain! I also listened regularly to Itzhak Perlman's recording of the work; as he has always been my inspiration on the violin.

'The Beethoven violin concerto is a very lyrical piece, perhaps not as difficult as the Tchaikovsky for example, but as you know, it's still scale laden and challenging in the higher positions.' Her voice was resonant as she recalled the feeling of euphoria at the completion of her debut solo performance. She always experienced a rush of energy immediately after every performance, but none since that first night had affected her quite so profoundly. It was as though her premier of the Beethoven had opened up to her a realm of possibilities and self-belief she dare not consider before that moment. In the glow of her memory it felt like yesterday rather than fifteen years previously.

The obstinate male student remarked, 'I read the critics labelled you "Beethoven's Babe"?'

His expression was smug, certain his comment would embarrass her. Isabelle obliged and her cheeks flamed for a brief moment. She had forgotten about the reviews. Her butterflies were flying in formation now and she established deliberate eye contact with him.

'Yes, I believe they did. I was very flattered at the time because he is my all-time favourite composer. He was such a genius, and I don't use that word lightly.

'We can all learn from his self-belief. I mean, to stay true to his artistic integrity in the shadow of Mozart, and write the works he wanted to, regardless of public opinion or against what was popular at the time, the "done" thing, that takes courage. He was so radical and innovative, and to produce the works he did with the loss of his hearing is almost beyond comprehension. I could go on all day, but needless to say I was so proud to have played his only violin concerto and to have done it justice. I haven't really played much Beethoven in my repertoire since then, with the exception of the Kreutzer Sonata in

A Major. Every artist has to vary their repertoire and try new things.'

The student finally relaxed his face and nodded in appreciation.

It seemed like only yesterday Isabelle had been in their shoes herself. She had made history by becoming the youngest ever winner of the BBC Young Musician of the Year Competition. It naturally followed that she was offered a scholarship to study at the Royal Academy of Music, and then she had completed her training at the Conservatoire in Paris, blossoming as an artist under the guidance of the legendary Jean-Christophe Charpentier.

Affectionately nicknamed "The Carpenter" by his students, and acknowledged by all his protégés as a master of his craft, he sculpted players into their own unique style. She remembered learning French very quickly. On her return to London Isabelle met Gerry Goldberg; a mature and experienced agent, but who still had a knack for new trends. He quickly became her mentor too, and rapidly she found herself on the international soloists' circuit, playing in concerts all over the world. Her first record deal with Decca swiftly followed. It was a heady time in her life, a whirlwind of success, all by her early twenties.

But her happiness was tinged by the fact that her mother had not been there to see it. She kept her grief inside, determined to make the most of her opportunities as homage to the sacrifices made by her parents.

Another question was being directed to her. 'At what age did you start playing?' Asked a sweet Japanese girl.

'Well, I was four if I remember correctly, and I didn't have much say in the matter! My mother was a soprano and my father taught music at the local comprehensive.'

She went on, explaining how her mother had pushed her hard after her first teacher had extolled the virtues of her talent with a little too much zeal. Her parents had worked hard to pay for regular lessons. They had insisted that she learn the Suzuki method, and there had usually been background music playing in their home. Isabelle had always espoused this method as it had enabled her to enjoy the music and play with competence and fearlessness. There was much nodding of heads as the group related to her remarks on sacrifice. To be the top of your field in any endeavour meant giving up so called normal activities. Like most of her contemporaries Isabelle had missed out on the parties that her peers had enjoyed. She was being prepared for a life on the stage. Whenever the family were invited to social events (usually because of their mother's connections) the Bryant trio of Jack, Isabelle and Lily were frequently asked to perform a musical recital in front of total strangers. Then the knot in her chest reminded her that it was painful to think about her family.

Looking round the newly built David Josefowitz Recital Hall, she noticed that the principal was now thankfully standing and bringing the session to a close. He praised Isabelle for her valuable time and insights. An enthusiastic applause echoed around the hall. Relief flooded over her, and for the first time she could appreciate her surroundings. She noticed how the light was reflecting on the wood panelled walls and floor, giving a warm atmosphere to the room. The acoustics had certainly been very crisp and resonant.

She reached for her semi-fitted, single-breasted tweed navy blazer, which was lying draped across the back of her chair. Gracefully she slid her arms in and buttoned it up over her sleeveless white shirt and smoothed it down over skinny fitting beige chinos, which flattered her long, slender and shapely legs. She had been right to wear her nude, flat ballet pumps which had kept her feet cool and comfortable for the duration of the Masterclass. Nonetheless she was savouring the prospect of a long soak in a warm lavender oil bath later that evening.

For two hours Isabelle had played excerpts of the major violin concertos and some of her favourite show pieces, as she gave practical coaching to a few of the students on their violins, and afterwards offered them advice and candid recollections of her path to virtuosity. It was a small price to pay for her current success, and she hoped she may have inspired some of the students to follow their musical paths, whether that meant careers as soloists, chamber musicians or as part of an international orchestra. She only wished that she hadn't felt so damn insecure, after all, her own success was irrefutable.

Maybe it went better than it felt. They seemed appreciative at the end. Hopefully I've made an impact.

With her case slung over her shoulders like a backpack, she made her way south on the underground from Regent's Park to London Victoria Station. The dreary grey sky hung like a heavy cloak over the platform. As the train jolted to halt, she quickly found a seat by the window and nestled her case vertically between her feet and knees. As more passengers entered the carriage she touched the edge of her violin case lightly, smiling with resigned humour as a passing stranger made a joke about her carrying a machine gun.

Her violin represented another limb to her, it was that precious. It felt so natural, like an extension of her body. She gently rubbed her neck which was feeling a little sore. The rough, red patch of skin on her neck just below her jaw was often mistaken for a love bite, when in fact it was what she affectionately referred to as a violinist's hickey. Many hours of gruelling practise had left their marks.

Her mind drifted to her earlier private viewing of the Academy's museum, where she had been shown round by the curator in person. She had spent a blissful afternoon paying particular awe and reverence to their recent acquisition of Italian virtuoso Giovanni Battista Viotti's 1709 Stradivarius, renamed as the Viotti ex-Bruce to honour its British donor, which the Academy extolled as one of the most important and well preserved Stradivarius violins in the world.

She had studied the sheen of the dark, pinky brown maple; picturing the old master craftsman huddled in his workshop in northern Italy; surrounded by the distinctive wooden shapes that would become so valuable over three hundred years later. Sadly there were so few of them remaining.

Her own violin, a modern Nagyvary, was crafted by the eminent Hungarian professor Joseph Nagyvary, who had spent his life studying the craftsmanship of Cremonese violin makers; namely Stradivarius and Guarnerius.

Nagyvary violins were made as closely to those of the ancient genius as possible, and there had been many debates about whether or not they actually sounded as good as those of the master. Isabelle adored its sonorous tonal qualities and projection power. If a Nagyvary violin had been good enough for Yehudi Menuhin to play for fifteen years, then it was good enough for her. Gerry, in his nothing is too much of a challenge for me attitude, had managed to do a deal with Joseph Nagyvary to loan Isabelle the instrument indefinitely. It was her most precious possession - except that she didn't own it.

Isabelle reflected she had been fortunate enough to have played on a Stradivarius at a couple of concerts; firstly at Carnegie Hall with the New York Philharmonic, for a programme of American composers. The slow movement of the Barber Violin Concerto Op. 14 had sounded particularly heart-breaking on it, with the silence in the room mirroring the audience's enthrallment. The

American Institute for Music had lent her the instrument for the occasion and she had been reluctant to return it.

The other time had been in Prague for the European Festival of Classical Music, almost a year ago. She and Howard had not long been married and a fierce debate had started in the music press about the tonal quality of the Stradivarius versus the Nagyvary. The scientific community had been the only objective party, with each opposing camp determined to prove their superiority.

The stuffy carriage and the gentle movement of the train as it trundled along were beginning to make her eyelids feel heavy. Her thoughts switched back to the students, they seemed so full of hope and ambition. She suspected they would trade places with her in a heart-beat. She knew she should be happy and she was - but there was a void in her life; and it seemed to be widening by the day.

Isabelle drifted into an elated sleep, unaware that the man opposite had, after one too many yawns, opened the window before continuing to read his book. The sudden burst of cold air roused her, and also her sim-mering irritation that Howard had not wanted to accom-pany her to the Royal Academy for the Masterclass. He too had been a student in their conductor's programme, and as far as she knew, there had been no other engage-ments in his diary. She was surprised he hadn't wanted to catch up with his old friends and combine some busi-ness with pleasure. After all, they had such little time together.

Her despair at his lack of support turned to resentment. *I'd do the same for him, especially if I knew he was feeling scared half to death.*

But she had coped without him, and basked in the satisfaction at having completed the session under her own steam. The principal had asked after him and expressed his approval at Howard's appointment with the London Sound Company. They were a rising contemporary orchestra, planning bold and exciting programmes, with the added bonus of positive media attention. Guest conductors had helped to raise their profile further, with performances given under some internationally respected figures.

He had enthused about what a handsome couple they made; but Isabelle knew all too well that appearances could be deceptive.

For a start, he couldn't know that Howard had delusions of grandeur about being the next Simon Rattle, because he was careful to hide his ambition in public. Howard's mother Celia had pulled some matronly strings, and his ensuing appointment to the LSC had been both lucky and inspired.

Then there was their marriage.

It had all started so promisingly. From their meeting backstage after one of her performances, they quickly progressed to a serious romance. At the time it seemed like a match made in heaven, but she had little experience of the opposite sex. Just like speaking in public, dating had been an activity avoided. Lately their relationship had been spiralling out of control and the honeymoon period was now a distant memory. Her chest tightened again. *How can my professional career be up in the stratosphere while my personal life seems to be breaking faster than some tabloid salacious scandal?*

They had been arguing of late about Isabelle not taking the Miller family name. She tried to reason with Howard that it was in her maiden name of Bryant that she had excelled as virtuoso, and to change it now might damage her reputation and her position as one of the most popular musicians in the world. After so many years of intense study and hard work she considered her artistic identity as sacrosanct.

Howard of course had a different perspective. Secretly he hoped Isabelle's popularity would rub off on his career, and also saw it as an affront to the stature of his family that she was being so stubborn in this matter. His mother had berated him for not agreeing the issue with Isabelle before the wedding, pointing out that the new Mrs Miller was showing disrespect and disloyalty to the family. After months of wrangling they had agreed to disagree, but the issue hung in the air like a discordant note.

Isabelle leaned against the window and took in the rolling Downs that passed her window every few seconds. The cloud had cleared progressively as the train reached further south to reveal areas of piercing blue sky.

She had found living in the Sussex countryside a refreshing change from living in London. Still, she never quite felt that she belonged to the clique of gossiping neighbours apparently under the spell of Howard's fearsome mother Celia. The countryside however, was stunning, and now even more so as the leaves were turning to vibrant hues of orange and red. She loved watching them dance in the wind as gusts whipped round the trees, sending them into swirling masses of colour, marvelling at the beauty of nature's choreography.

In a moment of nostalgia, Isabelle pictured the penthouse apartment she had lived in during her early career. The art deco building had a faded facade of dark bricks which was adorned by jade green balustrades around the exterior of each level. It was a familiar landmark on the corner of Grosvenor Place, overlooking Dorset Square, offering a small sanctuary of greenery. From her flat Isabelle could see the Victorian architecture of Marylebone Station and the skyline of North West London.

She knew that dwelling on the past wasn't helpful at the best of times, but she found herself wishing for the good old days before she was married; when she and Gerry made all the decisions surrounding her career. There had been no distractions then, no arguments and no jealousy to erode her confidence.

Howard's hatred of Gerry was another area of friction in their marriage. In Howard's mind Gerry hadn't helped with his persistent opinion that she should remain as a Bryant, assuming he was only thinking about his commissions. Howard detested agents in general.

His cynical view of them being leeches on the professional skills of performers did not endear him to the musicians, who viewed them as a necessity in order to enjoy successful careers that were well managed.

Howard's conducting career had taken a while to get going, and even now it wasn't comparable to Isabelle's success as a virtuoso violinist. He was determined to keep up with her at all costs it seemed, and his obsession with his reputation stemmed from his rampant ego, which she guessed his mother had fuelled from a very early age.

For months Isabelle had sensed something eating away at him. He was always snappy if a rehearsal had gone badly, and several violinists had walked out lately in a fury over his rants. Maybe they could take it from a more distinguished conductor, but this baton holder was barely thirty two, and didn't have the musical pedigree to get away with being a prima donna just yet.

She had tried to broach the situation and talk him round to being more amenable, but he had cut her short, saying that she should stick to what she was good at and not interfere with his career. His barely audible parting remark, as he turned on his heel to avoid her probing was;

'Bloody string players!'

Her cellist friend Sebastian knew one of the offended violinists, who had vented to him about Howard's ego and his lack of respect for the musicians. What annoyed him the most was the fact that Howard took all the credit when the performance was going well, but he yelled at them mercilessly if things weren't going exactly how he wanted them to. He told Sebastian in no uncertain terms that a conductor who didn't appreciate that it was the musicians that brought the music to life wouldn't get very far and furthermore, his intellectual snobbery was alienating half of the orchestra.

They all understood that the score itself wasn't the work. You had to play the music, not the instrument. The subjective experience of the audience was what the composer intended, and Howard should "get over himself" for thinking he alone could make the score come alive.

Isabelle agreed with him. Howard seemed to have a romantic notion that his conducting skills alone afforded him special status regarding the interpretation of a piece of work. *So much for humility!*

It reminded her of a particularly embarrassing episode during their time in Prague, when a nosy journalist had been sitting at the next table in the Four Seasons' Hotel restaurant, and had overheard Howard bulldozing her and Gerry and the conductor for the concert.

Howard had been drinking steadily all afternoon, but she hadn't noticed his heavy consumption due to her hectic practise sessions, and by then it was too late to avert a scene.

Howard was convinced that the Stradivarius sounded better, and was arguing with Gerry, who postulated that it was hard to tell the difference. Isabelle and the conductor had exchanged worried glances across the table, and some other diners in the vicinity had begun to stare at Howard's red face contorting as he blustered at Gerry.

When Howard had paused for breath Gerry casually remarked in his deep drawl,

'Look Howard, the average person in the street who comes to listen to these concerts, or buy the music, aren't going to have that good an ear. Maybe amongst us professionals we can have a calm debate, but surely the punters are the ones who matter, after all without them there is no music industry.'

Isabelle's stomach sunk. Howard was approaching nuclear fall-out, but she felt helpless as to what she could do to limit the damage.

Howard had taken off his small round-rimmed glasses and suddenly exploded.

'What the fuck do you know Gerry? You're just an agent, not an artist. Keep your goddamned opinions to yourself!'

Their mouths had fallen open.

'Howard! That's enough,' Isabelle had interjected; shooting Gerry an apologetic look.

Howard's foul temper always made him lash out like an injured animal.

His chair had tumbled backwards as he stood towering over Gerry, who didn't bat an eyelid. Then he had snorted and stormed off to their hotel room; leaving Isabelle to explain his actions to a bewildered conductor and her old friend, who knew only too well what he could be like.

An article covering the Prague Festival had been printed the following week in the Sunday Times.

The comments concerning Isabelle's performance of The Lark Ascending and other selected pieces had been complimentary, but were unfortunately accompanied by a scathing sentence or two highlighting the behaviour of a certain English conductor. Although the writer hadn't named Howard, he had made life very unpleasant for him. It had finished on the words, "A conductor who doesn't know how to conduct himself!"

Yet again Howard had blown his stack, threatening to sue the paper for libel; until Isabelle had persuaded him that he'd have a hard time proving they were making defamatory remarks about his character – his name did not appear once.

The train juddered as it approached the station, bringing Isabelle back to the present with a jolt. She looked at her watch. *Oh God!*

Her stomach was churning, she felt sick at the thought of being on the end of Howard's wrath again. He would be furious that she had kept him waiting for so long. Ironically she had always admired his promptness, but not today. She doubted he'd even be there still; he would have lost patience long ago and returned home.

I'll probably have to take a taxi back, but how am I going to call one with a dead phone?

She gathered her case and handbag and stepped into the cool air which revived her a little, and then that familiar voice, laced with contempt, greeted her on the platform.

'Isabelle! What time do you call this?' He tapped his watch and folded his arms. 'you're late!'

Isabelle flashed him a contrite smile. 'I'm sorry Howard.'

'Mrs Miller you may be a talented violinist but you can't manage your time to save your life. I've wasted an hour sat in this bloody car park!'

'You have every right to be cross Howard, but I couldn't help it. You know what a sucker I am for ancient Italian violins. I didn't want to miss seeing the Viotti Strad at the academy, but it meant I missed my original train.'

'Ever heard of a mobile phone?'

Isabelle remained conciliatory. 'I tried to call, but my battery died. I meant to charge it last night but I forgot; I was so pre-occupied with preparing for my first Masterclass.'

Not asking how the Masterclass had gone, he simply grunted and said,

'Did you remember me to the principal?'

She chose to ignore his question, knowing it would wind him up further. 'It went well, thanks for asking.'

Howard raised an eyebrow, muttering something under his breath before turning his back on her. *What a pig, he was acting like he had his baton shoved up his arse.*

They started walking towards the car. Howard began to button up his waistcoat in the brisk wind. Isabelle on the other hand didn't feel cold from the elements, but his icy greeting was another thing altogether.

They drove in silence back to Causeway Cottage, the Miller family ancestral home passed down through many generations. She had to admit, it was a beautiful sandstone Georgian country house, with picture book sash windows and wisteria adorning the front wall. The view from the rear of the house was simply magnificent, overlooking the South Downs in all their grand, undulating glory.

As soon as they got home Isabelle put her violin back into its cupboard in the music room, just off the first floor landing. Two large windows offered views of green rolling fields. She had fallen in love with the room at first sight. She was quite particular about her playing environment. The sun would set at the back of the house, casting a warm glimmer and reflection through the glass that was magical. It had been Howard's study before they were married, but after relentless pestering he finally moved out so that Isabelle could practice there. Her favourite print of Beethoven composing and deep in concentration, painted by Josef Stieler, hung on the wall alongside Andy Warhol's more colourful version. The sight of Ludwig looking down on her gave her inspiration every morning when she came in for practice.

The painted jade green walls were lined with book cases and piles of music scores. A Bösendorfer piano sat in the corner, which was mainly used when she needed to collaborate with a pianist for sonata performances. The wooden floor boards creaked in certain places, and her treasured, sumptuous Persian rug added a touch of luxury to the room. Isabelle was staring out over the downs when Howard popped his head round the door. 'I've still got some last minute programming to do for the Petworth Charity Concert, which no doubt will take me a few hours, so I'll see you tomorrow.'

'Okay. Maybe it would be nice for me to help you? After all I am supposed to be one of the featured soloists. I don't even know what you want me to play yet-'

'You don't need to worry about that.' He was terse. 'We can talk about it in the morning. I have to run everything past mother first. You know she's employed by the council, so the pressure's on me to come up with something special on our home turf.'

Isabelle sighed. She tried not to show her frustration at being excluded from their home concert; but it hurt her to feel that she was not deemed suitable to contribute to the concert's repertoire, or to even have a say in her own performance. Being side-lined by Howard and his domineering mother was a frustrating end to a successful day.

Before she could protest further Howard had vanished into his study downstairs. He was becoming more reclusive of late and she felt she had lost her connection with him. Her jubilant mood was waning fast. She was anxious that he didn't want to spend as much time with her as when they were first married. The sex had been okay to start with, but now it was irregular and mundane, and usually all over in a few minutes of frantic grunting. Isabelle craved cuddles, loving attention and true intimacy - but now there was no warmth.

Pulling out her mobile from the bottom of her bag she wandered into the bedroom and put it on charge, so she could send a quick text to Hortense. She needed their friendship more than ever at the moment. She had no family nearby and she rarely saw her cellist friend Sebastian, except when she was working with the London Philharmonic on a project.

Hortense was her oldest and closest friend, the daughter of a Louisiana French jazz singer who had worked with her own mother Julia. Together they had grown up in a quiet, leafy Beaconsfield street in middle class comfort.

Isabelle had studied the violin, while Hortense had trained her vocal cords. Although Hortense was ten years older than Isabelle, and had come from a very different background; their love of music and life had drawn them together. In fact, she often felt closer to Hortense than to her own sister Lily. Hortense had always been a somewhat motherly figure in Isabelle's life, but she seemed to take on the role even more so after her mother died. She'd had difficulty pronouncing the French name in childhood, and so it had been abbreviated simply to "H".

They looked very different too, with Isabelle's creamy olive skin, long brunette hair and skinny frame, she'd been a late developer; not getting her first period until the age of fifteen, only to fervently wish it had been even later when the event that signalled her womanhood had finally arrived.

Hortense was of African American descent, and usually wore her hair in braids. She was shorter and plumper than Isabelle, but what she lacked in stature she made up for with personality. She was as strong as an ox, with a beguilingly husky voice, and she projected a booming laugh that infected anyone in its vicinity.

H had cautioned Isabelle only once in her life; and that had been prior to her marriage with Howard. She remembered the conversation with a shiver as she undressed and slid beneath the sheets.

'Issy, you gotta think this through more. I know you've enjoyed his company, and he mixes in the right circles, but there's more to marriage than companionship and connections. Trust me, I know!' Her own marriage to jazz music producer Raymond Lafayette, had been the subject of a Channel 4 documentary aiming to extrapolate the components in a successful marriage. H always said it boiled down to alignment.

'Have you discussed important issues like children?'

'Sort of...'

'Kids are a big part of your relationship, it's a fundamental issue. Do you both feel the same about it?'

Hortense had an uncanny sense for deceit, and Isabelle, worried she would guess the truth had blurted out, 'H I'm too busy with my career to think about it at the moment. I guess some time in the future it would be nice, but Howard needs to concentrate on his career too. It would be a distraction at the moment.'

'Isabelle Bryant, my bullshit-ometer is redlining! You're starting to sound like his mother now. What has gotten into you? Don't you think it would broaden your perspective on life, give you something else other than music to live for?'

Coming from anyone else Isabelle would have told them to mind their own business, but she had too much respect for Hortense.

They had always stayed in close contact, even when Hortense and Raymond had moved back to New Orleans for two years. After that they'd decided to adopt an orphaned young boy called Louis. During that time Isabelle herself had been touring the world, establishing her musical credentials.

'H, that's just the way it is. I'm sure Howard will come round to the idea in time.'

Hortense had smiled and put her arm around Isabelle,

'As long as you know in your heart that this is right for you and he makes you happy Issy, that's all that matters.'

The thing with self-denial was that you never saw it until it was too late. Deep down she had known Hortense was right. There was a difference of opinion that she couldn't see a way round. At thirty-two she was beginning to feel her body's biological clock craving motherhood, and she didn't know if she could wait forever for Howard to change his mind.

She had always suspected there was a hidden agenda behind Howard's proposal, but hadn't paid any attention to the fleeting troublesome thoughts that interrupted her new found happiness. Loneliness was not an option for her. Always impatient to tackle the next big thing in her life, she had jumped in both feet first. She wasn't going to be one of these highly successful but single career women.

A wave of repressed intuitions carried her on a current that she feared might crash her onto the rocks at some unknown date in the future, but still she had chosen to ignore it. She justified to herself that Howard might not be her twin soul, but they seemed to get on well enough to start with. Her blistering schedule gave her no time for romance, and it was a breath of fresh air for someone up and coming in the industry to pay her some attention. She persuaded herself that she would be able to talk him round to having kids. It was to be an assumption made amongst many that would take her life off its plotted course and into uncharted territory.

Isabelle could make out Howard's voice on the phone, and sat up in bed to strain her ears. It sounded like he was talking to the director of the London Sound Company. Because of his connections Howard had been in a position to choose his own orchestra to perform at the Petworth charity event. Howard and his mother had persuaded the council to use the LSC based on a no fee arrangement. This would be the first time they were due to collaborate together on a project, and Isabelle was wondering why she felt so apprehensive about it.

I've got to hold it together and hope nobody spots the cracks; or more likely, the crevasses in our relationship.

The cream of West Sussex society would be there dressed in their finest, as well as honest hard-working locals, who went every year for some high calibre entertainment in an historical setting. The outdoor stage would be covered, with the sound travelling to the far reaches of the spectacular park and its surroundings. Even the deer would be serenaded that night.

Her sense of foreboding was holding back the sleep and she tossed and turned for an hour, eventually curling up in a comforting foetal position. Her mind slowly quietened, although she was still conscious of the empty space beside her; before finally succumbing to an uneasy slumber.

2

Isabelle stirred, rubbing her slightly puffy and itchy eyes as sunlight peeked round the edges of her gold damask bedroom curtain. Her phone bleeped.

Howard rolled over. 'Can't you switch that fucking thing off at night?'

'Sorry darling, did you get a late one?' Her tone was deliberate. As a peace offering she leant over to kiss him on the cheek and when he didn't move, she slid out of bed and headed into the shower. The warm, steady flow of water slowly revived her mind and body. She came out of the bathroom wrapped only in a towel, her dark hair sticking to her glistening shoulders. Howard appeared in front of her. He was holding her mobile up with a look of controlled fury. A reddish colour was seeping up his neck and his eyes were bulging. Suddenly her heart was pounding.

'How could you say those things about me to that
interfering black bitch?'

'Well, I'm not going to converse with you while you're
being a racist bastard!'

She snatched the phone from his grasp, almost dropping her towel in her haste, and retreated to the bathroom; slamming the door. She fumbled the lock, but
it seemed Howard had gone downstairs in disgust. She
perched on the edge of the bath, her face burning. She
could feel her indignation and rage at Howard's actions
a few months prior flaring up again. *I should have known
better than to leave my mobile lying around. He's already
proved what a reprobate he is after the stunt he pulled over my
U.S. tour.*

She recalled vividly the sick feeling in the pit of her
stomach when she happened to be looking through her
sent items on her email account, only to find that she'd
sent a message marked as high importance to Gerry that
she couldn't remember writing.

Her mind ran back over their ensuing argument:

'Howard! How could you?'

He had been watering the roses when Isabelle had
appeared flushed and agitated on the patio, clasping a
tear stained printout that was flapping in the breeze.

'Oh, that-'

'Is that all you've got to say?'

'Yes, I cancelled your American tour. I was acting
in your best interests Isabelle, but I know you won't believe me. Goldberg is fleecing you. He arranged for

you to perform with five orchestras on each side of the continent, with only four weeks to fit it all in. Not to mention, the time it would have taken you to learn the different repertoires they wanted. I've done you a favour.' Isabelle glared at him. 'It's been a long time since you last did a gruelling foreign tour like that. Plus we have commitments at home you know.'

'No I don't! Exactly what commitments Howard? What could be more important than me doing my job, especially during the times when I'm in demand? These opportunities don't just pop-up every day.'

'Well, neither does the LSC's and my first appearance at the Royal Albert Hall. We've been asked to play Elgar's Serenade for strings. It's a programme purely for British composers. I need you with me.'

Isabelle raised her arms in disbelief. 'That's just about the most selfish, unscrupulous, perfidious thing you've ever done Howard.' He looked sheepishly away, accidentally tipping the water over his feet.

'I'll tell you what favour you've done for me Howard. I've just come off the phone with Gerry. He can't reinstate the bookings. It sounds like they've already lined up Joshua Bell to replace me. Your actions have prompted the American organisers to think that I was wantonly messing them around. Tongues have wagged, and now it appears that I'm no longer welcome stateside.'

Howard had seemingly ignored her rant and continued to pull his secateurs from the nearby gardening kit. 'Let's tell the whole village shall we?'

'No wonder Gerry has been off with me lately. The only thing I've managed to salvage out of this whole fiasco is my professional friendship and credibility with Gerry.'

Howard adjusted his glasses. 'More's the shame. You should let me manage your career, you don't need him.'

Isabelle's eyes widened. 'I can't believe you Howard. Gerry's done a great job and besides, loyalty is something I value. If I don't have my professional integrity I don't have anything. Would you have decided that my performance in the BBC Last Night of the Proms last month wasn't in my best interest as well?'

'Now you're being truculent. Anyway, last night is different.'

'I don't see how,' Isabelle said through gritted teeth.

To add insult to injury Celia had been lurking in the conservatory, having eavesdropped on their row after hearing Isabelle's raised voice from her nearby annexe. Naturally she had sided with Howard.

'A wife's place is by her husband.'

Isabelle knew she had no choice but to accompany Howard, but she flung one last gripe into the air. 'I feel like a prisoner more than a partner.'

Her attention finally flooded back to H's text message, she clicked onto the text icon:

> **Issy call me after lunch, lecturing this am. Hope that idiot isn't upsetting you again. Love H.**

They ate breakfast in stony silence, until Isabelle could bear it no longer.

'Howard, I'm sorry if H's text has upset you, try not to be mad with me. I was only trying to understand how I could support you better and at the same time not lose myself. You know that H doesn't mince her words, and I have no control over what she says. I simply told her that I was feeling a bit left out of late, like I couldn't get through to you. Marriage is meant to be a two way street, and I feel like you've been shutting me out of whatever has been bothering you lately. I just want to help, and it makes me feel redundant that you won't let me.'

She gulped her orange juice, trying to gauge Howard's reaction but his expression was inscrutable.

'What's happening to us? I don't know if you still love me or not. When we do make love you don't show me any tenderness. We don't go out and socialise like we used to. We don't talk about having children, and at this rate my ovaries will wither and perish! You sacrificed my US tour so that I could support your career, but I can't neglect mine completely. It makes me sad that our lives are being pulled in opposite directions, but it's not fair for me to do all the giving and you all the taking.'

She blundered on. 'I'm beginning to feel like I'm just a trophy wife! You and your mother show me off to your friends when it suits you, and then discard me when you want to focus on your own agendas. We should be able to share our triumphs and our disappointments together. It's almost like there's some competition between us.' He still did not say anything. 'You haven't got anything to prove to me, only that you still love me.'

She placed her empty bowl in the deep sink and started to rub his rigid shoulders.

'Have you quite finished?' His tone froze her to the spot. 'How can you be so selfish? The world doesn't revolve around you, although I guess you think it should. You may be used to your sycophantic fans and that bloody Goldberg treating you like some goddess, but round here we just get on with things.'

Her heart sank. He brushed her trembling hands away from his neck where she could see the veins beginning to swell, fearing they might burst with the force of his anger.

'The honeymoon period is over, you need to grow up. I can't be doing with your constant neurotic blubbering - I've got to get my head down and make an impression at the LSC. I should make principal conductor in two years if I work hard. It's okay for you, you've already made it to the top of your tree. Just give me some fucking space to get to mine.'

'But surely the joy of life is in getting there? Together...' Her voice started to waver. His neck twisted round like plasticine and his eyes bore into hers.

'All I ask is that you talk to me about your pathetic little fantasies, rather than involving that Lafayette woman. Before we know it the whole of London will be gossiping about us. That's the last thing I need right now.

She's got a mouth as wide as the Dartford Tunnel, and she certainly knows how to use it.'

'Firstly, I would talk to you more often if you would just listen. Secondly, they're not fantasies; they're feelings and thirdly, I don't appreciate your unfounded criticisms of one of the most revered jazz singers on the planet, who you know full well is my best friend.'

Howard raised his eyebrows and sneered.

'Does it bother you that she's black? Or is it because she's successful as well and she doesn't take any crap from you or anyone else? Tell me Howard, what exactly is your problem with H? Do all black people make you feel insecure, or is it because you might actually be a little bit scared of her?'

'Now you're being over imaginative,' he said. 'I just find her brash and abrasive. It's nothing to do with skin colour. She just irritates me. Listen - our marriage is nobody else's business, and you shouldn't let her influence you so much. It's up to us how we run our lives.'

'So basically what you're saying Howard, is that I only do the projects that you deem suitable, do as I'm told and be grateful I married into such a perfect family!'

Howard had already turned his back on her and was heading for the hallway. 'This is going nowhere!' He grabbed his jacket and briefcase.

'We'll talk again tonight when you've calmed down. Whining and insulting me and my family will just make me lose my temper, and you don't want that do you?'

A few seconds later the door slammed, and she heard the familiar sound of his Jag purring out of the drive. Isabelle paced up and down past the grandfather clock that stood in the hallway. Their little spats often left her feeling frustrated and full of nervous energy.

Her head was at bursting point when the phone rang and Gerry's dulcet tones were soothing in her ear.

'Hi Issy! It's Gerry. Can you talk?'

'I can now that Howard Hitler has left the building. Sorry Gerry, we just had a humdinger, my head's spinning. I should really go and tackle the Brahms concerto now, but I'm just not in the right frame of mind.'

'Well, fear not, for I am the bringer of glad tidings to my favourite client.' He paused slightly. '*High Notes* Magazine readers have voted you as the sexiest classical musician of the year, and James Jackson from BBC radio 3 wants to interview you on his musician of the month spot at 7pm.'

'Gerry, I want to be known for my talent, not my looks. Anyhow, you know I'm a nervous wreck when it comes to public speaking and stuff like that.'

'Issy, it's all in the studio, there's only you and him. Besides, you know it only matters that the critics continue to write about your talent. My job is to make sure you remain popular, and in the public eye, or even ear... on the top spot my dear.'

Gerry had a knack of persuading her to do things that she didn't really want to do. He was practically her surrogate uncle. He wasn't handsome as more cuddly, with his twinkly brown eyes set in smiley round features, topped by a balding head. His short stocky body had on occasions almost squashed the air right out of her lungs with one of his affectionate bone crushing hugs.

Isabelle couldn't help but point out that millions of other people would be eavesdropping on their conversation and that constituted public speaking in her book. Reluctantly she acknowledged to herself she'd have to overcome her media phobia sometime. After all, she had managed to run a two hour master class only the day before. It would certainly give her a much needed confidence boost especially after all the recent unpleasant exchanges with Howard.

'Okay Gerry, you twisted my arm again. Can you email me the details? Remember I agreed to play a week on Saturday for the Petworth Charity Concert, with Howard and the LSC, so as long as it doesn't clash you can confirm it with James.'

'That's my girl. You know it makes sense. They want you in three weeks, so that should give you plenty of time to prepare. It'll be an ideal opportunity to promote your performance of the Brahms violin concerto next month at the Festival Hall.'

'I know; you rascal. I know. Speak soon.' She hung-up and went to make herself a cup of Earl Grey tea. She felt her mood lifting and the tightness in her chest had eased. She headed up to the music room.

She sat for a while in quiet meditation, a habit she had employed ever since Hortense had mentioned how much it had helped her to focus before singing. Isabelle had found it surprisingly helpful too in clearing her mind before a session. A few minutes passed and she opened her eyes and fixed her gaze on her hands.

They were wiry with long graceful fingers, although keeping her nails short made them look a bit more rugged than she would have liked. Regular manicures meant that they didn't pluck on her strings or interfere with her vibrato. Her fingers knew every inch of the Nagyvary's neck. She could place them accurately on the strings, motioning her wrist in varying degrees of intensity to achieve a heavenly vibrato while her right hand and lower arm directed the bow across the strings with perfect precision. Big slow Adagios were her speciality, but she was equally adept at faster movements and soloist's Cadenzas that crossed the strings frequently, requiring amazing dexterity, intonation and speed.

Aside from impeccable technique and being true to the score, she knew that artistic interpretation and a unique personal style was what made the top soloists stand out. They all had their own particular flair; hers was more akin to the likes of legendary masters like Yehudi Menuhin, Jascha Heifetz and Itzhak Perlman, rather than the modern pyrotechnic displays by some of her contemporaries.

The practice session did not go well. Her intonation had been dubious, and it felt like the Brahms D major violin concerto was going to be elusive in her mastery of it. She was working at the very top of the finger board. She angled her elbow in towards her chest to allow her fingers to reach the highest notes of the melancholy second movement. She couldn't imagine why Brahms himself had referred to it as a "feeble Adagio". The violin had to share the limelight with the oboe in singing its sweet and poignant melody.

The whole concerto was challenging, and the multiple-stopping, chord laden, scale-electric third movement, which had provided the inspiration for the evocative song "Don't Cry For Me Argentina" for the musical Evita, would probably be played well-below par in her current emotional mire.

Her concentration waning, she decided to break for lunch, and after a hurried bowl of soup she dialled H's number.

'Hi Issy, how are you doing?'

'Oh H, I've had the morning from hell! He took my phone while I was in the shower this morning and saw your text. Needless to say he wasn't impressed that I'd involved you in our problems. Every time we converse now its effing this and effing that.'

'Slow down Issy and tell me what happened,' Hortense said, in her deep husky tone.

'He started insulting you, and just brushed over my concerns like I meant nothing to him. I know I'm being selfish but H, I don't know what to do...it's just one battle after another at the moment. It's like he's hiding under a veneer of self-loathing and ambition; if ever there was a paradox. He's completely shut me out and turned into a control freak.'

'Turned? That's debatable. He's always had those tendencies; it's just that now you can really see them. The impression I get is there's a little boy inside desperately wanting approval, but he's not willing to let go of him yet. He has too much unresolved anger and his over inflated ego means he can't love anyone without strings attached. He's what I would call an emotional vampire.'

'You can say that again; he sucks the joy right out of my life. What should I do H?'

'Other than divorce him you mean? I'm sorry Issy, I don't mean to be flippant, but there's probably not much you can do to change a narcissist whose sense of entitlement and self-importance have made him cold and withholding. The only thing you can do is avoid him, but that's not really conducive to marriage. Mind you, neither is Howard.'

Isabelle was silent.

'Listen, why don't we meet up? Sounds to me like you need cheering up after all this aggro with Howard.'

Isabelle always felt energised after being around Hortense, she was one of those people who could lift your mood with just a smile.

'Thanks for your concern. Actually I'm coming up to London three weeks on Saturday for a radio interview with James Jackson. Perhaps we could meet up in the afternoon beforehand? I'll come to you in Notting Hill if you like.' She could hear the faint rustle of the pages flipping in H's diary.

'Great. I think Raymond is taking Louis to see the Gunners play Spurs, some North London Derby. I don't mind being a football widow if it means I can catch up with the sexiest classical star of the year.'

Isabelle could barely contain her excitement. 'So you read the article then?'

'Sure did honey. It's about time too. You don't just dazzle them with your playing. Look after yourself and don't get down. You can't afford to lose your edge.'

'I'm going to the newsagents in the village now to pick up a copy of *High Notes*. When Gerry told me this morning I was in a real stew, but now I'm curious. I'll call you on the day just before I leave. Thanks H, for putting up with me. See you then.'

'Look forward to it Issy.'

As Isabelle strode down the road she felt better for some country air, and anticipation mingled with the fresh oxygen in her lungs.

The landlord of the Angel Inn was sweeping dead leaves from the path as she walked by, and she recoiled from the pungent smell as smoke rose like a grey snake from the chimney. Eric nodded and smiled at her as she passed his popular watering hole, with its freshly cream painted Georgian façade and wide bay window. She waved back. He was one of the few genuine neighbours she liked and trusted in this village. He appeared more haggard than usual, dark circles hung heavy beneath his kind hazel eyes, and his hair seemed greyer than ever in the bright daylight. Too many late nights and smoky atmospheres had taken their toll on his health. But for all that he was a strong person, emotionally more than physically she thought and he always had a smile for her, like a kindred spirit in a town bereft of friendly faces.

On the rare occasions she ventured into the Angel for a drink he would lift his glass and offer a toast to her talent, then whisper to her over the bar about how stuck up he thought Celia Miller was, and how she had upset a lot of people in the village; and that Isabelle must have the patience of a saint to put up with her as a mother-in-law.

Isabelle could never be unequivocally honest. She might be even more compromised in the Miller family if she had been overheard bad mouthing them in the Angel Inn, only yards from their home. She had appreciated his obvious affinity more deeply than she could show. She wondered when and how Celia had alienated herself from such a kind man. Thank God Celia had her own annexe at the back of the house and was rarely around to disturb her.

Caught up in her thoughts, Isabelle was now at the entrance to the newsagent and on reaching the magazine section, she deftly lifted the lone copy of *High Notes* from the shelf. She paid the assistant and was back out the door in seconds. It was silly not wanting anyone to see her, but she quickened her step as she returned to Causeway Cottage.

Back inside the kitchen with the kettle boiling, and the familiar sound of the grandfather clock chiming from in the hallway, she opened the magazine. Her dry thumbs flicked through the glossy pages until she found the page referring to the annual reader awards. She skimmed over the various different categories: most influential composer, best conductor, best solo performance, best newcomer, most popular orchestra and finally the sexiest musician of the year. Her gaze settled on the print. Just as Gerry explained, there was her name in bold. She couldn't help thinking it was a shame that she hadn't been chosen for the best solo performance category, but that honour had gone to a relatively unknown pianist. Each of the category winners had a brief resume written about them and hers read:

> *Isabelle Bryant, AKA Beethoven's Babe! She is a beautiful young star who started her amazing career with what is now widely regarded as the most heart wrenching and reflective recording of his one and only Violin Concerto in D Major, giving a performance of maturity that belied the inexperience of the young virtuoso. Since her debut Isabelle Bryant has performed all the major violin concertos and mainstream repertoire in venues across the globe, in an outstanding career that has shown no signs of stagnating. She particularly wowed audiences*

in Milan with her interpretation of a thrilling Paganini number attired in a red lace shift dress.

As Isabelle scanned the page she saw that beneath their resume each nominated artist had their own "fact sheet" that listed important recordings, details of performances and some historical background. She was stunned at what they could find out about her. Then Gerry's verbal mastery sprang to mind and she was thankful they hadn't printed her inside thigh measurement. Her eyes fixed on a picture of her with the Nagyvary pressed to her jaw, dressed in a black silk playing gown. It was strapless and figure hugging, on account of Gerry's insisting on a more contemporary look for her. In his view, "having it and flaunting it" were not mortal sins.

During a previous discussion about her performance attire, Howard had vehemently pointed out that it detracted from her musical pedigree if the audience thought she was just a sex symbol. Isabelle ignored his comments as the music media had mostly written about her playing talent. Sales of her latest album, *The Virtuoso* had been healthy, and it had given her some satisfaction to know that she and Gerry had decided together what repertoire to record for it.

She couldn't help but notice someone must have done some serious research to find the early reference to Beethoven. It reminded her of the male student's comments mocking her at the Royal Academy the day before. She felt a burst of pride, but wasn't sure if Ludwig might be turning in his grave at the thought of anyone being labelled as his "babe", except for perhaps the secret identity of his Immortal Beloved. It was a story she had almost become obsessed by.

Despite many theories and deductions based on the letters of the time and the women known to Beethoven, scholars could only make an informed guess as to her identity, with no consensus of agreement on one individual from the list of contenders. Beethoven had left the world one last mystery after his death. Tearing her thoughts away from Beethoven's tempestuous love life she peered up to the conductor nominations. Howard's name was not among them.

She glanced at her watch, time was pressing on and Howard could be back any minute. Panic erupted inside her, she didn't want to be caught poring over what her husband would consider a trashy publication and a vain waste of time. She stashed the folded magazine in the pine table draw, and leaned back into the pine rocking chair with her drink.

3

'And now, ladies and gentlemen; The Petworth Charity Concert in aid of the British Red Cross is pleased to announce the arrival of our very own local celebrity and violin virtuoso – Isabelle Bryant!' The Mayor almost sung into the microphone.

She saw Howard's jaw twitch when her name was mentioned. Her apprehension grew. A soft breeze was blowing, and she ventured onto the stage, with her gown of red silk organza flowing gracefully behind her. As she reached the front of the stage and smiled to the audience Howard winked at her. His gesture caught her off guard, but it had a calming effect. She felt her stomach start to settle. People sat huddled on their blankets, with picnics and champagne to accompany the music that would soon resonate from the stage. Normally the concert would be held in the warmer summer months, but this year it had been delayed due to the unforeseen extension of maintenance and preservation to parts of Petworth House's exterior.

Despite the cooler autumn air many people had come. Dinner jackets and formal evening wear were still evident on some of the more hardened concert goers, but in the main most people it seemed, had opted for warmth and comfort and had come dressed in trousers, jumpers and coats. She scanned their expectant faces and knew she would have to play to the best of her ability to live up to her reputation.

Just as she was about to raise the Nagyvary to her chin, Isabelle caught Eric's eye. He was sat to the front left of the stage with his arm draped over his wife's shoulders. He looked excited and was smiling up at her. Isabelle's stomach somersaulted. She always felt like a part of history when she played in stately homes or their grounds. The fact that this one was on her doorstep was even more poignant.

Howard had planned the evening with a Spanish theme according to his mother's instructions, as the performance had coincided with the visit of the Mayor from the Spanish town that Petworth had recently been twinned with.

Rehearsals had been steady, just a bit of tweaking here and there had yielded confidence for all concerned. She had been pleasantly surprised to find Howard more respectful of her in their professional environment. Apparently forgetting their home battles, he was trans- formed when faced with an orchestra. There had been no sign of the rancour that she was sure Howard had felt with certain players in the LSC on other projects. She had been impressed with the way he had managed to separate out the different sections of the orchestra and concentrate on how their parts contrasted or complemented each other, and where they were meant to be in unison or responding to the others' musical phrases. But now the rehearsals were over. This was the moment of truth, and they all had to perform.

Isabelle's time on stage passed in a blur, and she gratefully soaked up the applause for her recital of the lively fourth movement of Lalo's *Symphonie Espangnole* and the *Rondo et Introduction Capriccioso* by Saint-Saens, which had been rounded off with her encore of Sarasate's popular gypsy theme, *Zigeunerwisen*. She lowered her bow and clasped the violin under her arm and bowed again. Howard couldn't deny she and his orchestra had set the tone perfectly for the rest of the evening.

Next on the programme for the main orchestral piece the LSC played Wagner's *Overture to Tannhauser.* German or not, Howard had made no apologies to his mother for introducing his favourite piece to the event. The beginning had an ethereal quality as the soft, deep tones of melancholy brass built up to a crescendo, then the strings came to the fore and expertly executed their plunging semi-quaver scales, only to be replaced with a warm brass melody. Shimmering strings then picked up the mantle again and it felt like they were being surrounded by legend and mythology. Just like Wagner's operatic theme, she wondered was hers and Howard's a sacred, or a profane love?

Dimitry Vassily, a young brooding Russian, played the adagio of Rodrigo's *Concierto de Aranjuez* on the Classical Guitar, which had also been well received by the audience, and to finish the evening Eduardo Hernandez wowed them all with Beethoven's Piano Concerto number five. The second movement had been played so exquisitely that she found tears welling up as she sat quietly backstage.

Eduardo was a very young Spanish pianist who had left his studies in Madrid to progress his tutelage in London and make a name for himself on an international level. She thought he possessed oodles of passion, and once his technique was perfected there would be no-one to rival him.

Throughout the evening Isabelle observed Howard intently. She had never really seen him in action before, as their schedules hadn't been conducive to joint collaborations. It was one of the few times his normally furrowed face was free of lines and just animated. He waved the baton rhythmically, first low by his waist when the music came to a quiet section, and then as the tension built and it came to a crescendo he was more forcible; also using his left arm, raising it, and sometimes shaking it slightly to indicate to the strings that he wanted more volume or intensity. It was certainly a skill that she greatly admired. No matter how good the individual players in an orchestra were, the resulting experience of the audience was also impacted largely by the role of the conductor. He was the sculptor shaping and carving the flow of time and the form of the music, living and breathing the notes with his orchestra. But it was a skill that involved so much more than beating out time. Part of his job was to embody the character of the music, as well as to deeply understand the tempo and phraseology of the work, and how the abilities and ranges of his musicians and their instruments could express the essence of the music in each moment.

It was a delicate eco-system she mused; the conductor could have all the mechanics and knowledge at his disposal, but without the attribute of being able to physically communicate his feelings as they were evoked by the music to his players, through the meaningful actions of his baton; his arms, his hands, his fingers, eyes and the gestures of his personality, and have them all respond accordingly, it would not elevate them as group to an exalted performance. Most conductors were also proficient or virtuosic on an instrument themselves. These were the attributes that were needed to be a really great conductor.

She had been impressed to learn that Howard could listen to a score as he looked at it, hearing the printed notes in his head before a single note had been played. She knew he was fastidious about preparation and could anticipate where his musicians might make mistakes during a performance. He had quoted Leonard Bernstein to her on one occasion.

'Isabelle, conducting is like breathing; the preparation is the inhalation, and the music sounds as exhalation. I have to always be a breath ahead of them.'

What was it that set apart the big names from the ones who didn't quite make it on to the world stage? The likes of Karajan, Barenboim and Bernstein who had achieved their iconic status had an intangible magic about their relationships with their respective orchestras. She wasn't sure if Howard shared their passion, he seemed to exhibit more of a cold ambition.

Respect on both sides was essential, but it had to be more than that. It had to be total commitment. Love for the music created an energy that brought it to life for the audience. The vibrations that flowed from the conductor bound him to his players and soloists in every split second, with each of them responding to the rise and fall of the music on a current of deep understanding and love. She could recall many such goose bump moments from her concerts.

She understood that every conductor also had his unique way of verbally inspiring his orchestra: using elements of praise, cajoling, demanding or at times, raging; his own way of making the orchestra love the music as he does. But where she felt Howard let himself down was in his dictatorial style, his tendency to impose his will on his players rather than projecting his feelings around him.

She longed for Howard's success, but not for the reasons she knew she should. If he got the accolade he craved, he would be easier to live with, and probably less critical of her. She was certainly selfish in that regard. *Howard would agree with me on that score.*

She glanced back up from the wings to see Howard's arms coming together and down in one last swift motion. The final note had been played. The crowd were in raptures. Isabelle and her co-performers made their way back on to the stage alongside Howard and the LSC to accept their standing ovation. The event had gone better than either she, Howard or Celia could have hoped for.

As the clapping slowly died down Isabelle and Howard turned towards each other and smiled. He had been a different man tonight; he was the man she married once again. Something within her had rekindled; her love and admiration for the person he had become in his moment of glory had shown her that whatever they had; it was worth fighting for.

Isabelle and her fellow soloists made their way backstage, where they were handed a chilled glass of champagne. She closed her eyes and savoured the atmosphere and the sweet tingling of bubbles on her tongue. Then a heavy waft of perfume filled her nostrils. She coughed. There was no mistaking the sickly familiar scent that regularly permeated the house. It could mean only one person - Celia. Her overpowering application of Lily of the Valley sank deep into Isabelle's throat and clung on to her taste buds.

'Well done my dear. I must say, Howard and I are proud of your performance tonight. I thought that Howard and the LSC did exceptionally well throughout. What a marathon of music. Mayor Gomez was most delighted.' Celia's silk lilac gown swished by as she passed to speak to someone more important; even before Isabelle could utter a sound.

Isabelle had to admit that playing with Howard and the LSC had been more enjoyable than she had expected. A zealous journalist interrupted her contemplation by grabbing her arm. He thrust her upon the swarthy and portly Mayor Gomez for a picture that would feature with an article about the event in the Petworth Gazette. Howard, who was already engaged in conversation with the cigar smoking Mayor didn't seem to mind the attention, and reached out his hand to welcome her arrival.

Isabelle glanced furtively at Howard, who made a dashing figure in his cream tuxedo and black bow tie. Her dark hair was piled up on her head, with wispy ringlets draped around her oval face.

'Eres muy bella Isabelle,' said the Mayor as his beady eyes swept over her figure. She tried not to choke on the acrid smoke that was emanating from his every pore.

'Tonight you resembled a Pre-Raphaelite Spanish princess with your grace and beauty.'

'Gracias, Senor Gomez.' She couldn't help thinking how wonderful it would be for any woman to have been immortalised on canvas by Millais or Rossetti.

In an instant the camera was clicking and flashing; capturing their smiling faces. They looked like a happily married, successful couple. It was a snapshot of how things could be and for that second she forgot her woes. She still hoped that one day they could live up to their promises made at the altar.

Her mind kept jumping ahead to the article's possible headline: VIOLINIST AND CONDUCTOR PARTNERS DO PETWORTH PROUD! She mused that if they knew about the problems in their relationship they might come up with a more ominous version, such as: PRELUDE TO DISASTER...

That night, as she carefully placed her violin case into its storage cupboard in her music room, a chill coursed through her entire body; every hair stood on end. She shivered and then without warning, a feeling of nausea began to rise like a fountain of burning lava. She managed to quell the surge by breathing deeply and slowly.

It felt like a premonition, but she had no idea of what. Not wanting to entertain any unpleasant thoughts she convinced herself it was down to tiredness. Her nerves had been on a knife edge all day, and the chilly autumnal evening air had seemingly penetrated her bones. She hadn't felt it while on stage, as all her attention and energy had been poured into her performance.

Isabelle dismissed her initial sense of foreboding. She did not know, that much like the theme of Beethoven's iconic fifth symphony; fate was about to knock on her door.

4

James Jackson was a ferret of a man. His slender frame was dwarfed by his exuberant curly hair and thick dark rimmed glasses. He had a voice that conveyed a sort of deep, maturity – an almost hypnotic quality that had made Isabelle feel instantly at ease. Seeing this popular DJ in the flesh had been a shock of symphonic proportions. She had pictured a quintessential macho type, suave with a cravat and probably educated at Oxford. She had to mentally berate herself not to look so bewildered every time he spoke. His cord jacket drooped around his slim shoulders and she wondered how he coped with the inevitable disappointment of his fans, once they set eyes on him.

'Isabelle, are you alright?'

She clasped her sweating hands and shuffled in her leather seat, hearing every creak of the material as she moved.

'Yes, sorry James. I'm just not used to doing radio interviews, or any kind of interview for that matter. Gerry may have mentioned I'm a bit media phobic. I know it must sound a bit lame coming from a performer, but that's me.'

'Lots of artists suffer from some type of nerves, just stay cool; you're in good hands. Feel the fear and do it anyway, as they say.'

He looked down at her notes. The jingle was coming to a close and Isabelle's stomach somersaulted. She watched James leaning in towards the microphone.

'Good evening folks, and welcome to the James Jackson show. You are all in for a treat tonight as my guest for the Saturday Evening Interview is the exceptionally talented violin virtuoso Isabelle Bryant.'

He turned to her and smiled, 'Isabelle, thanks for coming on the programme, I'm delighted to have you with us. We've had lots of excited emails from listeners waiting to hear from you. We are going to be talking about your stellar success at such a young age, some of your musical influences, and of course we'd love to hear some of your personal insights. We'll also be playing a small selection of pieces chosen by Isabelle.'

'Thank you James, it's a pleasure to be here with you and all your listeners.' The saliva in Isabelle's mouth was evaporating fast.

'But first, let's kick-off with one of your musical favourites; the slow movement of Beethoven's epic Ninth Symphony.'

James passed her a glass of water while the music was playing, and she took a few sips.

'Relax, you're doing great. I love your selection by the way.' James appeared not to look directly at her as he spoke, concentrating on the numerous dials and switches in front of him, his bulky headphones and wild hair framing his somewhat skeletal face. His skin appeared taut and stretched over his cheek bones, like he'd had cosmetic surgery that hadn't quite gone according to plan.

The minutes went by in a blur, and before she could get carried away with the music the On Air light turned green. Her insides were in free-fall again.

'So Isabelle, following your debut concert you have in the past been referred to as "Beethoven's Babe", and your love of his music seems to cement this nickname in more ways than one.' His voice tailed off transforming the statement into a question. A second passed...

'Yes, well he is the composer I admire most in the world. But a label, even a complimentary one, can be detrimental to a career. I didn't want it to affect the kind of repertoire I would be asked to perform.

'Don't get me wrong, I absolutely adore his work. He was one of the greatest geniuses of the nineteenth century, a true innovator and visionary, who stayed true to his artistic nature. His music sounds as fresh, inspiring and passionate today, as it did around two hundred years ago in the theatres of Vienna. It can't have been easy living in Europe during the Napoleonic Wars, and under the significant figure of Mozart who had dominated the late Baroque and early Classical era. For me, what stands out is his suffering and his passion. Unfortunately he didn't write a great deal of music for solo violin. I regularly performed the D Major Violin Concerto and his *Spring Sonata*, and sonatas eight and nine; the latter being named the *Kreutzer*. My repertoire after my Royal Albert Hall debut varied enormously.'

'What is it about the Adagio of the ninth that touches you particularly?' His voice was soft and encouraging.

'I think it's because there had been so much water under the bridge at this point in his life, so much pain - he was profoundly deaf and probably very lonely outside his music. It's just unbearably moving, full of anguish and torment, yet at the same time dignified beyond any words you could use.

'Beethoven supposedly once said, "I must confess that I live a miserable life...I live entirely in my music." When you understand his state of mind, it brings you closer to his music, and the way he expressed himself in that medium. He is recognised as the trailblazer of the Classical Era. He set the benchmark for the composers that followed him, and his late works paved the way for the Romantic era.'

James nodded, as if in silent agreement with her. 'Of course your big break came when you won the Young Musician of The Year Award, and were the youngest person ever to do so I understand; which was followed by your first recording with Decca of the Beethoven Violin

Concerto. How did you cope with such success at such a young age?'

'Well, I was lucky enough to have a very support-ive and worldly-wise agent in Gerry Goldberg, plus of course the grounding of my family and friends. I re-ally didn't view myself as any kind of superstar, I was just on a whirlwind of music, doing what I loved and what I had only ever done from as far back as I can remember.'

'Tell us more about what projects you have been work-ing on recently, and your plans for the future.' James's voice was lulling her into a relaxed state.

'I'm at the Royal Festival Hall next month with the London Philharmonic, and I'll be playing the Brahms Violin Concerto.' Isabelle took another sip of water. 'Over the years my schedule has never allowed me to play in the BBC proms cycle, but just last month I was fortu-nate to have performed in the Royal Albert Hall again for the last night of the proms. The atmosphere was electric and it was such an honour to be part of such a celebrated and popular event. I've also participated recently in a charity concert at the glorious Petworth House and Park. It's organised by the local council and this year we were fortunate enough to have the London Sound Company on stage...'

'And how did you feel collaborating with your hus-band, the conductor Howard Miller, who has recently joined the Company?'

His fidgety eyes watched her intently.

'It was our first professional performance together and it worked well.'

He signalled to her with his hand to give more of an answer to the microphone.

'Howard is a great asset to the LSC, and he's not afraid to try new things. I suppose we don't work together very often, so we can't get on each other's nerves in that way!' She glared back at James.

'How do you feel about the recent poll in *High Notes* Magazine, where you were voted as the most attractive classical star of the year?' He winked at her.

'It's wonderful and completely unexpected. I always felt like the ugly duckling compared with my sister when we were growing up. My mother died of cancer just before I won the Young Musician of the Year competition, and that terrible loss made me respect my health and body as much as I could.'

His voice softened. 'That must have been hard for you?'

A lump formed in her throat. 'Yes, almost unbearable. My dad and my family were rooting for me, as well as having their own grief to deal with. I definitely felt like mum was there in spirit. It was my love for her that infused my winning performance.'

'Even so, that's quite an achievement under those kinds of circumstances.'

'Well, mum was a performer herself, and a great believer in the motto "the show must go on" it was only what she would have expected.' Her eyes were stinging.

'I like to think she was looking down on me from heaven, whispering into the hearts and minds of the judges. It was an amazing feeling, winning such a prestigious competition, but of course I would have given anything to have been able to share it with mum. Without her I never would have gotten that far.'

James gave her a sympathetic smile. 'Of course- and it's good to know you had such comforting thoughts to help you through that time in your life.' He paused, and deftly changed the subject.

'What sort of health regime do you follow Isabelle?'

She was grateful for his new direction and responded candidly. 'I love holistic therapies and try to have a massage in between touring and concert dates or recordings. This helps me unwind during my hectic schedule. I like walking in the South Downs and going to the movies is a favourite pastime of mine too.

'Although it's wonderful to have been given the award, to be honest; I realise the voting was done from a relatively small cross section of the population, so I'm not letting it go to my head. My father always used to say that "beauty is in the eye of the beholder", and I truly believe that.'

'Judging by your recent record sales and packed concert halls I'd say that many people think your violin playing is beautiful as well.'

'Thank you James. That's the only thing that's important to me.'

'Now I understand that you have quite eclectic musical tastes, and that you also enjoy jazz, blues and rock?'

'That's right, but classical is my main interest, and even now I'm coming across new pieces from composers like Hummel, who have slipped into obscurity somewhat; but he was a brilliant pianist and composer in his own right, who just had the misfortune to be around in Vienna at the same time as Beethoven. I always enjoy making new musical discoveries. Just lately I've really been getting into opera. It's taken me a while to appreciate the power of storytelling that the drama of music and voice can convey. I think it can affect an audience in a way that no other medium can match. I'd love to do an album of arias that are suited to a violin and piano transcription. It's not a new concept, but still one that interests me. The violin is so close to the human voice and therefore the whole gamut of human emotion.'

'We'll all look forward to that Isabelle. It's time now to play your second choice of music; Rachmaninov's second piano concerto, the first movement. This recorded version is performed here by Russian pianist Sviatoslav Richter and the Leningrad Philharmonic Orchestra.'

The deep and sonorous chords sounded softly at first, building up to a crescendo when the main piano melody and the orchestra took the theme to a fullness that always captivated Isabelle. She was lost.

Afterwards he asked,

'What is it about this concerto that you love?'

'It's just so romantic. After Beethoven he's one of my favourite composers and this movement conjures up a serene feeling in me. It's lush and intense and makes my imagination soar.'

'Yes, I believe this concerto has reached the hearts of so many classical music lovers in the UK, it has been consistently voted as one of the most popular pieces in the nation.'

Then James was playing her last choice of music, the *Fantasia on a theme of Thomas Tallis* by Vaughn Williams. They listened in rapture, and when the airwaves were silent once again, James waited for a second before speaking.

'Of course you've also just released your third album titled, *The Virtuoso,* which is accompanied by Charles Stanley on the piano and also with the LPO on some tracks. I must say it's a refreshing look at shorter but brilliant violin romances, rhapsodies and sonatas. I like the way there is an equal partnership in some of the sonatas with the piano, and what stands out for me is you have a very pure tone and a very authentic but fresh interpretation of some very famous pieces.'

'Thank you James. It was hard work but incredible fun, and it was such an honour for me to work with Charles and the LPO.'

James fondled the shiny disc cover, flashing Isabelle a glimpse of the black and white image of her smiling in a cream silk strapless ball gown, clutching the Nagyvary like a guitar at her waist.

'*The Virtuoso* can be purchased at all good record stores or online at Amazon and for all you MP3 users it's also downloadable on iTunes. Sit back, relax and enjoy track number three, a much loved show piece; the Waxman Fantasy on Carmen by Bizet, played by my guest today, the violinist Isabelle Bryant.'

As her violin's warm tone began its virtuosic airing Isabelle felt a wave of relief. James was motioning to her a thumbs-up sign, and a big broad smile crossed her face. She closed her eyes and remembered recording the piece. Soon, its frantic last few notes were upon them, and the dramatic ending signalled the end of the interview.

'Thanks again to you Isabelle, for coming in and sharing with us. It has been both fascinating and fun. From everyone at BBC Radio Three we wish you every success in the future.'

'My pleasure James, thanks for having me on your show. I'm a regular listener myself.' Isabelle sat back squarely in the worn leather seat and exhaled. James shook her hand firmly.

'Well done Isabelle, I know that wasn't easy for you, you did great.'

It was over. She gathered her handbag and exited the studio along with James. He turned to her in the corridor.

'I'm gonna nip to the gents while the news is on. Listen, it was a pleasure to meet and chat with you; all the best for the future Isabelle.'

'Cheers James. Thanks for guiding me through that so expertly, I feel like I can do anything now. Never mind carpe diem, I feel like gaudeamus igitur!' Laughing she wandered down the corridor, smiling at everyone who passed her.

She stepped out of the renovated lobby of the original Art Deco Broadcasting House and passed beneath the statues of Ariel and Prospero into Portland Place, glancing up at the new glass wing to admire the fusion of traditional and modern architecture that now housed the BBC's broadcasting operations. She wrapped her scarf around her neck and faced into the exuberant wind that tore through London's streets. Her heels clicked purposefully as she strode along the pavement with renewed bounce, heading south towards Regent Street. Her phone buzzed in her bag and she fumbled it quickly to her ear.

'Hello?'

'Hi, it's me, fab interview darling.'

'Sebastian?'

'You were amazing.'

'Thanks Seb. I'm so relieved I got through it without talking gibberish.'

'Does Senor Miller know about this yet?'

'Err, not yet. Not unless he was listening. He would have been working on the LSC programming and scores, so I thought I'd surprise him afterwards. He might not mind so much when I explain how well it went.'

'I can't imagine he'll be proud of his wife outdoing him in the media spotlight, he always struck me as someone who wanted the attention himself.'

'You must be kidding, he's so critical of anything like that. He detests celebrity types, says his musical integrity comes first. He hates me wearing anything remotely slinky when I'm performing, but I listened to Gerry's advice on that. Mind you, look where that's got me!'

'Isabella, is everything okay?'

'Oh Seb, I don't want to burden you...'

'You know I have broad shoulders. Besides, I wouldn't have asked if I wasn't prepared for the answer. Spill the beans Senorita.'

'To coin a well-known phrase, it's all going "Pete Tong". We've been having terrible fights lately. It's like I'm married to a different person. He's moodier, more morose and has this morbid fascination with success. I'd go as far as to say it's an obsession for him. I feel like an ornament gathering dust, just sitting in the background. I mean I'm busy, and work is going well, but I feel lonely. I didn't tell him about the radio interview because I knew he wouldn't approve. I've hidden the *High Notes* magazine, I'm sure he'll be critical about that too. It's as much a surprise to me as it will to be him, but he won't see it like that.'

'Why don't you come to see me in Fulham, we can take Delilah for a walk and catch up properly. Not that I'm one to give advice on relationships, Marcus and I are going through a rough patch at the moment. How about meeting up straight after the LPO rehearsal?'

'I'd love that Seb. Sorry to hear you're going through the mire as well. Apart from you and H there's no-one else I can really open up to. Gerry does his best bless him, but I feel I should retain a certain professional distance if you know what I mean.'

'Si Senorita, I do indeed. I was proud of you today; don't let "you know who" spoil your moment of glory.'

'Easier said than done, but thanks for the vote of confidence. He's been drinking late every night at the Angel this week. I think rehearsals at the LSC are going badly; he's really tense. My stomach turns at the thought of telling him, but as soon as his mood improves I'll find a way to drop it into the conversation. Sorry Seb, I'm blabbering on.'

'Isabella, you don't have to ask his permission for anything, try not to worry.'

'I'll try...but I can't shake off the feeling that I'm in a prison without any bars, it's just the invisible constraints of anxiety setting the boundaries of my life at the moment.'

'Now sounds like a good time to break free.'

'Yes. See you straight after rehearsals.'

She rang off and scribbled the date in her pocket diary before heading home.

5

Isabelle squinted, the sun was blazing full in her face as she walked tentatively up the flower lined path to the doctor's surgery. Apart from the small garden at the front the dark brick building was not at all inviting. She swallowed and pulled on the cold metal handle of the poster laden entrance door. A good night's sleep and a morning of productive practice had made her feel more confident about taking back control of her life.

The smell of disinfectant hit her as she approached reception, with its bland magnolia walls and green carpet tiled floor. A solitary brochure rack stood by the seating area and a couple of faded, frayed posters clung to the walls. She had been ignored for a few seconds longer than was polite by the peroxide receptionist, who obviously wanted patients to see every lump and bump protruding from beneath her tightly bound, low cut leopard skin top.

'It's Ms Bryant. I have an appointment with Doctor Russell at two thirty.'

'Take a seat; he'll be with you shortly.'

She pretended to read *Country Life.*

Glancing furtively around the waiting room she took a mental snapshot of the other patients. She desperately hoped no-one had recognised her.

An elderly woman sitting opposite her was busy with her knitting, walking cane propped by her side. A young mother played nearby with her toddler, building up plastic bricks only for him to knock them down in fits of giggles. Her breath caught as she spotted Eric loping in through the entrance, and just then a stern voice protruded into her thoughts. It was getting louder and more impatient.

'Ms Bryant... Ms Bryant!'

She hastily walked through the double doors held open by Doctor Russell, who seemed irritated that he'd had to call her name more than once. His tall, spindly body appeared to be mainly supported by his wide shoulders, much like a coat hanger that held the body of a shirt in place. Wisps of thin grey hair were receding from his barren forehead. His watery grey eyes were sunken behind his frail spectacles that balanced precariously on the bridge of his narrow, pointy nose. He followed her down through the inner hallway.

Once in his treatment room he bowed his head and looked at her coolly over the rim of his glasses.

'What can I do for you Ms Bryant?'

Isabelle paused. 'Well, it's more of an emotional problem than a physical one. I feel like I'm slipping into a depression.' She was looking for a smile or a warm gesture, but he stared back at her with a blank expression.

'I feel embarrassed to say that Howard and I are having marital problems. I know you can't get involved in our disagreements as such, but we are having a particular issue over starting a family. It's affecting my sleep, and now my playing is starting to suffer. Recently I've been forgetting notes, my concentration is poor and worst of all my confidence is ebbing away. I'm scared Doctor Russell, this has never happened to me before.'

'You surprise me Ms Bryant. I would have thought a successful person like you would be able to avoid a "victim" state of mind. I suggest that you and Mr Miller go to marriage guidance counselling if your disagreements are having such an effect. Talking and compromise are generally the best ways to overcome these sorts of difficulties. In the meantime I will prescribe you a course of anti-depressants to help boost your serotonin levels. They'll take a few weeks to kick in and may make you feel a little drowsy. Taking positive action in my experience is the best way to overcome feelings of helplessness and fatigue.' He handed her the prescription, and pinned her to the spot with his accusing eyes.

'None of us can blame others for our predicaments. You need to look for the solutions within you. Good day to you.'

Isabelle stormed past the receptionist, her blood running hot, not noticing Eric raising an arm in greeting towards her.

She marched resolutely past boutique shops, the bakery and post office, her fists clenched, oblivious to the people milling around her, with doctor Russell's contemptuous expression burned into her mind. In a few minutes she found herself stepping from the pavement and into the sterile surroundings of the chemist. She handed the prescription to the assistant with a forced smile, and stared at the vast array of bottles and vitamins that lined the shelves as she waited.

'Isabelle? What are you doing here?' The voice sent shivers down her spine, as she spun round to see Celia walking towards her; newly coiffed and wearing thickly applied makeup. She was holding her large wicker bag in the crook of her arm, with fresh white lilies poking out of the top; she was frowning at her.

'Hello Celia.' Isabelle tried to sound enthusiastic, but inside she was dreading a public grilling from her mother-in-law. 'I'm just getting some medication.'

'I thought Howard had his ulcer medicine replenished the other day?'

'He did. These are for me. It's nothing serious though, there's no need to be concerned.'

'You must keep in good health my dear. Howard needs your support while he's trying to make an impression at the LSC.'

Isabelle made a polite farewell, but underneath her forced smile she was fuming. She left Celia gossiping with the manager of the chemist; she wanted to get home.

Petworth was a labyrinth of old buildings and cobbled streets that clustered around the main square: a jumble of antique shops, the Town Hall, small grocers, fashion boutiques, churches, book stores and cafes, overlooked by the seventeenth century palatial Petworth House and Park courtesy of Capability Brown's landscaped gardens. Sometimes Isabelle liked to discover new streets and alleyways that she hadn't noticed before, but this time she had driven straight home.

That evening back at the house, Isabelle pulled out the bedside draw. The packet of anti-depressants lay there unopened. She hesitated and then closed the draw.

Isabelle flung back the bed covers and made her way to the music room, taking her violin from its case. She had a sudden urge to stroke its wooden curves, and hold it like a confidante close to her body, as if it knew all her secrets and desires.

A few minutes passed, and then she raised the Nagyvary up to her jaw, reciting the Beethoven violin concerto once again, her fingers finding every perfect note as they moved fluidly on the strings.

Buoyed up with energy from her session she was in no mood to sleep, even though it was past midnight.

6

A loud crash woke Isabelle with a start. With bleary eyes and a pounding heart she glanced at the bedside clock. It was two in the morning. She rubbed her eyes.

'Howard? Is that you?'

There was no reply, and the darkness that surrounded her suddenly felt oppressive. Isabelle staggered through the bedroom on to the landing, arms out stretched as she entered into the blackness. She reached for the banister and tentatively descended the stairs. She could hear nothing but her now erratic and raspy breathing. Her heart was racing at the thought of what she might find lurking in the shadows. Her hands began to shake slightly as fear took hold. Her dishevelled hair hung languidly around her smooth olive shoulders. Each stair creaked as she slowly placed one foot in front of the other.

Moonlight streamed in through the half crescent window at the top of the front door, lending an even more eerie feeling to an already creepy atmosphere.

Negotiating her way past familiar objects in the moonlit hallway, she entered the kitchen and switched on the light. For a brief second she blinked as her eyes adjusted to the brightness, and then she could make out Howard slumped over the pine table, whiskey glass in one hand and a magazine in the other.

He raised his head menacingly.

'Howard, you scared me. I thought the house was being broken into! Where have you been?' As she approached him she noticed he looked dishevelled. There was no foliage, but the stench of alcohol hit her nostrils and she recoiled.

He fumbled with the buttons on his waistcoat and glared at her.

'When were you going t-to tell me about this?' He slammed the *High Notes* Magazine onto the table.

'Today, as it happens. I was hoping that you'd have been home earlier so that we could have a chat. It's late now and I can see you're not in the right state of mind. We're certainly not going to resolve any of our marital problems while you're filthy drunk!'

She turned away from him to go back upstairs, but had only moved a few yards before she felt his vice like grip on her arm. Unbelievably he'd travelled like a gazelle across the kitchen, knocking his chair over as he lunged towards her. She pulled away and he moved closer, stamping on her foot as he asserted his hold. His heavy walking boot left a muddy mark.

The pain was excruciating. Isabelle bent down to rub her foot.

'Howard! For God's sake. You're hurting me!'

Howard marched her over to the fallen chair. He picked it up with one hand and then pushed her roughly down with both arms.

She was shaking all over now and feeling more vulnerable. She sat shivering in her silk night slip with her foot throbbing. He pressed his knees over hers and stooped over her. She didn't look him in the eye.

'It's time we had a talk now, isn't it you little t-tramp?' His face was inches from hers. His complexion was sweaty and pallid. Isabelle turned her head to the side and her neck flushed with the warmth of his stinking breath.

'This debacle has Goldberg written all over it. You've become one of those fucking celebrity whores!' Spittle sprang from his mouth.

He lowered his voice. 'When did fame become more important to you than art? You're married into a respectable family now; you can't go flaunting your body around like some cheap slut! Do you have any idea how embarrassing this is for me and my family? I will not let you tarnish our reputation.' His breath was overpowering.

'Howard, I think you're being unreasonable. I didn't ask to be voted for, I didn't even know about the poll until Gerry told me. There are plenty of other serious musicians in the same category. It doesn't mean I'm of dubious morals or wanting to spice up my image.'

'I suppose James Jackson had a good gawp over you this afternoon. I thought we agreed that you'd run any publicity past me, you selfish b-bitch!'

'Howard, listen to yourself. You're being abusive.'

'You deserve it, you lying slut.'

He slapped her hard across the cheek, and Isabelle's head followed his blow. A red welt mark instantly formed on her cheek. She could taste salt now that tears were streaming down her face. She glared up at him in defiance.

'Don't f-fucking give me the waterworks, you think I've got any sympathy for you?' He sneered and stood up fully, pushing his tousled hair away from his forehead.

Seeing his slightly relaxed stance she kicked out with all her strength. Howard groaned as she made contact with his testicles. By now her adrenalin was surging and she pushed him back a few paces as he was doubled over. It had given her enough time to get to the other side of the table, where she stood facing him.

'Look Howard, we can talk about this calmly when you've sobered up. I don't want to fight. I thought you might at least be pleased about the radio interview, I've finally overcome my fear of public speaking.'

'You've made yourself look like a s-s-silly tart and it's going to s-stop, or else…'

She bolted towards the stairs with Howard in pursuit, still wincing from the blow to his groin and gripped by blind rage.

Isabelle had reached the fourth step, but then felt him tug firmly on her bruised foot and she cried out. Howard dragged her back down and she grimaced in pain with each bump. He pinned her to the bottom of the stairs.

'You whores are never content with what you've got.' His features contorted. 'You're insatiable, always wanting more. I'm going to give you more than you bargained f-for.'

She glimpsed his mad eyes, his broken glasses from the tussle and just as his intention sunk in his vice-like mouth was on hers, practically biting her lips.

She vainly struggled, but he had gravity on his side. His hand was ripping the delicate silk and clutching her exposed breast. She cried again in pain. He took his arm away to undo his flies. With one last burst of anger she pushed him backwards and he lurched, temporarily losing his balance on the step.

Without thinking Isabelle threw herself past him, grasping at the wall where the car keys hung. She pulled frantically to unhook her keys. Fumbling in her haste, she almost dropped the keys as she flung open the front door.

The cold night air hit her bruised flesh like another slap in the face, but all she could think of was getting to the safety of the car.

She hobbled over the gravel in her bare feet and pressed the fob. It bleeped and the car lights flashed. She opened the driver's door and turned towards the house to see how far behind Howard was. Her left hand was resting on the rim of the door as her body leaned on the rear passenger door.

'Where do you think you're going s-slut?' His voice cut through the dark.

'Away from you Howard, you demented bastard! I can't live like this anymore!'

They stood inert for a second, staring at each other. For an inexplicable reason Isabelle felt rooted to the spot. Her legs were numb and leaden. She just couldn't move fast enough. Howard, sensing her delay, propelled himself toward her in fury. He was suddenly upon her and pitched himself at the car door with all his body-weight behind it.

She could not avoid the high velocity door. Impact was inevitable. Then she screamed in agony.

She looked down, but her eyes didn't register what they saw.

She felt and saw the warm spray of gushing red liquid as she held up what remained of her left hand in front of her. Her eyes were fixed on her torn jagged flesh and protruding bones, now bathed in blood. Throbbing, searing pain shot through her hand.

Her two middle fingers had fallen to the ground, and her little finger was dangling from the first joint, like some gory model from a horror movie special effects workshop. She was looking at her knuckles inside out. Disbelief filled her entire being at the sight before her.

She was staring at her exposed joints. In a reflex action she tried to bend her fingers, even though they weren't attached to her hand any longer. More blood flowed out. She couldn't take it in.

Although shock had lessened the initial agony, her breathing had become fast and shallow. She staggered and watched her breath swirl and spiral upwards into the freezing night air. She felt light-headed and her balance faltered. Isabelle thudded against the car and slid to the ground, holding her mangled hand out in front of her.

Two of her decapitated slender fingers lay on the ground next to her, a pool of crimson gathering around them.

Her red and sodden silk gown felt cold against her body as the saturated material from her warm blood had rapidly cooled in the freezing night air.

The colour drained from her face and her head began spinning. Suddenly she couldn't breathe. Howard's face became blurry, and all she could make out was the crescent of the moon. Above her the stars were glimmering in all their candescent glory.

The last thing she thought she heard was Eric calling her name - just before she passed out.

7

Hortense was pulling into the driveway when her phone rang. Isabelle's mobile number flashed up on her screen. Clicking the answer button, she waited a second.

'May I speak to Hortense Lafayette please?'

'That would be me. Who is this? Where is my friend Isabelle Bryant? You are calling on her phone.'

'My name is Jonathan Tasker and I'm a consultant plastic surgeon at Hammersmith Hospital.' As he paused for breath, Hortense gasped. His tone was solemn. 'I've just operated on a woman called Isabelle Bryant. It appears that her husband has been detained by the police, and when I asked her if there was anyone I could call for her, she said just "H". To be honest I thought I'd misheard her, she was in shock when she was admitted, but when I scrolled down her contacts I found you.'

'What's happened to Issy?'

'She was involved in a horrific accident, apparently trying to get away from her drunken husband. Her hand has been very badly mutilated.'

'Not her left hand? Please God, not her left hand!'

'I'm sorry, so sorry, but I'm afraid it is.'

'Do you know who she is?'

'I'm afraid not, no. Her face looked vaguely familiar to me, but I couldn't place her. I'm guessing I should be aware of who she is by the tone of your voice.'

'There's probably no reason why you would know she's a violinist, albeit a famous and highly skilled one. I suppose you can guess what I'm going to ask next?'

'I'm a highly skilled surgeon, but unfortunately not a miracle worker. I'm also no expert on musical matters, but in this case, unless she re-trains to use her other hand, then I'm sorry - no.

Hortense swallowed hard. 'Shit! I'm sorry Mr Tasker, I'm sure you did your best for her. Can you tell me exactly what the situation is?'

'Well, she's regained consciousness from the operation now, but she's still very drowsy. I'm sorry to say that when I came to operate on her she had already lost her middle and fourth finger, and her little finger had been so badly mutilated I had no choice but to amputate it at the proximal phalange.'

'The what?'

'Down to the first main joint of the finger, basically it's a stump. There was a fracture to the metacarpal bone and acute strain on the transverse metacarpal ligaments of her little finger. She has also sustained bruising to other areas of her body consistent with a physical attack. Try not to worry, we've patched her up, she'll be fine.'

'Fine? Perhaps you'd like broaden your definition of fine? Is it fine to lose most of your fingers and therefore your livelihood?'

'I'm sorry, I didn't mean to sound blasé and uncaring. Physically she will make a full recovery, but mentally and emotionally, it could be a long-haul. The effect of the injuries on her lifestyle will probably scar her more than the severity of the actual wounds themselves.'

Tears fell onto Hortense's plump cheeks.

'I want to be with her. She can't deal with this alone. I don't care what the time is, I'm coming over. I've got to be there for her.'

'I understand completely,' he said. 'That's only a natural response when you hear this kind of news about someone very dear to you. But honestly, you can help her better in the morning when you've had some rest yourself and have been able to integrate the news to some extent. The more you can handle the situation with equanimity the more it will help Isabelle too. I'll personally come and talk with you then.'

'Okay... cos wild horses won't keep me away longer than that Mr. Tasker. Thank you for everything you've done for her.'

Hortense stood on her marble doorstep, unable to move. An owl was hooting in some nearby trees, and she instinctively looked at her watch. It was four twenty-five in the morning and soon the world would carry on with its daily routines as if nothing had happened. The grand Edwardian homes in her street were quiet; their sleeping residents blissfully unaware of her pain. She noticed that foxes had disturbed their rubbish bags again, with some of the leftover food trailing from the front path into their side passage and garden. It was deathly quiet; there wasn't even a whisper of a breeze. She turned the key in the lock and stumbled into the entrance hall. Her keys jangled as she placed them on the small table beneath the window by the door. She walked in darkness across the solid wood floor of their wide hallway, where from above her she could hear footsteps padding across the ceiling, too heavy to belong to Louis.

Raymond found his beloved Hortense in the kitchen, her usual graceful movements replaced by automatic robotic limbs instead. She was reaching for the coffee. Her coat was still on and her arm was shaking as she spooned the aromatic brown powder into her overused mug with "I Love Jools" in faded print on the side of it. Her tears reflected under the light.

'Hey babe, you look like you've seen a ghost, what's up?' He placed his hand on her shoulder.

'Oh Ray, if only I'd kept in closer touch with her. I knew she was unhappy, I just never realised how serious it was.' Sobs started racking her generous chest and Raymond pulled her into his arms.

'Isabelle?'

Hortense nodded, and reached for a tissue that had been lurking in her pocket to stem her flowing nose. Raymond squeezed her hand and waited patiently for his wife to gather her composure.

'It's over. Her career is over. I just got a call from this surgeon guy called Tasker, telling me her left hand has been mutilated. Fingers are gone. The violin has been her whole life.' Her voice tailed off and she sunk her head into her husband's warm and comforting embrace.

'I just can't believe this has happened. It's such a waste! She sounds...sounded, like an angel when she played that thing.'

'Jesus! I'm so sorry honey.' Raymond stroked her hair as he spoke. 'Listen babe, I'll take care of your engagements for the next few days and make sure Louis gets to and from school. Why don't you take her to our apartment in Madeira? I think we need to keep her out of the limelight in the immediate aftermath of this tragedy.'

Hortense managed a feeble acknowledgment. He gave her another squeeze. 'She'll be in shock for a while, and knowing the media they'll probably hound her and it'll only make things worse.'

'C'mon, let's get you to bed.'

Isabelle opened her eyelids, blinking away the misty edges to see chestnut brown eyes staring back at her. She didn't recognise the rugged tanned face they belonged to. The man had neatly cropped wavy blonde hair and a warm smile.

'Hello Isabelle, my name is Jonathan Tasker; I'm a consultant plastic and reconstructive surgeon...'

Overwhelmed with panic she looked across at her aching hand, now hidden behind bandages. The terrible sight of her fingers on the ground flashed back into her mind.

'I'm so sorry about the accident. We did all we could, but the fingers...well, they were too badly mutilated to sew back on, and we had to amputate most of the little one because of complications. We repaired you as best we could. I'll be along later to discuss the rest of your treatment and recovery, but for now you should get some rest. It must be a terrible shock for you.'

A lump formed in her throat. 'The Lord giveth, and the Lord taketh away.'

She caught sight of H, striding towards her. She was wearing black trousers and jumper, covered by an oversized dark brown poncho. She could never recall H ever wearing such dark and muted colours; she looked like she was on her way to a funeral. Her eyes were barely visible within the dark circles that surrounded them. The ward was slowly coming to life, with nurses checking-up on patients and breakfast was being given to those who could manage it. Hortense sounded a little breathless as she came up to her bedside.

Almost crushing Isabelle with her hug, she said,

'Issy honey, I'm here for you!' Gently holding her upper arms she looked into her pale, forlorn face.

'If I ever clap eyes on that husband of yours again, he'll wish he'd never been born. I'm so sorry this has happened to you Issy. Isabelle was mute.

'Does it hurt very much? Try not to think about your violin just now, we need to concentrate on healing you first. Whatever it takes.'

'Every now and then life can take a tragic and unexpected turn, and even though we can't discern if it's for the best, we have to trust that there's something else out there for us.'

'H there is a difference between discernment and disaster!'

Hortense smiled at Isabelle. 'I'm sorry; I didn't mean to start sermonising.'

'You've been my closest friend, you know that don't you? I know you want me to be brave and fight this, but I just can't. A part of me died last night.'

'But not all of you,' Hortense replied.

'Listen girlie, you get some sleep, I'm going to grab a coffee, and then I'm coming right back and I'm going to stay with you. Oh, I nearly forgot, here's a card from Sebastian, he dropped it round early this morning after I told him what had happened. He's going to call you later.' She placed the pink envelope into Isabelle's right hand and headed towards the reception.

Isabelle stared at the card for five minutes. Securing the corner with the base of her thumb on the left hand she managed to tear along the top with her right hand.

It was one of those funky cards, bright purple with sequins, it had a picture of a cartoon lady all dressed up listening to headphones, with music coming out. The caption read, "GROOVY MUSIC DIVA." As Isabelle opened the card she jumped as she heard the opening notes of Beethoven's fifth. His immaculate handwriting was elegantly scrawled across the page:

Never mind Beethoven's babe; you are my babe
too, and you are worth so much more than your
considerable ability to enthral audiences!
Love you lots, will catch up soon,
Seb x

Isabelle drifted back to sleep and when she woke H was sitting as promised by her bed, reading a hefty paperback titled How to Raise Your Consciousness.

'H, when can I get out of this place?' Her voice didn't sound like her own. It was feeble, Hortense moved closer to the bed.

'I spoke to Mr Tasker after you went back to sleep. I think they want to check you over again, and then later on this afternoon we should be able to leave. You'll have to come back to outpatients for check-ups and for the dressings to be changed at regular intervals. They wanted to keep you in for observation because they felt you may have suffered mild concussion.'

'Come to mention it I had a splitting headache earlier, but it's gone now,' Isabelle managed a faint smile.

'I've nipped out to Fulham and bought you some clothes to see you through the next few days. You're staying with me and Ray.'

'Thanks H.'

'I think the police are going to want to speak to you about what happened. They'll probably recommend you press charges against...Howard.'

'H, I don't want to talk about it. I don't want to relive any of this crap!'

'That's perfectly understandable Issy. We don't want to see you suffer; but usually in my experience, denial normally prolongs it. What we resist; persists. Once you've accepted what's happened and grieved for the loss of your fingers and your career, you can overcome it and move on to pastures new. Create a new life.'

Two burly policemen called into the ward to speak to Isabelle. For privacy the nurses had given them access to a private waiting room, kitted out with a small circular wooden coffee table, a drink and snack machine and low level sofas lining the walls. There was a window, overlooking the modern extension to the famous teaching hospital.

Hortense ushered Isabelle in first, and guided her to a corner sofa, sitting down beside her, as the two policemen introduced themselves.

'My name is Officer Mike Jones and this is my colleague; Officer Barry White who, as we like to joke; is my first, my last, my everything!'

Hortense smiled up at the two towering and grinning officers.

'I can see you two are pros at this interviewing business,' she quipped.

Isabelle gave a faint grin, but her painkillers were beginning to wear off and sharp tingling sensations were radiating through her gauze-clad hand. The men sat down adjacent to Isabelle and Hortense, while Officer White pulled a lined pad from his jacket pocket. Mike established eye contact with Isabelle and said,

'Ms Bryant, please can you tell us exactly what happened last night, as best you can remember? Take as long as you need.'

Isabelle's mouth felt dry, so she signalled to H for some water.

'Howard and I have been having marital problems for some time...'

Hortense interjected. 'She means ever since she tied the knot with that egotistical bastard!' Her nostrils flared. Officers Jones and White smiled at Isabelle to continue.

'I suppose if I'm honest, we did have difficulties fairly early on in our marriage, but just lately things had deteriorated rapidly. He's been having some issues at work and it's made him pretty overbearing and neglectful. I've been feeling like I'm walking on eggshells the whole time, wondering when his next outburst would be. He's always been fond of a drink or two, but he seems to be resorting to the bottle a lot more these days, and he came home tanked-up at about two am. At first I thought maybe we were being burgled, but when I entered the kitchen I found him slumped on a chair with a whiskey, and a copy of the classical music magazine *High Notes*, which I was featured in this month. We hadn't discussed the article before that evening, I was waiting to catch him in a good mood, but he must have opened the drawer and seen my article.'

'Yes and he can't stand that his wife is more talented, successful and popular than he is. Every time he looks at her he sees his own perceived failures. No doubt the alcohol fuelled his anger,' added Hortense.

'Go on,' said Officer Jones.

'H is right. He was totally steamed up; he hurled abuse at me, which I thought was as far as it would go. It was in the past whenever his temper flared up, but last night...last night was different.'

The policemen exchanged concerned looks.

'Before I knew it, he just sprang from his chair and had grabbed my arm and stomped on my bare foot, and then he shoved me into a chair; slapped me, told me what a tart I was and how I was asking for it.' Isabelle took another sip of water. 'I'm sorry, I feel so humiliated having to repeat the horror of it all, please bear with me.'

'No need to apologise to us Ms. Bryant, we're on your side, it's your husband who should be feeling embarrassed about his treatment of you,' replied Officer White, who was grasping his pen tightly.

'I managed to kick him in the nuts and somehow make it out to the hallway. I was still in my nightwear and I tried to get upstairs to our room which has a bolt, but unfortunately he caught hold of my foot, pulled me down and tried to rape me. I don't know where I found the strength, but while he was trying to get his penis out of his pants, I caught him off balance and ran down past him, grabbed my keys; thinking that at least if I could get to the car I could escape from him. Somehow my adrenaline carried me out into the driveway, I got the car unlocked and opened the driver's door, but then for some reason, perhaps it was the freezing air, I just sort of stalled. It was like I was in some kind of lucid nightmare and I was watching it unfold, as both the observer and participant. It was that pause that cost me dear.

'The rest is history as they say. Howard took advantage of my sluggishness, and before I even realised that part of my hand was still in the open door, he had used his body weight to slam it shut, with my fingers still in it.'

Officer Jones clenched his jaw. 'I'm sorry Isabelle. Can you remember anything after that?'

'It all gets a bit blurry after that. Of course I remember the pain, the shock of seeing my fingers on the ground; blood squirting everywhere. I sort of fell to the ground, I found it hard to breathe, but thought I could hear our local landlord calling my name. Then everything went black.'

'Isabelle, is there anyone else you know who could corroborate his tendency to lose his temper, anyone at all who might also know about his increased alcohol consumption?'

'Eric, the landlord of The Angel would be able to tell you about his drinking habits, certainly I've found bottles of spirits stashed all over the house. I tried to help him see that drinking wasn't the answer, but how can you help someone who refuses to acknowledge they have a problem? As far as his temper goes, you could try asking members of his orchestra, the London Sound Company, they would have been exposed to his various outbursts.'

Officer White lowered his pen, as his colleague fixed Isabelle with a sympathetic gaze.

'You can press charges for assault, attempted rape and grievous bodily harm. Luckily, it's not just your word against his, your injuries notwithstanding; but we also have an accurate testimony from the landlord you mentioned; Eric Campbell, who happened to be out giving his dog a late night walk after closing time. He gave us a statement saying that Howard got blind drunk whilst at his pub The Angel, and that he felt uneasy about it. He saw what happened to you in the driveway, but sadly he wasn't close enough to be able to intervene before...'

'It's okay Mike, if I can call you that?'

He nodded. 'Eric called the ambulance and made sure that Howard didn't bolt from the scene. He honestly was your saviour. I don't know what would have happened if he hadn't been in the vicinity Isabelle. Probably that husband of yours would have left you unconscious, bleeding and freezing to death in your driveway.'

'God bless Eric. But he doesn't know I'm a lost cause now.'

Isabelle studied the earnest faces of the policemen.

'We're confident we've got enough evidence for a successful conviction Isabelle, but we need you to start the ball rolling.'

'Will it entail a trial, you know; court appearances and the like?'

'Yes, but that's the same with any prosecution. I'm sure the public will have great sympathy for you.'

They waited and watched her distant expression.

'No. No thank you. That won't be necessary.'

They stared at her, urging her to change her mind, but Isabelle was not one for vacillation.

'Gentlemen thank you so much for your advice and concern,' Hortense said. 'Personally, I agree with you. This maniac needs to be punished, but I also think Isabelle now needs to focus on her recovery, and even a relatively short trial would deplete her precious remaining energy.'

'Okay. It's a shame as we'd like to help.' They handed her their contact details. 'You know where to reach us if you should have a change of heart. In any case the CPS may decide they have enough evidence to prosecute regardless.'

8

Isabelle sat quietly in the front passenger seat as Hortense battled the West London traffic. She watched shoppers and suit clad executives going about their business on the crowded pavements, all seemingly with a purpose.

'What are you thinking Issy?' Hortense's voice interrupted the melancholy silence.

'Only that everyone seems to have a purpose in life except me.'

'You already have one honey; the task ahead is to find out what it is. But all in good time.'

Isabelle snorted. 'Time... Well, I seem to have plenty of that H. Everything's fallen apart; my career; my marriage. I'm in constant pain and on top of that I feel like a freak; condemned to a life of ineptness.'

Hortense swung the wheel as they rounded a sharp bend and accelerated away from the built-up area.

'We'll be home soon. Listen, I don't know how I'd react if someone ripped out my vocal chords. Probably much the same as you do. It's only natural to feel anger and self-pity. To wallow even. You've got to grieve, it's a natural process. Ray and I will do what we can to support you while you figure out where your life is going.'

'Thanks H, but that's nowhere with a capital N right now.'

'I know it's a cliché but Rome wasn't built in a day, and neither will the new Isabelle Bryant.'

'H, when can I get my violin?'

'Not sure that's a good idea…'

'I can't leave it there H. I don't trust Howard or Celia not to… well, to dispose of it or something.' She could feel her agitation rising. 'I know I won't be able to play it, I just want to hold it and see it.'

'Tell you what; why don't you give me Celia's number. I'll call her and tell her I'm coming over to collect the Nagyvary and some of your things, and I'll tell the Millers if they know what's good for them they won't give me any attitude.'

'Thanks H.'

'Even with your violin it's not going to be easy Issy. You'll just have to take it a day at a time. Shall I put the radio on?'

'Yeah, sure.'

The music came on it was Beethoven's Violin Concerto. Hortense was about to change the frequency when Isabelle patted her hand to leave it. By the time Hortense had steered the BMW into their driveway, Isabelle's face was awash with streaks, her eyes red rimmed.

Hortense carried her bags and they entered into the spacious hallway. Hortense showed Isabelle to her room; a double mahogany sleigh bed sat beneath a wide bay window, and to her right the wall was lined with shelves, mostly filled with books and photographs. A mahogany wardrobe and dressing table were placed on the opposite wall, and a chaise longue upholstered in a champagne coloured silk jacquard material that matched the bedding set across the foot of the bed.

'Ray and Louis will be home soon, so I'll get some food on the go. Creole chicken sound okay to you?'

'You know me H, I'll eat anything,' replied Isabelle. She stretched out on her bed, occasionally getting a waft of garlic and Cajun spices. She could hear H singing At Last by Etta James as she prepared their dinner. Exhaustion took over again and she drifted off to sleep.

Isabelle's windowsill had filled up with get well cards. Alongside Sebastian's colourful musical card, sat one from Gerry and various friends and musicians had followed suit in wishing her a speedy recovery. Isabelle was re-reading them all when H poked her head round the door.

'Issy, do you fancy going to the theatre today, we could catch a matinee?'

'I suppose so. Do you mean you've had enough of me moping round the house?' She managed a smile.

'Not at all, but I think it will do you good to get some fresh air and venture out. Have you had your pills yet this morning?'

'Yes I have, but you know I'll never get a glove over my hand with all this...padding. The cold really makes it sting and I get numbness all around my joints.'

'We're only a ten minute walk from the tube and we shouldn't need to be outside for long. I'll book the tickets now while you get ready.'

Isabelle sighed and pulled off her dressing gown. She sat on the edge of the bed and held her knickers with her right hand, carefully looping the right hole over her right foot, before sliding her left foot in. She pulled them up slowly, also using her left thumb to help get them up to her waist. Her jeans were a tougher undertaking, and being a close fit they were hard to get over her backside. Using her left thumb and forefinger as a pincer she guided the belt into its usual notch. A heavy pain emanated through her forefinger as the movement strained her severely bruised connecting ligaments. She had taken to wearing her night bra during the day as well, which she could step into and pull up much like her pants. She felt too embarrassed to keep asking H to hook her up at the back. She slipped her shirt on and called for H to do up her buttons.

'H, I don't think I'll ever master buttons one handed.'

'Nonsense, you won't have to. Once the dressings come off and the muscles and tendons settle down you'll be able to use your thumb and forefinger much like before. But for now we ought to get you some warm jersey tops; that should make life easier.'

'Sorry I'm such a cripple.'

'You're not, stop it.'

'It must remind you of when Louis was young and you had to do pretty much everything for him?'

'Kids learn to be independent gradually, and so will you Issy.'

They descended the spiral staircase. Isabelle held on carefully to the railing with her right hand.

'Why don't you try putting on some makeup before we leave? Just give me a shout if you need any help.'

Isabelle pulled her makeup bag from her handbag and went into the downstairs cloakroom. The mirror was backlit, which was the main source of light in the tiny dingy room. The small window was virtually covered by foliage that was growing up the side of their house, cutting out the natural daylight.

She held onto the base of her foundation compact with her right hand and opened the catch with her left thumb nail. She then transferred the compact to her left hand, carefully setting it between her thumb and forefinger as she used her right hand to sweep her fingers through the rich emollient. She applied it in sections over her face. Although she was unused to applying it with her right hand she felt she had managed to cover her face evenly without any heavy patches, like the ones she could usually spot smeared over Celia's face. Isabelle used her forefinger and thumb to grasp her eyeliner, but the mass of gauze and bandage loomed large in front of her, and she dropped the pencil in the sink with a clatter. The lipstick fared a little better.

'How you doing Issy?'

Isabelle emerged from the cloakroom looking sheepish.

'That's better. Not bad at all for a first attempt. You've got some colour in your face and lips.'

'It's just as well I didn't try and use my right hand for my lipstick or I'd end up looking like a clown!'

They laughed, and Hortense guided her to the front door.

'C'mon, I'm taking you to the Old Vic.'

Isabelle slumped into one of the comfy lounge chairs. Hortense, who had heard her collecting the letters from the hallway, came looking for her.

'What's up Issy?'

'Apart from the fact that I'm not a virtuoso violinist anymore you mean?'

'What's that?' Hortense grabbed the letter from Isabelle's right hand and read with horror.

'It's from the Philharmonic Society asking me to play Mozart's Adagio in E Major.'

'You know they would have posted this before they got news of your accident Issy. It's just a combination of bad timing and slow post.'

'How could that happen? My accident was even featured on the news. How could someone in charge of programming for such a long established and respected musical organisation foul up so badly? They just twisted that fucking knife a bit further into my heart H!'

'Swear if it makes you feel better, but deep down you know this was an honest mistake. I know it's rubbing salt into the wound in a seemingly callous manner, but please don't let this incident upset you so much. It's still early days...'

'That's easy for you to say H. Your life couldn't be better right now. I just can't take any more proselytising. Everything is not going to be wonderful. I can't do the only thing that gave me joy, the only thing that I was good at, the only thing I know.' She looked up. 'I may be breathing, but my life was over the second my fingers were detached from my body.'

Isabelle stood and brushed past Hortense who was still trying to gather her thoughts. 'I don't mean to sound ungrateful H, but I just want to be left alone.'

'Okay Issy, have it your way. I've got to get ready for the drive to Sussex to collect your violin, but this conversation isn't over. We'll talk when I get back...'

Isabelle went back up to her room and sat sulking until she heard the front door slam and the revving of the engine as Hortense departed.

She didn't know how long she sat on the bed for, she tried to cry but her eyes were dry. She looked at the invite again and the thought crossed her mind that perhaps she could post her fingers back in reply.

Outside, the cold November sleet battered the pale orange brick facade of the Lafayette household, and the wide tree-lined road was relatively empty, as residents had rushed to their cars shivering and huddling under the onslaught of the watery hail.

As she sat simmering on her own, Isabelle could feel her depression rapidly deepening. She was grateful to H and Raymond for their unconditional love and support, but she observed her despair more keenly in the light of their close knit family unit and fulfilled professional lives. Discouragement whispered to her this was something she would never know. Every time she looked at her bandaged hand utter desolation filled her being. She decided she had suffered enough.

Thinking more clearly than she had for days, Isabelle donned H's hefty flying jacket and headed out to the local convenience store. Hortense had tied her greasy hair back in a pony-tail; she had dark circles under her eyes that were even more pronounced against her pale complexion and clothes were now hanging off her dwindling body. As she crossed the street the weather began to worsen, and she grimaced at the sting of the hail as it pelted against her skin.

Once in the shop Isabelle attracted some stares from young and older men alike. Holding the basket in the crook of her left elbow, careful not to catch her hand, she shovelled food in, with no particular thought to what she was buying. The Paracetamol had gone in first. Once at the till she smiled sweetly at the spotty teenager who was serving her.

She looked at him. He paused briefly when he came to the numerous packets, but after staring at her bandaged stumps he passed them through the scanner. Isabelle made her exit, running back across the street to the warmth and safety of the house.

She dropped the plastic bag in the hallway, leaving the contents scattered across the floor, taking only the pills up to her room. She sat on the bed with her bottle of water and caught sight of herself in the mirror. There was no sign of her former vibrant self, just a tortured soul staring back.

Isabelle took the first packet and started taking each pill out of its plastic cover as best she could with her right hand. Putting them in a pile on her bedside table she counted sixteen. Then she started to empty the next packet. She padded downstairs and shuffled through H and Raymond's extensive CD collection, where her eyes rested on the spine of a reddish CD. Reading the title: *Great Performances Edition*. It was Alfred Brendel playing live and the music was inevitably Beethoven, his piano concerto number five, dubbed the "Emperor". It had always evoked a melancholy response in her. Her shaking right hand placed the shiny disc into the player. All she could hear was the sound of her heart beating and the poignant melody of the piano against the warmth of the strings.

Isabelle searched through the study and found some A4 paper and a biro. Closing her eyes and travelling back to her childhood suddenly forced tears to the surface, and as she put pen to paper the words began to flow in spidery but purposeful fashion;

Dear Dad, Jack, Lily, H, and to all my friends,

I want you all to know how much I love you. My life could not have been the rich experience it has been up until now if it weren't for having had all your influence on me at some stage in my life. Dad, I never appreciated the times you coached me when I was a child, it was probably the deciding factor in my pursuing a musical career.

Jack and Lily you were wonderful to grow up with, as was my best pal H, who understands me better than any other living soul. I know we had our disagreements Lily, and yes: you were right about everything.

Sebastian, mi amigo, I never told you how much joy it gave me just to sit in your lounge with Delilah on my knee listening to you bring Bach's music to life.

H, sorry I let you down, you and that old deaf maestro have been my inspiration. I am honoured to have been your best friend.

My will to live evaporated when my fingers were taken from me, along with the joy of making others happy. What I have, I leave to H. Please tell Gerry Goldberg he was a faithful friend and the most decent agent I ever knew.

I'd like any further royalties from my latest CD (The Virtuoso) to be donated to the Nordoff Robbins Foundation.

I was lucky; I reached a level of success that most people only ever dream of, but I'm quitting the game now. You may think me cowardly, but I simply have nothing to live for other than unbearable pain, which by its very nature – is unbearable.

Think of me whenever you hear my beautiful instrument, for music is the language of the soul.

Love Isabelle.

Folding the note she placed it on the bedside table.

She began swallowing the pills. A sense of peace prevailed over her. She scanned the room. Numerous bookshelves lined the walls, and her eyes rested on a black and white framed picture of Hortense singing alongside Jools Holland at the piano. It was faded.

She stilled her mind and listened to her breathing. Feeling strangely more alive and aware than she had been since her debut performance, she was surprised at how being so close to death could have this effect.

Her long dark lashes swooped down onto her cheek as she lay back on the bed and finally closed her eyes.

9

Hortense sat in her car just crawling along. The roads were too congested approaching London, she'd never get home in-time. She pulled into a lay-by. She rang the number to her house and listened to the unanswered rings. She waited a few moments and dialled the number again. The rings buzzed in her ear. Her stomach was in free-fall as she dialled Ray's number.

'Ray Honey, you gotta get home right now, it's a matter of life and death!'

'I am going now,' said the voice. There was movement over the line before going dead.

She then dialled 999. There was a pause.

'Err... Ambulance please.'

Raymond pulled up in his own driveway. The house looked deserted. He paused for a moment taking in the scene before getting out of the car and walking up to the door. He turned the key in the front door. The house was silent. Their home felt bleak.

'Isabelle? Isabelle? Are you okay?'

He almost tripped over the plastic bag with its spilled contents of margarine, milk and various tins scattered across his path. As he climbed the stairs, the sound of the piano became clearer.

'Isabelle?'

He ventured into Isabelle's room. She looked like she was just taking a nap, her face peaceful in repose. He noticed the glass and empty pill packets. A paper note sat on the bedside table. Light was streaming in from the window. As suddenly as it had started the hail had cleared and the sun was now shining on her pale features. Her injured hand hung limply over the side of the bed.

He stared as panic infiltrated his muscles. Catching his breath, he finally regained control and ran over to her bedside to take her pulse. It was there: but very weak.

'We've got to get you to hospital my lovely,' he whispered, stroking her cool cheek.

He grasped his mobile from his pocket when he heard an approaching siren, which came to a crescendo outside the house. As he leaned across Isabelle and peered out the window he saw the welcome neon blue flashes cast from the ambulance in his drive.

A few seconds later voices were calling from the open door in the hallway and Raymond ran onto the landing.

'Quickly! She's up here! It looks like she's taken an overdose.'

10

'That was a lucky escape Issy.'

'Was it?' Isabelle replied with a sullen stare.

'If Ray hadn't got to you when he did...'

Hortense led Isabelle through the bustling hospital foyer. 'It's getting to be a habit visiting you in a hospital bed! Still, the doctors are happy that all the toxins have been pumped out of your stomach; you just need some rest and a change of scenery. I'm going to start planning our trip to Madeira.'

They passed through double sliding doors and out into the bright but chilly afternoon.

'Madeira?'

'Yes, Ray and I have a holiday home there.'

'I didn't know that. It's a sweet gesture H, normally you know I love to travel, but I don't think I'm up to that yet.'

Hortense unlocked her black BMW which was glinting in the sunlight. 'I don't want you running into Howard, or anyone in the media, or risk getting another request to play from a well-meaning orchestra, or anything at all that's going to interfere with your recovery. You've been to hell and back, but there's still purgatory to go through.'

Isabelle sank into the leather seat and sighed.

'Whatever you say H, I'll be like a docile lamb from now on, promise.'

'It'll be your defining moment Issy, when you figure the reason it wasn't your time to go.'

'I guess.' Isabelle heard the words, but she couldn't envisage their fruition. Her hand was throbbing and her throat was burning. 'Like you said H. One day at a time.'

Still feeling sleepy she closed her eyes and soon the motion of the car had sent her to sleep. Isabelle awoke as Hortense parked the car. She turned to her and smiled. 'Ray's taken Louis to afterschool football club, so we've got the house to ourselves. I thought we could have an afternoon chilling in front of the box with my secret stash of Galaxy bars.'

'I've got nothing better to do H.'

Hortense had bought a bunch of classic movie and at the top of the pile was; it's a Wonderful Life with Jimmy Stewart. It brought a wry smile to her face. H didn't do subtle.

They sat with their backs to the bottom of the sofa; with their legs and feet outstretched enveloped by the warm wool of the large cream sheepskin rug. Hortense had poured an assortment of chocolates into a bowl, and they sat chewing in silence as the black and white pictures flickered into life on the screen. By the end of the film tears were running down her cheeks as Jimmy Stewart raced to be with his family, having realised the futility of wishing his life away.

'We never realise how much we touch each other's lives,' Isabelle commented.

'So true Issy. Especially in the midst of a crisis; when our focus is on our own misfortune. Gratitude lifts the heart and clears away the fog of self-pity. No matter the vicissitudes of life, if you can find something to say thank you for every day, you'll get through life and look back and realise that on the whole, it wasn't so bad. Joy, sorrow, it's all from the same well of emotion.'

Isabelle sniffed and was tempted to wipe her nose on her bandage, until H produced a hanky. 'H, you've just reminded me of that poem If, by Kipling. Doesn't it say something along the lines of treating triumph and disaster just the same?'

Hortense pulled out her phone and Googled the poem. 'Someone was paying attention in class. '

'So, somehow, I've got to treat those two imposters the same. Any ideas on how I do that H?'

'Maybe it will come to you when we're away.'

'Maybe.'

Hortense kneeled forward and removed the DVD, replacing it with Gone With The Wind.

'This ought to keep us occupied! Issy this is my favourite film. I just love that scene at the end, where a tearful Scarlett looks up to the camera with an earnest expression and says, "After all, tomorrow is another day".'

Hortense and Isabelle were absorbed in Scarlett and Rhet's love affair when they heard the key turning in the door. Raymond and Louis arrived home in a jovial mood and the smell of Chinese takeaway was pervading the air.

'Hello my lovely ladies,' called Raymond. 'Come and get some supper. Mr Wong does a bloody good set meal for four.'

'It's true,' Hortense concurred. She halted the film and they headed for the kitchen. Ray was laying knives and forks on the table.

'Have a seat my dears. Louis has gone upstairs for a quick rinse and change. He's not a pretty sight after footy.'

'How'd he do?' Hortense asked.

'Pretty good. No goals tonight, but coach is saying he could have a future as a premiership player if he follows the right path and stays injury free.'

'You must be very proud of him,' Isabelle said.

'Yep.'

Raymond uncovered the foil containers and put clean plates out. 'Let's get stuck in then.'

'Thank you Ray, my taste buds are tingling.'

Louis entered the room with a waft of Lynx following him. Isabelle observed how muscular he was for a fifteen year old boy, his movements suffused with confidence.

'Hi Louis, well done honey, dad says you did great tonight?'

'Yeah, okay. Looks like I might be good enough to get into an academy.'

They ate in silence for a while, with Isabelle lagging slightly behind as she grappled with her fork.

'H, have you got the Nagyvary?'

Her question took Hortense by surprise, and she choked slightly on her rice.

'Yes. But I haven't really had a chance to talk to you about it, 'cos you were a guest of her majesty's infirmary.' She grinned.

'S'pose I asked for that one,' Isabelle retorted. 'Howard and Celia didn't give you any trouble I hope?'

'No, they didn't. But let's not talk about them. Your violin, music, clothes and some personal items are all locked away in our bedroom at the moment.'

'Do you think…is it possible for me to see it later?' Isabelle asked.

Hortense lowered her fork and exchanged glances with Raymond. 'I don't see why not. Are you sure you're ready to do this Issy?'

'I think so. I just need to touch it, to see and feel something that was such a huge part of my old life.'

After their meal Hortense led Isabelle into her bedroom where she had already opened the case of the Nagyvary. Isabelle gasped as she caught sight of its deep brown shiny surface. The resin from her bow had saturated the strings and a white sheen was still covering the lower part of the fingerboard and the surface beneath the strings.

'We need to wipe the resin off the wood. I was so tired after my practice that night, I forgot to clean it.'

She signalled H towards the inner pocket where a small cloth was neatly folded. Isabelle held it in her right hand and carefully wiped beneath the strings until all the sticky white dust had been removed.

'That's better, now she looks pristine,' remarked Isabelle staring intently at the instrument she loved so much. She plucked the strings with her left forefinger. It could have been like any other practice session. She closed the lid.

'It only took a split second for my life to be ruined.'

Hortense zipped and popped up the covering so that the Nagyvary was secure inside its red velvet home.

'Not ruined, just temporarily...derailed.'

Isabelle sighed. 'Yes but it's going to take longer than a split second to work my way out of this train wreck.'

'It doesn't matter how long it takes, as long as you're making progress Issy. To me it feels like you've turned a corner already?' Hortense studied her, hopeful for some kind of acknowledgement that she was off the suicide watch.

'I'm still heartbroken H. I can't even put it into words.' Isabelle sat on the edge of the bed and returned her gaze. 'It all got too much for me, and I just succumbed to a moment of intense grief. I can barely comprehend what's happened to me.'

Hortense put her arm around Isabelle and gave her an affectionate squeeze.

'Perhaps you were right though H; I owe it to myself to find out why I'm still here, whatever that entails. I haven't got a clue how, but I do know that I don't want to give up anymore.'

The night before they were due to travel Isabelle sat wrapped in Hortense's oversized fleece bathrobe on the sofa, gripping her warm milky drink in her right hand, her still heavily bandaged left hand resting in her lap. Hortense sat next to her.

Isabelle stared into the open fire, mesmerised by the dancing orange flames as they engulfed the small logs of wood in a tender, scorching ferocity. The warm light it projected flickered onto Hortense's feet as she slipped forward onto the thick beige carpet and sat with her legs stretched out in front of her and began jotting down notes into her small diary. Several minutes passed, when without warning, Hortense pulled the folded piece of paper from her dressing gown pocket, and moved her hand back behind her head in Isabelle's direction.

Isabelle recognised her suicide note instantly. She swallowed, laid down her drink and took it tentatively from H's grasp. She rubbed her fingers over its smooth surface, and without opening it she got up and thrust it into the fire. She watched as it blackened and crumpled, sending wisps of ash up into the chimney.

She turned back to Hortense, trying hard to overcome the lump that was forming in her throat. 'H, I'll never be able to thank you enough. I'm so sorry for all the hassle and worry I've caused. Can you forgive me for being so selfish?'

Hortense tugged her right hand, motioning her to sit down by her side.

'Issy, you mean the world to me. I'd do it all again if I had to, don't ever worry about putting me through stuff.' Her voice was unusually hushed.

'Thanks...but I just wanted you to know I was in a very dark place and I couldn't see my way out of it. But thanks to you and Raymond there's a glimmer of light, and I hope it will get brighter if I follow it.'

'Honey I just wanna see you regain your "joi de vivre". Take it one day at a time. You know, you're the most wonderful and amazing person Issy, it's time you realised that.'

Isabelle's face was flushed from being so close to the heat, but she cocked her head to the side and rested it upon Hortense's shoulder.

'Am I about to benefit from one of your profound insights H?'

Hortense flashed a smile. 'You sure are Isabelle Bryant! During hard times I've always found it helpful to think that when God closes a door he always opens a window somewhere else. I know in your case it was a gate, but by God we are gonna find that window!'

A warm sensation was flooding through her stomach, replacing the knotted ache she had felt since her stomach was pumped. Isabelle ventured her thoughts.

'I guess we'll have time to talk more when we're in Madeira. I'm actually looking forward to doing some sightseeing.'

'We sure will. It's good to get close to nature when life gets too much. Nature has such an unwavering and primordial beauty you can't help but marvel that everything is connected. That same energy runs through our veins. We are all a part of the essence that created the universe. If you can harness that power nothing will ever destroy you.'

'I wish I could be more like you H...'

'You're perfect just as you are, being you. You're one of a kind, just like we all are. Self-love is the key; it's the precursor to loving others.'

Isabelle sat up. 'You just always seem to know the right thing to say at the right time H. Is there any end to your erudition?'

'You know Issy, I always admired your talent and how you made other people's lives better from working hard and developing that talent – but mostly I love you for who you are, regardless of what you did and can do.'

Isabelle's eyes began to pool with tears. 'You've been such a blessing and a joy in my life; and for that I'll be eternally grateful.'

11

The plane journey passed smoothly, with virtually no turbulence and no screaming children to rattle Isabelle's jaded nerves. The cabin crew had been friendly and efficient. One particular steward had taken a shine to Isabelle, and he asked reverently for her autograph.

'I'll try. It might look more like a child's scrawl than the signature of a virtuoso!'

She held the pen between her forefinger and thumb as firmly as she could. There was no pressure or support to rely on from the other fingers, but she managed to keep the pen upright and write her name. 'I haven't quite got the new muscle memory going yet, but here it is.'

She handed the in-flight magazine to the steward, who had gone very pale.

'Please forgive me Ms. Bryant, I…I had no idea you were actually left handed. So stupid of me. I'm so sorry for the intrusion. That was most insensitive of me.'

'That's okay, it's no problem. I'm flattered that you knew me and my music. You know, you remind me of a very good cellist friend.'

He smiled and raised the magazine in acknowledgement. Isabelle and Hortense hadn't wanted for anything as he served them with a devoted fervour for the rest of the flight.

The captain's smooth voice sounded over the speaker.

'Ladies and gentlemen, we trust you enjoyed your flight with us today. We are now on our final approach to Funchal; we should have you on the tarmac in ten minutes. The outside temperature is a very respectable eighteen degrees, compared to the two degrees we left behind at Gatwick. The forecast for the next few days is similar, warm but windy. We wish you a pleasant stay in Madeira and hope to see you soon. Cabin crew please cross-check and take your seats for landing.'

Isabelle felt a quiver of excitement as they descended through the clouds and before them was a view of verdant green hills surrounded by a vibrant dark blue ocean.

The final approach over the nearby island of Porto Santo, situated off Madeira's south east coast revealed a drier more barren landscape; and she could feel that prick of excitement breaking through her depression like sunlight through clouds.

The airstrip was nestled at the base of the side of a steep hill, probably the only piece of substantial flat land on the entire island. With the ocean lapping closely on the other side of the runway, it didn't leave any room for error.

Hortense closed her book and peered across Isabelle's shoulder to look out the window.

'Ray and I have had many a happy holiday on this island – even before we adopted Louis. It's pretty unique. Are you enjoying the rugged scenery Issy?'

'I was, actually H. You know this place wasn't at the top of my must see list, but only because I didn't know anything about it...I think that could change very soon.'

A brief jolt interrupted them and they found themselves speeding along the runway, their bodies pushed forwards into their safety belts by the force of the jet's air brakes slowing them. Soon the ocean wasn't passing so fast in the window, and they gradually came to crawl as the aircraft taxied to the terminal.

A sturdy local man with thick black hair and a full moustache had gallantly loaded their bags into his canary yellow Mercedes, he nodded compliantly when Hortense showed him the address.

Pastel coloured houses with terracotta roofs perched on steep hillsides that overlooked the craggy inlets along the meandering coastline. Large and small were jumbled together, villas, apartments, and hotels all broken up, only with scattered patches of dark green foliage. To her left, flashes of shimmering ocean winked at her as they sped towards Funchal on the main coastal highway. It appeared to Isabelle that every conceivable spare plot of land had been developed or was in the process of being built into a luxury villa. The island seemed crowded yet organised, the towns huddling cosily into the mountainside.

'Madeira has been benefitting from money from the EU, there is a lot of investment being made in, how do you say, our roads and houses.'

Isabelle smiled as he watched her in the rear view mirror.

'Yes, I think the term is infrastructure. Your roads are better than the rough pot holey ones in London.'

He nodded. 'We are making hay as the sun shines,' he quipped.

Combined with a thick accent he sounded almost comical, but at the same time immensely proud of his heritage.

Isabelle noticed his gaze had been drawn to her bandaged hand, and she was about to say something to put him at his ease when he muttered,

'I am sorry for your pain; I hope the island will help you to make a speedy recovery.'

'Thank you, me too,' she replied.

Forty minutes later the Mercedes pulled up in the driveway of a low rise apartment building in the fishing village of Camara de Lobos. Isabelle instantly fell in love with its quaint horseshoe bay and bobbing boats that had once captivated Winston Churchill's artistic eye.

From Hortense and Raymond's apartment the view was beautiful, beyond Isabelle's imagination.

Hortense pointed towards a sheer cliff that dominated the skyline.

'That's the Cabo Girão, claimed to be the second steepest cliff in the world and one of the highest in Europe.'

The French windows of the lounge led out to a small balcony, where they sat in awe, taking in the view. They watched the fishermen return from searching the depths of the Atlantic, laden down with their hauls. The light had begun to fade and a chill travelled on the breeze. Isabelle felt goose bumps on her bare arms. She went back inside to explore her new home for the next few days.

The apartment was simple and minimalist, without feeling bare. The lounge was airy and decorated in pale grey tones, complete with chaise longue and a lengthy curving sofa. A flat screen television was fixed against the largest wall, directly opposite the sofa. There was also an expensive sound system wired up, and a brightly woven rug in the centre of the room, providing colour and depth to an otherwise plain decor.

A glass coffee table was positioned on the rug between the sofa and television, and was buried under various brochures and books.

She noted that there were two double bedrooms and a decent size kitchen that lead onto the dining area, with shiny parquet flooring. The bathroom was equally ample, in simple white tones and a white marble effect floor, with pale blue mosaic tiles in the shower and white borders. Plush carpets adorned the bedrooms, which had built-in wardrobes and sleigh style wooden double beds taking centre stage. There were also mahogany chests and a full length mirror in each.

Hortense and Raymond's room was painted in sensuous pink and red, while the guest room (which she guessed Louis slept in when they were on holiday) was more muted, with dark stone walls and mocha coloured curtains.

On closer inspection Isabelle noticed the pictures adorning the walls. They were mostly family portraits, with some jazz club shots of Hortense in action, one of New Orleans taken from a helicopter, which must have been taken long before the fateful hurricane Katrina had struck the city with such deadly force.

Her eyes were drawn to another picture by the main lounge windows. The photograph showed Isabelle in full flow on her violin; engaged in the music, elegant in her black halter neck gown, her slender frame bent over slightly, surrounded by the tips of the orchestra's first violins' bows behind her. The lights were bright above her head, casting shadows over the stage. The backdrop was unmistakable; it was the Sydney Opera House.

A wave of emotion swept through her, as she remembered the night it had been taken. She recalled playing the Bruch Violin Concerto number one in G minor, a popular choice in any soloist's repertoire, followed by the Beethoven Romance in F for her encore. The Australians had been an enthusiastic crowd, and she had loved every minute on stage. She could almost hear the applause in her head and feel the sweat trickling down her temples and between her breasts after completing the energetic third movement. As well as Hortense, her father, Lily and Jack had been in the audience that night.

With a pang of longing she experienced again the euphoria that they had all felt after re-uniting at the concert after years of separation. Relations had been cordial but uncomfortable with her father. Jack had found himself in between flights and Lily was in Sydney as part of a round-the-world trip with her new husband, so a memorable evening had transpired between them.

The flashback felt like another world, almost light years away, but paradoxically, safe and familiar, not like the world she now faced.

She flinched when Hortense intruded on her reminiscing. 'C'mon Issy, let's go and grab ourselves a fine meal, I could eat a horse! There are some wonderful restaurants in the village.'

Hortense hooked her arm through Isabelle's, moving her away from the picture in the direction of the door. As she turned her attention away from the past and onto her hunger a gurgling sound suddenly erupted from her stomach, causing them to burst into laughter. They strode out along the main road, where the street lights were twinkling in the dusk, and the sun slowly sank like a molten ball into the sea, its vivid glow casting an ethereal reflection onto the vast face of the Cabo Girão.

Over dinner Hortense went over their plans for the next day. In the morning she would send Isabelle up to the top of the Cabo Girão, while she finished a few chores and in the afternoon she would take her into the capital Funchal, to sample the sights of the city. Finally, when their feet would be aching and they would be gasping for drinks after their avid explorations, they would settle into an old British tradition on the island – institution even – of tea on the terrace at Reid's Hotel.

12

Isabelle woke at eight thirty. A Single shaft of sunlight poked through the curtains, beckoning her to view the splendour of its morning glory. Isabelle yawned, rose, and drew back the curtains to reveal a sharp blue sky. The soft breeze from the open window brought her the scent of the sea. Wandering into the lounge and dining area still in her pyjamas she noticed Hortense was already dressed in a floral printed loose dress, whispering encouragement down the phone to Louis about his forthcoming mock exams.

'I miss you too honey, I'll be thinking about you. Bye for now.' She clicked the receiver down and smiled up at Isabelle who was already looking for some cereal to feed her grumbling tummy.

'Sleep okay?' Hortense enquired.

Grabbing a bowl and a carton of milk and packets from various cupboards Isabelle absentmindedly nodded in the affirmative. 'Did you?'

'Like a log. Sorry to rush off Issy, I've got to go into Funchal for some business. Ray has asked me to visit our bank out here. I've arranged for Miguel, the guy who drove us here from the airport yesterday to take you to see the stunning Cabo Girão shortly after ten, and then he'll bring you into Funchal so we can meet up and do some sightseeing together.'

Isabelle showered, dressed, and was carefully applying makeup when the doorbell rang and a deep voice sounded from the entrance phone.

'Bom dia Mrs Bryant, this is Miguel. Mrs Lafayette has asked me to take you to the Cabo Girão this morning.'

Snatching her small shoulder bag and camera she shut the door to the otherwise empty apartment and slid into the comfort of the rear seat of the canary yellow Mercedes.

'You look very beautiful today Mrs Bryant,' Miguel said, his sweet face creased with lines around his mouth and eyes as he smiled.

'Thank you Miguel.'

She sat and admired the lushness of the island as they rounded the bends, each becoming more precipitous than the last, exposing more of the ubiquitous red roofs and tiny patches of banana crops. Although it was a clear sunny day, the clouds were gathering ominously in the distance, over the highest peaks on the island, and the sea was darker than yesterday, spewing white foam as it crashed against the coast.

'It's beautiful no?' Miguel asked.

'Very,' replied Isabelle, 'it must be quite challenging for you driving round these sharp narrow bends all the time.'

'I know it like the back of my hand,' he said. 'In the spring the roads are lined with wild flowers, and in summer they are adorned by Agapanthus, Hibiscus and Lily of the Valley.'

'It must be amazing. But the vibrant colours of the trees and the winter shrubs is still impressive viewing material,' Isabelle said.

'You know, even Eucalyptus trees grow in abundance on this island.'

They pulled in to a crowded car park, bustling with people, cars, taxis and coaches. Tourists clamoured to get to the edge of the cliff for the view from the heights of the Cabo Girão, apparently unperturbed that it might collapse before them at any moment. She welcomed being among throngs of people that she didn't know, and who didn't know her...

As she neared the cliff, the fresh smell of pine infused her senses, and enthusiastic local traders called and waved their arms to her as she passed, in an effort to persuade her to look at their wares. Wonderful lace tablecloths and hand woven wool hats lined the route, alongside tacky tea towels and baseball caps. The hubbub had now cleared ahead of her and she was able to slip into a gap at the edge of the cliff, up against the railings. She gasped in awe.

The sheer drop seemed to go on forever, and she could see the rocks beneath the pale turquoise ocean. She could make out some terraces on the land immediately at the foot of the cliff, which could only be reached by boat. The industrious islanders did not appear to waste any of their valuable land, especially virtually non-existent flat land.

She turned her head to take in the equally impressive view of the now distant coastline leading towards Camara de Lobos and beyond.

After a few minutes, she turned around, and made her way back to the taxi through throngs of people. She covered her left hand with her right, anxious that it might get knocked about in the fray. She waved at Miguel.

As they sped along the main coastal road into Funchal Isabelle began to feel her stumpy joints throbbing. They rode in silence until they reached the terminal of the cable car, where Hortense who was ready and waiting, opened the door. She grasped Isabelle's arm to help pull her out of the car.

Isabelle smiled at Miguel, and raised her arm to wave as he drove back in the direction he had come from.

'How was it?' Hortense was bubbling over with excitement.

'Thanks H! That was amazing...better than any sky-scraper I've been up! God's epic handy work really took my breath away.'

'I think you've just described most people's reactions to the Cabo Girão. You'll enjoy the cable car too, it's just been built and it takes you right up over the city to the Monte Palace and gardens up in the hills behind Funchal. Even Ray, Louis and I haven't been on this yet. I've got our tickets already.'

They strode through the entrance into an immaculate transparent car. As they sat the doors closed and it swung forward at a steep angle as it rose swiftly up from the ground.

Both women gazed avidly as they passed over homes and offices, treetops and roads. A sea of terracotta roofs spread out before them, which seemed to melt into the horizon as they continued their sharp ascent. As she looked up towards Monte Isabelle could see tall dark trees, interspersed by new homes perched on ledges as they drew closer to the looming hills. Hortense thrust a guide book into Isabelle's right hand. 'This is for you.'

The car pulled smoothly into the station at the top of the mountain, and as they stepped out a strong wind pulled at their skirts, and the sounds of the city's distant cars, cranes and people were almost inaudible in its breath.

They strolled round the lush gardens, enjoying each other's company, pointing in wonderment at the array of tropical flowers and plants prospering within the garden walls. Isabelle had felt particularly peaceful exploring the Japanese Garden. As they began to tire H had suggested they go back into the city, it was almost time for their afternoon tea appointment.

'The air is so fresh and fragrant up here. How long have we been walking round these botanical gardens H?'

Hortense glanced at her watch. 'Just under two hours.'

'It's gone in a flash. Just seeing and listening to these lovely waterfalls has been so calming, but I must admit my feet are aching a bit now.'

'Mine too. Now, Issy - do you want to go down the hill the boring way or the fun way?'

'I suppose boring is out of the question?'

As they rounded the corner she realised with a sinking stomach what H had in mind.

Tall, broad shouldered men in white trousers, shirts and straw hats were congregated at the top of the hill, next to a small queue of nervous looking tourists. One by one they clambered into wicker chairs secured on wooden runners. The men stood on each side of the back of the chair keeping one foot on the runner while pushing away with the other. To gather more speed they then jumped off it completely, still pushing hard and running to keep up with it as it sped down the steeply inclined road.

Isabelle began to tremble. 'It's perfectly safe,' Hortense said.

'H, you've got to be kidding! I've already had one near death experience lately. I don't want to be squished like a Madeiran mosquito on the road!'

'You know they wouldn't do it for the tourists if it was in any way dangerous.' Hortense's brow furrowed.

When their turn came around they climbed in gingerly and sat down, and before Isabelle had a chance to change her mind, their male escorts pushed away. Hortense turned to her, her brown eyes flashing, as she yelled,

'Welcome to Carros de Cesto Issy!'

The houses on either side of the road were passed rapidly as they hurtled down the street. Isabelle's tangled hair flew out like an unruly ribbon behind her. They simultaneously shrieked with laughter and terror as the city became ever closer with their increasing velocity. They arrived at the foot of the hill with shaky limbs and pounding hearts, and hair looking as if they'd been skydiving.

'Wow,' Isabelle exclaimed as she climbed out of her seat, 'we made it down in one piece.'

A waiting taxi took them into the city while they readjusted their hair and clothes. The air-conditioned leather clad interior had a calming effect.

Hortense grappled with her handbag and pulled out a compact mirror, studied her face for a few seconds, and seemingly satisfied with her appearance, she handed it to Isabelle.

'A girl has to look her best, after all, it's none other than the illustrious Reid's Hotel next on our agenda,' Hortense feigned a posh accent.

'That's easier said than done when one has just been on an adrenaline pumping, high speed descent through the city H.'

Still flushed, Isabelle applied some lip gloss with a quivering left hand. She only just had time to close her eyes and slow her breathing before the Mercedes peeled into the hotel driveway and she caught her first glimpse of its famous pink walls.

13

Smartly dressed doormen opened the car doors, and they almost floated into the cool foyer. Isabelle was struck by its rather faded thirties grandeur, and as they walked through towards the terrace she noticed that the chandeliers and the antique furniture all reflected the epoch of its heyday.

Reid's was a manmade feature of the emerald isle of the Atlantic, and she was warming to it with every step. The waiters wore pale cream jackets, and displayed impeccable manners to each guest. Hortense relayed their names and appointment time, and as they were ushered on to the legendary terrace, Isabelle wanted to take in the wonderfully relaxed yet sophisticated atmosphere. The black and white prints on the terrace inner wall conveyed a snap shot of the hotel's illustrious past. She pondered images of Winston and Clementine Churchill in the post war years, and to her amusement, George Bernard Shaw learning to dance.

The waiter gently pulled out their chairs to a table overlooking the bay, right on the curve of the balcony. Isabelle sat down and closed her eyes, feeling the sun warm her face as the sea breeze ruffled her blouse. When she opened them, she noticed Hortense peering over the balcony towards the swimming pool below, which was visible through gaps in the mature garden foliage. A waiter approached them and Isabelle sat back as Hortense ordered their tea and cakes. Isabelle continued to take in the sights of the terrace. The floor was tiled with simple black and white squares, which along with the pale pink walls adorned with arches gave the terrace an Art Deco feel.

The wind had fanned the clouds out to sea, and the view over Funchal Bay was spectacular. From their elevated position, she could see the curve of the bay, populated with its customary red roofs surrounded by sloping green hills. Isabelle's gaze settled on the harbour, which was busy with yachts and catamarans carrying expectant tourists out into the bay for dolphin watching excursions.

Isabelle found herself drawn to the guests on the neighbouring table. When she realised that she was staring, Isabelle averted her eyes from the two men. Hortense was reading the guidebook, so she glanced back surreptitiously at their fellow guests. The man facing her appeared to be a very wealthy European, with jet black hair and orange leathery skin, wearing a very animated expression and smoking a cigar. She could not make out the features of his companion who had his back to them, sitting directly behind Hortense. From what she could make out he appeared to be fairer skinned, and broad shouldered with cropped wavy brown hair. She noted there was only one other couple who appeared to be having a romantic tryst, the other guests were wearing business suits and occasionally answering mobile phones.

The waiter presented them with a large tray containing Isabelle's Earl Grey Tea, Hortense's coffee and the most comprehensive silver tray of sandwiches and cakes that Isabelle had ever seen.

'Hope you're hungry girl,' Hortense said, as the waiter laid everything out onto the relatively small table surface. They stared in awe at the mountain of food that lay before them.

'I'll have to start my diet when I get back,' Hortense declared as she swallowed a full mouthful of carrot cake.

'This tea is so fragrant! I've never tasted anything like it.' Isabelle sipped with a satisfied air.

'Issy I know relations are strained with your sister, you never really told me what happened between you, but I'd like to know, maybe I can help? At some point you've got to tell them what's happened. Have you considered how you'll react if they read it in a newspaper and then they call you up out of the blue?'

Isabelle's shoulders dropped as she sighed, 'H do we have to do this now? I was actually having fun today.'

'We have to talk about things sooner or later.'

'I doubt very much that my family will be aware of my misfortune H.'

'Tell me anyway...'

Isabelle inhaled. 'Okay, but I don't see what good dredging up the past will do.

'It all kicked off a few years ago, and I suppose I just buried it because it was too painful to deal with at the time. And now, after what's happened, Lily will just be full of reproach...' Her voice tailed off and her eyes glazed over the white bandage resting in her lap.

'It seems to me you Bryants are just as stubborn as one another. Life's full of surprises as we both know, but you can't go through your whole life second guessing the universe, it will always outsmart you.'

Isabelle pursed her full lips. 'I can see there's no use trying to occupy the moral high ground. What the hell, I might as well tell you the whole sordid tale.'

Hortense sat forward and crossed her forearms in anticipation.

'It's hard to think about my own shameful conduct in the relationship breakdown.'

'I know that coming out of denial is a sobering feeling, but it's liberating too' Hortense said.

'Lily and I were pretty close as you probably remember when we were kids growing up. After mum died, being the eldest, she was very protective of Jack and I. But especially over me being the youngest. By then I was gaining momentum in my career and she helped me get through the Young Musician contest. We found a place together in Marylebone. She began to do a lot of travelling with her interior design business, visiting wealthy clients in New York and the Middle East, even Dad's hometown of Sydney. I was going places with my violin, and we'd catch up with each other's adventures every few weeks when either of us was in the same city.

'I suppose the first sign of disagreement came when dad decided to move back to Australia. She was very supportive of him and I guess I was more selfish, I'd always been close to dad and I couldn't bear the thought of him going. It just felt like a betrayal, like he was abandoning us.'

She glanced up searching Hortense's face.

'Anyhow, a few years later, she married an American entrepreneur called Paul Kramer and they bought a place in Islington as he was working in the City at the time. She was busy creating their love nest and was heavily pregnant to boot, so we didn't see as much of each other. Looking at that picture in your apartment yesterday reminded me of our last meeting in Sydney before our fall-out.'

She looked round.

'The month before her baby was due she called me to meet up with her to talk baby things, or so I thought. We arranged to have a quiet dinner at a fancy bistro in Islington. She'd known about me and Howard for a while, but instead of being excited for me she had a weird reaction. She kept probing me about how serious were we, and how well did I know him? I got the impression she was trying to put me off him. I'd not talked to her that much about our time together, it was still relatively early days so I didn't want her lecturing me. I found it really odd she didn't ask to meet him.'

Isabelle frowned, leaned forward took the tea cup from the table and sipped at the contents. She then replaced the cup onto the bone china saucer.

'She sort of gave me a funny look and told me not to rush into things. Looking back with the benefit of hindsight, I can see that her behaviour was way out of character. She'd normally be nagging at me to find out all the gory details and wanting to be the first person to check him out. I think it was her overbearing "I'm the older sister" tone that got my back up, and from then on I became defensive and I didn't question her motives for being so negative about our relationship. She started being critical about all things related to Howard, basically doing a complete character assassination on him. I was happy; I didn't want to hear it. As a consequence I didn't pick up the warning signals.

'Three weeks later she gave birth to Maia. I was in the hospital visiting when she noticed my engagement ring. She accused me of not sharing things with her and I told her that if she was going to try and run my life she could keep out of it. We both said things in the heat of the moment that we regretted, but instead of apologising we just ploughed on, trying to preserve our pride.

'She pointed out that I was making a dreadful mistake, and how could I ruin my life when I'd worked so hard to get where I was. I couldn't understand why she hated him so much and so I dug my heels in further, and said that we were getting married and there was nothing she could do about it and that she and Paul would not be invited. She gave me an ultimatum, saying that I should trust her and she couldn't watch me throw my life away. She said if I didn't listen to her then we weren't really sisters anymore.'

A lump had formed in Isabelle's throat, and now she was struggling to hold back the tears. Hortense fumbled for a tissue in her handbag, and Isabelle proceeded to wipe her moist eyes and blow her nose as best she could with one hand.

'Are you ok? You can stop if you want.'

'No… It's fine.' Isabelle wiped at her eyes with the tissue. 'Howard and I got married, and six months later Lily, Paul and Maia moved to New York - his hometown, and we haven't spoken since.' She took a few deep breaths in an effort to compose herself.

'We can talk more about it tonight, but you mustn't blame yourself. The question you need to ask is this: do you want to re-establish contact with Lily? It sounds to me like she had good intentions for your happiness.' H cupped her face involuntarily as she rose from her chair.

'To quote the bard, there are no hopeless situations Issy - only people who've gotten hopeless about them.'

She gave Isabelle the sort of look a proud parent would do for a child who had just taken a brave step, then shuffled conspicuously. 'This coffee's gone through me like a dose of salts. I need to visit the ladies room.'

Isabelle watched Hortense loping across the terrace and then smiled at the waiter who began to clear away the empty plates and cups. She sat in a semi daydreaming state for a while and then decided to stretch her legs. Standing slowly she straightened out her denim skirt and pulled her soft cashmere cardigan over her smooth bare shoulders. The breeze had suddenly picked up and her matching silk sleeveless blouse was no longer sufficient to keep out the chill.

From the corner of her eye she could see that the European gentleman that had been facing her had also made a temporary exit, and the man with his back to her was leaning against the terrace wall.

Isabelle wandered over to get a closer look at the black and white prints on the inner terrace wall. She was drawn to their glamour and portrayal of headier times. It struck her how life could be frozen in a brief moment, captured on film, ensuring those precious seconds were immortalised on paper and not just lost in a fleeting memory. She was so deep in thought that she didn't hear the footsteps behind her. Then she heard a voice, like that of a baritone. It was steady and reassuring, without a hint of hesitation.

'Excuse me, I don't wish to intrude...'

She spun round to see who had interrupted her, and to her bewilderment found herself staring at the handsome face of the man who'd had his back to her from the next table.

14

'Forgive me – my name is Daniel Carter, I'm a director of Hudson Publishing and you must be the violinist Isabelle Bryant I presume?'

He held his hand out towards her, and she responded awkwardly with her uninjured hand. Her irritation of being put on the back foot had faded: she couldn't take her eyes off his ruggedly handsome face. His hand felt warm and powerful as it enveloped hers briefly. They looked at each other for a fleeting moment, and then his gaze wandered over her body and rested on the dressings covering her disfigured left hand. He was at least half a foot taller than Isabelle, probably about six feet four in height, she guessed, and his build was slender but muscular. She admired strength in a man, not just physically, but emotionally and mentally too.

'I'm sorry for disturbing you. One of our publishing outlets is *High Notes* magazine, I recognised you from this month's edition, but I'm also a fan and I think I've got all your albums. It's a pleasure to meet you.'

'Thank you.' She smiled.

'I'm afraid these are not very happy circumstances for me Mr Carter...'

'Please - call me Daniel,' he touched her arm and for a split second she felt an exquisite thrill pass through her. She flicked her hair away from her face with her right hand in a sweeping motion.

'Daniel, as you can see I have sustained terrible injuries to my left hand which have sadly proved rather fatal for my professional career. I'm here with a friend to recuperate while I try and get my head round the situation.'

It struck her from his response that Daniel Carter was a kind and intelligent man. That rare breed among males endowed with confidence and humility. He was showing no signs of possessing an oversized ego like Howard.

'I did notice your injury, but I didn't want to comment. I figured, if it was as serious as it looked, you must be feeling absolutely devastated. I can't imagine how you must be suffering...' He gave her a compassionate smile and his eyes remained on hers.

'I'm pretty numb at the moment actually.'

'Shock can do funny things to a person and everyone responds according to their own individual makeup. There is no hard and fast rule about how you should react. I'm a firm believer that given the right support, a person can overcome all sorts of adversities.'

Isabelle was suddenly rendered dumbstruck. Daniel filled the pause.

'I am truly sorry for your loss. This situation is a very great shame for all lovers of classical music, and especially of the violin. I hope you can take heart from the amazing career you have achieved so far, and from how many lives you have enriched - and will continue to do so in whatever you decide to do from this moment onwards.'

Isabelle's heart was pounding like never before.

'That's the problem Daniel; I haven't got a clue what to do next. I can't even contemplate a life without music at the moment.'

His eyes sparkled as he smiled at her and she eyed him with abandonment, not wanting to miss any facial feature or expression she could recall later in a quiet corner of her mind.

'Well, there's no reason to discount any further involvement with music, perhaps you'll be able to enjoy it in a different way. Have you any experience of writing?'

'The idea hadn't occurred to me so far, but now you mention it I had a reasonable ability back in school, it just didn't feature prominently because of my musical focus.'

'Great.' Daniel fished in his jacket for something. He retrieved two business cards, and held them out towards her.

'Please take my card, if I can be of any help with future plans, do get in touch. Also here's the card of my editor in London, Lucy Green. She does a great job at *High Notes* and I'm sure she could work with someone of your musical pedigree.'

She moved her hand towards his, conscious of the rapturous sensation flooding through her. 'That's very kind of you, when I get back to London I'll give her a call.'

Hortense came back onto the terrace, and bounded up to them like an exuberant child.

'Daniel, this is Hortense Lafayette, otherwise known as H!' Isabelle's arm rested on her sturdy shoulders. 'H is my dearest friend and the best jazz singer on the planet!'

Hortense shook his hand. They heard a few brief staccato words and noticed the gesticulation of hands as his returning European companion signalled to him from inside the lounge that they should be leaving.

'Listen, best of luck with whatever you decide to do Isabelle. Keep in touch.' He clasped her right hand. She didn't want him to let go. But he did, and in a few decisive strides he was departing with his swarthy companion. Isabelle found herself standing alone with Hortense, who had raised her eyebrows and was giving her a teasing look.

'Don't you dare say a word Mrs Lafayette!'

'C'mon, let's go home Issy, we've got some talking to do!'

They ate their pizzas together in the fading evening light, mulling over the events of the day. But Hortense couldn't contain herself until the end of the meal, and wiping melted cheese away from her lips she said,

'Daniel Carter is rather dishy isn't he?'

'Very.'

'So what did you two talk about so avidly on the terrace?'

'Just small talk really, he recognised me from *High Notes*, he's one of the publishing group's directors.'

'That's all?'

'He also gave me his card and said I should think about contacting his London editor.'

'He liked you a lot,' Hortense said, tilting her upper body forward slightly as she rested her ample bosoms over her crossed forearms.

'I'm sure he was just being polite. Directors of large publishing empires usually have a certain amount of charisma and people skills, wouldn't you say?'

Hortense smiled.

'Any way H, I'm still so raw. I can't handle any rejection right now, so I'll have to admire him from afar.'

'I saw the way he touched you when he left, and the way you almost leapt out of your skin!'

The pair of them pushed each other in jest, mocking each other's reactions.

'He was kind H. He helped me to think about my future, that until now I've dared not dream of.'

'Dream on I say. You've got to start somewhere Issy, and see where these ideas lead you.'

'H, don't you think it's weird that I haven't been able to cry?'

'No, that's quite common actually. It will take time to fully integrate what's happened to you Issy. When you are emotionally ready to grieve for your loss they will come. They will wash away your pain bit by bit.'

'Something else has been bothering me as well H, to do with Lily.'

'What's that?' Hortense asked.

'Lily would have to have known Howard, or at least about him, to have held such strong views. She's not prone to making quick and unfair judgements, especially about virtual strangers. What I don't understand is why she couldn't tell me if she knew him. Whatever the truth behind it all is, it worries me. I've just got a nagging feeling about it. Either way Lily knew something that I didn't...and I was too arrogant to listen to her.' Isabelle took a sip of her red wine, and savoured the warm sensation as it slipped down her throat.

'Well, there's only one way to find out.'

'I guess. I just need some more time before I take that step H,' Isabelle said. 'But one thing's for sure, I made a huge mistake marrying Howard.'

'H, I'm going to bed mate, it's been a wonderful day, but I'm going to try and get some sleep while I'm in the mood. I'll need my strength if you've planned another full day for me tomorrow.' She hugged and kissed her friend before retiring to the bedroom.

15

The mini bus scuttled along Madeira's north-west coast and Isabelle and Hortense had been transported into another realm. Verdant cliffs overflowing with waterfalls lined the winding road, while on the other side of the road the ocean virtually came up to the concrete.

Their journey had taken them through the core of the island, between its highest peaks, which had been shrouded in mist, and during a brief stop in the centre they could see both the south coast and the Northern hills. The trip had not allowed for a stop in São Vicente where Hortense had enthused about the lava caves from a previous visit with Raymond. They sat in amiable silence for the most part, there was only one other elderly couple on the mini bus who appeared to be equally impressed with the rugged landscape.

Isabelle had been reading her guidebook, nudging Hortense in the ribs when she found an interesting fact that she felt Hortense should be reminded of. So far she had discovered that the Island had been colonized by the Portuguese explorer Zarco early in the 15th century.

'It's so impressive how they managed to build any roads on this terrain. They must have literally hewn from the mountainside with little more than sheer strength and determination. It's impressive they've got this level of infrastructure considering what they were up against,' said Isabelle as she gazed out the window.

'It's amazing what the human spirit can accomplish,' replied Hortense.

'H, I can't believe Madeira's only really been on the tourist map since 1950. It's easy to see why they named it the Hawaii of the Atlantic.'

'Yes, those early sea planes started the aerial services. But it's still not commercialised on the scale of other European islands...thankfully.'

'I know I haven't properly thanked you for bringing me here yet H, but this oasis has given my somewhat tortured spirit much needed refuge from the world.'

Hortense clasped Isabelle's hand and smiled. 'That's the idea Issy.'

They found a pretty spot for lunch on the coast in Porto Moniz, where they admired the tumultuous waves crashing against the rocks. As Isabelle and Hortense sat on the balcony of the cafeteria Isabelle noticed a stout and balding middle-aged man striding purposefully towards her. She could feel herself tense. Not wishing to be rude she looked up, and as he spoke, her jaw dropped.

'Oh my God! It's really you isn't it? Isabelle Bryant! My wife and I are big classical music lovers, and we especially admire your work. We've seen you in concert several times, even that time when you were at the Carnegie Hall in New York. Just wait till I tell Hilary I've met you. She'll be thrilled when she comes back from the shop.'

Isabelle glanced round, and then stared back at him.

'We're so excited that we got our tickets early to see you play at the Festival Hall for the Brahms Concerto. It's Hilary's favourite. We just love your playing. This is such an honour for us. Would be you be kind enough to give us your autograph? I don't suppose you hang around after these concerts to sign programmes.' He pulled a pen and paper out of his rucksack and as he did so Isabelle raised her bandaged hand up from underneath the table.

'Thank you for your kind words, it's nice to know that I've helped you to enjoy the music of the great composers, but I'm afraid my performing days are over.'

The man's smile faltered, the colour drained from his ruddy, and slightly puffy cheeks, he stepped backwards and hastily retreated to his table. Isabelle and Hortense watched as Hilary returned and sat down next to him. Still red faced, he appeared to tell her about meeting their idol. She glanced up at them and flushed as Isabelle nodded in acknowledgement.

'I know he didn't mean to be, but sometimes people can be so ignorant,' Hortense said. She was about to carry on grumbling when she noticed a trail of tears flowing down Isabelle's pale cheeks. Her eyes sparkled like intense emeralds surrounded by red puffy rims. By now her whole body was taken over with convulsive sobs as the release of pain surged and intensified. Hortense ushered Isabelle away from the restaurant as she cried relentlessly for the next half an hour on a wooden bench.

Hortense stroked Isabelle's hair and felt the energy slowly ebbing away from her body. Cuddling her like a child she whispered, 'It's good to let the anguish out. Now you've truly started the healing process. You're on the road to recovery.' Isabelle didn't say anything. 'I remember from my own chequered history that ultimately, only acceptance and owning the experience of the loss can liberate us from the wretched demons that beset us.'

16

'This guidebook is brilliant H, I never realised there was so much to this place. The ingenuity of the early settlers and the vast network of Levadas they had built to harvest the natural rainfall on the Island is genius. It must be a hiker's paradise with all these miles of Levada walks, even the ones in steep and perilous locations.'

'Yeah, Ray, Louis and I did some on our last visit, it was beautiful, 'Hortense replied. 'We'll have to return together in happier times and spend more time enjoying the outdoor pursuits that Madeira offers.'

'You were right about the flood gates H. I've been feeling a bit lighter since my outburst in Porto Moniz yesterday.'

'To me it feels like your release has paved the way for you to have a more detached view of your situation.

Kinda like you're still in the fire; but you're not being consumed by it.'

'Sometimes you are so profound H, you blow me away. The pain is still there, but it's not as intense. I doubt it will ever completely vanish. I guess I owe that man some gratitude, after all, he was the catalyst.'

'I'll never forget the look on his face. He was absolutely mortified when he saw your hand,' Hortense said.

'Perhaps now you'll feel up to getting in touch with Lily when we get home. Also I think it would be helpful if we made a list of priorities to help you sort through the mire of confusion that's probably still in your head.'

'You can say that again H!'

'So, if you agree, I think you should focus on your physical and emotional recovery, before you give too much thought to your future in general. Daniel Carter has already given you a suggestion to mull over.'

'I'm going to start divorce proceedings fairly soon as well,' chipped in Isabelle. 'Funnily enough I don't feel any malice towards him, not even pity really, it's more like indifference.'

They sat in silence for a few moments.

'I spoke to Gerry this morning...'

'And?'

'He said that my album sales were having a boost after my accident was reported on the major the news channels. Thankfully, these royalties will help to support me along with whatever financial settlement I can negotiate from the divorce. Gerry assured me that he knows a matrimonial lawyer who would be happy to represent me and get fair compensation considering what Howard did to me.'

'Well, it's not just the normal dividing of assets after a marriage break down, he's got to factor in Howard's actions, the cause of the accident and subsequently your livelihood being destroyed.'

'My head is spinning already H. I've got to find somewhere to live as well.'

'All in good time Issy, you know you can stay with us as long as you need to. Ray and I want you to be emotionally stable and confident before you commit to buying a home.'

'I just can't thank you enough H. I hope someday I can repay you.'

'Just seeing you happy again will be enough for me Issy.' Hortense passed a glass of local wine to Isabelle and poured one for herself. 'Have you had any more thoughts about the alluring Mr Carter?'

'A few. Well, more than a few actually,' she laughed. 'But seriously H he's unattainable. I looked at his business card, seems his business HQ and main residence is in Manhattan, but he's also got a London address. I'm guessing he spends most of his time in the States.'

Hortense booted up her laptop for Isabelle who typed tortuously slowly with her left index finger and her right hand, as she perused the Hudson Publishing Inc. website.

'Looks like in addition to *High Notes* Magazine which is published in the UK, they own many other magazines from fashion to cookery, and in the US their mainstay is publishing non-fiction books. Daniel's title is Director Overseas Publications.'

'He must have strong ties in New York to remain there even though he has responsibility for *High Notes* and other foreign titles,' Hortense mused.

'He has all the qualities of a mysterious and success-ful man,' Isabelle replied, 'but as I've learnt the hard way, appearances are not always the best indicator of true happiness and fulfilment.'

'True, we shouldn't judge a book by its cover, but it's the front cover and back cover description that attract us to its contents.'

'Many people looking in at me and Howard would not have been aware of the sinister undercurrents at work, especially his secret contempt for my success and his constant approval seeking and egotistical nature.'

'Indeed, it's only when we look beneath the surface we see the truth. And I'm ashamed to say that even I didn't know the full extent of the abuse you suffered from him.' Hortense sighed.

'H, your insights during this break have been a reve-lation to me. It's clear to me now that I was too focussed on living out and planning the perfect life, to the detri-ment of hearing my inner voice. I ignored those uneasy feelings to my peril.'

'We all make mistakes, just gotta try and use them to our advantage after the event.' Hortense gulped down more wine.

'I've made a promise to myself H; I'm going to let life happen to me a bit more. You know, go with the flow. Live in the moment.'

'That's a great philosophy for life. Most of us are too busy doing instead of being. I understand why you were so driven in your career. I know better than most the pressures of being a professional musician. Ambition is such a double edged sword: it can also obscure our enjoyment of success. I've turned down many a tour because it would have taken me away from Ray and Louis for long periods, and I just wasn't going to accept that.'

'Well, I've got all the time in the world to reflect on my past achievements,' Isabelle said as she pursed her lips.

'I've had the wake-up call that fate was preparing for me.'

"The barriers are not erected which can say to aspiring talents and industry, 'Thus far and no farther'."
~ Ludwig van Beethoven

PART II - EROICA

17

Brightly coloured indigenous fresh cut flowers were everywhere in the airport's duty free shop. Isabelle touched them gently, trying to figure out which ones Hortense would like best. While she was ruminating over whether to choose the Passion flowers, Arum Lilies or the Bird of Paradise, she felt a light tap on her shoulder. She turned and found herself facing Daniel Carter and an exotic looking young woman, whose doe-like eyes narrowed as she stared at her. Every bit the image of sophistication in her skinny jeans and white T-shirt she oozed sex appeal. But Isabelle found her eyes drawn to her mouth. Her red lipstick shimmered as she nonchalantly chewed gum.

Isabelle could feel her cheeks flush and hoped Daniel was not a mind reader. After a second of open mouthed staring she composed herself enough to smile, trying not to look too delighted to see him again. Daniel returned her gaze with an intense look, eyeing her as she held bundles of flowers in her arms.

'Isabelle! What a co-incidence. Are you and Hortense flying back to London today as well?'

'Yes, we only had use of the apartment for a few days. I believe it's rented out from next week. Plus I need to get back and start sorting my life out.'

'Let me introduce you to Maria Alves, my partner. Her family have a holiday home here also. She's the reason we're on the island actually.' He glanced back to Maria who didn't smile. 'One of my European fashion publications organised a photo shoot in the mountains. We are travelling back to London for a few days and then on home to New York.'

Isabelle looked directly at Maria and held out her hand. 'It's lovely to meet you.'

An awkward silence ensued, as the two women warily studied each other's reactions. Isabelle noted that she was quite petite, certainly not as tall as she was, and she seemed to take an instant dislike to Maria's air of arrogance. Her sleek black hair hung in a bob around her oval face, and her skin was glowing like a goddess who had been born in the sun. Her almost skeletal frame was arranged with her hand on one hip, with her other arm coiled through Daniel's forearm. A more than decent amount of jewellery hung from her fragile neck and bony wrists.

She turned and faced the sales lady as she heaped her flowers on the counter. 'Thank you for the *High Notes* referral Daniel, it was nice seeing you again and good luck with the modelling Maria. I'm sorry I just have to get these flowers for H...'

'My ears are burning! Are those for me?' Hortense suddenly reappeared by her side. 'Oh Issy they're gorgeous!' Hortense gave Maria a cursory look, sizing her up instantly, she beamed at Daniel.

'Well, this is a welcome co-incidence. Hello again!' She looked towards Isabelle who was waiting patiently for the assistant to wrap her bouquet. 'I'll get her back on the straight and narrow soon. I suspect a new project will keep her out of trouble. I hope we'll meet again.'

Still watching Isabelle, Daniel replied, 'Yes, I'm sure we will. Take care, both of you.'

Isabelle managed a half-hearted wave and shot a longing look towards him as he made one last glance back in their direction before following Maria into the TAP Air departure lounge across the crowded departure floor.

'Maria's beautiful isn't she?' Isabelle remarked to Hortense.

'Mark my words, that one's beauty only runs skin deep - whereas you my child also have inner beauty, which is far more potent. When he's had enough fooling around he'll see through her.'

The glass building that housed Goldberg Brown & Dempsey on the Chiswick High Road glinted in the winter sun as Isabelle strode through the revolving doors. After a short wait, Gerry's compact and podgy form entered the foyer and he hugged Isabelle like a concerned parent. His bald patch shone under the lights and his trademark quick smile revealed dimples in his chubby cheeks.

'It's so good to see you Isabelle, my favourite virtuoso!'

'Thanks Gerry. It's been the worst few weeks of my life, but H bless her heart, has helped me to start thinking about the future now.'

'Come on. Let's get you up to my office. It'll be more comfortable there. Saskia will make us a cuppa and we can have a chat. It's so good to see you.'

Isabelle's heels clicked as they strode in unison across the pale marble tiled floor to the lift.

Once in his top floor office, Isabelle settled herself on the leather sofa positioned by the window, and gazed wistfully out towards the lofty tree tops of Kew Gardens. She had always loved his homely workspace, more like a lounge than an office with its plush cream carpet and Pre-Raphaelite art prints adorning the walls. The glass coffee table next to her was clear except for a pile of glossy magazines and his hefty bookcase containing volumes of hard back literary classics stood against the wall.

Gerry muttered some instructions to his PA and busied himself shifting mountainous paperwork off his cluttered desk.

'So my darling, just to put your mind at rest there's no contractual obligations with the Festival Hall performance of the Brahms. They're going to refund all the tickets if they can't find someone else to fill the spot. I'm not saying you are replaceable in any way of course. I'm sure your fans will be disappointed enough as it is when they hear about your misfortune.'

'I guess it's one less thing to worry about,' she said, smiling at Saskia as she diligently laid tea and biscuits on the table before them.

'That girl deserves a medal working for you Gerry,' she tapped him on the shoulder and motioned towards his strewn and elevated piles of paperwork. 'If it weren't for your desk resembling a burglar's handiwork there would be a feeling of total Zen in here,' laughed Isabelle.

'Yep, she sure does. Her English is impeccable you know. The most baffling thing is she seems to enjoy organising my chaos. She's been with me almost six months now, but I think she still gets homesick for her folks in Warsaw.'

They sipped their tea together in amiable silence for a while, and presently Gerry's expression grew more serious.

'I'm afraid I've got some bad news Isabelle.' He paused.

'Go on.'

'The Nagyvary...I'm afraid it's got to go back. I've looked over the contract and have been on the phone to them this morning, and if it can't be used they stipulate it must be returned so that it can be put into circulation again.'

'Gerry, it's okay. I prepared myself for this outcome. To be honest, it might be easier in the long run to let it go. If I see it every day knowing I can't play it,' her voice strained with emotion, 'well, that would be mental cruelty beyond words for me.'

He gave an affectionate rub of her arm. 'Shall I come by tomorrow evening to collect it?'

Isabelle swallowed hard. 'I didn't think I'd have to let it go so soon. Still, I suppose there's no point prolonging the agony.'

'There's something else I've been meaning to ask you Isabelle.' Her heart missed a beat as she averted her gaze from his sweet enquiring face. 'It's nothing to be alarmed about, but I was just wondering if – if you had any kind of insurance?'

Isabelle frowned. 'Insurance?'

Gerry pushed the point home. 'Were your fingers covered? I know some of your contemporaries have them insured for sizeable sums.'

The word came out of her mouth no more than a whisper. 'No.'

Gerry shook his head.

'No, don't be silly Gerry! The worldly wise and successful Isabelle thought that was unnecessary. Nothing was going to happen to her! She was riding the crest of a wave that was taking her all over the world. But she failed to see how vulnerable she really was. Her husband abused her and then her worst nightmare came to fruition.' Gerry looked down and shifted uncomfortably in his seat.

'The new "I've had the crap kicked out of me" Isabelle acknowledges it was her own fault. The new Isabelle won't spend any more time recriminating herself for her mistakes.'

Gerry studied her intently.

'You just have to move forward Isabelle. Guilt and regret must be the most energy sapping and soul destroying emotions known to man - and woman for that matter. I have a feeling that interesting things will start to happen for you my dear.'

'Thanks Gerry, but I'm not getting my hopes up. I'm just taking life one day at time for now.'

'Isabelle – I don't really know what to say about all this.' He gestured at her white swathed hand. 'I'm just so sad for you, but I want you to know that I'm sure you'll be successful in whatever you decide to do next. And you know I'll always be your agent, it takes more than a life changing accident to get rid of me!' Gerry's eyes twinkled, 'maybe God has something even more important in store for you.'

Isabelle's eyes misted over. 'I wish I knew what. Not sure anything will come remotely close to performing with an orchestra in front of an appreciative audience. Maybe God would be kind enough to reveal this new "higher" purpose to me soon and put an end to my suffering.'

'Have faith,' Gerry replied. 'From what Hortense has told me you've already turned a few corners. Perhaps there's a big crossroads waiting to be negotiated soon.'

'Perhaps. If there's one thing I got out of the trip to Madeira with H it's not to be so impulsive and controlling. I'm just going to take things slowly for a while, see what life presents to me.'

'I do know one thing though.' Her voice was steady and firm.

'Let me guess?' Gerry stroked his chin in mock confusion. 'You and Howard are no longer an item?'

Isabelle nodded. 'I nearly forgot, would you like my lawyer's number?'

'Yes please.'

Gerry wandered back over to his desk and delved into a drawer, triumphantly pulling out a slightly crumpled card.

'Patrick Hill & Sons were brilliant when I was going through my break-up with Margaret. They don't charge the earth either, compared to some of the sharks out there. Do tell them I sent you.'

Isabelle grasped the card and felt its texture in her right hand rubbing the corner with her thumb and forefinger.

'Thanks, this will be a good start to getting my freedom back.'

'I think I mentioned on the phone, your CD sales of *The Virtuoso* are going through the roof at the moment.

I'll do what I can to keep the PR positive. Presumably the royalties can still be paid into the same bank account?'

Isabelle nodded. 'We've always had single bank accounts. He was always pretty cagey about his money, especially when I was earning more. At least that's one thing I did right.'

'It's odd isn't it?' Gerry scratched his hairless forehead.

'What is?' Isabelle asked.

'I was just wondering why your sales were going so well now. It seems that your permanent absence from playing has invigorated demand for your albums. You know, like the dead artist syndrome.'

'Are you trying to kill me off Gerry?' She smiled.

'Never - but you know what I mean. Great composers, painters and musicians are always more in demand after their death, as if people can't really appreciate their genius while they are alive, and then when they are gone, they want more, so they clamour for the work that's left. It's your basic supply and demand theory at work, except in a more cultural rather than economic sense.'

'Except I'm not dead.'

'Thank God! But maybe in your case Isabelle your sudden departure from the public eye has made your fans crave for something that can never be repeated again.'

'They're not the only ones craving!' Isabelle clutched her handbag tightly as she positioned it across her shoulder, her voice wavering.

'But it's a very erudite observation Gerry. I better dash. I've got some calls to make.' She embraced him once more. 'Thanks for everything. I don't know what I'd do without you and H. Well – I'd probably be dead.'

'There, there, no more morbid talk. You look like you are on the way up now my dear. Keep in touch. Call me anytime.' Almost as an afterthought he added, 'I'll see you tomorrow night then?'

She nodded.

She pulled the Nagyvary gently out of its case and placed it in the middle of the bed. With her right hand she caressed its polished wooden surface, and plucked the now silent strings. Tears flowed down her cheeks.

She held it up under her chin, and her bandaged stumps protruded garishly as the neck of the violin sat in the dip between her thumb and forefinger. She moved the bow smoothly across the open strings. The instrument had become part of her physical being, and losing it would be almost as painful as losing a limb. When she played it, they were one – she didn't know where the Nagyvary ended and she began.

Their parting had played out like a scene from a film. Gerry arrived, kissing her and Hortense. He then took the case from her shaking right hand, apologising that he couldn't stop and that he didn't want to lengthen Isabelle's pain. As soon as Hortense closed the door she turned to a distraught Isabelle and held her.

That was it. In a matter of minutes Isabelle's most coveted possession, except for it wasn't really hers – was gone.

She had lain in the bath for an hour afterwards letting the warm water melt her tensions away, sobbing and wailing until she felt she could have filled the bath with her own brand of salty water.

Gerry's parting words were still ringing in her head.

'If you excuse the pun, this violin has played such an integral part of your life Isabelle, and nothing will ever change that.'

18

The *High Notes* office nestled above a mobile phone shop on Oxford Street, not far from the 100 Club where Isabelle had watched Hortense sing to eager jazz fans on many occasions. Sitting in the busy reception area she flicked through the last edition, the one that had sparked Howard's temper on that fateful night.

Staff meandered around her like ants. Each person with a duty and task to perform, but looking from the outside in, they interacted in a seemingly chaotic effort. She particularly empathised with the young work experience girl who looked like she was on the verge of kicking the photocopier or collapsing into floods of tears, when she felt a formidable presence bearing down upon her and holding out a firm hand; she recognised the Australian twang from her earlier phone call that accompanied the outstretched arm.

'I'm Lucy Green, nice to meet you Isabelle.'

She peered into a warm freckly face with pale blue eyes that were framed by masses of vibrant red curly hair, and she felt immediately at ease. Before Isabelle could muster a reply, Lucy was hollering into the office;

'Can someone please get that dickhead engineer to come back and fix that bloody machine again?'

She turned back to Isabelle and they shook hands. She ushered them into her office overlooking the street. It was a light and airy office, lined with large framed prints of previous front pages, book shelves and stacks of magazines. Her cluttered desk was almost in the same league as Gerry's, but something told her that despite appearances this forthright woman was on top of her game.

'It's very kind of you to see me, I know you must be very busy,' Isabelle blurted out almost before she had sat down.

'No worries. Dan phoned me to say that you would be in touch, and besides, I wanted to meet you myself. We write about classical musicians and soloists in all our editions; but not all of them are in your league Isabelle.'

'That's very kind of you, but I'm just an ordinary person, especially nowadays,' she glanced at her hand, 'and to be honest, I'm like a fish out of water at the moment. I don't really know how useful I can be to *High Notes*. On the other hand I can't imagine my life without music, it's my...' she struggled for the right word, '...opiate. It's strange how when fate deals you a difficult card, it forces you to re-evaluate everything. But I have been blessed with amazingly supportive friends.'

'I think anyone would feel the same in your shoes. I hope I never have to deal with such a blow. I'd like to help, and I think there's a project that's perfect for you.'

'Really?' Isabelle leaned forward.

'We're doing a big feature on Beethoven as next month's Composer spot. Being as you were the expert on his violin composition, nobody would be more qualified to write the piece. You can approach it from any angle you like.'

Isabelle's eyes widened in excitement, and she leaned back in her chair digesting Lucy's proposal.

'I...I'd love to. I know I launched my career on his violin concerto, but I love all his music, he really is my musical hero, so this would be such an honour for me. You've given me a glimmer of hope.'

'Great. That's settled then. I presume you've been to Vienna before?'

Isabelle nodded. 'I played a few times in Vienna, but because of my performance commitments I never had much time to explore the city and I've always wanted to go back, it's such a beautiful place. It would be wonderful to go back and discover Beethoven's musical home, get a feel for his environment and see where he lived and the theatres where his work was performed. It would be a kind of homage for me, a musical pilgrimage.'

'I'm excited for you Isabelle. Book your flights and hotel, tour guide, anything within reason, and you claim back these expenses from us. The deadline for the piece would be before the end of the month. We've got to go to print before the first of January for the February edition.

Lucy's phone rang, but someone picked up the line.

'One thing I would suggest though is getting a high quality tape recorder. You might find it difficult typing, so perhaps record the article first and then get a secretary to type it up before you start making amendments.'

'I hadn't thought of that,' Isabelle admitted. 'I can't wait to spend Christmas in the musical capital of Europe.'

'You know with everything you've been through, I think you'll be able to bring a personal parallel to Beethoven's music and his life. You don't strike me as a quitter either!'

'I've had my moments,' Isabelle said, and they smiled at each other in understanding.

'Whereabouts in Australia did you grow up Lucy? My father and brother live out in Sydney, and I'm half Aussie myself.'

'The harbour city. No place like it on earth. Maybe my lot know your lot? Wouldn't that be cool? You should go and visit your folks.'

Isabelle gazed out of the window where throngs of tourists and Christmas shoppers were milling about below them.

'Yes, I'm certainly overdue. My brother's a pilot for Qantas, so I should be able to organise something. I think the Opera House was the most awesome venue I ever played in, such wonderful acoustics there. Mind you, the Royal Albert Hall on my first professional solo has to be right up there; the history of that place gets right into your bones. Do you play an instrument Lucy?'

'Yeah, I learnt the flute at school and I played in an amateur orchestra for a while. I don't get time now though. I did media studies and this job was perfect, I could combine my love of music and publishing.'

'I just want you to know how much I appreciate this opportunity Lucy, I won't let you down,' Isabelle said.

'I've a feeling this will be the start of a lifelong friendship Isabelle. I'm looking forward to working with you too. And remember you can call me anytime or email me if you need to.'

'Thanks Lucy. I'll get cracking then.'

At first there was a stunned silence on the other end of the phone, and Isabelle could hear a young girl shouting in the background. After her initial shock Lily finally spoke.

'Belle?'

'Hi Lily, yes it's me, your long lost sister.'

'Oh my God! How are you? Paul only just told me last night about your accident. He read it in the paper. I was trying to pluck up the courage to call you!'

'Ditto sis.'

'I'm so sorry Belle. I never wanted this for you. That sicko was never good enough for you. But now isn't the time for recriminations, I'm just so happy to hear from you. How are you coping? Do Dad and Jack know?'

'No, not yet, at least not from me, unless they read it somewhere like Paul did. I'm only just getting myself together. You probably don't know about my attempted suicide afterwards?'

'What? You are kidding me right?'

'No, but it's behind me now. I just want to get on with my life, mend the rifts I created. I wish I hadn't let my stupid pride get in the way of our relationship Lily. Can you forgive me?'

Isabelle heard more shrieking in the background. 'Hold on a sec Belle. Maia! Please get off of there before you fall and hurt yourself! Mummy is on the phone, now play nicely.' Then back to Isabelle, 'of course, you're my sister. I just want you to be happy.'

'It's been such a long time. I bet Maia's grown. I only remember her as a baby.'

'Yes, well, she's a whirlwind of a toddler now; into everything and…Maia! I won't tell you again. Please go and play in the other room!'

'A trifle mischievous?' Said Isabelle.

'Indeed. I'm sorry about this Belle, once you have children you get used to things like never being able to have a conversation without being interrupted, or going to the toilet in private, or getting a decent night's sleep.'

'Can't wait. Listen, I can tell now's not a good time. Why don't we talk again when I'm in Vienna. I've got so much to tell you, I'll call you again in a few days.'

'That would be great. Maia's determined to topple the Christmas tree. Take care sis.'

19

Isabelle's hotel was located in the old part of Vienna, a pale yellow neo classical building close to the museum quarter, and a haven of modern convenience on the inside. Pretty lights hung over the foyer and its setting in a seventeenth century cobbled street made her feel for a split second like she could have been there in Mozart or Beethoven's heyday.

The receptionist had dispensed her room key in a charming and efficient manner, and Isabelle entered her double room on the top floor. Her accommodation was modern and comfortable, with smart minimalist furnishings and a marble bathroom that to her delight featured under floor heating. She exulted that her notorious poor circulation would not be causing her feet to go blue here.

Isabelle quickly unpacked and scurried down to the lobby to book a guide for the next day. She had reserved the room for four nights, and was due to travel home on Boxing Day. The anticipation of sampling the cultural delights of the heart of the once mighty Austro-Hungarian Empire had awakened her inner child, and she was almost skipping towards the front desk.

Johanna, the head receptionist, had made some phone calls after Isabelle described her Beethoven project. 'I am pleased to say that a gentleman named Hans Moser will be your guide for the day. He is very knowledgeable about Wien's musical history, and he will take you anywhere you need to go for five hundred euros for four hours.'

'Danke Johanna, that's great. Shall I meet Hans at 9am in the foyer?'

'Very good, yes, Mr Moser will be here.' Johanna smiled.

Isabelle jumped into a waiting taxi just outside the hotel entrance.

'Can you take me to the Café Landtmann please?'

The taxi driver nodded. 'That's a good choice.'

'Thank you. I quite fancied having tea at one of the most famous eateries in Vienna. I really love your café culture and relaxed coffee houses where you can sit, eat or drink and read a newspaper, or simply watch the world go by.'

It was only a few minutes by taxi, situated on the Ringstrasse close to the Rathaus, which was gleaming under a mass of different coloured lights. As they drew nearer she recognised the imposing and revered

Burgtheater, a larger, grander building than the original construction on the same site that had hosted premiers for Mozart and Beethoven prior to 1888. Snow crunched beneath Isabelle's feet as she made her way through the empty courtyard. She visualised the area shaded by an awning in summer, full of tables, chairs and enthusiastic diners eager to drink in the unique ambience and architecture of Vienna.

An elderly waiter showed her to a small table in the café's art deco interior, near to a counter of mouth-watering pastries and cakes. It was a magical atmosphere with the Christmas markets beckoning from across the Ringstrasse sprawled before the mighty Gothic Rathaus. She brushed the melting snow from her coat and draped it by her lap. Before long she was enjoying a hearty meat broth followed by a light but sumptuous apple strudel.

Finally, with her hunger sated and feeling more rested from her tiring journey, Isabelle sat contented with her pen and pad and the books she had collected for the trip. She wrote as best she could the list of places that she wanted Hans to show her.

She imagined standing in some of Beethoven's homes, looking around the same rooms that he had no doubt spent endless hours in, engrossed in his compositions. Satisfied with her venues, she paid for her meal and carefully put on her coat and gloves. She had bought a pair of men's gloves at the airport, so that she had one big enough to cover her bandaged left hand.

When Isabelle opened the door she noticed the snow was falling harder than before, and a fierce wind was driving the cold chunky flakes directly into her face. Squinting through the white haze she saw two men approaching the doorway. In her haste to get out of the café entrance she slipped on some ice and lurched towards them.

'Oops, there you go...'

A familiar voice echoed into the night as a hand steadied her flaying arm. They recognised each other in that electric moment.

'Daniel?'

'Isabelle! We must stop meeting like this my dear.' He was still holding her forearm. 'How are you? How is the research going?'

His companion smiled, as she tried unsuccessfully to regain her dignity.

'My research?'

'Lucy told me you were coming to Vienna to do some research for an article on Beethoven.'

'Yes, yes of course. We had a good meeting and decided it would be a mutually beneficial project.' Her tone was both defiant and grateful. 'Thank you so much for putting me in touch with her.'

'Have you been in Vienna long?'

'I just arrived this afternoon. I must say the cold takes a bit of getting used to. My hand is pretty painful and numb. I absolutely love the snow but it plays havoc with the nerve endings that were damaged.' She inadvertently clasped her bulky left glove. 'I've hired a very reliable driver and guide I'm told, and so the adventure starts tomorrow.'

'Great. I only just arrived yesterday evening myself. Perhaps we could arrange to have dinner tomorrow evening when you've had a chance to recover from your busy day?'

'I'd like that very much.'

'I'll pick you up at eight. Where are you staying?'

Isabelle panicked as she felt her mind go blank and her teeth began to chatter. 'Err... it's in the old city, close to the museum quarter. I think it's the Maria something... K&K Maria Theresia, that's it. Excuse me, my brain is freezing too.'

He smiled and walked past her. She waved feebly as they continued into the café. The meeting had taken her by surprise, just as their first encounter had on Madeira.

The day started out brightly. From her small balcony Isabelle peered over the numerous rooftops, her eyes sweeping over the narrow pavements lined with historical houses, each with their own unique story she pondered. Snow lay undisturbed on the pavement below her in Kirchbergasse, still fresh from the heavy fall the night before. She filled her lungs with the wintry air and then made her way to the lounge for breakfast.

Suitably filled with rolls and orange juice, she pulled her handbag across her shoulder and waited for Hans in the hotel lobby. It was dead on 9am. A tall dark figure stood erect and patient by the front door. She smiled at him. He smiled back at her, and in a few strides he was by her side greeting her with an outstretched hand.

'Good morning Frau Bryant, my name is Hans Moser. I am your guide for the day. I understand you wish to visit some of Beethoven's Houses?' His slow and clipped accent immediately warmed her heart. She looked up at his strong features. His wide set jaw, olive skin and dark moustache that gave him a strangely Latin appearance, while his large brown eyes were framed by substantial eyebrows. Isabelle guessed he must have been about forty.

'Good to meet you Mr. Moser. That's right. I'm re-searching the composer for an article I'm writing.'

He signalled towards a smart black Mercedes waiting at the entrance and pulled open the rear door for her.

'Is this is your first visit to Wien?'

'Not exactly,' she mumbled, clambering into the seat.

'I used to be a concert violinist, Mr Moser. I've been to Vienna once before, I was on tour playing with the Vienna Philharmonic, and most of my time was spent at the Wiener Musikverein. It was just for a couple of nights and unfortunately I didn't get to see anything of the city. I spent large chunks of my time rehearsing and preparing. I- I had an accident recently, so I can't play anymore.'

Hans' eyes caught hers through the rear view mirror. He had already noticed the dressings on her left hand and bowed his head.

'I am sorry for your loss. I wish I had been able to see you play. I am a great lover of classical music and especially of Beethoven. I will do my best to make an enjoyable day for you. Also, please call me Hans.'

'Thank you Hans, I really appreciate your help. I probably could have made it round the city on buses, trams and by foot, but I'm on quite a tight schedule and I don't really have time to get lost.' She raised her left arm. 'My injury isn't too good in the cold weather either.'

'It's a pleasure for me to assist you in such an important task,' Hans replied.

Isabelle showed him her scribbles of some of the venues she wanted to see and he looked thoughtful.

'I will take you to the Beethoven Platz first,' he said, 'followed by the famous Theater an der Wien, before stopping at the Memorial Rooms in the Pasqualati House, and perhaps the site of the Schwarzspanierhaus, where he died. Beethoven moved house over eighty times during his time in Wien, so there aren't many houses that we know of left standing. Also in the city is the Palais Lobkowitz which houses the Eroica Saal and the Palais Pallavicini which is opposite the Spanish Riding School of the Hofburg Palace.'

'That's great. If there's enough time afterwards I'd also like to visit the House of the Heiligenstadt Testament, and the Church of Holy Trinity where Beethoven's funeral was held.'

Hans gave an accommodating nod. 'I am at your service, we can go wherever you would like.'

They drove in silence as dark clouds gathered in the sky above. Hans pulled the car into a lay by and proudly pointed towards an imposing statue of Beethoven sternly surveying his eponymous Platz.

Isabelle got out and wandered up to the statue. He looked regal and rightly honoured in pride of place in his own little square. Groups of young students came and went as Isabelle took in the scene. To her left was a gothic building containing a performance hall and rooms, and on the opposite side of the square the view was dwarfed by the towering Intercontinental Hotel, and next to that was an ice rink and some construction cranes. The wind whipped around her like a mini tornado but she felt exhilarated.

She took a few pictures and climbed back into the warm interior of the waiting car, brushing her hair away from her face as Hans sped off further into the city.

Their next stop was the Theater an der Wien, a relatively innocuous looking building amongst the classical finery of the city. Its early nineteenth century yellow façade appeared a little shabby, but the theatre had seen thousands of Viennese concert goers through its green doors during its history. She studied the guidebook to see that it had been built in 1801 and the statues above the doorway were in fact depicting Papageno, from Mozart's Magic Flute. Reading further she saw that it had also premiered Beethoven's Fidelio in 1805.

'It's hard to believe Hans, but his violin concerto, which was my favourite, premiered in this very theatre on the twenty third of December 1806, after a rushed completion and next to no rehearsal. The Viennese didn't take to it, and it wasn't performed for about another four decades. These days it's in every soloist's repertoire as one of the great violin concerti and has even been transcribed for the piano.'

'It seems even the best of us sometimes have to wait for success,' concurred Hans.

Isabelle studied her book. 'Luckily his grand Symphony number five in C minor fared a lot better in December of 1808. His pastoral Symphony and the fourth piano concerto were also premiered in this unremarkable looking building. What I find amazing is that it's still in use for concerts in the twenty first century.'

'The concert hall interior is magnificent.'

'Can we go in Hans?'

Hans disappeared into a small door around the back of the theatre. Isabelle could hear lots of banging and drilling going on inside. He emerged a few moments later shaking his head.

'I'm so sorry, but unfortunately they are doing renovations ready for Mozart's two hundred and fiftieth birthday celebrations in the New Year, and so it is closed to the public.'

Isabelle's shoulders dropped as she sighed, 'What a shame.'

Hans led her back to the car, and she obediently followed him as he opened the door for her. This kind, tall, strong Austrian man had a grace of movement that was masculine and yet gentle.

The snow began falling again as the engine roared back to life, and they drove towards the Palais Lobkowitz.

'Hans, I understand Prince Lobkowitz was a great patron of the arts, one of Beethoven's strongest supporters?'

'He was indeed, Isabelle, along with Prince Karl Lichnowsky, Count von Fries and Archduke Rudolph. If you like, I have an interesting anecdote to tell you about when Beethoven was making a reputation for himself in Viennese society as a virtuoso pianist.'

'Oh Hans, yes please, do tell. I need insider information for my article. I'd love to know what happened.' Isabelle leaned forward slightly, stretching her seatbelt.

'You may know it already, but Prince Lobkowitz organised an improvisation contest between Beethoven and a Prussian pianist popular in Vienna in 1800 called Daniel Steibelt.'

'I've never heard of him, Hans. How cool, a salon duel on the ivories. Please go on.' Isabelle strained her neck a little closer to Hans.

'In fact they met twice, firstly at the von Fries residence, the Palais Pallavicini. Steibelt was already an established virtuoso on a tour of European capitals and wanted to make his mark in Vienna. He was known for his, how do you say, tremolandos. The first time they met I'm afraid Steibelt apparently impressed the aristocracy more than Beethoven with his fancy performance of his own Piano Quintet. By all accounts he was condescending in attitude towards Beethoven, who refused to play again on that occasion.'

'Knowing what an irascible temperament Beethoven had, I'm sure his blood must have been boiling after that,' Isabelle said.

'Most certainly, Isabelle. A rematch was planned a week later at the Palais Lobkowitz.'

'Oh! The anticipation! What happened Hans?'

'I'm pleased to tell you that Beethoven got his revenge on Steibelt at their second meeting. The aristocracy must have been on the edge of their seats under such an atmosphere of hostility. It is said that Beethoven parodied his precious tremolandos and indeed Steibelt's entire composition. He imitated Steibelt's Quintet for the ordinary piece it was and exposed it in a humiliating fashion. He then began to improvise on it with such brilliance that the audience could barely believe what they were witnessing.'

'Bravo Beethoven!'

'Steibelt stormed out of the salon while Beethoven was still playing, indeed, mocking him.'

'Game set and match Ludwig,' replied Isabelle.

'Beethoven was known for having small but very intense and bright eyes. They must have surely been blazing that night,' Hans concluded.

'Wow. It would have been incredible to have seen him in full flow, going hell for leather against the opulent backdrop with all his unrefined clothes and mannerisms, trumping some posh, over inflated big wig,' Isabelle said.

'Yes. He so comprehensively showed up Steibelt, that he left Vienna with his pride in tatters and went straight back to Berlin, refusing to ever play in Vienna again if Beethoven were present.' Hans pulled the car to halt. 'And here we are, in front of the very building where it all happened.'

'Thanks for sharing your knowledge Hans; that was completely fascinating. It certainly has a grand exterior compared to the Theater an der Wien,' Isabelle remarked as she stared up at its immense pale stone façade.

'It was built in the baroque style of the seventeenth century and is now a museum,' said Hans as he opened the car door for Isabelle. They rose elegantly up the sweeping white stone staircase. Marble floors glistened beneath them and daunting chandeliers hung above them as they walked along the hallway and the first floor hall. Turning left at the top of the stairs, she was rewarded with her first sight of the legendary Eroica Saal.

An inestimably high ceiling commanded awe as its painted frescoes peered down at Isabelle and another tourist already in the middle of the great hall. With a sharp intake of breath she stepped onto the symmetrical patterned wood floor, which creaked softly under her reverent steps. Her neck arched back and she spun round to try and see the ceiling in its entirety, but she almost became dizzy. Her eyes were drawn to the tall windows, overlooking the street below. The snow outside did not detract from the ethereal light that filled the room. Isabelle sat down on one of the plastic chairs that had been lined along one wall, and sat quietly picturing a chamber orchestra at one end; and the highest echelons of Viennese society at the other end, with Beethoven somewhere in the middle, furiously directing the rehearsals of his ground breaking third symphony.

Only time separated them. It was history in the flesh. Isabelle could feel his legacy in this room.

She recalled what she knew about the Eroica Symphony: the symphony had initially been dedicated to Napoleon, as tumultuous times hit Europe with the start of the Napoleonic wars. But like all pure idealists Beethoven had become disillusioned with Napoleon's narcissistic tendencies, and had emphatically crossed through the dedication on his original score. Beethoven was the real hero she decided. He brought joy to many, and even though his own life was far from happy, he produced such spiritually transcending music that although revered in his day, had also stood the test of time to be even more respected and loved in modern times.

She remembered a sarcastic comment that Hans had made earlier in the car. 'I think Austria wanted to adopt Beethoven as a son of the nation, and give away Hitler as a son of Germany.'

She got up and gave one last scan over the beautiful frescoed ceiling and the marble walls, and headed back down the staircase to Hans, who had gone back to the entrance to wait for her.

As the weather worsened further Hans pulled the Mercedes up in front of the Palais Pallavicini, and Isabelle peered at the façade. It was not as impressive as the nearby Hofburg Palace, and looked somewhat grubby coated in a tincture of dark beige. To her it was still large by mere mortal standards, spanning eleven windows across. Huge wooden doors were flanked on each side by two pollution stained female statues clearly of noble Roman origin, standing on a white pedestal, at each end a lady with one with arm raised, as if supporting the heavy lintel that hung over the entrance.

'Here we are at the von Fries residence, number five Josefplatz. Count von Fries was a wealthy patron of Beethoven's, and his family were bankers. After the von Fries family left it was owned by the Pallavicini family. You probably spotted their majestic family coat of arms on the roof. I know the outside needs a good clean, but inside it is beautiful. There are long mirrors, extravagant gold leaf chandeliers and high ceilings. It's used as an art gallery and café now,' Hans explained.

'I'm sure it's lovely inside Hans, but I'd like to get to the Beethoven memorial rooms before lunch. It's enough for me to take in the surroundings.' She scanned the cobbled square. 'Who is that?' She pointed towards a large equine statue of a Roman Emperor in the centre of Josefplatz.

Hans smiled, revealing perfectly straight, white teeth in comparison to his neatly trimmed dark moustache. 'That is the monument of Emperor Joseph II, built by Franz Anton Zauner, who also created the beautiful entrance to the Palais Pallavicini by the way.'

'He looks Roman rather than Austrian.'

'What can I say, the Habsburg dynasty had an obsession about being descended from Roman emperors,' Hans replied. 'As you can see, sections of the Hofburg Palace enclose three sides of the square, along with the Spanish Riding School, formerly the imperial stables, or Stallburg, here in the north west corner.'

Isabelle squinted as the white stone of the Hofburg seemed amplified by the reflection of the snow.

'The architecture is stunning. Thanks Hans. Can we go now?'

Back in the comfort of the Mercedes Isabelle jotted down some brief notes that she could refer to later when she came to write the article. They passed the now familiar Gothic Rathaus, and the Landtmann Café, and soon Hans was parking up again on a street corner.

Isabelle got out of the warm car and followed Hans's directions to walk alongside the old city wall, which had been mostly demolished in the construction of the Ringstrasse.

'These bulwarks below and in front of the Mölker Bastei facing the university are one of the only two surviving portions of the ancient city fortifications.'

'Those bricks do look old,' Isabelle replied.

Climbing up another steep cobbled path she reached the whitewashed corner building located at Mölker Bastei 8 that housed the Beethoven Museum. Panting slightly after ascending a dark winding staircase up four floors, consisting of one hundred and five stone steps, she rested at the top and peered down into an internal courtyard, also whitewashed and dotted with wooden shuttered windows.

Although sparsely furnished, the five rooms that once constituted Beethoven's home were respectfully arranged, all with whitewashed walls, low ceilings and real wood floors. She moved slowly through each room, struck by their generous size and expansive views towards the city. Prints of Beethoven and his family and friends were positioned in each room, along with copies of original scores and wooden tables that held headphones. Isabelle listened carefully to the Allegretto of the seventh symphony; its brisk and foreboding vigour always reminded her of some impending disaster. It had been one of the symphonies written in those rooms. Checking her guidebook Isabelle noted that Beethoven lived in the rooms over two separate time spans. The first had been from 1804 until 1808, and then again in 1810 for a further five years.

One section of the third room had shown the original wall tiles that would probably have adorned the walls in the master's day. Layers of cement had been scraped away to reveal a darker, flowery sort of pattern that was faded and dreary.

The fourth and largest room housed his five-pedalled klavier, now sitting silently in the middle of the room. Isabelle longed to touch the worn ivory keys, but they were covered with a clear plastic plane. The ornate inlay on the front was startlingly beautiful, and she noticed that the piano was longer and narrower than its modern compatriots. A music stand kept it company, again made of wood and ornate in style.

The last room felt more eerie, and inexplicably Isabelle was drawn towards the cast of his life mask. She hadn't expected to see one here, although she was aware that one had been made shortly after he passed away by Dannhauser. She felt compelled to stare at it for minutes on end, noting the contours of his face. It was the closest she could get to seeing him in the flesh. Suddenly she felt stifled and headed back down the stairs, where she gasped for air on the pavement at the foot of the building.

After a brief look in the shop she bought a copy of Beethoven's famous Heiligenstadt Testament, with an English translation and also the original in his own handwriting.

Hans was giving her a concerned look. 'Perhaps you would like to get a baguette now? He led her to a small takeaway café nearby for much needed sustenance.

In between mouthfuls she said, 'I'm sorry Hans, this must be very dull for you...'

'No, not at all, I love to show off the cultural gems we have here in Wien. I hope these visits are proving useful for your work.'

'Yes, very, thank you Hans. I'm really enjoying myself. You know, the first major piece I ever played professionally was Beethoven's violin concerto, and I've always been fascinated with his music and his life.'

After they had eaten Hans got her back on the road, and before long was bringing the car to a wide street further out from the city centre. She noticed the road sign, Schwarzpanierstrasse. He pulled up in front of a line of shops.

'This is the site of the Schwarzspanierhaus, meaning house of the Black-Robed Spaniard, but alas this is not the original building. It was built by Benedictines from Spain, hence the name. Beethoven's apartments were located along the second floor, and had good views across the inner city and out towards the Prater. Sadly, it was demolished sometime after Beethoven's death. None of the structures opposite were here in Beethoven's day; the building and street faced the Glacis, which was an expanse of open ground around the inner city.'

'I suppose that explains how thousands of mourners were able to congregate in the street outside on the day of his funeral. You are a treasure trove of Beethoven nuggets Hans.'

Isabelle looked up to the second floor windows; there was absolutely nothing that indicated his later works had been composed there, except a small brass plaque on the wall.

'I read a book by Gerhard von Breuning called "Memories of Beethoven" it's very moving,' Hans said.

'That sounds interesting. Can you tell me a little more?'

'He was a twelve year old boy at the time he became acquainted with Beethoven. He lived in the building adjacent, the Rothes Haus, with his family. His father was Stephan von Breuning, an old childhood friend of Beethoven's from Bonn. He was the last living person to have known Beethoven, and he wrote down his memories of Beethoven's time at the Schwarzpanierhaus to give an accurate account of the composer's daily life during his last years. Apart from information he was given by Anton Schindler it is considered accurate.'

'Schindler was the fellow who tampered with and destroyed his conversation books wasn't he? Known to be dishonest and unreliable,' added Isabelle.

'Yes indeed. Although we will never know, I like to believe his motives would have been entirely honourable, at least in some instances. Beethoven and the young Gerhard became very fond of one another, and Beethoven gave him the nick-names "Hosenknopf" meaning trouser button and also "Ariel" after the spritely messenger in Shakespeare's Tempest. He writes about how Beethoven would often have lunch with him and his family and how they would go for a stroll in the grounds of the Schönbrunn Palace afterwards, and about his domestic arrangements and his relationship with his nephew Karl, his circle of fellow musicians and composers. The book has been translated into English; I think you would find it a fascinating insight into his daily life at the end Isabelle.'

'I'm sure I will. I'll definitely purchase a copy when I get back to London. In fact, I think you are more qualified to write this article than I am Hans!'

He raised his hands in objection and shook his head.

'I remember seeing a black and white print of Beethoven at his Graf piano, covered in manuscripts in the midst of composing in what must have been the Schwarzspanierhaus. It reminded me of my agent's office, which can be somewhat... chaotic. And when I listen to his string quartet number fifteen, I think it's the opus one-three-two, specifically the adagio, "Heiliger Dankgesang" it makes me feel that Beethoven had glimpsed immortality and the true nature of the human soul.' Isabelle felt her eyes well-up. She looked again at Hans and thought she could see his eyes were red-rimmed also.

'There is a road nearby that is named Beethovengasse, where you will find the restaurant Beethovenstrüberl.'

Hans waited again while she retraced his steps to the café Stuberl, where he had been a regular patron. Hans turned to her as she settled back in the seat. 'And now I will take you to the Holy Trinity Church on the Alser

Strasse in the eighth District, where his funeral took place.'

They rode in silence until he pointed to the towering façade of the church as they passed by the entrance in the car. Hans parked in a side street and walked with her to the entrance. She gazed up in awe at the sheer height of the pale yellow and cream baroque façade and the two imposing black domes crowning each tower.

'The arches and extensive buildings facing the church were once a hospital in Beethoven's day, but they are now used to house students from the university.'

A plaque on either side of the large wooden entry doors explained in German that both Beethoven and Schubert had had their funerals held in the church. They walked down a wide corridor with tiled floors and plaque lined walls. Hans pointed towards the numerous memorial plaques to the fallen Austrian soldiers from both wars, and translated some of the epitaphs for her. A side door took them into the main body of the church.

The ceiling stretched away from them, and a huge oil painting dominated the space above the altar. The sound of the hefty organ almost reverberated through her bones, as an enthusiastic organist suddenly began a recital.

The air was damp. Isabelle walked slowly down the red carpeted aisle, passing the wooden pulpit and looking through white archways she studied the devotional side chapels that spanned the length of the church.

Wooden pews sat on either side of the aisle much as they must have done on that fateful day. Light was streaming in. She looked up to see the full spectrum of the stained glass window above the entrance. The atmosphere was so serene, she could picture Beethoven's coffin resting at the altar, with the Kyrie from his Mass in C being sung to the heavens.

Although the church was grand in every sense, after a while Isabelle began to feel an oppressive shiver run down her spine, and waving at Hans she left the organist pounding his keys and headed for the Mercedes.

'I would have liked to pay my respects at his grave, but I won't have time today. I understand he was buried at the Währing Cemetary?'

'That's correct Isabelle. Franz Grillparzer wrote a very moving eulogy for Ludwig, and his oration was read in solemn tones in front of thousands of mourners at the cemetery gates by Heinrich Anschütz. Were you aware that Beethoven's grave was moved?'

'I wasn't actually.'

'Both Beethoven's and Schubert's remains were exhumed in 1863 to be cleaned and reburied in lead lined coffins. During the cleaning process, the now adult Gerhard von Breuning, who had known and worshipped him as boy, and who was now a physician himself, kept Beethoven's skull by his bedside.'

'That strikes me as somewhat macabre doesn't it you Hans?' Isabelle scrunched her face.

Hans smiled. 'Beethoven's remains were moved from Währing to pride of place in the Zentralfriedhof in 1888.'

She sat in silence once again as Hans drove her through the outer suburbs of Vienna. He pointed towards a dark mottled house to their right, positioned almost level with the road.

'Here is the Eroica Haus in Oberdöbling.'

'Hard to believe that's where he composed his revolutionary third symphony,' Isabelle said. 'I would have passed this plain building and been none the wiser, save for the memorial plaque.'

Shops and houses eventually became interspersed with trees and shrubs, and soon Isabelle was admiring the palatial homes that now lined the road.

'This is a very expensive part of the city, mostly inhabited by Wien's more wealthy citizens,' Hans said.

Isabelle loved the way his English was so formal, so well spoken. A true gentleman she decided.

'In the time of Beethoven, many of the suburbs we have driven through from Vienna were fields. He came to Heiligenstadt for rest, and how do you say... recuperation? He was a great lover of nature.'

'I can see why Hans, it's a charming neighbourhood,' replied Isabelle, admiring the quaint houses nestled together with old churches and quiet roads, surrounded by steep vineyard covered hills.

Hans pointed to the sign for Grinzing,

'This is also a picturesque town popular among tourists in the summer, especially for the local wine.'

The snowfall had ceased and billowing clouds ushered each other speedily across the sky, as the winter light began to diminish.

A few moments later Hans brought the Mercedes to a halt in Probusgasse, opposite the Heiligenstadt Testament House and archway. It was a quiet residential street with no extraordinary features.

'Shall I come back in an hour Isabelle?'

'Yes, that should be fine, thanks Hans.'

She crossed the road and looked back. Hans called over to her.

'If you get time do visit the church over there,' he pointed towards a spire. 'Michaels-kirche is lovely. Also just along the road is a good restaurant.'

Isabelle instantly felt a peace and tranquillity descend over her in the courtyard. The Linden tree was poised stoically without its leaves, and the courtyard walls were whitewashed. Isabelle climbed the main stairway that wound around the tree up to the main museum and house. She imagined that in the summer it would have been magical. An elderly lady gave her a welcoming smile and she paid her entry fee.

Isabelle entered the long rectangle room at the top, and stepped slowly across its solid dark wooden floor. At the far end she could see a piano, and there were sections of manuscripts on display, including the front page of the Eroica score - with the infamous scribbling that accompanied Napoleon's fall from grace with the composer.

She pondered the antique prints of local scenery that were dotted around the room. She closed her eyes to try and imagine what it must have been like there in the summer of 1802.

She read with interest how a local river walk was said to have inspired him in the composition of the sixth symphony, affectionately referred to as the Pastoral.

The room was cold, and her stumps began to throb, so after a while she crossed back into the courtyard and ascended the shorter wooden steps that were opposite the main building. Here there were two rooms that served as another museum, and Isabelle was transfixed by a lock of his greying light brown hair. She remembered reading somewhere that some of his hair taken a day after his death had been recently analysed, showing high levels of lead. It was a suffering that only one who had suffered greatly in some way, could begin to understand. A few minutes later Isabelle sat down in the courtyard by the tree and began to read the Heiligenstadt Testament that she had purchased in Vienna.

The letter to his brothers was heart rending; his impending deafness was obviously completely overwhelming him; such was his desperation that he might never fulfil his artistic destiny. The depth of emotion he felt in order to write such a document at the age of thirty two, must have been overcome by an even stronger will to pursue his art no matter what, as the document had lain in his desk undiscovered until after his death in 1827. Tears welled, and then fell onto the page. Isabelle recognised his despair. She wiped her streaked face hoping no-one had witnessed her little episode.

Breathing in the chilly winter air, Isabelle huddled quietly, watching an animated group of young Japanese students pass her on their way to the museum. She didn't know how long she had been waiting, completely lost in thought, unaware that she had been shivering, when she suddenly noticed Hans's brown eyes peering at her through the archway.

'It is okay for me to arrive now?'

'Hi Hans, yes it's good to see you. I think I had better head back to my hotel, it's getting dark and I'm frozen.'

'I trust you had a good experience in the Beethovenhaus?'

'It blew me away just being in the room where he lived and worked. It was incredibly moving. I could imagine him composing there. I think it was here that I especially got a sense of what he went through, just to follow his art. It's his isolation that really affected me.'

'It is to our very great fortune that he did not give up,' Hans replied.

He drove her back to the city, and despite her stumps throbbing as her left hand began to thaw, Isabelle drifted into a light sleep. When they arrived back at the hotel Isabelle gave him a hug and Hans blushed slightly.

'I wish you good luck Isabelle; it has been my utmost pleasure to drive you today. Here is my card. If you are ever in Wien again, please give me a call.'

'Thank you, I definitely will. I couldn't have asked for a more helpful, friendly and lovely person to help me with this project. I will always remember this day Hans.'

She handed over his fee with a generous tip and strolled into the warm foyer.

In her room; emotional and physical exhaustion had begun to take hold, and with her bare feet warming on the underfloor heated tiles she ran a hot bath to revive her senses for the evening ahead.

She decided on skinny fitting black jeans and a gold silk halter neck top, covered by a black lace cardigan, and her black suede heeled ankle boots. It was too cold to look completely glamorous, and she didn't want to give off the wrong signals. After all, she reminded herself; he was going out with a supermodel and probably just wanted some intelligent conversation.

Finishing her lip gloss with a rather shaky left hand she headed down to the lobby, and caught sight of Daniel almost immediately, sitting comfortably in a soft chair, apparently engrossed in a magazine. Her heart quickened.

He looked up as she approached him.

'You look lovely,' he stood, and kissed her cheek. Isabelle almost buckled at the knees.

'Hi Daniel.'

Daniel's blue eyes glinted. 'Hungry?'

'Hungry doesn't cover it, I could eat a horse! I've walked up and down stairs, trodden every floor board of every Beethoven museum in the city, so you could say I've worked up an appetite!'

He lightly touched her elbow guiding her to the hotel entrance, and they walked in silence to the waiting taxi.

'Imperial Hotel bitte.'

They sat in silence for the short ride. Isabelle was all too aware of his strong physique next to her. On arrival he held his hand out for her as she got out of the car and as they touched she felt a primordial energy course through her.

The busy Kärntner Ring that fronted the magnificent neo classical building of the Imperial Hotel bustled with tourists and locals heading towards the inner city. Isabelle stared in awe as they entered through the revolving doors and into the large frescoed ceiling foyer. Art work adorned the high walls and a large elaborate crystal chandelier hung over them. The Hallensalon was plush and opulent, resplendent with marble pillars, wide cushioned sofas, wall seats and yet more chandeliers. Sumptuous curtains were draped in aesthetic fashion around the room, and a Bösendorfer piano was placed in the corner.

She followed Daniel through a corridor to the art deco restaurant lined with intimate booths. A waiter with impeccable manners seated them, and deftly lit the candle on their table. The linen was starched white, with not a single blemish or crease. Silver cutlery sparkled.

'I've stayed in some pretty amazing hotels during my career Daniel, but I don't remember any being quite as palatial as this one.'

'Palatial is the right word actually Isabelle, it was built in 1863 as the Vienna residence of the Prince of Württemberg.'

'The company looks after you when you travel then?'

'It's a perk of the job.'

'Hmmm… A gold plated perk,' she joked, and they chinked glasses brimming with chilled champagne. She hadn't even noticed the waiter fill their glasses as she had been so absorbed with the magical surroundings and Daniel Carter staring at her from across the immaculate table.

'How was your day? It sounds like you covered a lot of ground?' He studied her animated face, radiant with glowing rosy cheeks and sparkling emerald eyes, complemented by a full and inviting mouth.

'Where do I start? I'll never forget today. It was completely fascinating! I mean, I know a certain amount about the man, but to be there, in his rooms, amongst his surroundings and some of his possessions, it was just a dream come true. It's probably the first day since my accident that I haven't had any "woe is me" thoughts. My attention had a welcome diversion. My guide; Hans was really sweet, and as it turned out, he was also pretty knowledgeable about Mr B.'

He looked intently at her. 'From what I can tell, you seem to be coping well with your new lifestyle.'

'Maybe... It's early days yet, it just feels like I'm on holiday, having a break from practising.' She shuffled in her seat. He continued to gaze at her.

'I miss the Nagyvary, more than words can express. I miss holding it to my neck, and pressing on the strings. I miss the buzz of walking out on stage, performing and then appreciating the audience's rapture afterwards. I miss being able to play. I miss interacting with the orchestra. It's like I've been stuck in this virtuoso identity all this time... and now I feel lost.'

'Perhaps you don't need a new identity; you just need to be you. I know we all derive a certain amount of self-esteem from what we do, but it shouldn't define who we are.'

'I'm going to be indescribable,' Isabelle said with an air of fake grandeur.

'Indeed you are,' said Daniel, 'but you know what I mean about letting the past rule us, and I'm as guilty as the next person for living on auto-pilot and basing my decisions on past experiences.'

'Looking in the rear view mirror instead of watching the road we're on,' chimed in Isabelle.

'Exactly. There's a saying about getting "paralysis of analysis" or something like that. Traumatic experiences make us open our eyes and our hearts, sometimes. Every now and then I find it quite liberating to go by my gut feelings, just be in the present moment and see what comes up.' His blue eyes narrowed in on her face like a hawk. 'Perhaps we should both let go of our identities for the evening.'

'What about Maria? Surely she didn't decline a visit to one of the most romantic cities in the world with you?'

'Maria isn't really a romantic person, plus she had to work on a Christmas shoot in New York, then she's going straight back to Lisbon to be with her family over the holidays. I'm going to join them after Christmas. I had to come to a major publishing conference in Berlin a few days ago, and rather than flying back to New York and then back to Europe again I thought I'd bolt on a meeting with my contact in Austria, Carl Zeiss. He runs the classical outfit in Vienna. He was with me yesterday evening when we bumped into you at the Landtmann café.'

The waiter politely interjected with menus. 'I can thoroughly recommend the salmon.'

'So tell me Daniel, why do you live in New York, when you are responsible for UK and European titles?' Her cheeks burned.

'It's simple really. I like New York. It's where I grew up. My mother's English and my father's American. They met in New York and so that's where we spent most of our lives. I was sent to Oxford to study for my degree, followed by a brief stint at the Met Art School. Mum was a painter and Dad was an art and antiques dealer. He was partner in a firm off Fifth Avenue, and it was expected that I would follow suit in the world of art dealing.'

'I take it you had other ideas?' Isabelle asked.

'I did. The bottom line was I didn't have enough talent to be an artist, and I didn't really have the desire to be a dealer. But I do love literature, philosophy and culture. It helped that I had a strong sense of business, so I was drawn to publishing.'

'You'd probably get on well with my friend Sebastian. His mother loved art, especially Frieda Kahlo, being a patriotic Mexican.'

The waiter quietly set down their steaming plates and they ate hungrily for a while. Daniel shot her a teasing glance.

'That's what I like to see – a woman who likes her food!'

'What's not to like? That was an incredible dinner. Mind you, I've always had a healthy appetite. H used to tease me that she and I were in the wrong bodies for what we ate.'

He grinned and raised his glass. 'Here's to healthy appetites!'

'Cheers!' Isabelle took a sip of her champagne.

'I used to live life in the fast lane when I was making a name for myself on the soloist's circuit,' her eyes glazed over. 'I loved travelling, and I still do, but there was no urge to settle down or think about the future. I revered the old and contemporary masters like Menuhin, Heifetz, Stern, Oistrakh and Perlman. They had long prestigious careers and there was no reason to think that I wouldn't have.'

His hand came to rest softly on top of her right hand.

'It's true that I neglected my spiritual path on the way to the top. I was so hungry for success that I missed the warning signs that showed up in my personal life. H helped me to figure that out in Madeira. I could blame Howard for the rest of my life, but that isn't going to help me heal. I made a decision to just go with the flow for once in my life, and not get so uptight about everything being perfect. Qué sera, sera as the song goes.'

'There's supposed to be perfection in everything, or at least that's what the teachings of the east pertain to.' He started stroking the back of her hand. It was like a wave of sheer ecstasy washing over her.

'Do you have any room for dessert?' Daniel asked, as he noticed the waiter approaching them again.

'Why not, it's nearly Christmas. Anything chocolate will do me.'

'In that case, we'll have two Imperial Torte's please.' Daniel handed the menu back to the waiter who nodded and departed.

'Now, where were we before puddings caught our attention?'

'Well, in broad terms we were discussing the evolution of the soul. Not a subject as light and fluffy as an Imperial Torte.' Isabelle studied him for a second. 'But I don't understand the perfection in my predicament.'

'Isabelle, have you ever heard of the Chaos Theory?'

'Chaos Theory? I do know my life is chaos at the moment!' She laughed.

Daniel leaned closer as though just about to impart a top secret tip. His voice lowered.

'Have you ever wondered what your life would be like if things had been different? You know... if you had pursued a different career, made different choices? Kind of like a parallel universe?'

'You've reminded me of that film Sliding Doors based on that idea. Recently I have. So many times I've gone over in my mind, why I didn't leave Howard earlier, or comprehend his agenda. I think fear held me back. Maybe I'd still be playing. I'd still be playing...'

'Ah, but that's the thing. In the Chaos Theory there's a dynamic called sensitivity to initial conditions and it's been branded as the "Butterfly Effect".'

This time Isabelle leaned forward until their faces were only a few inches from each other. 'I do love butterflies. Perhaps you can elucidate Daniel?'

'The "Butterfly Effect" suggests that the flapping of a butterfly's wings might create tiny changes in the atmosphere, which could, over a period of time cause a tornado to occur. The flapping wing represents a small change in the initial condition of the system, which causes a chain of events leading to large-scale phenomena. Had the butterfly not flapped its wings, the trajectory of the system might have been vastly different.'

She sat thoughtful for a moment, and then said,

'So you mean, if a butterfly flaps its wings in Brazil, this could set off a Hurricane in Hawaii?'

'Exactly right. Of course in context, it applies to the weather, and Lorenz came across it when learning how to forecast the weather, but I think you can apply it to the physical universe. It appears as though there's no order to the universe, but really even our thoughts lead us to where we're at, not just some strange twist of fate. An event happens, someone does something and then cause and effect take over. Have you ever thought that if either of us did anything differently, we wouldn't be sitting here right now?'

Isabelle could feel her heart pounding. She leaned back.

'Poor Beethoven thought that fate had it in for him.'

'Cue his fifth symphony,' Daniel said.

'Yes. But when you look at what he produced in his later years, you wonder if he would have left the musical legacy he did, without the physical and emotional suffering he had to endure. And out of that spiritual growth, music was created that is so intrinsic to the human spirit. He composed such towering works of genius that have a way of affecting each of us now as much as they did for nineteenth century listeners. The themes of catharsis, going from darkness into the light ran throughout his symphonies and sonatas. And even at the height of his despair, he showed such courage and innovation in his art. He was a true inspiration to us all.'

'I think your article will be superb Isabelle.' Daniel was looking at her intensely.

Their eyes met.

20

Isabelle's vision gradually came into focus in the darkened room. She was aware of Daniel's breathing steady and soft beside her. The full experience of their union was still luminous in her mind.

Images flashed to and fro; their clasped hands, an exchange of intense looks, Daniel taking her hand, leaving the table before the waiter returned with their desserts, then their slow walk up the marble Imperial Staircase to his room, never once taking their eyes off one another.

She knew that nothing could prevent their longing and passion from being expressed in physical terms. Her body was on fire, tingling under every touch, while their mouths had been glued together as they kissed fervently against the slammed door.

They were so engrossed in each other's bodies that clothes had literally been torn and discarded, in their haste and desire to be united. She couldn't remember how they made it across to the bed.

Daniel had been the perfect lover. His hand had grasped the back of her hair and pulled her head back as his tongue lightly dusted her neck as he showered her with kisses, slowly moving down her body tracing every smooth curve of her form, as his hands had caressed her hungrily. She had revelled in his strong embrace, running her hands over his muscular frame, cupping his neat yet powerful buttocks. The moment of ultimate intimacy when he entered her willing body had been exquisite. His every movement sent her into orbit. It felt like he had merged into the very depths of her soul. Her long lithe legs were wrapped around his waist, as he held firmly on to her shoulders, their laboured breathing and soft moans escaping into the high ceiling above them.

She had lain in his arms afterwards, smoothing and stroking his dark wavy hair back from his forehead, as he drifted into contented sleep. Filled with the elixir of love and lying quietly in Daniel's arms in the afterglow of their lovemaking had been a bliss she had never before experienced. She didn't want their contentment to end. She knew whatever feelings she had for him, were far more potent and intense than she had felt for any other man. It was as if a drug had taken over her entire being.

The second time she awoke Daniel was watching her. She rubbed her eyes, and smiled back at him.

'Good morning, my little virtuoso!' His finger started to trace along her breast and around her hardening nipple. 'You are so beautiful Isabelle. Thank you.' He kissed her breast and she squirmed, flushing a little under his haze of affection.

'Daniel, I...Words aren't really sufficient right now. I'm so happy.'

The second time they made love more deliberately, and although she didn't think it was possible; even more intensely. Afterwards they stayed entwined in their position, their sexual energy spent for the time being. Isabelle straddled him, gently resting her breasts on his heaving chest. He sat against the headboard, their flesh now slightly slippery against each other as their sweat began to cool on their skin.

Daniel's phone rang and he cursed over the intrusion. Isabelle showered while he took his messages, and he followed her into the palatial marble bathroom after a few minutes.

Isabelle stood naked, her skin glistening with water droplets in front of the mirror, studying her own complexion.

'Still think I'm sexy?' she teased, holding up her hand, 'with mummified fingers?'

'Especially with mummified fingers.' Daniel kissed her forehead and climbed into the shower.

As they dressed Isabelle was faced with her first awkward moment. Hastening towards the door, she turned, unsure of what to say next.

'Well, I suppose you have a busy schedule for today, and I've got my article to write up, so perhaps we can see each other later?'

He sat on the edge of the bed buttoning his shirt and looked earnestly at her.

'You really want to spend the day alone?'

'No, well, of course not,' Isabelle replied.

'Work can wait. How about we spend the rest of the day together, after all it is Christmas Eve - and in Europe they celebrate Christmas on Christmas Eve.'

'I can't resist, when you put it like that.' Running towards him she pushed him flat onto the bed. 'Are you going to show me a good time?'

'That depends on how well you behave!' He moved her right hand over his now firm groin.

'I think you are the one not behaving Mr Carter!' Isabelle pulled away and attempted to straighten her hair which was tumbling out of its grips. 'C'mon, Vienna is waiting.'

They started their sightseeing at the Hofburg Palace, gasping in awe at the splendour of the baroque surroundings. Even the porcelain collection had been mind boggling in its sheer size and intricate detail. They became engrossed in the story of the ill-fated Princess Sisi, told in an exhibition in the state apartments. They passed through rooms with high ceilings, adorned with gold leaf and sumptuous red curtains and carpets.

The tour had been followed by some punch to warm them, ready for their ride in the open air carriage. A gruff looking Viennese man gave them a blanket, and his horse strolled sedately around the inner city. They got on in front of the magnificent elliptical library, and even that building with its majestic pillars filled her with awe. Passing the Rathaus, Isabelle had to pinch herself. Despite all the heartache she felt, the moments in Vienna and Madeira had been etched into her memory forever. Isabelle reclined in Daniel's arms as they watched their breath float away in the cool air, enjoying each other's company and the beauty of Vienna's architecture gleaming under the snow. Eventually the horse came to an abrupt halt in St. Stephen's Square.

It was late afternoon when they entered the Gothic Cathedral, and inside the lights were dimmed. Still masses of tourists flocked to its altar. Daniel had steered her towards a small flight of stairs leading underground, whispering,

'The medieval catacombs will be more interesting than another church altar.'

After a few minutes a guide appeared, followed by a handful of other tourists and before she had a chance to object, they were passing through a heavy wooden door, where the air was cooler and the dim light even less evident.

Fear and fascination gripped her in equal measure. They started with the coffins of past bishops, before moving into a cave like atmosphere of underground tunnels, where they came face-to-face with rooms filled to the brim with ancient bones and skulls piled on top of one another. Old grey bones that had lain undisturbed for centuries. She had found the plague pits disturbing, there was something so undignified and terrifying about the huge piles of bones. It was death on a horrific scale.

They approached a room where the founder of the cathedral rested with his family. Copper coffins lay in all sizes, and in the room they passed by giant urns that sat on shelves. Daniel seemed to be revelling in the macabre nature of the tour, but Isabelle was shivering now and her hand began to ache.

The guide was talking again. 'Here we have the family's entrails that have been removed and placed in the copper urns for preservation.'

Isabelle looked up at Daniel. 'I can't help but wonder about medieval customs.'

The final staircase took them up and out into the square beside the cathedral, and they gratefully acknowledged their guide. On Isabelle's part, it was more for not leaving them stranded under the ground with centuries old skeletons dumped in dank dark rooms.

'Well, that was gruesome,' Isabelle pinched Daniel's cheek.

'Gruesome yes, but you should be used to gruesome by now.'

Isabelle's smile faded, and he said, 'I'm so sorry Isabelle, that was very thoughtless of me.'

'So you can do crass after all. And here's me beginning to think you were the perfect man.'

'Far from it,' he admitted, 'but you do bring out the beast in me Isabelle.'

'I'm starved, let's get some Schnitzel.' She grabbed his hand and they headed for a nearby café.

The day was rounded off by wandering among the quaint Christmas markets in the old city, close to Isabelle's hotel. The cobbled streets were slippery and hard underfoot, but it added to the festive atmosphere, along with wafts of roasted chestnuts, softly falling flakes of snow, and happy Viennese families socialising and buying their gifts.

They spent a delirious night in her hotel room, making love and caressing each other into blissful orgasms. Daniel discovered how ticklish her feet were, and Isabelle had located a sensitive spot behind his ear, which she had been happy to exploit.

As they both drifted in and out of sleep, Isabelle became animated and wanted to talk. Daniel lay peacefully, apparently letting her words flow over his satisfied body.

'It struck me tonight how music mirrors life. Fleeting ephemeral moments, made up of beauty, sadness, joy, hope and despair. Melodies which are written in both major and minor keys. Flowing and fleeting. You can't hold onto it, or keep it from changing. Our emotions possess the evanescence of a note.' Daniel nodded, but kept his eyes closed.

'I remember all of my performances. But not so much the finer details, as the feelings and atmosphere.

They could even be figments of my imagination, but the soft gristly lump under my jaw where the chin rest chafed my skin was proof they took place, that I once was a violinist, a virtuoso...'

'You certainly struck a chord in me Ms. Bryant,' Daniel said, as a grin curved onto his mouth.

'You know, it never occurred to me before, the madness of spending hours in practice and study - all banked in the school of hard work for those never to be repeated minutes in a concert hall somewhere, creating sounds to be enjoyed. And it was perfect in the moment. The recordings made of my live performances never evoked the same emotional response in me, as the times they actually unfolded.'

'You swallowed a philosophy manual.' Daniel shot her a teasing glance.

'Haha, very funny Mister Philosophy. You must be a good influence on me,' she countered, nuzzling into the crook of his neck.

'My love of music and performing has at least taught me that being an artist, in whatever genre, means expressing yourself. Although I can't do that on the violin any longer I intend to do it in my writing. Thank you Daniel, for giving me the opportunity to do something vaguely useful...'

Christmas morning came and went. Isabelle and Daniel had spent the morning oblivious to the occasion; they were naked in bed, Daniel once again inside her in rapturous delight. Later they woke with hunger and wolfed down their Christmas dinners Isabelle had ordered on room service.

They spent the afternoon walking in the gardens of the grand Belvedere Palace, built as a summer residence for Prince Eugene. It was cold and crisp but clear, and bound in warm jumpers and coats they marvelled at the impressive views of the city spread out before them. The prominent spire of Saint Stephens rising above the rooftops reminded her of their afternoon tour in the cathedral's chilling depths.

Hand in hand they enjoyed the art exhibitions, testing each other on their European history, which to her dismay, Daniel had an almost obsessive knowledge of. As they strolled down the gardens in the direction of the Schwarzenbergplatz memorial and fountain Isabelle asked,

'Daniel, as we are both flying home tomorrow, I was wondering when we might see each other again?' She looked down at her frozen feet. 'I can't bear the thought of being apart from you. I realise we haven't known each other long, but I feel I've known you all my life. I...I never thought I could be remotely happy in this condition.' She lifted her left hand. 'Somehow you've given me back my zest for life.'

'That's quite a compliment, thank you Isabelle. I'd have to be blind not to notice the sparkle in your eyes these last few days that wasn't there in Madeira.'

He spun her round to face him, and they stood motionless in the garden surrounded by tourists of every nationality milling around in the winter sun.

'I understand what you're saying, I feel the same. But our situation is complicated, so I think we should take it one step at a time. I have to be back in New York next month with work and social commitments and then I can come back to London.' With a cheeky smirk, 'I'm sure I'll be desperate to stroke your contours long before then!'

She planted a kiss on his cold cheek.

'Don't worry. I'm not going to metamorphose into a bunny boiler. I believe in freedom. I have to finish my Beethoven article and source my next assignments, along with finding somewhere to live. I'm sure H won't kick me out, but I really need my own space now. I haven't told you much about my family, but I have a sister in New York, and well...let's just say we had a barren patch in our relationship, but before I came here we sort of broke the ice. I'd like to see her, so maybe if I make it across the pond I might just look you up...'

'For the record, I love surprises.' Daniel pulled her even closer to him. 'I'd like to know more about your family. Perhaps we can exchange stories next time? It will give us plenty to talk about.' He clamped his mouth onto hers and held her in a lingering kiss.

Isabelle's phone jumped into life.

'Hello H!'

'So tell all Issy. How was Vienna? I want all the gory details!'

'H, can't it wait till I get back; I'm in the middle of packing?'

'Sod the packing! You're not flying until tomorrow. I definitely can't wait.'

'It's been amazing, in more ways than one and I wish it could have lasted longer. But I'm coming back to the real world now. You'll be pleased to know I've got a sense of direction now H, and I'm going to start looking for a place of my own.'

'Whoa, back up a minute. Was Daniel Carter the "more ways than one"?'

'You don't miss a thing do you?' Isabelle laughed. 'Yes, actually he was, he was pretty much all the ways, but I have also been inspired by my guide Hans and my dear eternal Ludwig. I had a message from reception this morning saying Hans had popped in and left me his copy of a book he told me about called "Memories of Beethoven". How many people would do that, let alone on the day after Christmas Day?'

'Good for you Issy! Sounds like you made quite an impression.'

'Daniel and I might be lovers, but that doesn't mean he loves me. We shared something incredible, and that something will live with me forever, even if he decides to go back to New York and shack up forever more with Maria.'

'Did he leave without any commitment to see you again?'

'Well, no…sort of. But it doesn't matter. It's weird H, I feel like I've known him all my life, and yet there's not much I do actually know about him. We experienced the most intimate union possible between a man and a woman, yet he remains a mystery to me. Maybe that's the way it's meant to be. Not everything can be explained. I just know that it felt perfect in the moment.'

'It was quite a co-incidence that Daniel just happened to be in Vienna at the same time as you don't you think?'

'I don't know H, he was in Berlin beforehand. Whatever it was, it was meant to be.'

'You sound happy, and that makes me happy. I'll be at Heathrow in the morning to pick you up. I'm glad you weren't alone over Christmas.'

'Thanks H. I've got a Tyrolean teddy for you.'

Isabelle hung up.

21

Isabelle spoke into the microphone:
'I can honestly say that Beethoven is my hero. Not just in a musical sense, for his great works of genius, which have a spiritual and timeless quality as they perfectly express the human condition, but also for his persistence in bringing them to bear. He achieved all this, despite much personal strife and tragedy, set against the tumultuous backdrop of the Napoleonic wars in Europe.

'The opening bars of his fifth symphony in C minor are probably among the most often hummed and dramatic in musical history, written by a master in touch with the importance of music to the human spirit. He believed that music was more important than science and philosophy as a means of expressing ideas and reality as he saw it.

'My current circumstances have in some measure given me an even closer connection to Beethoven, two centuries notwithstanding. He never compromised his artistic integrity for what was "safe" at the time. He was innovative and courageous and his music bears testament to the character of the man - more in my opinion, than any other composer before or since.

'Then there was the enduring isolation that his deafness caused. He must have been conscious at a very deep level that his isolation would ultimately underpin his creative ability and his growing spiritual awareness. The essence of his works are infiltrated by his faithfulness to his experiences, it's what makes them so immortal.

'What I take from his music more than anything is this – the triumph of the spirit over despair and seemingly insurmountable obstacles. His suffering was eventually his salvation. Beethoven has helped me personally to come to terms with my own injuries – both physical and emotional, to arrive at a place where I'm ready to find new meaning in my life.

'The challenge as a musician, was always to play his music with a sense of discovery, and to capture the essence of his struggle to produce the sound that Beethoven had in mind. You have to go to the edge of the precipice with him. To do that enables the listener to forget that they know what's coming to some degree, and immerse themselves in a totally fresh experience.

'Certainly the spiritual qualities of the epic ninth symphony show us that he drew heavily from the well of his own life in being able to compose the most magnificent symphony ever written. Such illumination which originated in the profoundest depths of his soul can never be expressed in language.'

Isabelle felt herself welling up and couldn't complete the article in one go. She turned off the tape recorder and stared out the window, still immersed in her memories of Vienna.

22

'**M**ate, it's better than I imagined. It's bloody awesome!' Lucy bellowed down the phone. 'You managed to get into the heart of the man, his music and his life. I love all your photos, and the way you parallel your circumstances to his. It's nothing short of inspirational!'

'Thanks Lucy, that means a lot to me, I wasn't sure if it was good enough and I was wondering if you had a back-up plan in case you thought it was pants.'

'I had every faith in you Isabelle, I'm never wrong about people. Listen, I'd like to hire you as a freelancer, would you like to write for us regularly?'

'Yes, I would. If your hand was here I'd bite it off.'

'Get you; making jokes about missing hands already. I don't know what happened in Vienna mate, but you are definitely on the way up.'

On a quiet January morning as Isabelle sat at the desk in Hortense's study facing their snow clad back garden; watching a lively Robin pecking at the seed tray, whilst preparing her next article, her mobile phone rang.

'Hello Ms Bryant, it's Melanie here from Riverside Homes in Marlow. I hope you don't mind the intrusion, but I thought you'd want to know about a lovely period cottage we've just taken on near the Thames.'

'Hi Melanie, that's okay, are you able to tell me a little about it? I've got quite a lot of work to get through, but if it sounds like it's what I'm looking for, I'll drop everything and drive over.'

'Well, it's got two large double bedrooms, three reception rooms, including a kitchen/diner, plus a bathroom, utility room, a very small box room, which you could use for a study, and a reasonable garden. I took down the particulars myself earlier this morning and I thought about you straight away, I remembered you saying you wanted somewhere with character and lots of natural light. It's number 2 Watermill Gardens, just a stone's throw from the Thames. You've got the best of both worlds as it's in a nice quiet road, but you are only a ten minute walk from the High Street.'

'Thanks Melanie, it sounds perfect, and I know that these little finds go very quickly, so I can be there in an hour if the traffic flows. I'm still staying at my friend's house in Notting Hill. Now my wounds are healing, it's getting easier to drive. I'll give you a call if I get stuck anywhere.'

'Great. I think you'll like it. Let's meet in our office in the High Street, and then you can follow me there. Take care, bye for now.'

An hour later she arrived in Marlow and Melanie turned out to be just as agreeable in the flesh, with pale blue eyes and long flowing almost white hair, surrounding a well- proportioned and slightly square-shaped face. Her short and slender stature was bolstered by high heeled court shoes and Isabelle guessed she was in her mid-twenties.

With a warm handshake and due reverence to her injured hand, Melanie led the way and before long Isabelle was staring at the detached flint and stone cottage, fronted by a large bay leaded-light window and an oak front door.

Isabelle couldn't put her finger on what it was that most appealed to her about the house, certainly it was light and airy, with real wood flooring and exposed beams in the ceilings.

'As you can see it won't need any work doing, and the décor is tasteful and minimal,' Melanie said.

'Just to my taste,' agreed Isabelle. 'It's perhaps a little smaller than I would have liked, but it will offer me a cosy existence in pretty surroundings. Can I confirm that asking price is four hundred and ninety nine thousand pounds?'

'Yes, that's right,' Melanie looked at her sheet.

'Well it seems reasonable to me compared to other properties I've viewed in the area. They aren't a patch on this one for the same money. Melanie, I think you've found yourself a buyer! Am I the first to view it?'

'Luckily you are Ms. Bryant, but there are a few appointments booked in for this afternoon, but we'll inform them it's under offer if you want to proceed. I know the owner has already found somewhere and wants to move quite quickly.'

'Call me Isabelle please. I'm very grateful to you Melanie. It's perfect for me right now. I'll offer the asking price, I don't want to mess around, and I've got no chain. I can put down half the value as a cash deposit, and I'll need to organise the rest on a mortgage.'

'Great, thanks Isabelle. I'll call the vendor with your offer immediately I get back to the office, and I'll let you know as soon as possible.' With her spindly heels clicking on the narrow path leading from the front door she got into her car and sped away.

Isabelle sauntered along the road, keen to take in the surrounding area. She felt for her mobile which had been nestled in the pocket of her pink tweed jacket, and pulled up Sebastian's number. After a brief ring the line clicked and she took a breath ready to speak, but then she heard his familiar soft Spanish accent telling her to leave a message.

'Hi Seb! It's me, Issy! I guess you must be rehearsing. Sorry I haven't been in touch sooner, it's been kinda crazy since I got back from Madeira. In the meantime I've been to Vienna, and I recently got my first article published and put an offer on a house today, so things are beginning to look up. I hope everything is well with you and Marcus and Delilah of course. Give me a call...bye.'

No sooner had she hung up than her mobile shook with an incoming text. Her heart missed a beat. It was from Daniel.

Hello my lovely virtuoso, missing you so much. You did him proud! Loved your Beethoven article BTW. Let's speak soon, x Dan

She decided not to respond straight away. He'd left it nearly a week to contact her, although she knew he must have been busy, and she wasn't about to appear desperate.

After walking towards the High Street Isabelle crossed the road just before the bridge and entered Higginson Park. She passed the children's play area and sat on a bench facing the river as it rippled beneath the swans and ducks, all competing for scraps of bread that mothers and toddlers were throwing for them. Against the backdrop of the All Saint's Church spire and the striking white suspension bridge, tourists were embarking on a river cruise a few yards away, accompanied by the sounds of the engine spluttering into life and an occasional bark coming from further down the towpath. She had found the perfect spot for her new home.

She searched her mind for what she knew already of Marlow. Apart from being an upmarket riverside town it had been inhabited since Norman times. She leafed through the local information that Melanie had furnished her with earlier. She read that the bridge over the Thames was designed by William Tierney Clark and had been built between 1829 and 1832, replacing a collapsed wooden bridge further down the river and was the only bridge of its kind spanning the non-tidal section of the River Thames. The same engineer had used his design for the Marlow Bridge but on a much larger scale for the now famous Széchenyi Chain Bridge across the Danube in Budapest.

She continued reading and discovered that it was from the scenery in nearby Cookham that Kenneth Grahame had drawn inspiration for his much loved children's book, The Wind in The Willows. The town had been no stranger to literary residents, as the poet Percey Bysshe Shelley had lodged in the area with his friend and writer Thomas Love Peacock. With her head spinning full of facts she jumped slightly as her phone rang.

'Hello?'

'Isabelle, it's me, Melanie. I've got good news...'

That evening Gerry called in his usual affable mood, this time he really did have an offer she couldn't refuse.

'Isabelle, I've got a speaking engagement offer from the Met in New York. They want you to come and talk at an evening function as part of an Arts Celebration Week they're having.' He paused for breath. 'You'll never guess what – it's during the period when you are going to be in New York!'

'Gerry, I think I'm going to regret telling you about my visit to Lily.'

Then he added, almost as an afterthought to the kudos of the assignment, 'they'll pay a generous fee, and I don't need to remind you what a confidence booster this would be, as well as giving you a sound basis for the future.'

'What you're saying makes sense Gerry, but...'

'But what Issy?'

'There's so much going on in my life. I don't really have enough time to prepare and besides; what will I talk about? What if it's a disaster? What if my last vestige of respect and reputation is left in tatters?'

'I can help you with the content. I'll do whatever I can to help you make it a success. Look how well you did with the *High Notes* article, and now you're writing for them.'

'Issy, you gotta do this honey!' Hortense's voice chipped into the conversation. 'You may not feel confident now, but how do you think your reputation as a fighter and an inspiration to others will serve you in the long term? This is a fantastic opportunity. Lily can go with you for moral support. I'm sure Daniel will want to support you in this as well.'

'H, how long have you been listening in? Never mind, I forgive you, you're always so annoyingly erudite.

God I hate it when you're right all the time H! I know I should do it, but I'm still dealing with my depression, and I don't feel fully confident yet. Besides, the last thing I want is for Daniel to see me, in case I make a hash of it.'

'Hash of it my arse! Issy, courage isn't the absence of fear!' Once H had a mission nothing short of a natural disaster stopped her from seeing it through.

'I've heard some crap in my time, but this takes the biscuit! Issy you have played in front of thousands of people in your career, music critics, and art lovers the world over. The highest of social echelons have appreciated your talents, not to mention some of the world's most revered conductors. The only way you are going to beat the depression is by overcoming your fear. Only doing what you fear can liberate you. I for one will admire you whether you are a good speaker or not. It's the message that's important, not the messenger.'

Gerry remained silent, and they heard Isabelle sigh.

'It can go down on the record that I succumbed to your joint coercions! I don't stand a chance when you both gang up on me.'

'It's for your own good.'

'Okay Gerry, you've got yourself a deal. What's the date?'

'You won't regret this Issy. It's on Valentine's Day, be there for nineteen hundred hours at the Metropolitan Museum in Manhattan. I'll email you the full address and the name of our contact there. I just need to reiterate that there can be no backing out once we've accepted this, as the event is being publicised in art journals and circles across the city.'

'You know me Gerry, only another disaster of some kind will stop me from making an idiot of myself on the fourteenth.'

'I've got a feeling it'll be an auspicious day,' Hortense said.

'I hope so H. Feeling out of my depth has been a new experience since my accident. I knew that even before my accident, when I was testing my playing skills to the limit at every performance, there were still challenges in my life; but I never felt totally overwhelmed by them.

'But since that unspeakable autumn evening, try as I may, I just can't erase it from my memory.'

'It's probably something you'll never completely be able to shut out Issy, but the emotional charge that comes with such a traumatic memory at the moment will eventually disappear.' Hortense's tone was reassuring.

'Isabelle, I'll call you the night before to confirm everything's okay. Drop me a line with any ideas and if you need any help at all.' The line clicked and Gerry was gone.

Replacing the handset, she and H met in the hallway and hugged.

'It's satisfying and irritating at the same time, but thank God you always give me what I need rather than what I want,' Isabelle said.

'Yes, well, that's my job as your best friend, to give you a kick up the derriere when you need it,' laughed Hortense.

Half an hour later after dozing off in H's comfy armchair her mobile leapt into life, and this time Sebastian's exotic but nasally voice filtered into her ear.

'Hello darling, it's Seb, got your message.'

'Seb! How the devil are you?'

'Compared to what you've been through I can't complain. Isn't it about time we got together senorita?'

'Yes, when you can meet?'

'Why don't you come over Saturday, Friday is our last performance so I can relax properly.'

'Great. I'll be over about eleven then. I'm driving again now.'

Settling back into H's armchair, she let her head fall back into the enveloping cushions and closed her eyes. Seeing Sebastian again would be like old times, but in reality she feared they were both older, wiser and too world weary to pretend otherwise.

23

Sebastian flung open the door and greeted Isabelle with a forceful hug. Isabelle pulled back and looked into his tired brown eyes, noticing they appeared more set into his drawn face. Her smile faltered as she followed him into his apartment, his usual grace and ease seemingly replaced by an awkward gait. His handsome dark features were still evident, but in comparison to the last time she saw him, his face reflected a sickly pallor.

'Seb, are you okay? You look like you've lost weight?'

'Can't complain darling, I'm playing lead cello in one of the most respected orchestras in the world. I come and go as I wish.'

Isabelle frowned.

'I think my schedule has taken it out of me.' He glanced up at her, managing a half smile. 'It's good to see you looking so radiant Isabella.'

'A good foundation can do wonders. I've missed you Seb. How are things with Marcus?' Isabelle sat down on his armchair, her roving eye taking in all the luscious detail of Sebastian's immaculate flat. It was like sitting in a private art gallery, there were whole walls plastered with Impressionist, Renaissance and his beloved Frida Kahlo prints.

'Marcus left me.' Sebastian shrugged his shoulders. 'He decided to go back to his wife. By all accounts he wanted to have children with her. We split about two months ago.'

'Seb I'm so sorry. You never mentioned this before. Can't same sex couples adopt these days?'

'That was my argument, but there is more to it than that. I didn't mention it earlier as you had enough on your plate, and still do. I didn't want to burden you.'

'I hate to admit it Seb, but I probably wouldn't have been much comfort to you, I was too busy wallowing in my own self-pity.'

Sebastian brushed his hands through his short, sleek black hair and stared past Isabelle and out of the window.

Delilah came running into the lounge and rubbed herself against his leg before greeting Isabelle with her usual rapid barking and bionic tail. Isabelle held out a customary hand that Delilah nuzzled for an instant before she returned obediently to her owner.

'She's been a faithful mutt.' Sebastian ruffled her neck and knelt to be more at her level. She's kept me sane through the break-up.'

'Sebastian,' Isabelle rose and lightly touched her bandaged hand on his shoulder, 'promise me next time, that no matter what is going on, you will call me if you need an ear or a shoulder to cry on. I'm here for you. We've all been battle scarred, we can help each other.'

Sebastian's hand covered hers for a brief moment, but his gaze averted hers. 'Thanks Isabella, I appreciate that. Now, we have some serious gossip to get through, so I'll get the kettle on.'

They sat facing each other over steaming teacups. Sebastian crossed his legs and said, 'So how was Madeira, Senorita?'

'Madeira was amazing. The scenery was stunning and H, bless her heart, gave me plenty to ponder on. I've definitely turned a corner. I even met a tall dark handsome stranger...'

Sebastian almost spilt his tea. 'You did what?'

Isabelle smirked. 'Yes, on the terrace at Reid's. H and I were having afternoon tea, as one does when one is in Funchal.'

'And?'

'There's not much to tell really. He's a director of a large publishing group and was on a work trip. He gave me his card, but we only chatted for a few minutes, but boy did I feel an undercurrent.'

'Have you seen him since?'

'You could say that.'

'Now you are being coy Isabella. You said on your message that you made a trip to Vienna?'

'Sorry Seb. Yes, I did at Christmas. Fate must have been smiling on me, because I met Daniel there also, and yes, before you ask, we had a passionate affair. Vienna is one of those cities you never forget, and to see the main sites associated with Beethoven was really special. So you could say it was memorable.'

'I'm happy for you,' Sebastian said with glinting eyes. 'Are you and Daniel an item now?'

'It's complicated Seb. It's more unspoken, but we're not officially. I forgot to mention that he has a beautiful girlfriend, she's Portuguese. I know it was wrong of me to sleep with him knowing he's seeing someone else, but honestly, I got the feeling that his relationship with her was on the rocks. I felt such a strong attraction to him, such a powerful connection. It's hard to explain.'

Sebastian raised his eyebrows. 'Don't look at me like that Seb. It wasn't some cheap one night stand. Not for me, anyway. I'm probably going to surprise him when I go to New York. So, to sum it all up: I'm in love, and I've got a new career, and hopefully soon a new house.'

'And you deserve it Isabella. You can't keep a good virtuoso down! Have you told Daniel how you feel?'

'No...not exactly. He must know. You don't share that kind of connection when there's nothing underneath the physical attraction. Maybe it's different for guys though.'

Sebastian said with a sigh, 'The emotional attachment makes it just as real for us too.'

Isabelle sipped her tea.

'After all, isn't he shagging you and not Maria?'

'I'm glad to see you haven't lost any of your wicked wit Seb!'

'It helps me keep my perspective on life,' he smiled, 'otherwise I'd never get out of bed in the morning.'

'I guess you're right, if you can't laugh at yourself, it all gets too serious. I never thought in my wildest dreams I'd attempt to kill myself. Life was so sweet, for so long, that I didn't see it for what it was, didn't fully appreciate my blessings…'

'Gotta have the attitude of gratitude' Sebastian said. He moved like a lithe panther grabbing a copy of *High Notes* from his writing chest in the corner, dropping it casually onto the oak coffee table.

'Beethoven's Babe has done okay. I know you don't like it, but that sobriquet suits you. Have you had any contact with you know who?'

'Ha! Sounds like we're in a Harry Potter novel,' said Isabelle. 'He whose name shall not be spoken. But in answer to your question, no I haven't.'

Her stomach lurched. 'I saw my lawyer this morning to discuss what kind of settlement I can negotiate, and he's writing to Howard's solicitor. If we can agree on things then there won't be any need for court appearances. To be honest, I know he won't ever sell the house to pay me off; it's been in his family for generations. If I get a reasonable sum I'm not fussed. I'm only just starting to feel like my life is getting back on track, and I don't need the stress of any more acrimony.

'How's Yolanda?'

'Gracias. Sadly she's going senile. I called to speak to her this morning. The dementia has taken hold of her quite quickly, I'm not even sure she still recognises my voice.'

'I'm so sorry to hear that Seb. It must be a worry for you, being so far away.'

'Yes, and it's only going to get worse, so I've arranged for her to be moved into the best nursing home in Mexico City.'

She could see a measure of pain and regret in his face, and when his dark brown eyes met hers they held a resolute look. 'After the season has finished, I am going to take a month's holiday and go visit her. Make sure that's she's settled in okay. I should have visited her more often after papa died, but I was too wrapped up in my career and then I met Marcus, thinking that one day we would settle down in domestic bliss.'

'How long has it been since you were last there?'

'Too long. She hated living in London when I was a bambino, she never got used to the cold. Papa was running the British embassy in Mexico City when they met, but he wanted me to be born in the UK, and I grew up and attended various boarding schools here. We spent the summer holidays in Mexico every year. I have very fond memories of Los Muertos Beach.'

Isabelle wandered over to the window and gazed out.

'I hope you can be some comfort to your mother, and maybe it would be meaningful to get back in touch with your roots, mi amigo.'

'Darling, that is what I intend to do. Mama probably won't recognise me anyway, but I am going to play for her and all the old people who live there. I owe her that. Papa was always the academic one, but Mama instilled my love of art and music, and both of them sacrificed so much to give me the fabulous opportunities I had to study music in London.'

Sebastian lifted his china cup to his lips while staring in a trance like state towards his cello resting in the corner.

'I think I know how you feel. Both my parents were so supportive of my playing. Mum was the one that really pushed me, and I don't think I ever really conveyed how much I appreciated her efforts before she passed away...'

Sebastian sat forward slightly, 'What about your father? Isn't he abroad somewhere?'

'He's living in Sydney now. He grew up in the Blue Mountains as a boy, and when he came over to Europe travelling, he met mum and they made a life and family over here. I suppose after she died he felt a need to return to his roots also. As if the loss of mum wasn't enough, I made his life hell. I didn't want him to go.'

'That's understandable Isabella.'

'He was the music teacher, the one that was reliable, always there with a down to earth approach. I miss him. Maybe I should just turn up on his doorstep someday. It would be nice to catch up with my jet set brother too.

The last time I saw them both was at a performance I did in the Sydney Opera House.'

'You should darling. Get the house sorted and then go. It's always the things that we don't do that we end up regretting.'

'But not always,' said Isabelle staring at her hand.

He rose and took their cups into the glistening kitchen, which was decorated by a single translucent pink orchid.

Isabelle raised her voice slightly so that he could hear her. 'Did I tell you that I'm going to New York to see Lily? I really hope we can put the past behind us and get back to being close, like we used to be. Gerry's organised for me to do a speech at the Met while I'm there, but I haven't got the faintest clue what to cover. I could talk about the life of a virtuoso, but that's not who I am anymore.'

'Yo lo tengo!' Sebastian exclaimed.

'You've got it?'

'Why don't you talk about overcoming adversity? You have recent experience in that. Also you can add a personal perspective on how art and music can inspire people recovering from trauma.' Sebastian returned from the kitchen.

'Seb you are a genius! I suppose I can be myself on that subject. So, that is sorted then. Gerry will be pleased. By the way, I'm going to have a house warming once all the boring stuff is out of the way, hopefully you'll be back from Mexico by then.'

'You know I love a good party Isabella!' He winked at her and manoeuvred his legs into a more comfortable position.

'How are things really going on the Howard front?'

'Just thinking about seeing him or speaking to him turns my stomach Seb. But on the other hand, I am not the same person as I was before the accident. Patrick Hill, my solicitor, thinks we could be divorced in as little as six months. I guess I owe him really, I've seen a glimpse of who I really am as a result of these experiences, and I wouldn't be able to say that without Howard's contribution, no matter how awful it may have been.'

'Hortense has done a good job with you,' he replied.

'I have my moments, believe me. I only have to hear a piece that I've once played on the radio and it sets me off.'

Isabelle looked at her watch. Sorry Seb, I better get going. It's been wonderful to see you again, thank you for the tea and your illustrious company.'

'De nada Senorita,' he said gracefully.

As Isabelle was at the door, with Sebastian and Delilah bidding her farewell, she suddenly felt nervous.

'Seb, please call me, and email me some photos, I want to make sure you made it to Mexico. Oh, and I'll let you know about the housewarming.'

'I wouldn't miss it, I want to meet Daniel.'

With her right hand Isabelle clasped his arm tightly and said, 'It might be difficult considering he still lives on another continent.'

24

Lily's porcelain face grinned at Isabelle as she came through the security at JFK airport. She noticed that despite Isabelle's trauma, she still had her long wavy brunette hair and arresting features. She looked skinnier than before, but that was hardly surprising given the recent circumstances.

The only thing that gave them away as sisters were their incredible jade green eyes, but whereas Isabelle had her father's olive skin Lily was pale like their mother, with short blond bobbed hair. The anticipation and anxiety that had taken hold of her before her sister's arrival, had given way to joy as she launched herself at Isabelle who was struggling with her errant suitcase.

'Hi Belle! I'm so glad you made it. How was your flight?'

'Me too! Thanks Lily. You know I slept most of the way. My life has been like a whirlwind these last few weeks and I was absolutely exhausted.'

Lily pulled along Isabelle's suitcase and hand luggage and they walked in relaxed silence to the car park, where she slung the suitcase into the ample boot of her Chrysler.

Once inside the car, the warmer air began to melt Isabelle's somewhat frozen hand.

Lily's eyes were drawn to Isabelle's hand now that she had removed her gloves, and the garish red stumps were clearly visible underneath a thin layer of gauze.

Noticing her sister's startled expression Isabelle said,

'The dressings have only just been removed a few days ago, and it feels weird. I know the scars look pretty grotesque. I'm still getting used to it myself. The good thing is I'm gradually getting used to having more flexibility, even if my hand is a little vulnerable to knocks.'

'I'm sorry, I didn't mean to stare Belle, it's just…it's hard to see you like this.'

'It's okay Lily honestly, I'm used to being stared at. I'd expect it, especially the first time you really see my hand up close.'

Lily's eyes moved away from the stumps to the darker skin around the wounds, like a purple layer of bruising around her affected fingers.

'Is it badly affected by the cold?'

'Yes. They are this colour anyway, but the cold weather makes them go numb, which is fine, but when they warm up and the nerves start to tingle, it can be excruciating,' Isabelle nursed her hand softly. 'Where's Maia?'

'She's back at the apartment with our nanny. She's into painting in a big way at the moment, and also we're potty training, which has been interesting. I can't believe she's already two and a half.'

'My God, it's been that long? Here I am only just seeing my little niece for the first time since she was born. Motherhood suits you Lily, you look great.'

They sat quietly as Lily negotiated the New York traffic, and before long the ubiquitous yellow taxis were all around them, along with the monumental skyscrapers of the downtown area. Glass walls reflected in the crisp sunlight, as the city went about its relentless business. The splendour of the view still took her breath away, and she thought about Daniel. Lily pulled into the underground car park beneath their apartment block on the Upper West Side, and they ascended in silence as the lift carried them up to her penthouse exit on the top of the building. Lily turned the key in the front door and stood momentarily in the large square lobby as she set down Isabelle's luggage.

'Maia, please come and say hello. This is Aunty Isabelle from England. She has come to see us.'

Maia's reaction to Isabelle was one of indifference at first, but with a little more coaxing from her mother, she smiled sweetly at her, before running back into the lounge.

Isabelle stepped from the entrance hall into a palatial lounge, fronted with glass almost all the way along the opposite wall, offering panoramic views over Manhattan and Central Park. The dark cream plush carpet almost bounced beneath her feet, and the walls were decorated with ornately patterned seventeenth century style wallpaper. A chair that looked like it had been plucked from a French chateau with an elaborate wood design and gold brocade upholstery was placed against the left wall. Alongside it beneath a large gold guilt mirror stood a marble table with a large antique vase filled with fresh flowers. Moving into the centre of the room she sat down on a large corner sofa which was placed so that guests were facing the impressive skyline. A finely woven antique rug stretched out before her feet. To her right side a tapestry of Monet's water lilies dominated the wall. An antique wood bureau sat beneath it. Family photos had been dotted around the room, and a unit holding the flat screen television and DVD player was next to that.

'It's just stunning Lily. I mean, the view, the décor, everything. But I'd expect nothing else from the best interior designer in New York!'

'I'm glad you like it. Treat it like your home while you're here, please Belle. And yes, I never get used to that view, it always takes my breath away.'

'Paul and you must be doing well. It's quite an apartment. I'm glad to see you've made a good life for yourself Lily. You haven't made a hash of things like I have.'

Lily watched intently as Maia approached her auntie to show her a painting she had finished earlier.

Isabelle smiled at her.

'Why, thank you Maia, that's a wonderful picture. Do you like painting?'

Maia nodded, and seemed to be studying Isabelle's features.

'I've got a little something for you sweetheart.' She pulled a neatly wrapped present from her handbag. Maia's eyes lit up, and she took it gracefully without snatching. She scurried into her bedroom. Moments later squeals of delight filled the apartment as she ran to her mum waving a set of crayons and colouring book in the air.

'Yuanita, would you mind giving my little munchkin her bath before you leave? I need to catch up with my sister for a bit.' A comely woman with dark Hispanic features took the now babbling Maia to have her bath.

'I'm not sure who she resembles most,' Isabelle said. 'She's certainly got your spirit, so full of fun and innocence. Mind you, all that wonderful strawberry blonde curly hair must be from a few generations back!'

Lily paused for a moment.

'You know Belle I've decided that if we get the revelations out of the way now, then we can get on with being sisters again.'

'I'm glad you said that, I had so many revelations in Madeira and Vienna.'

Lily cleared her throat. 'That's not exactly what I had in mind Belle.'

'Now you're making me nervous.'

Lily sat down on the sofa next to her anxious sister. 'This is probably going to be one of the most nerve-racking conversations of my life.'

'I know we've had our differences Lily, but I came here to patch things up with you. We are sisters after all. What can possibly be so bad?' Isabelle asked.

'Do you know anyone in our family with the same colour hair as Maia?' She searched Isabelle's eyes for a spark of recognition. Isabelle seemed taken aback by the question. Frowning, she simply replied that she did not.

'But you do know someone with that colour hair.'

'Lily, what are you getting at? What does it matter? Maia is Maia, she's unique...'

Isabelle scratched her head. Lily remained silent. After what felt like an eternity, her confusion gave way to a startling clarity. With a gasp her hand involuntarily covered her mouth. Her voice was a whisper.

'Lily, is Maia Paul's daughter?'

'No, I'm sorry to say she isn't, but I think you've just realised that...and more.'

'Does Paul know?'

'Yes, Paul knows, and he's been one hundred percent supportive.'

'Lily – if it's not Paul, then who is Maia's father?'

'You know him already Belle...'

'No! Please no. It can't be Howard?' Lily pursed her lips and nodded.

'Oh my God Lily, it's Howard!'

Isabelle's bulging green eyes almost popped out of their sockets. She stood, as if the movement would help to steady her reeling head. 'I've hardly set foot in New York and you dump this on me?' Her tone was incredulous.

'I know it must be a shock for you, I'm sorry to do this sis, but it's only fair that you know everything. There hasn't been a day gone by that I didn't kick myself for not telling you before...well, before you and Howard tied the knot. I can't forgive myself for that and to some extent I blame myself for your accident.'

Isabelle's eyes narrowed. 'You mean all those warnings you gave me about being sure, all that grief about how well did I know him was all because you and he – you and he had been lovers?'

Lily bit her lower lip. 'I am a terrible coward Issy. I should have told you everything, then maybe none of this would have happened, but I was so scared, so ashamed...'

'And so you should feel ashamed. Sleeping with your sister's boyfriend is right up there Lily!' Tears began to fall slowly onto her flushed cheeks. 'It's not that I'm jealous, it's the deceit that hurts the most.'

'It wasn't like that. Don't judge me until you have all the facts. This all happened before you and he got together. And as for being lovers you are completely barking up the wrong tree about that too.'

'Do enlighten me then, I can't wait to hear this,' Isabelle said.

There was no sound from Maia or Juanita in the bathroom despite their raised voices, and Lily continued.

'As you know, the time span we are talking about was when I was just married to Paul and starting out on my interior design business.'

'What are you saying? Why can't you just get to the point?'

'Isabelle, I was raped. Howard raped me.'

'Raped? How? When? I – I mean what happened?'

'I met Howard because his mother contacted me to make over the lounge at Causeway House in Sussex. One day I was in there measuring up, drawing my designs, only she had to go out and then Howard turned up. Well, I thought he was quite nice at first, quite handsome, seemingly polite, smartly dressed in his shirt and waistcoat. We got chatting, he told me he was a conductor, and I mentioned I had a sister who was a soloist on the violin.

'It all happened so fast. I wasn't expecting it. I mean I looked a mess. I was just being my normal friendly self and he appeared to want to keep chatting, rather than let me get on with my job. I vaguely recall saying politely that I had to get on or I wouldn't be able to finish the work in the timescale I promised his mother, and when I turned away he was suddenly on me pushing me forwards over the table. The stench of alcohol as he got close was overwhelming. He had me pinned down. I yelled and he covered my mouth, but there was no one around to hear me anyway. Afterwards he threatened me, saying that he would twist things to make it look like I had seduced him, and he'd make sure I didn't get any more work as an interior designer. I was weak I know, but the fear of being brandished a whore and having my reputation destroyed stopped me from going to the police.'

Isabelle's mouth gaped open.

'My God I can't believe I'm re-living all this, hopefully you'll realise that I've suffered too.'

Isabelle buried her face into her hands.

'I left a note with my apologies for his mother saying that due to family matters I couldn't continue with the project, and left. God she was rude! I felt so guilty, so ashamed. I went back to London. I showered and went to bed and cried for hours.

'The most gut wrenching thing was that Paul and I were trying for a baby, so I wasn't taking any contraception. I told Paul that evening, he could tell I was distraught, and it was all I could do to stop him going round there and killing Howard. He tried to get me to go to the police, but I just couldn't face it. So few rapes ever result in a conviction, and I knew I'd end up being the humiliated one. After all, he was an eminent conductor in the city and I would have been made to look like some nobody flirting with the man of the house. I just tried to get over it, and with Paul's help I did. Of course when I discovered I was pregnant, I had a dilemma. I suspected that Howard was the father.'

Isabelle handed a tissue to Lily.

'Paul was so wonderful. I know I married the right guy. He said that it wasn't the child's fault who its parents were, and under the circumstances even if it was Howard's, that he would raise it like his own.'

She looked up, and her red-rimmed eyes bore into Isabelle. 'How many men would do that?'

Isabelle shrugged.

'Shortly after Maia was born I knew the awful truth. We did a paternity test anyway. I just wouldn't have had the courage to bring her up without Paul. He said that Maia was never to know that he wasn't her "biological" father, and that he would be the best father she could ask for. We moved here to start a new life. He works long hours at the New York Stock Exchange, but at weekends he's the most attentive parent I've ever seen. I love her so much Belle, it's not an issue where she came from. She's innocent, and we're going to bring her up in love. I don't want that monster to know anything.

'Paul had so much sympathy for you when he heard about what happened. He kept badgering me to contact you, end the rift and tell you everything. I was so scared. I thought you'd just have even more contempt for me. I'm so glad that you had the courage to make the first move, and now, somehow, I have the courage to see it through.'

'So let me get this straight Lily, you basically stood by and let me marry a rapist because you were frightened of what I'd think of you?'

'I know it's low. I can't forgive myself. But at the time I thought you'd listen to me if I did a sly hatchet job on him. I thought if I could put enough doubts in your head you'd think twice. I thought you'd eventually discover he was a sewer-rat for yourself.'

'Lily, I lost my fingers and my whole career because Howard tried to rape me in a drunken rage! Don't you think my tragedy and my utter despair could have been avoided if only you'd had the courage to – to tell me before I walked down the fucking aisle with him?'

'I'm so sorry Belle. I've had punishment enough knowing what a coward I've been and I'll regret it for the rest of my life. I don't know what I can do to make it up to you. I'll do anything you want. You deserved to know the truth at the time, but I'm only just telling it to you now. I hope you can forgive me someday...'

Isabelle was silent for a few moments. 'I don't know what to take in first; the fact that Maia is my niece, or that Howard raped you, or that you decided not to tell me about it before I married him. I can't forgive you right now Lily. I can't even get my head round what you've just told me.'

Lily's shoulders drooped forward as if her spine could no longer support her upper body; 'I don't expect you to; it's a lot to take in. I understand that.'

'I feel so angry Lily. I've been through all this, and yet it's not that I don't have any sympathy for you. I mean I'm not sure I would have believed you anyway, I was so determined to stick two fingers up at you for questioning my judgement.'

'Even so, I should have tried. Even if you hadn't of believed me Belle, at least I could have looked myself in the mirror every day knowing I'd done the right thing.'

'I know what H would say right now, and it's a whole lot kinder than what I want to say,' Isabelle said.

Lily looked hopeful. 'What would Hortense say if she were here?'

'H would detach herself from the situation and say that what has happened to you and me can't be undone, and that no amount of reproach will bring my old life back. H would have asked how I might have reacted in the same situation as you.'

'Belle, you still have every right to be angry.'

They clasped hands, and in that fleeting moment Isabelle felt closer to her sister than she ever had.

'We've both been at the receiving end of Howard's dysfunctional personality, and now we also share a secret that we'll probably take together to our graves. The irony is, I wanted children and Howard didn't. It's such a paradox that he has one, and she is also related to me. Truth really is stranger than fiction.'

In the corner of her eye Isabelle saw a family portrait of Lily, Maia and Paul that had been taken in the park.

'Don't worry Lily, I think she's a wonderful little girl, and despite Howard's problems I know she has a chance to fulfil her potential away from his toxic influence. I will always love her too. The main thing is, are you and Paul happy?'

'Yes we are. We've put it behind us, there's no time for dwelling on such negatives when you've got a child to raise. But when I heard about your accident I was beside myself. Paul and I agreed that I had to tell you. I feel a sense of closure now. These experiences have made us who we are.'

'That they have.' Isabelle sat down again and closed her eyes. Lily wrapped her arms around her neck and then said,

'I think we've had enough revelations for one day, I'm going to cook some supper for us.' She wandered through another door into the kitchen leaving Isabelle slumped on the sofa staring blankly over the New York skyline.

25

'You've got nothing to prove to any of the people there,' Hortense said, her voice muffled by the long distance phone call, 'by virtue of the fact that you have already reached the top of your field, and have had to face an adversity that ninety percent of them could not imagine.'

'Thanks H, that's helpful. Lily and Paul have given me some great tips too, such as keeping eye contact with the same person for a minute or two, before moving on to someone else. That way I'm only having a one to one conversation, at least that's the theory. Gerry has been pontificating about the do's and don'ts of public speaking as well. Truth be told, I'm absolutely terrified.'

'Even a seasoned public speaker gets nervous before a big speech, but content is probably more important than delivery, and no-one is expecting you to be polished, it's not what you've trained to do. Always remember Issy, what matters is progress not perfection.'

'Indeed. So to summarise what Paul said, all I have to do is know my subject matter, deliver the talk in a confident manner, not talking too fast, not reading too much from notes, and use his simple formula that he told me always worked from himself.

'Tell them what you're going to tell them, then tell it to them, and finish by telling them what you told them!'

'You'll be fabulous Issy.'

'If only it could be that easy. What if my nerves play havoc with my tone of voice? And what if I forget all yours, Gerry's and Paul's well-meaning advice under the spotlight?'

'What if nothing. The world isn't going to end. If they're there to judge you then they need your message more than anyone.'

There was a click as the key turned in the door.

'How was the Central Park Zoo?' Isabelle sat up on the sofa and tried not to look like she had just woken up.

'It was great wasn't it Maia?'

Maia, red cheeked and triumphant roared as she ran past Lily and Paul, tearing her hat and scarf off. 'Alex is lion.'

Paul smiled. 'She saw Madagascar recently and has been badgering us to take her to the zoo ever since.'

'Did you finish your speech?' Lily asked.

'I did thanks. I also ordered take out as I knew you wouldn't feel like cooking.'

'Happy Valentine's Day you guys!' Isabelle hugged Lily and made her way into the kitchen. 'Why don't you all get comfy, I'll bring in the noodles.'

They ate mostly in silence, watching the Manhattan skyline transform into its evening hues as twilight descended. Even Maia was quiet, concentrating on getting the noodles into her mouth as her mother alternately fed herself and her hungry daughter. Isabelle carried the empty cartons back into the kitchen, and when she returned to the lounge Lily and Paul presented her with a single red rose. 'This is for you Belle, from all of us,' Lily said as she held out the velvet red flower. Maia clapped.

'Aww it's gorgeous, you shouldn't have, but thank you both.'

'Paul and I can have a romantic evening anytime. I'm coming with you Belle to give you some moral support. We'll leave daddy cuddled up on the sofa with Maia.'

They stood in the hallway for a moment, watching a rampantly excited Maia, pointing at the dancing flowers on Fantasia; then doing her own version on the carpet to Paul's delight.

'That's just so sweet,' said Isabelle smiling.

She was wearing a simple and elegant black wrap around dress that Lily had purchased for her during their shopping trip at Berkdorff Goodman the day before.

'Grab your coat Belle. Have you got your notes?'

Isabelle patted her pocket, and felt the pack of small index cards that she had placed there an hour earlier in preparation. 'Let's go.'

They walked in silence along Manhattan's Museum Mile, and ascended the steps leading up to the pale pillared façade of the Metropolitan Museum. Isabelle stared in awe at the domed expanse of the Great Hall. The three window-topped spherical ceilings descended into white stone columns, each linked by smaller pillars along the sides like a magnificent Roman temple.

Lily made their presence known to a member of staff at the visitor's desk in the centre of the hall.

'Hello, I'm Lily Kramer and I'm here with my sister Isabelle Bryant who is scheduled to give a presentation in the Grace Rainey Roger's Auditorium in about half an hour.'

The heavily made up middle aged woman smiled warmly at them.

'Welcome both of you. We are so pleased to have you. Let me escort you to the Egyptian wing of the Met, where the auditorium is located. Our museum covers two million square feet. We wouldn't want you getting lost, now would we?'

Their guide escorted them through gallery after gallery until they found themselves in a corridor leading to the stage. They passed through a doorway, which opened onto the rear of the wooden stage, only half visible behind a closed red curtain. The wood panels at the back of the stage were softly lit providing a calming ambience for Isabelle. A man of medium build clad in a tweed suit rose from one of the wooden chairs and held his hand out for her.

'Great to meet you Ms. Bryant, my name is Maurice Caplan,' he said in a strong New York accent. 'I've been dealing with your agent Gerry Goldberg. From what he has told me it sounds like we're gonna be in for a real treat this evening.' His smile revealed slightly crooked teeth, but his bright hazel eyes twinkled with admiration from behind his spectacles.

'Thank you Mr Caplan, I'll do my best to live up to Gerry's hyperbole. Are there many people attending?'

'According to my numbers the auditorium should be about three quarters full, which should equate to roughly five hundred and twenty five guests. I just had a peep through the curtain fifteen minutes ago and we're filling up nicely. I'd say we'll be fine to get underway bang on time.' He glanced at his hairy wrist, mostly covered by a circular analogue watch face. 'Yep, we've got about ten minutes. Can I get you some water?'

'That would be lovely,' Isabelle replied, feeling the effects of her dry mouth.

'Please, have a seat.' Maurice held his arm out towards the three chairs. He disappeared through the rear door along with their guide, leaving Isabelle and Lily alone momentarily. Lily sat down.

'You okay Belle?'

'Yeah, just about. I can't sit down, I prefer to keep moving; it helps me to control my nerves.' She removed her coat and placed it on her seat and walked slowly along the length of the stage, back and forth, the floor boards creaking softly beneath her. She could hear a multitude of muffled voices and laughter emanating through the curtain. A few moments later Maurice returned and handed them both their drink.

'Ready?'

Isabelle gulped down her water and nodded.

Lily squeezed her hand, whispering, 'I'm so proud of you Sis, knock 'em dead!'

Before she had time to appraise the situation Maurice had slipped through the curtain and a hush fell upon the auditorium. He began to introduce her to the audience. Through the deafening pounding of her heart Isabelle thought she heard him say that she was the youngest ever winner of the BBC Young Musician of The Year Competition, a virtuoso who built her career on a much loved recording of the Beethoven violin concerto, and then something about her tragic accident, and after a moment an applause was ringing in her ears. She stepped tentatively through the curtains and came face to face with her audience. The light was brighter beneath the podium, which was placed at the front centre of the stage. She turned, and to her left stood a Steinway grand piano. But this was to be a recital of words.

She gazed across the room, and seeing what she interpreted as anticipation and admiration in some of the guest's expressions, she relaxed her muscles and deepened her breathing. She smiled as graciously as she could, and waited for everyone to sit and for the coughing to die out. Isabelle opened her mouth to speak when the sudden noise of a door shutting in the ensuing silence caught her attention, and heads in the audience turned in unison.

Distracted, she peered up towards the front row of the circle of the auditorium, and set eyes on Daniel Carter, who hurriedly seated himself and was staring back at her with equal interest.

She took a deep breath and leaned towards the microphone. 'It's quite unsettling having all your eyes bearing down on me with no violin or an orchestra to support me.' She pulled her shoulders back and grasped the podium with her right hand, grateful her knees were holding firm. 'But it makes it so much easier to speak to you this evening with such genuine appreciation. Thank you for such a warm welcome. I'd like to take this opportunity to thank The Metropolitan Museum of Art for asking me to speak.'

She fixed her gaze on a young and handsome man in the front row, who had been smiling at her since she had walked onto the stage.

'This is, in fact, my first speaking engagement since an accident that left me with mutilated and decapitated fingers on my left hand.' She held up her gauze covered hand and gasps echoed simultaneously around the room.

'This...accident finished my career as a virtuoso violinist, and very nearly my life,' she paused and switched her gaze to an older woman a few rows back. 'I tell you this, not to garner your pity, but rather in the hope that I can still do something useful with my life. I have come to realise in the few months since it happened that maybe I can use my personal tragedy to inspire others in similar strife. And that is what I'd like to share with you today.

'First I'm going to talk a little about what it took for me to get where I was, and then how I coped with my injury, a kind of a before and after synopsis.'

Isabelle looked at the sea of expectant faces before her. They all appeared genuinely interested, and just like a toddler learning to walk, she felt more confident with every step. Her voice became stronger as her fear dissipated.

'I started playing the violin when I was five years old. As time progressed, it became apparent that I had some talent that could be channelled. With some en-couragement from my parents I was practicing for up to five hours a day, and bar holidays and sickness I never missed my practice sessions. I worked hard, studied with some amazing teachers and students, won competitions and reached my dream of a recording contract early in my career. I was doing what I loved: playing a beautiful violin, travelling all over the world and being well paid for my efforts; I had a wonderful lifestyle.

'Music is a lofty form of art in my view, it can lift people out of a low mood, inspire memories, and it can heal hearts and invoke spiritual experiences. My main ideal when performing a very well-known work, such as the Beethoven Violin Concerto, was to reproduce the score into a musical first for the listener, so that they got something new and fresh from it, even though they were familiar with the notes that were coming.'

Isabelle switched her gaze across the room, taking in the friendly atmosphere.

'How much pressure was applied to the string, the level of vibrato, the style of bowing and my interpretation all impacted upon the experience of the listener. It was and still is my passion in life. Some of you may know that of all the composers in history Beethoven is the one I admire most. Not only for his musical genius, or the spiritual depth of his music, but lately just as much for his perseverance against adversity. The ninth Symphony was written in his mind, for he was completely deaf. I looked to his example when I couldn't play any longer. The agony was almost unbearable at first.'

She took a sip of water to try and ease a hard lump that had formed at the base of her throat. She caught the eyes of another guest.

'I felt useless, like my future had been squandered. I still get emotional when I see or hear other performers. Music's in my blood. I knew that I could take my Nagyvary and make it sing, but what could I do now? There was nothing that interested me - including living.'

She searched for Daniel's blue eyes, and finding them held his steady gaze.

'I went from being at the top of the tree, to the bottom of the pile literally overnight. At least that's what I believed back then. Reflecting on the circumstances of my private life I realised that I wasn't always happy and totally fulfilled, and despite outward appearances my life wasn't perfect. Maybe fate decided I needed a major wake-up call. Like Beethoven's deafness, my accident was a catalyst for change in all areas of my life.

'I've had so much support from my friends and even people I hardly know, I have started to use my knowledge and experience to strive forward to offer an example to others that life can be enriching, even after a bout of intense suffering - if we let it.

'I firmly believe that art has the power to show us a path to our higher selves, whether we are the artist, or the one appreciating the art. All forms of art, music and literature have the power to communicate emotions that its creator may have felt, enabling us to see, hear and read the world through their eyes, ideas and aspirations. Somehow they resonate within the individual, even though his or her experience may be different. The common thread of the spectrum of human emotion is encapsulated in each of us, waiting to be drawn out at just the right moment.

'Programmes that include art therapy for children have transported troubled kids into other realms, where their creativity was more important than their circumstances. Music can bring people together, as we have seen in the Middle East with the dedicated work of Daniel Barenboim and his formation of the West-Eastern Divan Orchestra.

'Shakespeare may have lived over four hundred years ago, but his characters and their dramas are timeless, universal themes, that can be adapted into contemporary settings. Michelangelo's genius will live forever on the roof of the Sistine Chapel, benefiting all who see its beauty and appreciate the feat of his achievement.'

Daniel was smiling at her now, nodding in encouragement.

'The arts offer us all a subjective experience and can therefore be viewed through each of our individual filters and levels of understanding. The Met is priceless in its role for preserving such timeless and precious artefacts for all humanity, and we should do all we can to determine its preservation.' A light applause rippled through the auditorium.

'To summarize then, I have been very privileged to have pursued a career doing something that I loved, which has hopefully given joy to all who saw and heard me play. More importantly, I am able to see my situation with compassion and some detachment now and, with a renewed hope for the future.

'A very special friend helped me to realise that my self-expression was not confined to four strings on a violin, but comes from my inner being; my very soul. Writing and speaking projects are providing me with an outlet to highlight art being used as a way of recovering from trauma, and it's my fervent desire to help others on their journey. I only hope there is something out there for me that I can develop that will leave an even greater legacy than even my playing career would have. The challenge now is to discover it!'

The audience were smiling at her in appreciation and empathy.

'I was very nervous before coming onto this stage this evening, but I can truly say that I have enjoyed speaking to you all. You are great people living in a great city; with a great museum. The Met has had a rich cultural history since 1870, and contains over two million works in its permanent collections. May you all continue to flourish! Thank you.'

There was silence as Isabelle took a step back from the podium, and then her ears rang with raucous clapping and cheers from the audience that she had not expected. One woman was wiping tears away from her cheek, and she caught Daniel's eye, and thought for a second that she could see admiration staring back at her.

Maurice was grinning at her, and holding his arm open respectfully as he guided her from the stage to a quieter area where waiters began to serve champagne, soft drinks and appetisers.

Isabelle was used to talking to people after a musical performance, but as this was such a unique and liberating experience, her body felt a rush of energy like never before. Shaking hands and thanking people for their kind words, with Lily standing quietly by her side. Gerry was a pain sometimes, but she murmured a secret "thank you" in her mind.

A hand came to rest on her shoulder, and instinctively knowing the touch, she shot Lily a sideways glance, wondering if she would pick up on their vibes.

'I should have told them Daniel, about how you were an ambassador for a wounded musician. You know I found it very hard to concentrate with you sitting at the back!'

Isabelle spun round and threw her arms around him, not paying attention to the surprised faces of members of the audience who were still mopping up the museum's culinary offerings. Taken aback, but enjoying her display of affection Daniel wound his arms around her slender figure. As they drew back from their embrace Lily's expression bore an enquiring look, but she remained silent.

'Lily, this is Daniel Carter, we met while I was recuperating in Madeira. Daniel is the director of the European publications for Hudson Publishing Inc.,' there was a pause.

'It's nice to meet you Daniel.' Lily held out her hand and they shook firmly. 'And thanks for helping my sister on the road to recovery. She's been through more than anyone deserves.'

A quick glance told Isabelle she approved.

'Isabelle mentioned she had a sister in New York, it's great to meet you too,' Daniel said.

'Please excuse me. I need to visit the little girl's room.'

Daniel's gaze followed her for a split second, and then he turned his piercing blue eyes back to Isabelle.

'She seems gorgeous,' and seeing a glimmer of jealously which emerged unconsciously on Isabelle's face, 'but not a patch on her sister with the mummified hand, or not so mummified now.'

He held her left hand gently and kissed the back of her palm.

'You were magnificent this evening Isabelle.'

Isabelle blushed. 'I must say, you made more of an entrance than I did.'

'That's not possible,' Daniel said in jest.

'I was surprised to see you, as I didn't even tell you I was coming to the Big Apple. After your solitary text I figured maybe you wanted some space. Besides, I was going to be the one who surprised you.' Isabelle put her empty champagne glass back on to the tray of a passing waiter.

'And what a nice surprise it would have been. Being a member of the Friends of the Met, I received a mailing two weeks ago promoting the event, and I've been able to think of nothing else since. I figured I'd surprise you.'

He lowered his voice and inched closer to her. 'Listen, are you staying with Lily while you're here? Would it be very rude if you came and stayed with me this evening?'

'Daniel, I... I don't know. Lily and I have just patched things up and I don't want to upset her. A lot has been going in the last few days, I'm not sure I'll be very good company. And what happened in Vienna... I shouldn't have succumbed. You're with Maria, it was wrong to go rushing in like fools.' Her voice was low so as not to draw attention to their conversation. She turned away. His fingers softly surrounded her jaw and tilted her head upwards.

'Look at me Isabelle Bryant. I know you don't regret what happened, and neither do I. Our time together in Vienna made me realise that I don't love Maria. I know I haven't exactly been beating a path to your door since then, but I needed some space to figure out a few things.'

'You can have all the space you want. I don't think I'm ready for another heartbreak just yet Daniel.' She looked directly into his baffled eyes.

Lily returned without either of them seeing her.

'Listen, you guys look like you could do with some catch up time. After all, it is Valentine's Day. Belle, I'll see you later. You have my address, here's a key.' Whipping the spare out of her handbag she thrust it into her hand. Isabelle stood mute as Lily leant over to hug her goodbye and whispered into her ear,

'Don't worry if you don't come home tonight.'

Turning to exchange pleasantries with Daniel, she was gone almost as abruptly as she had re-appeared.

Daniel took Isabelle's hand and led her through the waning crowds and into the cold but sparkling evening. Once again the sight of the brightly lit skyscrapers took her breath away. She watched as Daniel took control of the situation, hailing a cab almost instantly, and they cuddled in the back like teenagers. Just as Isabelle was about to fall asleep on Daniel's shoulder, the taxi pulled up outside a classically designed building with a tarpaulin and door man at the entrance. They made their way in silence up in the lift, and then paused outside the door of Daniel's apartment.

They gazed at one another, and both feeling the other's urgency to be physically united again, Daniel whisked her through the front door, and upon closing it Isabelle found herself pushed up against it as Daniel immediately lifted her dress. She felt him slide his hands beneath her stocking tops, running his fingers up the length of her suspenders, tugging on her panties and pulling them down to her ankles. He raised her legs level with his hips and she gasped as he entered her rather forcefully. His sweet breath warmed her neck and sent tingles down her legs. She was oblivious to everything except the feel of him. Shuddering in pleasure, they remained entwined for a moment, then staggered across the room and fell onto the sofa giggling, where they remained embracing each other as they drifted into a satisfied slumber.

When they eventually stirred Isabelle noticed a lamp was on in the corner of the apartment radiating a translucent light, and it was the first real opportunity she had to see his home. It was elegantly furnished in a minimalist style, but the real wood floor, giant vases and far eastern looking rugs gave it a sophisticated look. A book case lined one wall, and various paintings were hung around the lounge and entrance hall.

Daniel kissed her forehead before extricating himself from beneath her. He wandered in to the kitchen, returning a few minutes later with two glasses of chilled water. Quietly he led her into the bedroom. They removed the remainder of their garments and curled up under the duvet on his large bed in a blissful state. Isabelle was aware of a warm sensation slowly taking hold of her body.

The air was fresher in the bedroom, and she watched the curtain rustle in the cool breeze as it billowed in through the open window.

With her back to his chest and Daniel's arms wrapped around her she fell into a soporific state. As if in a lucid dream, she was suddenly aware of herself teetering on the edge of an abyss. She couldn't see the bottom of it, and felt herself tipping over the edge into the chasm.

"Music is a higher revelation than all wisdom and philosophy." ~ Ludwig van Beethoven

PART III –
'IMMORTAL BELOVED'

26

Isabelle awoke to the sound of her mobile phone bleeping and an aromatic smell emanating from the kitchen. Stretching under the duvet, she rubbed her eyes and slipped out of the bed. She delved into Daniel's comprehensive wardrobe. She chose the smallest and most casual shirt she could find, and grappled with her overflowing handbag for her phone.

The text was from H:

Gerry called, couldn't get hold of you!
Gr8 feedback from Met, well done xo

The clatter of pans in the kitchen brought her back down to earth, and she yawned. Her feet felt cold on the shiny wood floor.

Daniel grinned as she entered the kitchen. 'You're just in time for my speciality.'

'I can't wait. I don't fully wake-up until my taste buds are tingling you know.'

'Get stuck into this then,' he placed a substantial plate of eggs garnished with tomatoes and fresh herbs before her.

'Smells gorgeous, hope it tastes as good as it looks.'

Daniel watched her rather messy and swift consumption with an amused expression. When she had finished Isabelle glanced up, unaware that a tiny morsel of scrambled egg had smeared onto her chin.

'What?'

Daniel shrugged in an exaggerated joking way.

'Making love makes me hungry,' she smiled as she set down her knife and fork onto her empty plate.

'It certainly does my, little virtuoso.' He slipped his hand under the soft denim folds to caress her breast. Isabelle sighed.

The hardness of the surface did not register with her as he lifted her onto the table and took her there and then in the kitchen, accompanied by the faint noise of car horns and the city waking up far below them.

Their soapy bodies rubbed together under the warm water and all thoughts of work, or the future, evaporated into the mist. Isabelle still had instructions from the doctor to keep her hand dry as much as possible, and so left it dangling just outside the glass door. Vaguely dry, they collapsed onto his bed and pleasured each other with tantalising caresses, before Isabelle climbed on top of Daniel's muscular body. Their eyes locked as she rose and fell with his rhythm, slowly at first, building up in tempo and intensity as they approached the final release.

Exhausted she lay by his side with her head tucked under the crook of his arm, slightly resting on his chest. She could hear his heart pumping rapidly. Small beads of sweat had formed on his forehead, and Isabelle stroked the few softly matted hairs covering his pectorals.

'I've never made love twice in one morning before, God it feels so liberating.'

'You are beautiful Isabelle Bryant,' he murmured, resting his hand on her firm buttock. 'What is this power you seem to have over me Isabelle? I can't resist you!'

'Daniel Carter, thou art so virile, thou art an Adonis, and my quivering flesh can do nothing but surrender to you.'

Daniel squeezed her bottom and retorted, 'and surrender thou shall my lover.'

Isabelle didn't answer; she was happy deep down, but his words carried a tinge of disappointment, she was hoping he might utter something more profound one day. There was so much she longed to say to him, but the moment hadn't felt right.

Instead she closed her eyes and drifted into a contented sleep. When she woke, she was aware of the empty space beside her, and she glanced up. Isabelle's vision homed in on his tall frame in the doorway.

'You looked so peaceful, I didn't want to wake you. I've got to go to the office, I'll see you later. Make yourself at home Isabelle.'

'Have a good day,' she called meekly after him.

In the quiet of Daniel's bedroom she searched through her handbag until she found his business card.

Clothed in her still clean wrap around dress Isabelle pulled up outside the shimmering skyscraper that housed the Hudson Publishing Inc. offices off Fifth Avenue.

The huge marble foyer was slightly intimidating, bustling with suited men and women walking purposefully about their business. Checking the card again, she noted that he was on the 57th floor, and stepped into an already full lift. It was a smooth ascension, then a slight lurch as the lift halted and the doors slid open.

There in front of her, but not aware of her penetrating gaze, Daniel appeared to be in earnest conversation with Maria. He was holding her upper arms, and she was leaning towards him. Isabelle felt her body become leaden as the other occupants in the lift exited around her and new people filed in. She peered through the bodies and saw him hug her tightly. Her eyes widened as Maria turned her head towards the lift just before the doors began to close. Isabelle froze. The lift descended.

She felt her face flush and her heart pound so hard that it might leap out of her chest. As the lift reached the ground floor, she was the last to step out into the still busy lobby, trying to process what she had just witnessed. She paced back and forth in distress. Nausea gripped her for a few seconds, all traces of her former bumptious mood gone.

She was jolted forward by someone clipping her shoulder as they passed her. As she turned to see who had barged into her, Maria's sullen face contorted into a hateful expression. Lost for words Isabelle could only stare back, as Maria snorted at her through gritted teeth and a thick Portuguese accent,

'You are out of your depth English whore!'

Still reeling from Daniel's betrayal, Maria's outburst had caught her off-guard, but the vicious slap to her face that followed stunned her. Isabelle's hand involuntarily rubbed her now flared cheek, but her pride hurt more than the stinging.

Maria stormed out through the main entrance. Bewildered and desolate, Isabelle looked around but there was no sign of Daniel. Numbly she followed Maria's footsteps into the sunlight, and hailed a cab.

On the way back to Lily's the cab driver tried to make polite conversation, but became discouraged by Isabelle's monosyllabic answers and catatonic expression. He shook his head in tactful disapproval.

Isabelle strained to hold her emotions at bay as she ascended in the lift up to Lily's apartment, not wanting to startle the elderly lady in the lift with her. Half way up the old woman got out. Isabelle reached the penthouse level alone and by the time the doors had opened she felt herself bursting like a dam that had been held in by a rickety wall. Tears were streaming down her pale face, and her body convulsed with giant sobs. She fumbled with the key and entered the bright lobby, where she could hear Maia's soft voice coming from the lounge. As she walked surreptitiously past she could see Maia playing with her duplo bricks and dolls, as her mother sat with her cross legged on their carpet.

Lily turned and gasped as she saw Isabelle's swollen face.

'Belle? What's wrong? Look at you...'

Steering her distraught sister into the bedroom, Lily wrapped her arm around her hunched shoulders, and Isabelle wept without restraint. She opened a drawer on the chest and pulled out a box of tissues, which Isabelle gratefully took.

'What happened sis? Tell me everything.'

Isabelle could hardly bring herself to say the words. 'He betrayed me Lily,' she sniffed and then blew her nose. 'How could he?'

'I presume he is this Carter chap I met last night?' Lily asked.

Isabelle nodded and rubbed her drenched, itchy eyes.

'Oh Belle, will you tell me what happened? Start at the beginning, get it all out of your system if you can manage it.'

'We met shortly after my accident, in Madeira. H had taken me to Reid's Hotel for tea and he happened to be there on the terrace, sitting at the next table. And just like that we were talking, and my life hasn't been the same since that moment. For me it was like Pandora's Box had been opened, these intense feelings were let out, and I can't get them back in. Even though I had my recovery to think about he became a permanent fixture in my mind and before long, my heart. He put me in touch with Lucy his editor at *High Notes*, and she hired me to write a piece about Beethoven and his life in Vienna. I went over at Christmas, and he was also there meeting a colleague after a conference in Berlin. I mean of all the places, we bumped into each other on my first evening. I say bumped, I was careering across the snow and ice and nearly took them both out, and then I felt his hand on my arm and heard his voice. It's so deep...I love to hear him speak.'

Lily tilted her head so it rested gently on Isabelle's shoulder.

'You've probably figured out we became lovers in Vienna. The desire and attraction and admiration I had for him were completely overwhelming, and like an idiot I couldn't resist him.'

Isabelle sniffed somewhat feebly and put her fingers to her temples, jogging Lily's head.

'I was so weak Lily. I slept with him on our first date. It was like a scene from a fairy tale. We were at the poshest hotel in the city, surrounded by opulence and we had such a powerful connection I couldn't ignore it. It was far more potent than anything I had ever experienced with Howard. Being with him gave me a rush of exquisite energy that electrified me. When we merged it was just mind blowing, like nothing and no one else existed except for he and I, and our bodies in union. I've never felt such passion in my entire life.'

'Oh my God Belle!'

'Before I knew it I was head over heels in love with him, and I wanted to start my life a fresh. He reignited that spark, and suddenly my life had meaning again.' Isabelle's sobs subsided and her voice took on a brittle timbre.

'I really felt he was the one for me, I can't understand why he helped me so much only to break my heart in such a callous manner.' Her tone was dejected. 'We even made passionate love this morning, and he seemed to feel the same way I did.'

'What did Daniel do Belle?' Lily sighed, and squeezed her sister's right hand.

'He used me Lily. All along it was Maria he wanted. I felt so embarrassed, so sleazy, standing there in that lift, watching the pair of them together. Well- she's welcome to him! I'm done with men! At least with Howard he made his contempt obvious.'

Isabelle wiped her eyes and turned to Lily. 'He was so convincing, such a good liar. Those two were made for each other.'

'Did you actually see them kiss Belle?'

'No, but they were in an intimate embrace. You don't really snog one another in the office in front of everyone do you? I saw the way he looked into her eyes.'

'I'm sorry Belle, it's just so unfair that you should have to endure more woe on top of the bombshell I dropped on you a few days ago, and especially after you've been on such a high from your presentation at the Met.'

'I'm sorry Lily. I didn't mean to snap at you. He's not worth getting upset over. On the scale of important events in my life it shouldn't even register on the chart!'

Lily nodded in agreement.

'Why don't we spend your last day doing some sightseeing?'

'Okay. I didn't get to see that much last time I was here, apart from the Manhattan view, the Carnegie Hall and the inside of my hotel room.'

Maia came bounding into the room. She stopped, frowned and quietly hugged her, holding her teddy bear out for her to cuddle, as if it would magically cheer her up.

Somehow it did.

'Listen Belle, why don't you have a nap, I'll get us some lunch and then we can hit Manhattan later.' Lily took Maia's reluctant hand and led her out of the bedroom.

Isabelle obediently lay down and drifted into a deep sleep, transported in her ensuing dream to the stage at Carnegie Hall three years earlier, with the New York Philharmonic. All she could see were faces, bright under the lights, the black notes, her fingers on the strings, and her inner resolve that she, Isabelle Bryant was making a difference in people's lives. The dream progressed with her marvellous rendition of the Mendelssohn Violin concerto, but then she caught sight of Daniel in the crowd, and sitting next to him was Howard, and next to him Lily, Maia, and all her friends, until she stopped at Julia Bryant on the end, who was smiling at her accomplished daughter, and so was her father Bill. Basking in their haze of love and pride she stumbled and lost her place in the music. The audience gasped in horror. She looked down and could see blood oozing rapidly from her left hand. She could no longer hold the neck of the Nagyvary. Blood was dripping onto the instrument, her arm, her dress and the floor. Panic overtook her. Then the hall became silent, as the orchestra, unsure about what was happening stopped playing. Time stood still, but then seemingly in-tune with her suffering, the audience started to produce a strange cacophony that made her ears hurt. Screams and wails pierced the silence. She dropped the violin and it smashed into tiny shards of wooden shrapnel. She was floating up to the ceiling, looking down on herself and the carnage below. It was then she heard the voice. Her mother was calm, peaceful.

'Isabelle, my darling no-one can take away your talent or achievements. Be brave, life has more to reveal to you. I love you.'

The noised subsided, and for an infinitesimal moment Isabelle reached out towards the source of the voice, and started with a jolt as she felt a hand touch her.

'Belle! Belle! Wake-up! Are you okay? You were having a nightmare. You sounded almost delirious.' Lily's concerned face came into focus, and at once the dream vanished into the ether, leaving only the heady sensations it had aroused.

'That was a weird dream...'

Lily put her hand on top of Isabelle's drenched forehead. 'It was probably a mixture of all your topsy-turvy emotions over these last few months, all gathered into one freaky neurological place at the same time.'

'It felt so real though...' Isabelle's tummy rumbled loudly, and they were overcome with sudden laughter.

'Your hunger is definitely real,' said Lily smiling.

Isabelle watched as her breath coalesced and floated away in the crisp afternoon air. The horse and carriage, containing herself, Lily and an excited Maia, plodded through the trees of Central Park. As she enjoyed their genial company and the sights of the frost bound city, the disturbing images from her dream slowly faded. Their cab driver was pointing at the Plaza Hotel, telling them stories about its illustrious history. The pavements, grass and trees were all covered in a white glistening sheen, in stark contrast to the brick buildings that rose up around them, cocooning them in a winter wonderland, just like a glass paperweight encasing a picturesque scene.

As their genteel ride came to an end, they climbed out of the carriage and walked for a few minutes until Lily pulled them into a cosy café. Warmth was restored in the form of hot chocolate at Lily's favourite delicatessen, and then the three of them headed downtown on the subway to pay their respects at ground zero. They stood in silence contemplating the ghostly empty space that had previously been the site of the World Trade Centre. The construction area around the desolate ground was surrounded by fences, and Isabelle's eyes were drawn to their plaques and information about the 9/11 attacks. Many other people milled around them, each paying their own respects. It could have been any other building site were it not for the knowledge of the events that had taken place on that very spot only four and a half years ago. Horrific images that had been seared onto the minds of millions who had watched in disbelief as the towers were struck by the aircraft before collapsing and killing thousands.

Isabelle turned to Lily. 'I'm ashamed of my self-pity in the sight of such catastrophic suffering.'

'It's sobering isn't it? Belle, why don't you take a trip to Australia? Go and visit Dad and Jack.'

'I might just do that sis.'

That evening after their meal she sat with Lily and Paul on their sofa with a glass of wine, musing over her time in New York. The shimmering lights of the city twinkled before them, and Isabelle became transfixed by the night view.

Lily had her legs curled up by her as she snuggled up to Paul. Isabelle thought his chiselled features and dark curly hair resembled a Roman statesman, and both displayed a pensive countenance. Her hosts glanced at one another and nodded. Lily started the conversation.

'You know Belle, Paul and I have been doing some thinking lately. It's a bit of a morbid subject, but we've had to think very carefully about who could care for Maia if anything should happen to both of us.'

Isabelle's head snapped up. 'Jesus Lily, I hope you're not planning on emigrating spirit side just yet,' she replied.

'No, of course not, but we'd be irresponsible if we didn't think about Maia's future. We fully plan to be a big part of it, but should God have other ideas we'd like you to be her main carer Belle.'

Isabelle's mouth dropped open.

'We both know that you'd love and respect her, and that you'd instil in her the same values that we hold dear.'

'We know you appreciate her innocent charms despite of where half her genes come from,' Paul said.

'Yes, of course, I adore Maia, but I'm not exactly a good role model for her,' replied Isabelle.

'Nonsense!' Lily barked. 'You are her Aunty Belle, and there is no-one better.'

'Thank you guys, I'm honoured. I would do my best by her if the worst ever happened. But let's hope it won't!'

Isabelle watched the skyline fade into the distance as the aircraft climbed steadily. The megalopolis of skyscrapers and houses blurred into one grey mass, and then disappeared entirely as the aircraft eventually levelled out into clouds. New York and its inhabitants were now far beneath her. She tried to shut out haunting memories of Daniel and Maria, instead turning her attention to the dream, and her mother's voice that had lifted her out of a downward spiral.

Resolving to finalise the house purchase and her divorce as quickly as possible upon her return, Isabelle then busied herself by jotting down some notes for her next article. An incoming text interrupted her train of thought, and retrieving her mobile somewhat clumsily from her jacket, she saw that it was from Daniel. Her heart missed a beat. She held her breath as she opened the message.

> **Is everything ok Isabelle? Can't reach U. R you free for dinner 2night? Got something 2 tell you.**
> **Dan x**

She responded with a fervour she had previously reserved for her lengthy practise sessions.

> **Am on plane flying home. Don't contact me again. Have no wish to be told what I already know. Nothing wrong with my eyes! You will not break my heart again Dan.**

Isabelle switched off the phone and drifted in and out of sleep, eventually waking to see the familiar sprawl that was London as the aircraft descended through the early morning haze. Lights twinkled randomly as daylight began to illuminate the city.

27

It was a bright spring morning in London, as Lucy Green sat at her table in *Maison Novelli* in anticipation of Isabelle's arrival. She was enjoying a glass of wine and reading the newspaper when a slightly flustered Isabelle stepped into the bright indigo restaurant.

'Hi Luce, sorry I'm late, just not feeling that great, took me a while to get myself going today.' The two women hugged and Isabelle sat opposite her editor, facing the big bay window, where the light streaming in made her squint.

'No worries mate. Would you like a wine?'

Isabelle nodded. 'Sure, why not?'

They sipped their wine as Lucy ran over her Nagyvary versus Stradivarius piece.

'This is perfect Issy, just what I wanted. We should get some lively engagement from our readers on this, well done.'

'Thanks Luce. I was thinking that my next article could be about training to be a soloist, as it's something I've done myself, I ought to be able to make it helpful to young musicians.'

'Spot on mate. It's tough out there, any insider tips will be welcomed I'm sure,' said Lucy. 'I just wanted to thank you for your contributions to the magazine. The *High Notes* readership has increased by five percent since you came on board.'

'I'm sure it has nothing to do with me, probably a lucky coincidence,' Isabelle said.

The restaurant began to slowly fill up with other diners, and a relaxed atmosphere pervaded the room. Isabelle and Lucy ate their meals as they chatted.

'I think we create our own luck. And one thing's for sure, you're a lucky charm mate,' Lucy said with a mouth full of seared tuna.

'Maybe for others, but not for myself...'

'You should be on top of the world right now, it's all happening for you, which leads me to think your gloomy demeanour today might be something to do with the men folk?'

'Who told you that? Bloody hell, is it that obvious?'

'Ha! I sussed you out, didn't I? Well, it's none of my business,' and not pausing long enough for Isabelle to agree she continued with her prognosis. 'This Sheila knows a thing or two about the opposite sex. I know you've left the loser who caused your accident, so my guess is that some other bastard has infiltrated your defences, and penetrated your nerve centre, where he has short circuited some delicate wiring.'

Isabelle smiled.

'In my experience, men might as well bloody be from Mars, and us gals don't speak a word of Martian. It's a cliché, but treat em' mean, keep em' keen! Seriously, he's not worth the aggro, you've had enough on your plate lately, just...' Lucy stalled mid flow as Isabelle suddenly threw her chair back and ran with her hand clamped over her mouth towards the direction of the toilets.

Lucy eyed her with concern as she returned to the table.

'You okay mate? I've never seen you look so tired and pasty. And what's that red patch on your forehead?'

'I feel a bit better now, thanks Luce. I haven't puked like that since I got drunk on my eighteenth birthday party.' Isabelle reached up to her forehead. 'I was so desperate to get into the cubicle I was a bit heavy handed with the door and it bounced back and whacked me in the forehead. Almost knocked myself out.'

Lucy leaned forward over her finished plate. 'Was it a heavy night?'

'No, not at all. I'm only an occasional drinker. H wouldn't let me get plastered anyway.'

'Strewth Issy! Have you considered another possibility?'

'You mean stress?'

Lucy raised her slender eyebrows. 'You know...'

Isabelle stared at her with a blank expression.

'A bun in the oven!'

Isabelle froze, and felt a shiver run down her spine.

'What with the house buying, the travelling, the speeches and everything else I haven't been keeping track of my cycle.' She pulled her pocket diary from her overflowing handbag, and counted back the days. Six weeks had passed since she got back from New York, and around two weeks before her trip she remembered having her monthly.

'Oh my God Luce, if you're right that means I'm eight weeks pregnant!'

Overcome by panic Isabelle touched Lucy's arm in gratitude, but her mind was elsewhere; and the smell of seared tuna was playing havoc with her stomach.

'Luce, I'm sorry, I've got to go. I'll email you with the article next week.'

She knocked her glass over in her hurry to leave causing some of the other diners to stare at her.

'No worries Issy. If you need anything just give me a call.'

Lucy glared at the two businessmen on the table next to them and hissed with the most sinister Australian accent she could muster. 'Show's over boys. One of the most famous virtuosos in the world has more talent in her mutilated fingers than both of you put together. How about I wipe that smug grin off your faces? Pomme bastards!'

The waiter who was hovering at the other end of the restaurant couldn't hear what she said, but he noted it seemed to have the desired effect. The two men blushed and looked down, while Lucy paid the bill still glaring in their direction.

Other than the strange events of the morning work had been busy, but uncharacteristically Lucy had found it hard to concentrate. She had been unusually lenient on her staff that afternoon, which sent confused gossips around the office.

An email from her boss Daniel Carter had appeared at 4.30pm and she opened it unsuspecting of the content.

> *Hi Lucy,*
>
> *I know Isabelle Bryant is still freelancing for you, and you may or may not be aware that I met up with her on assignment in Vienna at Christmas and again in New York recently. How are things going there? Isabelle has not responded to any of my calls, so I am concerned about her welfare. She's been making great progress since the accident, and I just want to make sure she's alright. Please can you let me know if there's anything untoward I should know about?*
> *Regards*
> *Daniel*

Daniel sat in his leather chair staring at the skyscrapers surrounding Central Park. The air was heavy and misty, and the usual buzz of the city rose from below. He turned to the response from Lucy.

Hi Daniel,

Funny you mention that, Issy does seem to have been a little depressed in the last few weeks. As you know readership has increased significantly since she became a regular contributor, and I am keen to keep her on our books. Did anything you know of happen in New York that might have upset her? She hasn't confided any situation to me so far.
Bye for now,
Luce.

Caution got the better of him and he decided to probe Lucy a little further.

Dear Lucy,

I don't know of anything that might have upset her. I saw her speak at the Met when she did her talk, which was brilliant. She seemed happy and confident then...

I know that she has been staying with her estranged sister in Manhattan, and they haven't seen each other for some time, I can only think maybe they've had another falling out. I'd be grateful if you could dig around a bit (tactfully of course), and if you can shed any light on her mental state, please let me know.
Cheers
Daniel

'Coward!' Taunted his inner voice as he hit the enter key. His irritated mood was interrupted by a call from his secretary to advise him that Richard Hamilton was outside his office. He grabbed his Boss jacket from the back of his mahogany chair.

Seated at their favourite deli across the road from Central Park, they tucked into brimming bagels in quiet friendship. Richard had come straight from his practice, wearing his dark grey single breasted suit with a crisp, white tieless shirt. At six-foot-two he was both lean and tall with rugged features which were complemented by his immaculate grooming. Daniel was similarly athletic, but more casually dressed. Both men were unaware of admiring looks from female diners. As they sat on their high stools at the lunch bar by the front window Daniel asked:

'How's Nancy these days? Is she still running the modelling agency?'

'She's good thanks, and yeah, she's still whipping skinny asses into shape over at Paloma's.' After a few minutes of silence during which Richard eyed his usually gregarious companion with compassion, he blurted out,

'You can share it with me Danny.' His grey eyes were searching.

'Rich, don't you get bored enough of all the crap you have to listen to being a psychoanalyst to Manhattan's finest wealthy and paranoid citizens?'

'I've always got time for my best buddy,' Richard said flashing him a dazzling smile. 'Besides, I've known you since we were at Columbia University together. It's obvious you're not happy. You should unload your burdens and have the benefit of my expert advice. You know you won't get any BS from me.'

'Is that your diagnosis doctor?'

'Yep.'

'You got time?' Richard just waved his hand as if to imply he had all the time in the world.

'You've probably already guessed that it involves a woman, and I might add it's not Maria. I met the most remarkable, beautiful woman when I was in Madeira with Maria. I mean... I wasn't physically with Maria when I met her. I was having a business meeting with Carlos at Reid's Hotel that day, and this... this vision was on the balcony at the table opposite. I knew I recognised her from somewhere, but I couldn't place it until we were actually face-to-face and exchanging polite introductions.'

Richard listened patiently.

'Her name is Isabelle Bryant, the world famous virtuoso violinist. Or should I say- was.'

Richard's eyes widened perceptibly.

'I know of her Danny, and now I do remember seeing her perform at Carnegie Hall a few years ago. She had the whole place on its feet at the end. From what I can recall she was a real stunner, and talented to boot.'

'She'd just suffered a crippling accident at the hands of her husband, and lost three fingers on her left hand, which killed her career as a soloist. I know what you're thinking Rich, and it wasn't a pity job. I really liked her spirit. There was something noble and yet vulnerable about her. I know I've had this penchant for tortured souls before, but that's not the case with Isabelle.'

Richard took a sip of his coffee and nodded for Daniel to continue.

'I gave her my card, and I offered for her to get in touch with Lucy Green who runs our UK publication, *High Notes*, in the hope that she might have something to offer the readers, and help her get her joie de vivre back. I haven't been disappointed. To cut a long story short she went to Vienna to do some research for a Beethoven piece, and luckily I planned a meeting in the city during her stay. I bumped into her one evening quite by chance. Mind you, I did know she was going to be there, as Lucy had to put the expenses through. It was as though fate gave us a helping hand.'

'I don't believe there is such a thing as fate in the traditional sense. You created that fate Danny. You attracted her to you, and not just physically, but at the soul level.'

'I suppose so. That was the start of our passionate love affair. We had the most mind blowing sex, shared the same interests and I think at that point I was already a gonner. I knew she felt the same way, but she didn't have the same hang ups about the L word that I do, so her expressing herself so freely kinda put extra pressure on me. My feelings for her are genuine, but I couldn't really express them at the time. In the past it felt like an anchor I didn't want round my neck. But Isabelle is different. She stirred me.'

'Not just your groin I hope,' laughed Richard.

'No! Not just that. You said it earlier. It was at the soul level. I felt a powerful magnetic draw, like our energies had fused. Plus I felt guilty about cheating on Maria, but things hadn't been right between us for months.'

'So you didn't let on how you felt about Isabelle, and gave her just enough encouragement to fan the flames as it were?' Richard said.

Daniel let out a nervous laugh. 'It must infuriate Nancy that you are right all the time!'

'Ah, but I do occasionally concede to my wife.' Richard wiped his mouth with a serviette. I find it helps with the flow of harmony in the home and the bedroom.' He winked at Daniel.

'So you've established that I played hard to get. Lucky for me another chance came my way when I saw that she had been invited as a guest speaker at the Met, part of their "Artists on Art" season of talks. I went to see her, caught her completely off-guard. Again, I couldn't keep my hands off her. We made love that night at my place.

'She seemed dreamy and happy when I left that morning. I waited a day or so; then I sent her a cryptic text, which was the forerunner to spilling my guts.'

He stopped abruptly, frustrated and unable to make sense of the situation. Richard interjected. 'Then something went wrong?'

'You could say that. I got a text back saying she was on her way home and didn't want anything more to do with me. No explanation, just a cryptic message about not being blind!'

The world outside the deli was rushing about its business, oblivious to the two men engrossed in their mystery. A line of hungry office workers were queuing up from just outside the door and Daniel could make out impatient faces through the glass.

'I'd only just formally ended it with Maria the day before. We were already on the rocks, and after my time in Vienna with Isabelle, I knew it was over between us. She must have known it too. We had the most enormous row in my office, and then afterwards we kind of made peace. I think she at least appreciated my honesty, even if it was late in coming. So we hugged and parted. I didn't hear from Isabelle for the rest of that day or evening, but I thought I'd give her some space to be with her sister Lily, who she was staying with in Manhattan. I haven't spoken to her since. I can't get her out of my head, I can't concentrate at work, and she won't respond to my calls.'

Daniel sat back in his chair, and ran his hands through his ruffled hair. 'I hate to think of myself as one of those self-pitying schmucks that are like puppy dogs devoted to some mean owner who takes joy in tormenting them.'

'Bummer,' Richard remarked.

'You know Rich, I'm glad I'm not paying top dollar for this particular session.'

Richard looked thoughtful for a minute. 'You and Isabelle parted on good terms after your night together?'

'Sure, I left her in my bed sleeping like a baby,' his tone had changed to one of a person wronged without his knowledge.

'Danny, when you and Maria met at your office, were there any onlookers?'

'We met in private in my office, but we did say good-bye in the reception area, so my office staff would have seen us. Besides, they all know her, so there was nothing to hide.'

Richard sighed. 'If you weren't my best buddy, I'd smile at the Shakespearian tragedy of it all. Maybe it's just possible Isabelle was on her way to surprise you that day, and saw something she wasn't meant to see, in a context she wasn't meant to see it in, and concluded it was something that she didn't want to see either!'

'If Isabelle had somehow witnessed my goodbye to Maria, she might have assumed I was still in love with her, and that would explain the sudden withdrawal of her affections. Rich, that's the only goddamned explanation that makes any sense. What do I do now?'

'Hopeless situations are my speciality,' Richard said. 'What we have here is a melee of misunderstanding. Only considerate communication is going to resolve it. Danny, women like Isabelle Bryant only come along once in a lifetime.'

'True. She's beautiful, talented, compassionate, intelligent, successful and kind, but even more endearing

are her vulnerabilities; her fragile confidence and innocent ambition. If I'm not mistaken, she seemed to have
strong feelings for me as well.

'Why didn't I finish with Maria earlier? I hedged my
bets for too long.'

'Never mind that Danny, we need to figure out how
to put it right.' Richard had a determined expression on
his kind face.

'It seems that the butterfly's wings have flapped one
too many times and now the storm is swirling around
me,' Daniel said. 'Have you got an umbrella Rich?'

28

Isabelle reeled as she read the test result. Emerging from the bathroom she found H waiting curiously outside, concerned at all the commotion Isabelle had unintentionally created when she had arrived back at the house.

'Oh H, I know I wanted to be a mother, but not under these circumstances!'

Confused and frightened, Isabelle fell into Hortense's open arms, and sobbed uncontrollably. Hortense gently drew a handkerchief from her pocket and led Isabelle by the hand down their winding stairway into their large cluttered kitchen. She felt like a forlorn child as she sat at the end of their giant oak table and rubbed her swollen eyes. Hortense busied herself with making the tea.

'Have you re-established contact with Daniel Carter yet?'

'You know I haven't. I don't want to talk about him. He hurt me very deeply.'

'Has it occurred to you that he may have hurt Maria as well?'

She sat down opposite Isabelle and laid the tea on the table.

'You know Issy, even the best laid plans go awry. It's all very well planning the perfect life, but sometimes it just doesn't work out how we want. More often, what appears to be a problem can ultimately be a blessing.'

Isabelle's expression was vacant.

'Having a baby is a gift, no matter how it's packaged Issy.'

'What do you want me to say H? I already feel guilty at my sadness over what is supposed to be one of the happiest moments in a woman's life. It's easy for you to say, you have a loving husband, a great kid and a meaningful lifestyle. My circumstances couldn't be worse...'

'Now, let's see, you're writing wonderful articles for a popular classical music magazine, you are in the process of divorcing Howard and buying your own home on the banks of the river Thames. Not such bad circumstances as far as I can tell.'

'You know what I mean H. Daniel won't want anything to do with it. God, what an unholy mess! How am I going to cope on my own?'

Hortense was pondering her reply when her mobile phone leapt into life with its customary jazzy tune, and with an inaudible sigh she pulled the phone from her pocket.

'Unless it's Jools Holland offering me a night of passion or my darling Raymond they can get lost.' Peering at the display screen she noticed it was neither and swiftly turned it off.

'These are all pretty big assumptions Issy. You have to examine each fear and look at it in a balanced way. Firstly, you don't know that Daniel won't be interested, you haven't given the poor guy a chance to explain his actions; and secondly you've managed amazingly well with a life-changing accident, and are now carving out a new career for yourself. Financially you're doing okay, there'll be more money heading your way after the divorce, and at least what you're doing now is family friendly and can work around the little one. If things don't work out with Dan you'll always have a son or daughter to share your future with.'

'I know what you're saying makes sense H, but I can't forgive Daniel for breaking my heart. At least I knew where I stood with Howard.' She shook her head. 'It's too late H, the trust is gone. He doesn't have the right to know anything. Anyhow, Daniel aside, I'll be judged and maligned for being part of that collective of single mums and all the discrimination that goes with it.'

'Since when did what other people think bother you, apart from opinions about your violin playing?'

'Normally I'd agree with you, and I despise myself for being so fearful, but as soon as I clapped eyes on that thin blue line a surge has welled up inside me like a volcano, and no amount of common sense can seem to plug it.'

'That's understandable Issy, it's a big shock. Give yourself a chance, you only just found out ten minutes ago that you are pregnant.' Hortense gave her a sympathetic smile.

'I guess. I've been through so much. Isn't it enough that I'm dealing with a mangled appendage?' Isabelle raised her hand. 'It feels like I'm taking one step forwards and three back at the moment. It's like I've stumbled at the last hurdle.'

Slowly, as if on some safety mechanism Isabelle's mind emptied of its thoughts as they sat drinking their tea together at the table. She could hear the fridge humming in the corner and an exultant blackbird chirping outside.

'There's no question that I'll keep it of course. I'd never take a life. I've just got to get my head around it,' Isabelle said.

Hortense nodded in agreement. 'Well, you know that Ray and I will support you all the way. We've been there with Louis, and it's not easy, but nothing worthwhile normally is.'

'Thanks H. What would I do without you?'

'Issy, I know I sound like a stuck record, but I do think Daniel deserves to know. From an outside perspective it looks like you're cutting off your own nose to spite your face.'

The tea slipped down Isabelle's throat warm and comforting. H's big brown eyes and warm smile had started to lift her spirits.

'You're probably right, as usual. You know I really loved him. I still do, and that's what makes it so hard. He knew I'd been to hell and back and was vulnerable. He still risked everything - just for some carnal pleasure. I thought he was different. Maybe when I'm finally over him I'll tell him. He's been persistent in trying to contact me, but right now I can't face the possibility of being humiliated or hurt anymore.' Her words sounded hollow.

'The funny thing about perception is that we can bend it to our own views and beliefs. When we don't consider all aspects of a situation it blinkers us to a wider field of possibilities, and we can get stuck in negative cycles. I've found from my own experiences that the world generally gives you back what you believe about it, like a mirror reflecting our role in it.'

Isabelle scrunched her eyebrows together.

'For instance you could think that I'm an interfering old bag who wants to tell you what to do, or you could hopefully perceive that I'm your closest ally and friend, who is genuinely seeking to help you.'

Taking another sip of tea Isabelle said, 'of course it's the latter H.'

Hortense took a deep breath and exhaled slowly. 'Something very bad happened to me shortly after our family moved here from New Orleans. I've never told anyone except Raymond, but I'm hoping that by sharing

this incident with you Issy you'll realise there's always another way to view a situation.'

Isabelle leaned forward in her chair.

'I was teased mercilessly being the only black girl
when I first started at the secondary school. In the years
since then it's changed, there's a much higher percentage of coloured students. You hadn't long been going to
primary school when it happened. I think you may even
have been on holiday with your family when it occurred.
I was fifteen-years-old.'

H's bosom heaved. 'I think a little JD will help me
get through this.' Suddenly she bounded into the dining room and Isabelle could hear the chink of glass
against glass as Hortense reached into the drinks cabi-
net. Moments later she re-appeared wearing an apprehensive expression and sat opposite her.

'It's been a long time, but it feels like yesterday when
I re-live it in my mind.' She gulped down half the glass
of amber liquid.

'It happened just before the start of the summer holidays. I was walking back home, and on that particular
day it was hot and sunny so I decided to get some air
rather than take the bus.'

Isabelle eyed Hortense. 'I don't like the sound of
this H.'

'His name was Vince Clark.'

'Who was he?'

'He was my nemesis Issy. He was in the sixth form,
mostly despised as an obnoxious little shit. He had a

gang of cronies that followed his every word and terro-
rised anyone they didn't like the look of. Ray calls him
"that mongrel" if we ever talk about him.' H swallowed
hard.

'Well, Vince and his brainless buddies were also in
the vicinity that day, and they started whistling and yell-
ing obscene comments at me from across the road. I
tried to ignore them, but inside I was trembling as I still
had about half a mile to walk. I kept my head down
and carried on walking and eventually the voices died
away, so I assumed they'd gotten bored and gone home.
I couldn't see them. It wasn't until I got to the fields at
the back of our street and I was climbing over the stile to
get into the field that I felt a rough hand over my mouth
and I was being pulled backwards.'

Hortense was visibly shaking, and a single tear glistened on her dark skin.

'It was Vince. He pulled me down and began saying
the most horrible things to me, like he'd never screwed a
darkie before, and he wasn't going to start now. He said
I was ugly and he hated me, and he'd make sure I could
never populate the world with my filthy genes. I don't
remember much after that, except curling up as best I
could to shield myself from their kicks and punches.'

Isabelle noticed Hortense's hand was tightly
clenched.

'When they finished their brutal beating they
laughed and ran off, proud of their handiwork. God
knows how I managed to stagger home, at first I could

hardly move and there was a searing pain in my abdomen. It felt like I was having a period, except I wasn't. I had a bloody nose and cuts and bruises on my arms and legs. That was it. That was the moment my motherhood was taken away from me. My ovaries and womb were so badly damaged they said I would never be able to bear children.'

Isabelle took a sharp intake of breath.

'My parents were devastated too. I spent weeks in hospital being operated on and examined every which way from here to the moon by consultants. Luckily the police took the attack seriously. I mean a teenage girl being beaten-up in broad daylight in a supposedly upmarket town doesn't look too good for them. Vince was arrested later that day, and owned up to the crime under police interrogation. He'd still got my blood smeared all over his boots, which they took in evidence. It turned out he wasn't so tough after all. The school expelled him and the rest of his gang. He was jailed for twelve years.'

'Is that all?'

H's fist had unclenched slightly and Isabelle moved her hand to clasp her arm in support.

Hortense's tone grew more reflective. 'My parents never gave up hope of being grandparents and after seeing various gynaecologists it was declared that too much tissue had been scarred in my reproductive system and I wouldn't be able to have children. As if taking a vicious beating wasn't enough, they also took away my divine female right to bear children.'

'My God H, I had no idea. I'm so sorry. I think we must have all been on holiday in Australia at the time. I was so young, and I remember not seeing you for quite a while. Perhaps mum and dad thought they would try and shield me from the awfulness of it all, but now I'm older I would have wanted to be there for you H, I hope you know that?'

Hortense met her compassionate gaze. 'I was ashamed back then, and as time wore on it became harder to contemplate telling anyone. I just wanted to forget about it. You were my sweet little friend next door, and besides, it wouldn't have been appropriate anyway at the time.' She downed the remaining Jack Daniels and wiped her glistening eyes.

'I feel guilty now for burdening you with my pathetic self-pity party,' Isabelle said meekly.

'The purpose of telling you wasn't to get your sympathy or to re-live the whole miserable experience, although it has been cathartic after all these years; but to illustrate how I dealt with that adversity, to show you how it helped me later on in life. Sure, I was angry, frightened and suspicious for a while. But after I met Raymond, I became aware that not all men were like that. I was grateful to have found a partner who was fun to be with, kind and understanding, and from a similar background to me. Thanks to my darling Ray I had a normal loving relationship, which was something I would have never felt possible. We talked about adopting, and he supported me all the way. Louis is such a gift.

'I know that what happened toughened me up, and by the grace of God I managed to get through my teenage years without being eaten up by bitterness and hatred. Sure, I had some trust issues to get over, but I realised I was just in the wrong place at the wrong time. Their intent was pure evil and whoever had been in their sights would have gotten hurt that day. Had it been a white girl they probably would have gang raped her. It just happened to be me.

'I never even told Ray that I visited Vince in prison a few years later. It was one of the hardest things I've ever done, but it was worth it.'

'Why? What on Earth possessed you to do that?' Isabelle couldn't hide her incredulity.

'It was part of my emotional recovery. I saw what a broken person he was by then. All his bullish nature had been ground down by prison life. I heard he'd been treated to a dose of his own medicine inside, and was thoroughly unpopular with the other inmates. When it came to the real tough guys, the hardened criminals, he was the runt of the litter.'

'So he got his comeuppance then? How did it go?'

'He was very surprised to see me. I told him that I forgave him and that I hoped when he was released that he would find some peace. I said I hoped that he had examined the reasons why he felt he had to be a bully and hurt people. I suppose being on the end of similar treatment inside had focussed his mind somewhat.'

'Probably being buggered senseless made him repentant,' Isabelle said.

'I had a letter shortly after that, via the prison service, to say that he had topped himself. One less low life in the world didn't upset me.

'But the point is; life is too fleeting to do anything other than live it to the full. I love my life. Singing is my joy, my passion, and I used my troubles as a way to really appreciate what was great about my life. I used the experience to mould me into the person I knew I could be.'

She paused and stared into Isabelle's green eyes. 'If I can do it, so can you Issy - so can you.'

'But how can you justify it was for the best? They could have killed you H!'

Hortense tried to take a gulp from her empty tea cup. 'It's just a point of view that keeps me sane. While we're discussing this issue I may as well give you the whole shooting match.'

Isabelle shuffled in her seat, unsure if she could take much more.

'Have you ever considered that the universe is just one master cosmic show? That we are the participants, the actors if you like, who show up and play our parts. Like pieces in a puzzle we all contribute to the collective experience. There is no good or evil really, they're just states that either lead us towards or draw us away from our source, our higher Self. I believe that we don't just get born by accident, there's an intelligent design at work, and when we die, it's all been pre-arranged, it's our turn to take a bow.'

Isabelle was astounded. 'Your ideas are so expansive compared to the theological indoctrination that I was subjected to over the years.'

'When the student is ready, the teacher will appear. If you listen carefully to your soul you'll discover what part you came to play. You are in the director's chair. Everything that happens in life is all part of the plot. Evolution is the cosmic play's way of becoming more sophisticated.'

'God H, what have you been reading?'

'Whatever the reason we are here is, and however the universe works, you put me to shame H. It's a heart breaking story, but inspiring too. I know I'm lucky to be pregnant. I realise how upsetting my distress over the news must have seemed to you, and anyone who can't bear children would rightly be annoyed with me. I'll let things settle for a while and then decide what to do about Daniel.'

'I'm not upset with you Issy. Everyone deals with their challenges based on their own experience and beliefs. I just want to help.'

'You always do H…you always do.'

Hortense hugged her. 'Have you heard from Sebastian yet?'

Isabelle began searching the cupboard for some pasta, as her stomach lurched in hunger.

'No, I haven't actually. He was going to visit his mother in Mexico City and take a break afterwards on a beach somewhere. I got the feeling he wanted to get back to his roots. I've been worried about him; he seems really run down lately. I didn't know they were working them so hard at the LPO. Mind you, I think the split with Marcus has taken its toll too.'

Her voice trailed off as she emptied some shells into a saucepan. 'I wonder what he's done with Delilah, I forgot to ask. She will miss him terribly, poor little thing.'

They chatted over pasta, which this time Isabelle managed to keep down.

'H, as the house sale is due to complete in a few weeks I've decided to have a housewarming party to celebrate my new found independence. Would you and Ray come? I'd love for you to sing as well, it'll be the best entertainment.'

'Issy it would be an honour. Let me know the date as soon as possible. My diary is quite patchy at the moment but best to put it in there in case I start getting booked up.'

Isabelle Spontaneously touched her still flat stomach. 'At least there will be some part of Daniel that I can love.'

29

Daniel wandered aimlessly through Central Park, watching with interest families and business people enjoying the late spring air in their lunch hour. It was a picture postcard scene, with tourists clamouring for horse and carriage rides, open mouthed at the majesty and sheer enormity of the towering buildings rising above the trees that surrounded the park. Kids on roller blades whisked past, Japanese visitors posed for each other's photographs before an amazing backdrop.

Seized by a sudden urge to devour some art and quieten his mind, he turned on his heel and headed for the nearby Frick Museum off Fifth Avenue. It was his favourite art collection in the city, intimate enough to see in an hour or two; with just enough wonderful paintings to admire without being overwhelmed. The museum was housed in the former home of wealthy industrialist

Henry Clay Frick, an avid art collector in his lifetime, and in Daniel's opinion the greatest art collector that ever lived on his side of the Atlantic. His parents had taken him to the collection on numerous occasions. His father was especially fond of the ambience inside the house, and even though they had been many times he had always espoused the quality and origin of the paintings.

It was a breath of fresh air to step inside the nineteenth century mansion with its original features and paintings, sculptures and porcelain on display much as it might have been during Henry Frick's day. Daniel lingered in the long West Gallery, drawn by the great works of Constable, Rembrandt and Velazquez. He loved the colours in the Turner paintings; the Harbour of Dieppe always held his attention. It felt like a ray of light on his soul. His favourite was the Vermeer painting of the Mistress and Maid, the last acquisition made by the wealthy patron of the museum before his death.

The vibrant yellow of the mistress's cloak leapt out at him, their skin was translucent, alive, the lighting magical. It was almost like they were sitting in front of him in the flesh. Meandering through each gallery he finally arrived at the Garden Court, which was peaceful except for a disagreement between a young mother and her child, who was intent on showing her mother that she was less than impressed with being reigned into her buggy. Some of the visitors stared impatiently at her inability to shut the child up, and he noticed the older women who were nodding sympathetically, probably mothers reminiscing about their own experiences.

Daniel hadn't paid much notice to the scene, but after a minute he doubled back as something familiar stuck in his mind. Her hair, fair and bobbed, and those green eyes, she looked familiar, like he had seen her somewhere before but he couldn't recall where...

He spun round with his realisation, but it was too late. The woman had now made a beeline for the exit, and he swiftly followed her. Once outdoors the little girl had calmed down, content to be removed from the enclosed space. She smiled at him as he approached nervously. She looked the picture of innocence with her sparkly eyes and generous freckles. Her innocent face was framed by large pale red curls. Daniel came into her mother's field of vision.

Lily looked up, startled at first, then wary as her shock abated. She didn't smile as she recognised the man who had broken her sister's heart. She looked away in disgust, and busied herself with re-arranging the bags under Maia's buggy. She was about to set off down the road, when Daniel touched her lightly on the shoulder.

'Please, Lily, don't go, I need to talk to you.' He walked beside her as she began to stride down a bustling Fifth Avenue.

'I don't think we have anything to discuss Mr Carter. My sister informed me of your less than honourable behaviour.' Her green eyes flashed disdain, and for a moment he imagined he was looking into Isabelle's eyes.

'I'm sorry to say that Isabelle didn't understand what she thought she saw!'

Lily continued walking and gave a cutting smile as she said,

'I'm sure her eyes must have completely deceived her, as you appear to have done.' He flinched. 'What you did was unforgivable, especially after everything Belle has been through. Please leave me and my sister alone, she doesn't need you rubbing salt into her wounds.'

He quickened his pace and stepped in front of the buggy, half expecting Lily to ram it into his shins. She sighed and came to a halt, which delighted Maia, who let out peals of laughter as she reached out towards Daniel to touch him. Lily remonstrated with her, half pulling the buggy back, but it did not stop Maia staring. Daniel became more frustrated and gesticulated with his arms.

'I'm not suggesting that Isabelle was lying, she did see me hug my ex-girlfriend, but it was in full view of everyone in my office, and we were saying goodbye. I had just ended my relationship with Maria, and unfortunately it appears Isabelle was on her way up to surprise me when instead she got a surprise herself. I'm so sorry for hurting her, I love her and I just want one chance to make it up to her.'

Lily gazed steadily at him. 'Shall we?' She motioned him to cross back into the Park with her.

Once in the confines of the sheltering boulders and trees they found a bench, where Lily unhooked Maia so she could play on a nearby playground, leaving her sat next to a relieved and repentant looking Daniel.

Daniel ruffled his dark wavy hair with a hand, gathering the courage to open up to Lily.

'I've been trying for weeks to get hold of her; calls, texts but she won't reply or answer her phone. I was even going to fly to England to see if I could patch things up but I don't know where she lives, or who her friends and family are over there.'

'Well, as far as family are concerned it's just me over here, and Jack and Dad are in Sydney. Our mother died when we were teenagers. Did she ever mention H, her friend Hortense?'

'Yes, as a matter of fact she did, and I did meet her briefly in Madeira, but I never got her number. I could kick myself now.'

Maia waved at them, clearly enjoying her spell of freedom from the buggy. Lily waved back to her exuberant daughter and then turned back to Daniel.

'You know that ignoring you is Belle's defence mechanism? The only reason I know that is because she ignored me for a long time, and when she visited recently it was the first time I had seen her for ages, and since the birth of Maia. I'm sure she still loves you, but it was just too painful for her to be in a situation where she could be hurt again. There have been a lot more family sagas going on behind the scenes than you have been aware of Mr Carter, her nerves have been on a knife edge for a while. However, I'm going to give you the benefit of the doubt for my sister's sake, I just want her to be happy. Are you the man for the job?'

'Yes! That's all I'm asking for Lily, a chance to do just that. Please help me Lily, I can't bear another day without her, she's the one I want to spend the rest of my life with.' Clasping her hand he said, 'I won't let you down - either of you. I can't bear this purgatory anymore.'

'I believe you Daniel,' Lily replied with grace. She pulled a slim address book from her handbag. 'I'm going to give you H's telephone number and address, perhaps the two of you can conspire to sort things out. You might also want her agent's number, Gerry's a good guy too, I'm sure he'll help.' She scribbled the details on the back of his card.

Lily stood up and called Maia back to her. Shaking Daniel's hand she said, 'I wish you luck Daniel. Go and make Belle smile again.'

'My gratitude knows no bounds, thank you Lily.' As they parted he whispered, 'God bless you.'

Daniel made a beeline for his apartment, where he called Richard for some last minute advice before plucking up the courage to call Hortense. The phone seemed to ring for an age, and in between the rhythmic buzzing he could feel his heart almost beating a hole in his chest. He tried to stifle the fear that Isabelle might pick up the phone, then he would be back to square one. Finally, there was a click, and a breathy, low warm voice sounded down the line.

'Thanks for calling the Lafayette residence, unless you're Jools Holland please leave a message, otherwise you can call me on my mobile Jools baby! Raymond is available at Southern Records in Paddington and I'm just available full stop.'

He smiled at Hortense's jocular recording. Unwilling to leave a message, he was on the verge of hanging up when he heard another click, and the same voice boomed down the line.

'Hello, Hortense Lafayette.'

'Hi Hortense, this is Dan Carter. Can you spare me a few minutes please?'

A moment of silence followed.

'Daniel, this is a surprise! Issy isn't here at the moment, she's with her lawyer, but you can talk to me.'

'It's you I wanted to talk to actually. I hope you don't mind me calling, I had a chance meeting with Isabelle's sister in New York this morning and she gave me your number.' An awkward pause followed as Hortense waited to hear what he had to say.

'I know I'm not flavour of the month right now and as I explained to Lily, what Isabelle thought she saw was misinterpreted. I've not been able to get through to her to explain what happened.'

'You may not know this, but Maria rather put the boot in. She insulted and slapped Issy in the foyer on her way out, so you got a double whammy to deal with honey. I've told Issy that she's not thinking straight at the moment, but then love does strange things to you. How can I help?'

'I had no idea they bumped into each other. Shit! It's worse than I thought. Maria never was a graceful loser. We had parted ways just before that, so she would have been full of rage and jealousy no doubt. I don't know what to do, I think the best thing would be if I come over to London and try and meet up with her. That way she can't ignore me.'

Daniel waited.

'Dan, it's gonna take some doing to bring her round. She's stubborn as a mule sometimes, so good luck. I'm glad if what you're saying is true, that there was nothing untoward going on. I was very disappointed when Issy told me what she witnessed. I did warn her to be more open minded to other possibilities, but she wouldn't have it from me either.

'I suggest you contact me on my mobile when you arrive in the UK, and we can arrange something. It's best not to call the house as Issy is still living here, but probably only for a few more weeks.'

30

Isabelle sat facing Patrick Hill, with his large polished desk devoid of the mountainous paperwork that adorned Gerry's between them. Two photo frames, a telephone and one file tray were all that was on display for his clients. He was a striking man, with almost jet black eyes and short dark brown hair that was receding enough to leave a small patch of skin at the top of his head. His tall slender frame meant that he looked down on her slightly, and although he had always been genial towards Isabelle, she observed that his general manner was forthright and slightly aloof.

'The Miller family have agreed a financial settlement with you to the value of a third of Causeway Cottage, which, based on various estate agent valuations of the total sale value is around three hundred and seventy five thousand pounds. I know it's not half of the property value, but it's still a generous offer, and I strongly advise you to accept it.'

'Yes, of course, it's really a no-brainer. Thanks to you there are no lengthy court appearances to go through. Luckily we never had any children...'

'I'm sure Mr Miller is also counting his blessings at not being incarcerated for your assault, so it's the least I can do Isabelle. A friend of Gerry's is a friend of mine.' He smiled, and faint creases surfaced around his dark eyes.

'I'm astounded that they have that kind of money to part with without having to sell the family home, which I know Celia would never allow. The family name and tradition means everything to her.'

Patrick nodded. 'We also need to discuss the royalties of your album *The Virtuoso*, which is still selling well thanks to Gerry's efforts. Even with the cost of your cottage taken into consideration, you should be able to lead a financially comfortable life, thanks to this lump sum from the Millers, your album royalties and freelance work income.

'I'm expecting your decree absolute through in about six to eight weeks, and by then all the transfer of funds from your settlement should be finalised as well.'

'I'm grateful to you Patrick. Getting divorced from Howard has been a relatively painless process, but unfortunately I'm still suffering from the physical and emotional effects of his actions, and probably will for some time to come.'

The tyres of Isabelle's Golf crunched on the gravel outside Hortense and Raymond's majestic London home. Hortense opened the door with a smile as she walked towards the house.

'It's time for a mental spring clean H, I'm going to finally let go of my past.'

Hortense opened her mouth to speak but Isabelle was already halfway up the stairs, bounding up in two.

Her left index finger pressed the key for Howard's mobile. The line connected and his familiar raspy voice sounded eerie in her ear. Her mouth went dry.

'Isabelle? Is that you?' He sounded half panicked and half nonchalant.

'Yes, it's me.' There was another momentary silence, then Howard ventured,

'I wasn't expecting you... would it be very lame if I asked how you are?' Not waiting for her to reply, he babbled on nervously, 'I'm aware that had you decided to press charges, life would have been even more difficult and humiliating for me and mother. I swear I never meant to hurt you like that. It was the drink. Mother has suggested I join AA to try and kick the addiction.'

'Howard, the only way to move on is to take responsibility for your actions. Yes, the drink was the cause of your behaviour that night, but ultimately you are the one who made the decision in the first place, either consciously or unconsciously, to turn to drink to solve your problems.'

'Believe me Isabelle; you can't think any less of me than I do of myself. I hope you can be happy,' he said.

Isabelle concentrated on her breathing. It was a technique she had used during her time as a soloist. Her voice sounded controlled, with no hint of her sudden anger beneath the surface.

'I never thought I would be happy again after...after the accident. The moment you pushed that car door on my hand; my life as I knew it was over. I'm going to get this off my chest one way or another. I wanted you to know this Howard. But I've discovered that life has a funny way of showing you different dimensions when you least expect it. Such a sudden change, it forces you to re-evaluate everything.

'I've made a new life for myself, and even if I can't yet say that I'm happy, I can at least say that my awareness has been expanded. I forgive you Howard. I hope you can find some peace.'

There was a sound of raspy breathing as he absorbed her words.

'That's more than I deserve. I've done some terrible things under the influence of alcohol, and ruining your career was about the worst of them. I was in denial when I met you, and at first I thought I could keep it under control. I was too complacent. You probably heard they kicked me out of the LSC. Mother has threatened to disinherit me if I don't get my act cleaned up. The difference is this time I want to myself.'

'I'm sure you will Howard with enough determination.

'Good bye Howard.'

'Good bye Isabelle and good luck for the future.' There was a hint of humility in his voice.

The line clicked and she sat in stunned silence.

Hortense poked her head round the door. 'Is everything alright?'

Isabelle smiled. 'Yes, thanks H. I've just been chasing away black clouds from my past of dark skies.'

'Good stuff. I'm just heading off to Raymond's recording studio. I haven't had a chance to tell you, but we're collaborating on a new jazz album for various artists, one of which is me.'

'Have fun. I wondered why you were looking so chirpy. I know you are chirpy all the time, but you seem to be taking it to a whole new level today H.'

'Do I?' Hortense smiled with a self-satisfied air. 'Maybe I'm in the mood for cloud chasing too Issy. See you later.'

Her chest felt less tight, but the visceral ache she felt at being apart from Daniel had never really gone, and now visions of him in his tieless shirt and tweed jacket sitting opposite her in the Imperial Hotel in Vienna were haunting her. Overcome by wistful daydreaming she recalled their lovemaking and could feel her excitement start to build.

She picked out her Virtuoso CD and began listening to her own playing of the Beethoven Kreutzer Sonata. She wondered how much catharsis she could take in one day.

She had not listened to any violin music since the accident, it was still too raw, but now somehow she felt she had turned a corner.

The familiar double stopping chords of the opening bars sang out accompanied by Isabelle's profuse salty tears. The Nagyvary had such a sweet sound. Her intense feelings of joy and satisfaction at having recorded the album were mingled with the poignancy of knowing she could never do it again. That particular joy was consigned to her memories.

Isabelle opened up her laptop after stocking up on peanut butter and crackers to alleviate a sudden bout of nausea. Struggling to concentrate on her Secrets of a Virtuoso article she flipped over to her emails, and saw a reply from her father in her inbox.

> *My Darling Isabelle,*
>
> *Thanks for getting in touch, I know it must have been hard for you after we parted on bad terms, but I'm glad you did. I only wish I had known earlier about your situation, I would have come back to Britain to be with you, I feel devastated being all this way out here and ignorant of your suffering.*
>
> *I had no idea that life has been so cruel to you, but I was grateful to also hear from Lily prior to your message, and it warmed my heart to know that you two have made up. She told me that you are coping admirably,*

*and I wouldn't expect anything else from my
little girl. Jack is often away in some exotic
location with Qantas, but it sounds like they
are moving him up the ranks and he should
be flying the Kangaroo Route to London
shortly so maybe you guys can see more of
each other.*

*I haven't met anyone else who comes up to
scratch since your mother died, but I'm content
teaching music in a school in the suburbs of
Sydney. I'd love to see you if you're ever in these
neck of the woods, and please call me anytime
(except the middle of the night) if you know
what I mean!*
All my love always,
Dad

She pictured their family home in Beaconsfield. It was
summer; and she, Jack, and Lily were running around
in their swimming costumes. She was eight at the time.
Her father was chasing them round their large oval
shaped garden, aiming the hose pipe at their shrieking
bodies as they ran to escape the chilly spray. Somewhere
in the background, her mother was singing, rehearsing
for an Oratorio. Whoops of laughter echoed around the
lawn, and Julia, upset at the noise levels, took intermittent breaks to yell at them all.

Still consumed in her childhood memories, Isabelle
fumbled on the keys.

Dear Dad,

It's so wonderful to hear from you. Please try not to worry about me. I've got so much to tell you, I've missed you so much! I'd love to come and visit and I'll book my flight (one with a white rat on the tail anyway!) as soon as the purchase of my cottage is completed, which should be in the next few weeks. Tell Jack to dig out some eligible pilots for inspection!
Will be in touch soon,
Lol Isabelle x

She sighed, and tried to concentrate on the article but her breasts were now tingling, a sensation like someone had plugged a very low electric current into her nipples. She knew she ought to see a doctor, who would no doubt explain that this was all normal pregnancy symptoms, and that she was not some kind of hormonal freak, but decided it would best to wait until she had moved and registered with a permanent GP.

She had barely gathered her thoughts for the two thousand word article that Lucy had primed her for, when her mobile sprang into life, and Isabelle's heart missed a beat as thoughts of Daniel came to her mind again. She was simultaneously relieved and dismayed to see it was Gerry. Wondering what project he would almost certainly be cooking up for her, she reluctantly pressed the green button.

'Hi Gerry, how are you?'

'Hello Isabelle, I'm good thanks, and how is my favourite client doing?'

'I'm okay. You saved me from writer's block actually, I'm trying to write my next article but I'm not on the same page as my grey matter at the moment! You're not giving me more work are you?'

'How did you guess? Anyway my dear, they loved you so much at the Met, I've got another speaking engagement, and I think this one will be close to your heart.'

'You've piqued my interest Gerry, go on.'

'I've managed to secure an after dinner guest spot at a charity event run by several classical music organisations including the Royal Opera House in support of disadvantaged and special needs children in the UK. As you know, music lessons are declining in classrooms across Britain and the event will draw top celebrities in the field of music and drama to highlight the significance of music in education and also raise funds for such children to enable private tuition.'

'Gerry, I really do appreciate you thinking of me, but this is way out of my league. It's one thing to talk to a group of wealthy old cronies who've probably never played an instrument in their life, but it's an entirely new ball game in front of top notch musicians and music industry insiders. I absolutely don't want to talk to my peer group. I can't do it.

'Any way I've got such a busy schedule Gerry; I'm working on another piece for *High Notes* which I need to finish within the next five days, and I'm on the verge of buying my own place, and as soon as I've moved in to that I'm going to Australia for a few weeks to visit Dad. I just don't have the time to polish off a speech that I know I'd like to be perfect for such an important occasion.'

She could hear Gerry sigh at the end of the line. 'I know this is just your fear talking Isabelle. I know you've been through a lot, and that you're still trying to get your life back on track, and for my part I just want to help. After all, financially it would be unwise to turn down any offers. Despite your angst you seem to have a talent for public speaking, and that's not just my view, it's been corroborated by the feedback from your sister and the Met. Just think how many children you could be responsible for introducing to the joys of music...'

'Gerry, how can I refuse when you put it like that? I'm sorry, I don't know if I'm coming or going at the moment. Give me the low down, where and when etc.'

'Well, it's not for another ten weeks, and it's being hosted by the Royal Opera House. Hopefully that will give you time to get settled in your new home and make a visit down under.'

'So much for a quiet life. Thanks Gerry. That should be fine. Speak soon.'

31

'Here's the key to your new home Isabelle, we hope you'll be very happy here.' Melanie looked genuinely pleased as she handed the fob to Isabelle.

'Thank you so much.' Isabelle accepted the keys. A warm glow radiated from the pit of her stomach.

'Is this the first property you've owned?'

'It's the first home I've owned purely on my own, yes. I travelled a lot when I when I was a soloist, so I rented in London back then. When I got married, I just moved into his house, so it never really felt truly like home. This is a new chapter in my life, and this will be my very own bolt hole from the world.'

'It's a wonderful feeling isn't it?' Melanie was beaming at her.

'Ah Melanie, you are so right. I was lucky to have a very good friend who has put me up, and put up with me since the accident, but I'm ready to stand on my own two feet now. I can tell how far I've come, just by being able to talk about my tragedy to you, without becoming overly emotional. And here I am, standing on the doorstep of my own property, number two, Watermill Gardens.

'Thanks for all your hard work getting the sale through smoothly and swiftly Melanie. I've written to your employer recommending he promote you. You did a great job. Goodbye.'

Melanie blushed and waved as she climbed into her car.

Isabelle checked her watch. The removal van was due any minute. She faced the mahogany door for a second, and then slid the key into the lock and turned it gently. It clicked and opened with ease. She pushed the door open, and saw the cream coloured hallway, bare in front of her.

She strode across the parquet wood floor and surveyed the empty space. Sunlight illuminated the room through the French doors at the back of the lounge, and even through her sunglasses she struggled to make out the garden, with its well-manicured lawn and shrub borders. A magnolia tree swayed in the wind, which tugged at the shrivelling blossom and swirled it around in the air before depositing the petals onto the grass below. It was small, but it was hers, and it was beautiful.

That evening she sat slumped in her large enveloping beanbag. The day had passed with fervent activity, and now, as she sat with heavy limbs and eyelids she surveyed the boxes littered in every room. It looked like carnage, but she was too tired to care.

Her new flat screen television had arrived that morning. Raymond had put together some bookshelves for her and helped with moving in her furniture, including a dining table set that H had bequeathed her when she departed. She had known that Isabelle always loved the dark wood furniture, and she and Raymond had wanted a change for a while, so it had found its way to Isabelle's cottage. Upstairs she had one large wardrobe, plus her own fitted wardrobe in the master bedroom, a couple of suitcases of clothes, linen and towels, and her old pine dresser that H had rescued from Causeway Cottage, along with her new contemporary four poster bed and many pictures and photographs. All she needed was her new sofa to be delivered, and then everything would be ready for her housewarming party.

Isabelle mulled over the events of the day, thankful there had been no major dramas.

Whilst helping to unload the van Isabelle had bumped into one of her new neighbours, a rather skinny older woman who had introduced herself as Valentina. She listened intently as Valentina greeted her in English laden with a heavy Russian accent.

'Dis is a good place to live. Very pretty, very quiet. We like the quiet after Moscow.' She inhaled on her cigarette and stared briefly at Isabelle's mutilated hand. 'We can get to know each other eh?'

'That would be nice, thanks. Have you been here long Valentina? Did you come over for work?'

'Work, yes. My husband is very important man in Russian business. I was once a famous model in Russia, but now am making myself a how do you say… housewife. We have been here in the UK for a year.'

Her straw like dyed red hair sat perched on her shoulders and her skin was slightly wrinkled and orangey from too much sun and smoking. Isabelle almost had to squint she was so laden with gems. She decided her face must have been very beautiful in her younger days. Underneath the ageing process, she still had a magnificent bone structure and a twinkle in her eye. Isabelle guessed she was probably in her late fifties. She stirred from her reverie and decided that Valentina was the sort of woman that Gerry would find interesting: glamorous and worldly, but with a touch of vice and a tantalising history.

'You and your husband are most welcome to come over for drinks, I'm having a party soon,' Isabelle had replied, instantly regretting the invitation.

The nausea had subsided during the day, or maybe she hadn't noticed it because of the stress of getting everything in without any breakages or injuries, but now that she sat inert in a state of satisfied exhaustion on her beanbag, she felt the familiar rumblings of morning sickness. It was a quiet evening save the odd engine starting up and the hint of voices as pedestrians walked past. The removal men had long departed and a hunger pang had taken root alongside her nausea, begging to be noticed.

She sated it with a slightly stale sandwich and the last chunk of cheese that H had given her to get her through the first day. For dessert she ploughed through half a packet of ginger biscuits, bought en-route to help relieve her nausea.

She searched aimlessly through different bags, and unable to locate her pyjamas she cleaned her teeth and climbed into her newly made bed naked. The tiredness was overwhelming, and in an air of contented achievement she curled up and spent the first night under her own roof.

Isabelle was placing her favourite books into the bookcase when she saw Gerry's number flash onto her mobile.

'Hi Gerry, you just caught me unpacking. I'm finally in my new place.'

'Congratulations, my dear. In fact, congratulations are due all round...'

'They are? You're being very furtive Gerry.'

'You've always been successful, and even after your accident it hasn't taken away your star factor,' Gerry said excitedly.

'That's all very sweet of you Gerry, but I must get on. I've got to get straightened up before the party and sort out my stuff for my flight to Oz.'

'Whoa! Not so fast Isabelle,' his voice was reaching a crescendo. 'There was actually a point to my ramblings my dear. Your album, *The Virtuoso*, it's gone platinum!'

'Oh my God, that's fantastic! Thank you Gerry.'

'I've arranged a photo shoot in London for when I present the platinum disc to you, and I've taken the liberty of clearing some editorial space with Lucy in *High Notes* so that I can submit a few words about it and your career highlights.'

'That's very kind of you Gerry, and I'm under no illusion that I owe this honour, in no small measure, to your incredible marketing and dedication.'

'We make a good team Isabelle. It'll be either Tuesday or Wednesday next week, so keep your diary free.'

'Okay,' said Isabelle still in shock over the news.

'That's my girl. Accident or no accident your legacy is living on.'

'Gerry, can I ask you something?'

'Sure, what is it?'

'Well, I feel a bit silly asking, but I had a strange card in the post the other day. I've had lots of lovely new home cards, I haven't had one from you, and it doesn't matter, but I had one that wasn't signed.'

'No, I'm sorry Isabelle, I've been flat out, I bought you one, I just haven't sent it yet. Saskia's been back to Poland for a few days, so I'm in a terrible mess. Anyway, what do you mean it wasn't signed?'

'I'm relieved it wasn't you. It wasn't even posted with my regular mail. It had my name printed on the front with no address and it was put through my letter box. Inside there was a printed message typed on white paper stuck to the card that read; "Enjoy your new home. You may be single, but you are not alone…".'

'That's on the creepy side my dear.'

'I know. Forgive me for thinking you could have sent it, I thought maybe it was some kind of prank. You have been known to pull the odd stunt,' Isabelle said with contrition.

'Any other ideas who it could be from?'

'Well, there's this guy I met, but I don't think this is his style. Only my close friends know my new address, which makes it slightly freaky.'

'Keep an eye out. If anything else suspicious happens contact the police. Promise me!'

'I promise Gerry.'

The line clicked and Isabelle sat surrounded by books; her joy at Gerry's news tempered by the uneasy feeling in her gut.

32

The doorbell rang. Still putting the finishing touches to her makeup, Isabelle smudged her mascara. She abandoned her lipstick and descended the stairs in a somewhat flustered manner to welcome her first guest. She flung her arms around his rotund frame, and stood back to appreciate his clothes. Gerry was wearing black leather trousers and a bright pink silk shirt showing rather too much chest, adorned by a single gold medallion.

'Do you like it? I thought I'd make an impression with my seventies vibe,' Gerry said, flashing her one of his irresistible smiles.

'It's certainly more flamboyant than your normal attire Gerry. Forgive my staring, it's just that I've only ever seen you wearing your suit and tie,' Isabelle responded.

'I bought it especially for your party,' he said and handed her a large bouquet of roses.

'Thank you Gerry. You'll be the talk of the town that's for sure. Come in.'

Party goers passed over her threshold in fluent streams. Gerry had set up the music system and got the party going with his own compilation CDs. The party was in full swing as H and Raymond pulled up in their car.

Lucy had arrived shortly after, with a raft of *High Notes* employees, all of whom Isabelle recognised from her occasional visits to the office, but none of whom she could name, much to her shame. Lucy's strong accent carried across the lounge, and peals of laughter were soon ringing out as she told her usual anecdotes with uncanny comic timing and her typical uncouth slang.

'Strewth girl, you scrub up well!' Had been her opening gambit on arrival, followed by a discreet by Lucy standards; rub of her tummy.

Isabelle glared and whispered softly, 'Luce can you keep it quiet, nobody knows about the baby yet.'

'Mum's the word,' replied Lucy with a tap of her finger against her freckled nose.

As the evening progressed Watermill Gardens became blocked with luxury motor cars, but nobody seemed to mind. Most of her neighbours were in attendance, including the vivacious Valentina, who resembled an ageing Hollywood starlet wearing a little too much makeup, cigarette in hand, cavorting around in a backless sequined dress, which hugged her slender body. As Isabelle suspected she instantly caught Gerry's roving eye. Shortly after her arrival, he had approached her, and as Isabelle had made the introductions Valentina made it very clear that her husband was away in Russia and unfortunately she was all alone.

Some of her old pals from the Royal Academy had also turned up, and Isabelle felt like an excited school girl again, going back to her student days. She had been drawn away from their discussions about previous teachers and their foibles, when she noticed Sebastian and another well-groomed gentleman were being shown into the lounge. Making her excuses, Isabelle ran and launched herself at him, almost knocking him over.

After their initial hug, she was aware of how frail he felt beneath her touch, and his pale face and tired eyes only hinted at his vibrant former self. They hadn't spoken since he'd got home; she'd simply sent him an email invite, hoping he'd be around.

He read her lost expression and proudly introduced the stranger by his side. 'Isabelle darling, this is my very close friend and confidante Marcus Baxter.'

She gave him a subtle smile, trying not to show any sign on her face that she knew who he was, and held out her right hand for Marcus. Studying his face as they clasped hands, she noticed that he was tall, certainly a few inches taller than Sebastian, wearing a dark jacket over a grey shirt with smart black slacks. His face was oval and pale grey eyes smiled back at her. His olive skin was complemented by short greying hair and substantial grey sideburns. She could see why Sebastian might find him attractive, indeed she had. His distinguished appearance did not, in her opinion, betray his sexuality.

'Glad to meet you Marcus.'

She switched her gaze back to Sebastian, and guided them towards the drinks table. Despite the shocking way he appeared compared to the last time she saw him, he actually looked happier. Sporting a new goatee style beard and a cream dinner jacket, he still looked supremely elegant.

'So how are you? You look tired Seb. How was Yolanda? I want to hear all about Mexico.'

'It was wonderful Isabella. Mother was so happy to see me. I was worried she may have forgotten me, as is so often the case with dementia. I entertained the whole nursing home with my cello. After my two weeks in Mexico City, I left my cello in a safe storage facility and backpacked along the coast; then I went into the jungle in Oaxaca for a three-day trek. It was such an adventure...' Sebastian coughed violently and rubbed his forehead.

'Seb are you okay?'

'I keep telling him to go to the doctors,' Marcus said. 'He's been hacking away since he got back, and at times has difficulty breathing, as well as having night fevers.'

'It sounds like you have the flu, you must get it checked out Seb,' admonished Isabelle.

'I will, stop nagging you two. Yes I've been coughing and getting headaches, which started a few days after I got back.'

'Would you like to have a lie down Seb? You should be in bed, not partying the night away! But it's so good to see you anyway.'

Isabelle noticed Hortense walking towards her, and left Sebastian to talk to Marcus.

She turned to chat to H, who was grinning more maniacally than usual.

'I hope Raymond isn't getting you drunk H!'

'It's a great party Issy! Are you happy girl?'

'Do you know what? I think I am! I'm still feeling shattered from the move and you-know-what though.' she looked down at her slightly swollen abdomen.

'It makes me happy, to see you happy.'

'I'm so glad you could be here H, I never would have made it this far without you. She blinked tears away. 'I can't thank you and Ray enough for everything you've both done for me...'

'Nonsense!' Snorted H. 'You helped yourself, we just gave you the space to do it, and it was our pleasure Issy.'

Isabelle was showing Hortense how her stumps and little finger had healed when she was vaguely aware of another person arriving. Before her curiosity could get the better of her H had bellowed out that she would do a few numbers, and as silence fell her sultry low tones sounded out Isabelle's favourite Nina Simone song, and the whole room was humming and swaying along with her.

'Ain't got no home, ain't got no shoes...'

Isabelle glanced around the room and noticed Gerry wielding a video recorder, capturing H's rendition perfectly, with Valentina resting her bony hand on his shoulder. She couldn't help thinking, rather uncharitably, that she was a female version of a tom cat, marking her territory. A couple of minutes passed and H was on the final verse.

'I got my arms, I got my hands, I got my fingers, got my legs, I got my feet, I got my toes, I got my liver, Got my blood; Got life, I got my life...'

Wolf whistles and enthusiastic clapping filled the air, and it was then with a pounding heart, that Isabelle caught sight of the person who had been admitted shortly before Hortense began singing. She stared in disbelief at those unmistakable drowning pool blue eyes creased in laughter and the wavy dark hair. Daniel appeared to be oblivious of her intense stare, but then moved his gaze towards her, as she fixed her glowering attention on him.

Hortense had rattled straight on with another song, ignoring the sudden tension in the room. Isabelle couldn't hear, smell or see anything as she dived into the empty kitchen, gripped by panic.

Isabelle gulped down some water. Scanning her surroundings she took in the multiple cases of beer, bottles of wine, and soft drinks, which were scattered over the shiny granite work surfaces. Her small round pine table was strewn with empties, ashtrays and smeared glasses.

The gentle opening and closing of the kitchen door sent her pulse racing, and she felt his looming presence behind her. She kept her back to him, frightened that she would succumb too quickly if she looked into his eyes.

'H gave me the intel before you ask.' He spoke softly reaching out to gently touch her shoulder with his trembling hand. Normally his touch would have sent her into wanton convulsions, and although she felt a shiver down her spine, she kept her cool.

Stiffening slightly she replied, 'I guessed as much, which leads me to the obvious why are you here question?' Her tone was curt.

'I'm so sorry for the circumstances,' his hands rubbed her upper arms slowly, as he continued, 'it was the only way I could risk seeing you and have half a chance of explaining what happened.'

'Well you got that part right, my manners outweigh my better judgement sometimes, so you better start explaining, and don't give me any crap clichés, like "it wasn't you, it was me".'

33

'**I**'m not going to deny that I embraced Maria in my office. I presume that's what you saw that day?'

'Yes, that's what I saw. You made love to me and then you lavished your affections on her only a few hours later. After everything I'd been through, it was just too humiliating and too painful.'

'We were saying good bye Isabelle, I had just ended it with her. And before you ask, she didn't take it well. I haven't been very fair to her. To be honest, I was totally hung-up on you from the moment we met. I should have finished my relationship with her as soon as I got back from Vienna. I despise myself for being such a coward and prolonging the inevitable. I couldn't make love to her when you were filling my head and my heart.'

'So why didn't you end it?'

'I was scared. The intensity between us rocked me to my core, I guess I felt vulnerable. You had the power to destroy me.'

'Why on Earth would I want to do that? That's not the kind of person I am Dan.'

'I realise that now. I just had some emotional baggage to unpack first, before I could fully let you into my life. After I saw you again in New York, I knew I couldn't fight it any longer, I decided I wasn't going to sit on the fence anymore.'

'It looked like you were really into one-another.' Isabelle said with a hint of rebuke.

'I know it must have looked bad, but I promise you, I was just trying to part on good terms with her. Obviously she wasn't feeling very charitable towards you, and it must have seemed at best like a cruel twist of fate, or at worst, a planned shameful put-down, when she ran into you. I'm not surprised that she reacted the way she did. At the time, I had no idea that you had seen us, or that Maria had reacted so badly to you on her exit. All I know is that I'm going crazy without you.'

He grasped both her hands into his. 'God must have taken pity on me. I couldn't bear the thought of losing you to a stupid misunderstanding. But luckily I bumped into Lily and Maia at the Frick Museum, and I persuaded her to give me Hortense's number. I would have flown over anyway, but I had no idea where you lived.'

'So my sister trusted you then?'

'Yes, and H told me about the party. All I want to do is make you happy. How can I make it up to you Isabelle?'

'My heart wants to believe you Daniel, but my head is saying I'm a fool to open myself up to that kind of pain again.'

'It's you I've chosen Isabelle. There was never any contest. I'm prepared to make some pretty big sacrifices to make our relationship work. I don't believe anything in this life is a co-incidence, we make our own fate,' Daniel said as he stroked her deformed hand. 'Maybe this tragedy, although devastating for you in one sense, in another it has brought us together, and at the same time it has led you to find your higher purpose.'

'You've been having motivational lessons from H, I see,' she responded with a wry smile.

'Can you blame me Isabelle? I feel a connection with you that revives my spirit, and gives me faith in human nature, I wasn't about to give up on that without a fight.'

'Even when I thought you were a bastard, I was still on fire for you,' she said in a whisper.

Daniel lifted her into his arms. 'I do believe it's time to properly christen your new home.' She sank into his strong arms and he carried her up the stairs to her bedroom. Daniel shut out the music and the sounds of a party in full swing, as he bolted the wooden door behind them.

'You're mine Isabelle.' He pulled her to him, holding onto the back of her hair as he engulfed her in passionate kisses. Isabelle revelled under his every touch, wanting to preserve the ecstasy of being with him again. She responded with wild abandon, her body was moving and tingling as if it had a mind of its own, and her usual mind chatter evaporated under the onslaught of his mouth. Her hands roved across his taut back and shoulders.

He almost growled into her ear. 'My second home is right between your legs.' She gasped as she felt his hardened flesh vigorously thrusting into her, and surrendered herself completely to him. The sound of their moans and murmurs filled the air as they came closer to the moment of ecstasy.

Isabelle lay contentedly in Daniel's arms for what seemed like eons after their lovemaking, not wanting to move from his protective hold. If he had noticed her slightly swollen belly he hadn't let on. Then she felt his hand tracing over her breasts, and their desire was rekindled. This time they made love in a more languid fashion, caressing each other slowly as they built up to another satisfying climax. All the tension she had felt over the last few weeks had emptied from her body with each orgasm.

Isabelle slept soundly, only stirring when she heard Gerry calling her name. She inched out from beside Daniel who appeared to be comatose in a blissful sleep. She pulled on her bathrobe and stepped out onto the hallway. She greeted a sheepish looking Gerry. Isabelle walked gingerly down the stairs. She had no idea what the time was, but it was obvious that a hard core of guests had stayed through the night, and that Gerry was the last one remaining.

The house was quiet. The sun's rays were beaming through the patio windows casting light onto the carnage that was her home.

Gerry followed her, but was having trouble walking straight as he swayed over to his camcorder. He motioned for Isabelle to approach and held out the screen for her to see.

His voice had a hint of slur. 'My God Isssy! You had a face like a smacked arse when you clapped eyes on h-him!'

Isabelle flinched slightly at his obvious intoxication.

'Everyone had a good t-time. Nobody noticed that you mysteriously disappeared for the evening, but there was some g-gossip going around the room about the tall dark handsome stranger you were with.' Gerry gave her a sweet smile as he muttered, 'I hope you enjoyed yourself, you des-s-serve it.'

'Is that what you did with Valentina Gerry?' She asked.

'We all enjoyed ourshelves Issssy.'

'Gerry, I ought to tell you that Valentina is married to a very wealthy and powerful Russian, and I'd hate to read in the paper that you had fallen foul of the Russian mafia for the sake of a lustful encounter.'

Isabelle virtually forced Gerry into the street.

'Thank you for the music and the video Gerry. I think it's time you had a walk to the High Street and got a coffee, I'll run you to the train station later. It's probably best if we sort out the date for the platinum disc photo-shoot when you've sobered up.'

'Shorry Isssy, see you later.' He ambled into the street, and Isabelle felt a pang of guilt for exposing him to certain derision from passers-by, but at the same time wanting him out of the house when Daniel woke up. She turned back to the lounge and sighed in utter exhaustion. The sheer scale of the mess stretched out before her eyes. She decided to leave the cleaning up until a bit later and started to climb the stairs.

She had almost reached the landing when she felt herself wretch. She scampered to the bathroom and vomited what little had passed between her lips earlier in the evening. She washed her face and brushed her teeth before snuggling back under the covers next to Daniel's warm body.

Isabelle woke with a start to the sound of her landline ringing. She reached across to her bedside table and grasped the handset. She answered, still half asleep with her head resting on the pillow.

'Hello, Isabelle Bryant.'

Silence prevailed.

'Hello?' Still there was no sound at the other end of the line, and in frustration she sat upright and raised her voice further.

'Who's there? Hello?'

A few seconds passed, followed by an audible click, and the line went dead.

'What the?'

Daniel rolled over, 'Who was that?'

'I don't know - nobody spoke. Maybe it was a wrong number. But they must have heard me speaking; it's bloody rude not to say anything.'

'Can you trace the number?'

Isabelle keyed in the code only to reveal that the number had been withheld.

'That's really weird, I haven't given out my number to that many people.'

They sat in Isabelle's sparse dining room, in casual attire working opposite one another across Hortense's donated dining table, on their laptops. Isabelle glanced up at Daniel and studied his face as he typed. She was drawn to the crease between his eyebrows, which was accentuated whenever he was in deep concentration, and his lips, which were quite voluptuous for a man. How those lips had set her on fire...

'It must have taken a lot of courage for you to leave New York and come over here to surprise me.' Her statement came out with a questioning air. Daniel stopped typing and looked up at her.

'Where did that come from?'

Isabelle shrugged. 'It's been on my mind.'

'Well, it was worth it. The price I would have paid for being a coward doesn't bear thinking about.' He reached across and stroked her cheek with his fingers.

'And just like that day we talked about the butterfly effect; and how the physical universe has certain laws which are predictable, it struck me how human nature is inherently creative, and always has the capacity to be unexpected. It's what adds another dimension. We all invent our futures in the field of potentiality...'

'I swear you and H are on another planet sometimes.' She smiled at him with a bemused expression.

'Well, I'm feet first on planet Earth right now. Lucky I landed in your lounge when I did,' he grinned back. 'I got so bogged down in my mind and my intellect that I wasn't connected to my gut instincts; which were screaming at me that you were the best damn thing that ever came into my life.'

'Daniel, there's something I need to tell you...'

'That sounds ominous.'

Isabelle tried to formulate her sentence. To her alarm, she felt a warm wet gush pervading her groin. Panic rose in her.

'I need to go to the toilet!'

'What?'

She hastily made her exit.

As she lowered her pants she was shocked to see a pool of blood in them. She raised herself upright and felt a cramping pain.

She grabbed a pair of clean knickers and inserted a pad and sat on the seat for a few minutes contemplating what to do.

Footsteps sounded outside the door.

'Is everything okay Isabelle? You've been in there for ages.'

She opened the door and looked searchingly into his face. Tears formed and started to smear mascara over her cheeks.

'Isabelle, what on Earth's the matter?'

'I wanted to tell you...'

'Are you pregnant?'

Isabelle nodded. 'Yes, but...I'm not sure how long for, I'm bleeding. Oh Christ! Why does this have to happen now?'

She noticed him sway slightly, as if her words had exerted an imaginary physical force. He appeared to struggle with the magnitude of what she had just told him. Then, after a few seconds he seemed to take control of his emotions, and turned his attention back to her.

'We're going to have a baby? When were you going to tell me?'

Isabelle's eyes widened. 'That's what I was trying to tell you, just before... this.'

'I'm happy of course, and you shouldn't worry that I would have taken it any other way. I'm not one of those morons who would have mysteriously vanished. I just want to love you and give you support if you need it.'

He looked with concern at her pale features as she rested her forehead on his chest, not saying anything. Words were redundant at the thought of losing their baby.

'We need to talk to a doctor. How far along are you Isabelle?'

When she replied her voice was faint. 'Just under twelve weeks. I was beginning to think I might be out of the danger period.'

Daniel scrolled to her doctor's number from her mobile phone, and went into the lounge. A few minutes later he hung up and his expression was grim. 'She said that we ought to go to the hospital where they can monitor you more closely. She asked if the bleeding was being accompanied by cramps.'

Isabelle nodded. 'Why am I clinging on to false hope that everything will be okay? I'm being punished. I shouldn't have had those negative thoughts about the pregnancy in the early days.'

Isabelle looked up at the bright lights of the cubicle as the registrar said, 'I'm very sorry Ms. Bryant, it's gone. There's no heartbeat. There's nothing more we can do. We'll take another blood sample in a week's time to make sure your hCG levels have gone back to normal, and in the meantime, take Ibuprofen for the pain and keep an eye out for any large clots.'

Daniel gripped her hand.

'I'm so sorry Daniel.'

'It's horrific to feel and see the components of life breaking up and leaving my body; an utterly cruel and devastating blow.'

Her only comfort was that Daniel had been there by her side, silent and strong, suffering with her. It wasn't until after she finished bleeding, some ten days later, that the full loss had hit her. A follow-up ultrasound revealed that her womb was empty.

She looked at the nurse. 'I'm empty at my very core, that's for sure.'

'Unfortunately it's a common occurrence, but probably for the best. It was nature's way of dealing with problems in the embryo's development, and was most likely caused by abnormalities in the cells,' the nurse said.

Isabelle was curled up on the sofa when Hortense arrived. Her pale face was partly hidden by her long, unruly brunette tresses and she seemed to be hibernating into her fleece dressing gown. She didn't look up when Hortense entered the lounge. Her thoughts were trained on what sort of features her dead baby might have had, and its personality, that she would never know.

'Thank God you're here Hortense. I can't seem to lift her mood at all,' said Daniel as he hugged her. 'She's been mute on the sofa and has hardly said a word since we got back from the hospital this morning. I don't know what to say or do. I'm worried that she might slip back into a suicidal depression.'

'Don't worry Dan, I don't think she's quite that low, but she does need a certain kind of TLC right now. Never fear, Aunty H is here.'

Twenty minutes later Hortense had helped her to dress and led her out into the warm, balmy evening.

'C'mon, let's have a stroll by the river; the exercise will do us good.' Hortense began striding towards the Thames towpath.

As they walked in silence along the water's edge it was apparent that many others wanted to enjoy a summer evening by the river. Couples were having picnics on rugs, while families with young children had brought bread to feed the voracious swans that clamoured at the water's edge. As they strolled past the activity, the white road bridge that spanned the Thames from the bottom end of the High Street began to fade into the distance behind them. Just the sweet evening air and a few persistent mosquitoes surrounded them, complemented by intermittent sounds of boats passing through the water, causing delicate ripples.

'H, it feels like I'm being punished for not...well, you know. Not wanting it in the beginning. I keep thinking maybe I did something wrong, worked too hard, lifted too many boxes, I don't know what.' Isabelle frowned, and raised her arms in frustration, as if to question God.

H looked pensive, but didn't speak straightaway. Bumblebees wove in and out of the air between them, as if silently eavesdropping on their conversation.

'Haven't I suffered enough? I just can't seem to shake this feeling of guilt. Why can't the big guy up there give me a fucking break? My life is so twisted. I mean here I am, reconciled with Dan, my soul mate, I've finally got my own home, the divorce is almost through, and Gerry keeps telling me about fantastic CD sales, but I just don't feel I deserve any of it!'

Hortense paused, breathing deeply as the aroma of cut grass hit her nostrils.

'This isn't going to be easy for you to hear Issy, but I'll say it anyway. There's nothing to be gained by beating yourself up. There's no blame to attach. Like any loss there's a natural grieving process, and you mustn't resist it because it's painful. The healing starts when you fully accept your feelings.'

Hortense guided them both out of public view, away from the water's edge and they sat in the longer grass. Isabelle pulled her knees up to her chin and began plucking dandelions. She couldn't remember a time when H had been wrong about anything. She knew she had to try and absorb her friend's wisdom yet again.

'Poor Dan, he's not used to seeing me like this. I suppose I shut my feelings off because I couldn't handle it on top of everything else. I'm in a vacuum and I can't seem to get out of it.'

'The trick is to just feel whatever comes up Issy, don't try and resist it. Guilt, hate, fear, anger, whatever. Try and be an observer watching your emotions with interest; kinda like being in the fire without being consumed by it. This way you are not repressing your grief. Otherwise it will come back with a vengeance later on and consume you.'

'I'm getting a sense of deja-vu H. I know we've covered this before, but each time I make some progress, I get knocked down again.'

'No-one can know how painful it is to lose a baby until they've experienced it themselves. I feel your pain Issy, I really do,' Hortense said.

'It's funny - Lily said something similar on the phone the other day when I told her what had happened. She was sorry for me of course, but said that when she fully accepted that Howard was Maia's father she felt an even closer bond with her, like it had freed up some emotional space – so she could be more present with her daughter. I guess I need to stop resisting the pain and irony of it all.'

Hortense nodded. 'Don't put off dealing with your loss. It's the same for your injury. I notice you haven't been to a classical concert since it happened. That would be the acid test, to see how far you have come.'

Isabelle winced.

'Issy I don't mean to preach honey, but if you want to feel happier try and be appreciative of everything you do have. Gratitude will shift you into a higher vibration. Don't look at the shit, concentrate on what you want. Daniel has moved continents to be with you and shows no signs of leaving. You're still in your early thirties, so you've got time to have more babies.'

'In theory...'

Hortense picked a dandelion seed and blew the wispy white petals, which spiralled into the soft breeze.

'Can I offer you another perspective that might help with the guilt?'

'Please do H, no-one else comes close to your amazing insights.'

'This may sound a little far-out, but bear with me. I've picked-up this knowledge from an enlightened master. He suggests that the soul doesn't actually enter into a human body until at least the third month of gestation.'

'I don't understand. My baby had a heartbeat long before then.'

'The physical form did, but we can't be sure it was one with its soul.'

'You mean it decided not to come after all?' Isabelle's brows furrowed.

'I suppose that's what I'm getting at. What you lost wasn't real in a way, because the life force wasn't there in the first place, only the physical components that might house it. Imagine that there's this sentient being that has chosen to come into the world through you and Daniel, but it hasn't gone away forever. It's still there, just waiting for the right karmic conditions before it comes into a physical manifestation.'

Isabelle felt her eyes welling up. 'Oh H, I can't begin to comprehend what you've just told me, but it's a helpful way of looking at it. Thank you.'

Hortense tried to lighten the mood further. 'Maybe it would help to think of Arnie's Terminator line; I'll be back!'

Isabelle managed a feeble smile. 'Yes.'

Daniel wrapped his arms around Isabelle as they lay in bed. Isabelle had left the curtains open and the glow from the full moon was cast over them, illuminating their faces.

'Dan, thanks for getting H over this afternoon, she got through to me as usual.'

'I knew only H would be able to help you get through this loss.' He stroked her hair.

'You're wrong there, because I can't get through it without you as well. You've been my rock. You've both given me what I needed, and somehow we'll get through it. We've got time to have kids. I haven't even asked you if it's what you want...'

'Losing our baby has made me realise it's something I'd like, sometime in the future.'

'You'd make a great dad Dan.' Isabelle turned to caress his back. 'But you're right; we won't think about it until we're both ready.'

They lay silent for a few moments, before Isabelle spoke again.

'If it's okay with you I'd like to take a trip down under to see my Dad. Normally I'd love for you to come with me, but I think it's best if I go alone on this occasion. I don't mean to be selfish, but I have to set things right with Dad, and I don't want to drag you into our family sagas.'

Daniel grasped her hand. 'It's okay Isabelle, I understand. It's fine. I've been giving our situation some thought. I've decided to go back to New York to tie up some work issues, which I can do while you're in Australia and I can organise getting my apartment rented out so that I can come back and live here with you. I'll need a London office, but it means that we can be together for the most part.'

Isabelle kissed him on the lips. 'That's music to my ears.' Her hand slid beneath the covers to find him becoming aroused. 'Won't Hudson Publishing mind if you relocate to another country?'

'No. I've cleared it with my boss. I only need to be in New York once a quarter for our Directors' meetings. Most of my appointments are in Europe so it makes sense to be in London. The internet is truly a Godsend.'

He kissed her back and their mouths hovered and brushed against each other as they rubbed noses.

'I'm thinking I'll be away for about a month, and then I've got to prepare my speech for Gerry's big charity event at the Royal Opera House...'

Daniel closed his mouth over hers, and no more words passed between them.

Daniel wheeled Isabelle's case into the airport terminal building. Humid air clung to them like imaginary clothes, stifling their skin. Armed guards wandered the concourses in the wake of another threatened terrorist attack, among swarms of people.

The departure gate was crowded with families saying their goodbyes.

Isabelle turned to Daniel. 'You know I'll miss you desperately.'

'Ditto my lovely virtuoso. Don't worry about anything. I'll sort things out back in New York and in a week or so I'll be back to look after the house. You never know, I might just have a surprise waiting for you,' Daniel brushed a loose strand of wavy hair back from her face.

'Well, I've got plenty to keep me occupied on the flight. H has given me a wonderful book about Patanjali's Yoga Sutras and an Autobiography of a Yogi by some Indian guru!'

'Pity it's not the karma Sutra darling.' Daniel patted her bottom.

'Yes, well, we don't want the other passengers thinking I'm a sex fiend or anything.'

'But you are...' He pushed a crumpled piece of paper into her hand.

'It's from Lucy - her parents' address in the Blue Mountains, in case you wanted to meet them.'

He pulled her into a long embrace, and after a minute Isabelle backed away from him, with their eyes locked.

'I love you. See you when I get back.'

34

Isabelle relaxed into her spacious business class seat and began devouring the Yoga Sutras, which she soon realised were written more as guidance on how to live than to flatten one's tummy. She was fascinated by the succinct form of each aphorism. The philosophy covered Kriya Yoga, noted as action yoga, which focussed on losing attachment to the results, and the Ashtanga Yoga, made up of eight sections that encompassed the form.

After reading for a few hours, Isabelle pulled out her pen and diary. She had H's voice in her ear,

'It's a worthwhile spiritual practice to write what comes into your mind every day.'

Isabelle began to scrawl, gripping the pen in her now firm pincer grip.

I've learnt so much since my accident, but probably the most practical piece of advice has been this; if you change your outlook on things, then your experience of them changes also. I can let go of my past, and use it for the benefit of others, but I'm not sure how best to do that, other than to carry on doing what I'm doing. I'm looking forward to my stay in Australia, and seeing how things will unfold.

A memory of a conversation with Hortense shortly after their return from Madeira came flooding back into her mind. It had happened while Hortense was treating Isabelle to a retail therapy day. During their shopping spree Hortense had divulged that she had been meditating for years, alongside yoga classes when her time permitted. She often joked that for a big lady she had the suppleness of a nubile nymphomaniac, which Isabelle knew was no false brag. They had been rummaging in close proximity through the sales racks when Hortense had asked,

'Issy, I hope you don't mind me asking, and I'm not trying to be morbid, but what, if anything; did you experience nearing death?'

'I can't remember that much H. Honestly I wasn't aware of anything. It was like I was asleep, in a really deep sleep. There were no angels, no spirits, nothing I was aware of.' Isabelle frowned. 'What if there isn't anything – you know, beyond the body. What if we really do perish into oblivion at the end?'

'Maybe you weren't that close to the final doorway. Anyway, I thought you were a devout Catholic, where's your faith?' Mocked Hortense.

'Well, I was brought up in the doctrine of the Catholic Church. I used to believe that if you were good in this life you went to heaven, and if you were bad you would burn in hell. The hell-fire and brimstone teachings terrified me as a child. But now I'm not sure I believe that either exists as a place, rather as a state of being. I find myself questioning everything that I've been taught, not just in my religion, but my whole life.'

'That's not such a bad thing Issy. Religious dogma and righteous beliefs cause more wars and suffering than they do tolerance and unity. Searching inside one's own self for the answers, rather than blindly accepting what those in power, or who want to have power, espouse. When you are in commune with your soul, you realise that you don't need anything.'

'You're not afraid of death then?'

'No. Death is not the end, it's merely a process. You are not a body with a soul, but a soul with a body, and I believe that you simply pass back to the nature of your true self. The physical world is an illusion, and while you're in it, you gotta play the game.'

'And no-one plays it better than you H,' she had replied.

'I had an epiphany not long ago.' She pulled a bright red top and held it up to her generous torso.

'Oh H, don't keep me in suspense, do tell.'

'Let's just say I think I may have experienced what the Western mystics call a spiritual awakening.'

'You never mentioned this before.' Isabelle tried not to sound reproachful.

'I was waiting for the right moment Issy. You weren't in any coherent state just after the suicide attempt. Anyway, I'm not sure there are words to describe it.'

'Please try...'

'It happened at the end of a meditation session. I was in a lucid dream; a kind of trance, feeling totally relaxed, but still alert. Mind you, I couldn't hear Ray's snoring which is saying something. Next thing I know, my whole body starts to tingle with millions of bubbles of exquisite energy, and then I can feel myself floating above it. A strange sound entered my head, and bearing in mind I had my sleep mask on so I couldn't see anything, I became enveloped in the most incredible luminous light. It was pure and all encompassing, but it didn't blind me. It was sheer ecstasy, like being in a field of love so intense it transcended any explanation. Then like a fool I must have panicked about not being in my body and in an instant I was awake, and buzzing.'

Isabelle could only stare open mouthed. 'Did you tell Ray?'

'I sure did, I was just so amped up he thought I'd taken something at first. For months afterwards my whole body felt unbelievably energised. There's not a day goes by that I don't re-live it in my mind, especially when things don't go my way, it helps me to keep perspective. I'll lend you some of my books sometime.'

She had passed the remainder of the flight with a movie, a little sleep and a welcome stretch of her legs when they refuelled in Singapore. Twelve hours later she stood facing her father in the airport terminal at Sydney Kingsford Smith. He waved at her as she pushed her trolley into the arrivals hall. All around her fellow travellers were being greeted by family, colleagues and chauffeurs. A tall "Welcome to Sydney" sign glowed at them, and Duty Free stores, car hire offices and plush gift stores lined the concourse.

'Hi Dad, it's so good to see you, you look well.' Bill Bryant towered over her slender five foot ten frame, and hugged her. His hazel eyes twinkled and he shot her a warm smile. The remaining colour she remembered him having in his hair had been ousted by silver and grey, but his face remained relatively youthful, marked by only a few lines, and deeply tanned. Apart from a slightly softer belly he was still trim and looked younger than his seventy years.

After their initial hug Bill held her back at arms' length. 'Let's get a good look at you Isabelle Bryant!' His eyes swept over her. 'Well, at least you don't look as skinny as Lily said you were in New York.' His eyes fell to her side.

'Let me see your hand darling.' He lifted her arm and held her wrist as he inspected the scars across her stumps.

'Looks like it has healed well; considering. Does it hurt much?'

'Only in the cold, or if I use it too much, then the nerves start to tingle and all around the edge of the stumps goes numb.'

'My beautiful baby, I'm sorry you had to go through such a trauma. First, there was your mum passing, and now this. I'm so proud of you, the way you've pulled yourself together.'

'Cheers. My God, your accent has really thickened up Dad. I've never heard you speak with such a twang! I thought Lucy's accent was strong, but it's not a patch on yours.'

Bill smiled, took control of her trolley then placed a protective arm around her as they exited through the glass doors out into the pick-up zone. 'My car's just parked nearby in the short term multi-story,' said Bill as he guided the trolley beneath the white metal arches that shielded the entrance to the terminal. Outside, the morning air was fresh with a warm tinge, and a light blue sky devoid of cloud hinted at a mild winter's day in store for them.

'I'm taking you back to Jack's apartment in Pott's Point for the time being, it's closer than my place out in the suburbs, but also I thought you'd appreciate the harbour views.'

'Great, is Jack home?'

'He did plan to be, but then he had to do a friend's shift so he's taken a last minute trip to Tokyo, so it's just you and me kiddo.'

'Our hen-pecked younger bro has done alright for himself then?'

'You could say that. I gather he's very popular with the ladies too,' Bill said.

'I don't know how often he comes to London, but the last time I saw him was when I had my Opera House debut.'

35

'I'm not missing you yet, I mean much, I mean missing you badly! So how's it going down under my little virtuoso?' Daniel's teasing voice was clear down the line as Isabelle rubbed her eyes. With her right hand she puffed up the pillow behind her as she sat upright in a bid to feel more awake.

'Ditto Dan! Yes, it's been full-on so far. Dad and I did a harbour cruise, then we had lunch at the Hyatt, he also took me up to the top of the Sydney Tower, which has great views over the city. After a couple of days, he went back to work so I took a trip to the Blue Mountains to see Lucy's folks. They were just so welcoming and down to earth, and we shared some lovely anecdotes about Lucy. Her mum plied me with food constantly. It's no wonder Lucy isn't the size of sumo wrestler if that's how much she got fed growing up! I'll have to take you there one day: it's just stunning, the sight of the Three Sisters against the backdrop of escarpments and forested hills, tinted with a blue haze and infused with the scent of eucalyptus. Dad's place is out in the sticks so I've had time to read some more of H's Yoga books, and we've been going for walks in the bush around his house. When I got back to the city we had two days of torrential rain so I visited the aquarium, The Powerhouse Museum, and I even plucked up enough courage to go back to the Opera House, which brought back some memories.' Isabelle yawned.

'I envy you, it must be wonderful,' Daniel said.

'It is, and it's lovely to spend some time with Dad and put the past behind us. He's offered for me to sit in on one of his music classes, so I'm going back to school today.'

'Better make sure you pay attention then.'

'Don't worry I don't think it'll be too taxing. How is everything with you? Did you manage to get your apartment rented?'

'Yes, all sorted. Everything's fine my end. Enjoy yourself. Don't worry about anything. I got back from New York yesterday. I'm back at Watermill Gardens, keeping it cosy for when you come home. I'm off to bed now, I'll call again soon.'

'Thanks Dan, love you. Sweet dreams.'

Isabelle followed her father and streams of pupils through the wooden doorway. She scanned the room as they entered. The classroom was large, with a white board at the front, and an upright piano sat in the corner. Isabelle noticed a storeroom with a small window and she peered in as she passed. It was a jumble of violin and cello cases, along with a small selection of brass instruments. The wall opposite the entrance was lined with windows, and the sun cast its dappled rays onto the desks. A sound system had been installed in the classroom for playing music to them, and with the music block being situated apart from the main school building, it meant her father's class had a degree of privacy. She was glancing out of the window towards the playing fields when she heard her father's voice again.

'Morning everybody, how are you all on this fine day?'

'Good sir,' they responded in unison.

'You may or may not have clocked the family resemblance, but this is my daughter Isabelle Bryant, who is visiting me from the UK. Some of you may remember me talking about Isabelle before, but for those of you who don't know, Isabelle was one of the top violinists in the world, playing to packed concert halls in venues across the globe. I hope you don't mind her being here, but I thought it would be nice for you have a chat with her about the violin and music in general.'

Their faces turned simultaneously to look at her, and Isabelle felt herself colour up.

'Hi guys, thanks for having me, it's lovely to meet you. My Dad talks very highly of his music students.'

Isabelle guessed that the average age must have been nine or ten, and judging by their confident demeanour she guessed many of them were already quite proficient on an instrument, while some of them had probably only just started learning to play.

Watching him with his students, Isabelle regretted that she had never been taught by her father. She observed his gentle, humorous and captivating manner, and how he drew the children into his musical world. After a studious half hour of music theory, during which he had his students tapping and clapping different rhythms, with examples on the board of the opening notes of Beethoven's Fifth and Mozart's Symphony Number 40, they had also participated in singing note intervals as Bill played them on the piano. A few of the children had almost perfect pitch.

Isabelle found herself becoming preoccupied by the idea of grass roots inspiration. When she thought of other successful musicians, artists and entrepreneurs she realised their passion had mostly been cultivated in their childhood. Her musings were interrupted abruptly as she caught the end of a question from her father.

'Isabelle, isn't that true?'

'True?' Her vague response solicited a look of annoyance from her father.

'I was just saying to my budding musicians here, that if they study and practice and dedicate themselves to their art, that they will be successful, as you have been.'

Isabelle looked around the room at their hopeful faces.

'Yes, totally. But there's more to it than just working hard. Certainly, interests that are nurtured in childhood can translate into living that passion in life. It happened for me. I do feel that it's easier to maintain self-belief and follow your heart when you are a child. If positive self-esteem is ingrained early enough, before the onslaught of society's conditioning and well-meaning adult's opinions, then you have a fighting chance of creating your own definition of success.

'I was very fortunate to have had supportive parents and the right environment for my talent and dream to flourish. It has become apparent that in so many families children are told that they either don't deserve to achieve, or that they are somehow inferior, or else the parents are too busy trying to survive to be able to focus on their offspring's future.'

The room remained silent, and she could see her father grinning from the corner of her eye.

'You need to have a dream. I may have been a virtuoso, but in my quest for perfection and to some extent vanity, I neglected other important aspects of my life. I suppose all I would say is, by all means be dedicated, by all means practice, by all means love what you do, but don't forget your family, your hobbies, and your education, your faith. It's these things that add different facets to your personality, and your music will only benefit from that. I had oodles of passion for my violin, but outside of that my life was empty. And when my playing career ended, I had nothing.'

Her father shuffled.

'I'm not saying for one minute that you shouldn't be committed, but I am saying that everyone needs balance in their lives, no matter what you decide to do.'

Bill strode to the front of the class.

'Thank you Isabelle. Now, does anyone have any other questions for my daughter?'

The majority of the students smiled in appreciation, some of them obviously couldn't wait to get out of the class. Bill was on the verge of ending the lesson, as a girl raised her arm hesitantly.

'Yes Miranda, what would you like to know?'

'Sir, please, I was just wondering, being as how lucky we are that our parents can afford instruments and everything, and even if they don't, we can use them at school. How do the kids without anything get going? What if their passion is music, but they haven't had a very good education or they live in the bush, or their parents are broke, what happens to them? My mum says it's heart breaking that kids suffer from a lack of opportunities just because they don't have the right start in life.' Her neat oval face shone up at them, her pretty features highlighted by her long wavy fair hair.

She had spoken so eloquently that Isabelle and her father were momentarily speechless.

Bill offered, 'Your mum is right Miranda, it is tragic, and more should be done.'

Miranda appeared unimpressed by the lack of sub-stance in his response, and turned her penetrating gaze towards Isabelle.

Isabelle could only muster, 'You seem very caring and sensitive Miranda, thank you for highlighting such a worthy cause. I know there are lots of programmes for children such as these, and indeed music therapy for severely emotionally damaged children. The challenge as ever is to reach more kids.'

As the class emptied Isabelle wiped the tears from her cheeks. Bill wandered round the class tidying up desks and chairs, gathering their homework books to-gether for marking. 'It never ceases to amaze me what comes from the mouths of babes sometimes.'

Staring straight ahead Isabelle murmured, 'when the student is ready, the teacher will appear.'

Her father scrunched his substantial eyebrows.

'You know, children aren't stupid. Just because they're younger it doesn't mean they're any less intelli-gent or intuitive. In fact, they are more so, they don't have any of the excuses or justifications that adult minds are so good at creating,' said Isabelle as she turned to face him. 'Their simplicity is their strength.'

'You know I'm not a superstitious man Isabelle, my faith barely survived your mother's death, but I just can't shake the notion that somehow Julia's spirit has had an etheric hand in your new found purpose Isabelle.'

'I haven't even said what it is.'

'But remember I can read you like a music score...'

'So we have a lot to talk about then, because a new path has just been revealed to me.'

'Let's get home then, and I'll light the Barbie,' replied Bill.

They sat in quiet companionship in the car, with Isabelle staring out the window, watching the forest scenery pass by the window in a blur of muted greens and browns. The bush clamoured to the edge of the perimeter of the long, smooth tarmac road, with the trees and shrubs on either side of them providing a thick coverage of leaves, almost certainly hiding a plethora of wildlife living in the woodland interior she pondered.

An hour later, they lounged on Bill's veranda with their tummies full of chargrilled chicken, corn on the cob, salad and cold beer. The faded white washed wood veranda was adorned with colourful hanging baskets and looked out over a small field surrounded by trees, cut through by a single dirt track leading to her father's remote bungalow.

'You still do the best barbeques of anyone I know Dad.'

'It's in my blood Belle. An Aussie man prides himself on his culinary barbie skills.' His leg suddenly shot forward and his heel crushed a cockroach that had ventured just a little too far. Isabelle flinched as she heard the crunch.

'So what happened this afternoon?' asked Bill. 'You seem more focussed and determined than I've ever seen you – and that's saying something!'

'Really?'

'It doesn't take a brain surgeon to see that you've got the bit between your teeth again. I guessed that you plan to get involved with underprivileged children, but in what sort of capacity I don't know. That doesn't matter to me. The main thing is that your life has meaning again.'

'You know Dad? I never thought I would feel so alive and inspired again after my accident, but with hindsight, it hasn't been all bad. Meeting Dan was one of the most amazing blessings in my life. I feel closer to H, and to you and the family than ever before, and I've found a new talent for writing. I was even going to have a baby... for a while. Wonderful as it all is, there's still an empty feeling that haunts me sometimes.'

'I'm an expert on emptiness. I was filled with it after your mum died.'

Isabelle brushed his arm. 'The void mum left in us will never be completely filled though Dad.'

'No it won't...'

'This is going to sound vain and shallow,' ventured Isabelle, 'but nothing quite gives me the same satisfaction as a hard earned applause from a packed concert hall. It's not for the recognition, but the feeling that I really had touched the audience's lives somehow, brought something magical to them.' Looking at him to see if he'd understood, she baulked.

'God, I sound like a fucking diva!'

'No, you sound like a gutter rat. Swearing aside though, I know what you mean. There's been something missing in your life. It wasn't a gap that could be easily filled. I know that feeling. And now you've found a cause that stirs the same passion and drive, the ambition to make a difference in people's lives.'

'I couldn't have put it better myself.'

'Isabelle, listen to me. Even in the face of everything that's happened, you truly are a lucky person. Not many people go through life finding their passion. Ever. And to find more than one in a lifetime is very special. And if it's what I think it is then it will take you to an even more fulfilling place than you think possible right now. But don't think it will be easy.'

'Dad, I know I'll need everyone's support.' Isabelle leaned over the balcony. 'I can't help feeling terrified and excited at the same time. What if I fail? What if my peers scorn me and I end up making a terrible mistake?'

'These are just silly insecurities, and we all have to deal with them. The difference between life's achievers and those living lives of quiet desperation, are that they didn't let their fears stop them. The only way you can make a difference, or leave a lasting legacy is to forget yourself and put your attention onto others. Then you won't see the faults and weaknesses that you think you have; only the opportunities you have to serve.'

'Spoken like a true teacher Dad. I don't know where to start...'

'Start at the beginning Belle, formulate your plan and follow it, no matter what.'

'I do know this; one way or another I'm going to create an academy of music for exceptional and underprivileged children with no opportunities or hope in life. And I'm going to name it *The Bryant Miranda Foundation.*'

'That's it. Just take it one step at a time. The longest of journeys starts with a single step. Your mum would have been proud of you Belle. Not only for what you achieved as a musician, but just as much for the way you've handled your trials and tribulations.' Bill placed his palm between her hunched shoulder blades.

'I'm sure she'd have been thrilled that I tried to kill myself.'

'She would have understood your mental state at the time.' He lengthened his arm around her smooth, tanned shoulders. His wicker chair creaked.

'Oh my baby, I'm so glad you didn't succeed in that. I'm sorry I wasn't around to give you my support, I'll always feel bad about that.'

'Don't be Dad. You didn't make me take those tablets. But thanks anyway.' Isabelle gave him a peck on the cheek.

'At one time or another we all feel inadequate. We feel like we can't do it on our own. Nobody can do it alone. I'm just a teacher, but maybe this is the most valuable lesson I can give you Isabelle. Remember, a great symphony is played by a whole orchestra, not just one player. The teacher is the conductor and the ideas come from the composer. As musicians we are the ambassadors for the composers, and we try to ascertain what their intentions were and are. Forgive my philosophical BS, but you know what I mean don't you? Everything is connected, past, present and future.'

'Dad, has there been anyone special since Mum died?'

'Only a few brief romances. No one ever measured up to Julia. But I kind of went into a self-imposed loneliness when I was grieving, and it just sort of stuck. I had my precious students, and I have you three. I have all I need.'

They stood and leant over the rail to admire the sky, now infused with intense orange and red hues from the slowly disappearing sun. The air was quiet, with the exception of the occasional Kookaburra delivering what sounded like a raucous laugh from the top of a nearby gum tree.

The shrill noise of the phone ringing broke their quietude, and Bill left to answer it. He reappeared on the balcony motioning to Isabelle. 'It's for you, it's Hortense calling from London.'

He handed over the receiver and Isabelle sauntered into the house.

'Hello? H?'

There was a brief pause and then Hortense's normally smooth voice sounded brittle down the line;

'Sebastian's dead...'

36

Isabelle stood trembling before the congregation. The chapel settled into a respectful silence, and Isabelle drew strength from the familiar faces. They were in a small old church. Wooden pews sat either side of the aisle, and a high arched ceiling ran the length of the building. Stations of the Cross were lined along the walls, made up of tiny colourful mosaics, the most beautiful she had ever seen. The floor had been tiled with elegant patterns, and the windows were clear, providing a plain contrast to the mosaics.

The site of the coffin placed before the altar made her feel sick. She pictured Sebastian's vibrant smile, his love of music, his craft, and his faithful Delilah. Hortense's words were lurking at the back of her mind. 'Death is not the end but a process.'

Isabelle suddenly had the feeling that Sebastian was there with them in spirit, as the sunlight streamed in behind her through the large solitary stain glass window, casting multi-coloured light across the altar. She closed her eyes and bowed her head for a brief moment, then faced her fellow mourners and began.

'Sebastian Cortez-Smith was my very dear friend. We met while studying together at the Royal Academy in London. Sebastian as you know; on the cello, myself on the violin.

'Although our careers and lives took different paths once we qualified as professional musicians, we were always united by our love of music. One of the things I admired most about Sebastian was his zest for life. You always knew where you stood with him, and he always had a wicked sense of humour, which helped him through difficult times, and was a source of joy for all who knew him. He was never afraid to stand out from the crowd, and stand out he did. Unlike some, who live life behind a veneer of self-deception and lies, he was open and happy with who he was and what he stood for. How many of us look for approval of some kind in our lives, never really appreciating the uniqueness in ourselves, or being content with who and what we are? It is said not every man really lives, but every man dies. In my view he really lived.

'Sebastian's achievements as a musician are impressive, and he had many loyal fans appreciative of his talents. The last five years of his life were spent as the principle cellist in the LPO, one of the finest orchestras in existence. He was a loyal supporter of the Mexican football team and never forgot his roots. The kind of person he was eclipsed even his musicianship. He was never afraid to follow his heart, and would do anything for his friends. Selfish was not a word in his vocabulary.'

The congregation appeared deep in their thoughts, mulling over her words.

'We each have our own special memories of Sebastian, maybe some are of him smartly turned out in his tuxedo, or dashing around London in his black Mercedes, or the flamboyant parties he threw, or the devotion he showed to his dog Delilah and of course, his beloved mother, Yolanda. But for me, none are more enduring than a conversation I had with him at his apartment a few months ago, when we were both at a low ebb. He told me that it was mainly the things that we didn't do that we regretted the most. I know he didn't have any regrets, and sadly I don't think there are many who can claim this when they go to their maker.'

The lump in her throat began to feel like she had swallowed an apple, and her eyes were stinging.

'I'll miss you Seb. Thank you for the wonderful times we had together, and wherever you are, I hope you are happy and feeling excited about the beginning of another adventure.'

Daniel flashed her an encouraging smile. She wiped her soggy eyes with a tissue.

'And finally, our amigo lying there before us would not want us to mourn his passing excessively, I'm certain that Sebastian would rather we have a celebration instead, to remember his achievements and his impact on our lives.

'I think he would have liked this poem about the spiritual state of consciousness, from a book that my very dear friend Hortense Lafayette gave to me.'

Isabelle read slowly:

> 'Samadhi by Paramhansa Yogananda
> Vanished the veils of light and shade,
> Lifted every vapor of sorrow,
> Sailed away all dawns of fleeting joy,
> Gone the dim sensory mirage.
> Love, hate, health, disease, life, death,
> Perished these false shadows on the screen of duality.
> Waves of laughter, scyllas of sarcasm, melancholic whirlpools,
> Melting in the vast sea of bliss.
> The storm of maya stilled
> By magic wand of intuition deep.
> The universe, forgotten dream, subconsciously lurks,
> Ready to invade my newly-wakened memory divine.
> I live without the cosmic shadow,
> But it is not, bereft of me;
> As the sea exists without the waves,
> But they breathe not without the sea.
> Dreams, wakings, states of deep turia sleep,

Present, past, future, no more for me,
But ever-present, all-flowing I, I,
everywhere.
Planets, stars, stardust, earth,
Volcanic bursts of doomsday cataclysms,
Creation's molding furnace,
Glaciers of silent x-rays, burning electron
floods,
Thoughts of all men, past, present, to
come,
Every blade of grass, myself, mankind,
Each particle of universal dust,
Anger, greed, good, bad, salvation, lust,
I swallowed, transmuted all
Into a vast ocean of blood of my own one
Being!
Smoldering joy, oft-puffed by meditation
Blinding my tearful eyes,
Burst into immortal flames of bliss,
Consumed my tears, my frame, my all.
Thou art I, I am Thou,
Knowing, Knower, Known, as One!
Tranquilled, unbroken thrill, eternally
living, ever-new peace!
Enjoyable beyond imagination of expec-
tancy, samadhi bliss!
Not an unconscious state
Or mental chloroform without wilful
return,

Samadhi but extends my conscious realm
Beyond limits of the mortal frame
To farthest boundary of eternity
Where I, the Cosmic Sea,
Watch the little ego floating in Me.
The sparrow, each grain of sand, fall not
without My sight.
All space floats like an iceberg in My men-
tal sea.
Colossal Container, I, of all things made.
By deeper, longer, thirsty, guru-given
meditation
Comes this celestial samadhi.
Mobile murmurs of atoms are heard,
The dark earth, mountains, vales, lo! mol-
ten liquid!
Flowing seas change into vapors of
nebulae!
Aum blows upon vapors, opening won-
drously their veils,
Oceans stand revealed, shining electrons,
Till, at last sound of the cosmic drum,
Vanish the grosser lights into eternal rays
Of all-pervading bliss.
From joy I came, for joy I live, in sacred
joy I melt.
Ocean of mind, I drink all creation's
waves.
Four veils of solid, liquid, vapor, light,

Lift aright.
Myself, in everything, enters the Great
Myself.
Gone forever, fitful, flickering shadows of
mortal memory.
Spotless is my mental sky, below, ahead,
and high above.
Eternity and I, one united ray.
A tiny bubble of laughter, I
Am become the Sea of Mirth Itself.

'And now Sebastian, on behalf of myself and all who loved you, it's time to bid you farewell. Gracias por tu vida, tu amor y tu música.'

Her voice broke just as she finished, and avoiding eye contact with the congregation, she hurried back to her seat and leaned on Daniel who produced a timely hand-kerchief. They waited outside the church in respect as Sebastian's coffin was loaded back into the flower laden hearse to be taken to the crematorium.

A subdued atmosphere settled over Sebastian's flat as they all filed into his chilly lounge. Isabelle clicked on the thermostat and placed his iPod into its docking station, while Hortense busied herself in the kitchen preparing refreshments. Slowly conversations struck up among the guests. She set the volume low, and recog-nised the melody of a Beethoven cello sonata.

Marcus approached her as she perched on his stylish armchair. He looked elegant in a black suit and mottled grey polo shirt, but his eyes were heavy and dark rimmed, and he was unshaven.

'Thank you for your eulogy Isabelle, he would have loved it.'

'Thank you. How are you holding up?'

Marcus didn't appear as tall to her as he did at her house warming. His shoulders were rounded and hunched forwards. 'I can't believe he's gone.'

'Me neither,' replied Isabelle.

'Sebastian asked for his ashes to be scattered over the Pacific Ocean off the coast of Puerto Vallarta, his mother's home town. I've already booked my ticket.'

'Seb was only thirty six, but he crammed so much into his brief time. It was definitely a case of quality rather than quantity for him,' Isabelle said as she hugged Marcus. 'Good luck with your trip to Mexico.'

'Saying goodbye to Seb has made me even more determined to focus on the important things in life.'

She wandered into the kitchen for a drink and found Hortense.

'Well done Issy, you gave him a great send off.' Hortense patted her on the back. 'Sadly, even as we speak, thousands of youngsters are dying of Malaria around the world.'

'It must have been that jungle trek in Oaxaca that did it H. Oh my God, poor Seb. He was complaining of flu like symptoms at my housewarming.' Isabelle shook her head. 'Why didn't he take anti-malaria tablets for God's sake?'

'He probably thought he was immune to it as he'd been to Mexico so often. Maybe the trip to the jungle was a spur of the moment thing, and he just didn't think about it,' Hortense replied.

'I hate to think of him lying in hospital replete with modern facilities, still suffering and dying just because of some lousy mosquitoes!'

'If it's any consolation I think he went downhill very quickly, his pain was relatively short lived. The actual cause of death on his death certificate says renal failure.'

'Do you think he knew it was terminal H? He never told anyone what was wrong.'

'I expect he wanted to keep the horror of what he was experiencing from us. Marcus only found out a day or so before he passed on, so at least he had some support at the very end,' concluded Hortense.

'I hear you have another lost waif under your roof?'

'You mean Delilah? Yeah, she's a gorgeous little bundle. I've been singing to her but she's pining like crazy for Sebastian.'

'H, word will be going out across town that the Lafayette household is a bolt hole for strays and lost causes,' Isabelle said.

'They are my speciality,' replied Hortense.

'How's the new Jazz Legend's album going?'

'Not bad thanks Issy. Thankfully my singing engagements and walking Delilah have been keeping me busy.'

'I noticed that The Times has run an obituary, and it looks like the LPO are dedicating their next concert to him, which just so happens to be the Elgar Cello Concerto with none other than Yo-Yo Ma. You know, what with Seb's passing and all the funeral arrangements I haven't had a chance to tell you about my new music foundation.'

'Your music foundation? How did that come about Issy? I approve by the way…'

'Thanks H, because I'm going to need your help.

'It's a long story which I won't bore you with now, but suffice to say the inspiration came from one of Dad's music students, a bright and charming girl called Miranda. The aim of it will be to give instruction for violin, cello or piano, plus music therapy to underprivileged kids, and those with talent but no opportunities. It's about giving something back. But an idea has just crept into my head.'

'What's that then?'

'I can honour Seb by including his name as part of the foundation. I was thinking perhaps it could be called the *Bryant Miranda Smith Foundation*; or BMS for short.'

'It has a certain ring to it Issy,' Hortense agreed.

'I put it to the back of my mind when I got back because of Seb's death, but now, even though I'm devastated, it will give me focus and meaning.'

'I'll do whatever I can to help Issy.' Hortense bent down, donned a pair of musical oven gloves and pulled out the samosas, pizza slices and sausage rolls. 'It will do us all good to get on board.' Isabelle lent forward to breathe in the warm aroma wafting from the food.

'The only problem is I don't actually have a clue where to start. I've got so many questions to find an answer to like how will it be funded? Where will we be based? How will I source the expertise, and not least promote its creation?'

'Why don't you set up a meeting with me, Gerry, Dan and Lucy? We can tackle these questions together, do some brainstorming,' suggested Hortense.

'Good idea, I'll email everyone and we can arrange a date. Although it's my baby I don't want to do it alone,' Isabelle said.

'Other than that, how are you coping? How are things with Dan?'

'Seb's passing hasn't really hit me yet. I've been wandering around the house like a lost sheep, and I've been having trouble sleeping since I got back, but Dan's been absolutely wonderful. He cradles me in his arms and strokes my hair, and then I just drift off in a cocoon of love and security. He's had a lot to deal with himself what with the miscarriage and re-locating over here. I feel even closer to him since we resolved our *misunderstanding*. I have to pinch myself sometimes that I landed such a handsome, kind, intelligent and fun guy. He makes up for all those lonely nights with Howard.'

37

Isabelle smiled at her supporters. Gerry, Hortense, Lucy and Daniel all appeared relaxed and comfortable as they sat on the spongy sofas by the large window in Gerry's office. Chiswick High Road bustled beneath them, and the sun warmed their expectant faces.

'Thanks guys, for giving up your time to help me with this. I've been reading up on the various options open to us, and feel that the best thing would be a private foundation and we should definitely apply for charitable status. That way we can benefit from tax relief and claim gift aid on donations. We'll need to appoint a trustee as well.' Isabelle looked at Hortense.

'Issy I thought you'd never ask. It would be my pleasure.'

'Thanks H, I know you are the best person for the job, and I'm aware of the limited time input that you have. I'm prepared to do all the leg work and principal fund-raising, but if we can all meet, say every quarter, we can have a proper update on where we're at,' said Isabelle.

Saskia brought their teas and coffee in on a large tray and Gerry rose to assist her placing it on his glass coffee table.

'First things first, are we all agreed that it will be called the *Bryant, Miranda, Smith Music Foundation*, shortened to BMS in the logo?'

'Isabelle it's your baby and we wouldn't criticise anything you decide unless we feel it would have a detrimental effect on the foundation,' Daniel said.

'It's okay with me,' offered Hortense, sipping her latte.

'Me too,' chipped in Lucy, as she poked Gerry who nodded in agreement.

'As a matter of fact Issy, I've got a friend who works for the Charity Commission, so I can make sure that side of things goes through without a hitch. I suggest we do a big feature on its inception in *High Notes*, and Dan will probably suggest running the same feature in some of the other European titles and maybe *Manhattan Music*, which is the flagship publication in the states.'

'Thanks Luce, that's brilliant. I'm happy to write it.'

Daniel said, 'It will be your piece de la resistance Isabelle.'

'You'll need an accountant on-board Isabelle, especially if the investment and donations are over twenty five thousand a year,' commented Gerry.

'Yes, good point maestro. I'm aiming for us to make a quarter of a million in our first year. After all, the more we make the more we can help. I plan to invest ten thousand pounds initially as a start-up balance. I'm due some money from my settlement with you know who, and thanks to Gerry my album is selling tremendously well. I know the time input will be significant, but I think I can support myself with my speaking fees.' Daniel squeezed Isabelle's right hand.

'Issy, Ray and I know a good accountant; he's handled all our stuff for years. As Trustee I can contact him and organise that side of things,' Hortense said.

'Go for it H.'

'Isabelle have you decided how it will operate. I mean, will you fund other musical projects in the UK, or do you plan to open a centre in London for the kids?' asked Daniel.

'Ideally both Dan, but I think in the beginning we should mainly focus on various musical projects that are already planned and underway. Once we become more established I fully plan to open our own premises for tuition and charity concerts for the kids.'

'Yes, I agree Issy. Let's not run before we can walk,' said Gerry, as he gulped down the dredges of his coffee. 'I'm in a good position to pass on assignments that will help raise the profile of the foundation. I'll also set up another radio interview for you my dear. Your feet won't touch the ground once I get my well-oiled PR machine into action!'

'That's what I'm afraid of Gerry.'

'I'm sure we'll be inundated with requests once the word gets out,' said Hortense, 'and at first it's going to be a difficult job to decide who gets what.'

'It's a difficult job, but someone's got to do it H. Any charity or project that means a child with the desire to play music, but not the means to achieve it, is a deserving case in my book. I'm sure there'll be special projects that we will do specific fund-raising for, as well as our normal activities. Why don't we open the foundation's bank account tomorrow H?'

'Sure thing Issy.'

'I know it all sounds simple as we bounce these ideas off one another, but I'm still daunted by the enormity of the task ahead of us,' Isabelle said.

'Remember Isabelle, Rome wasn't built in a day, and nothing worthwhile is ever achieved overnight,' said Daniel.

'Touché.'

Silence settled. Lucy was the first to speak.

'We need a mission statement, any ideas?' She pushed her delicate glasses up the ridge of her freckly nose. She had tied her mass of thick, long auburn hair into a bun but wispy strands kept dancing across her face.

'Oh my God Luce, since when did you wear glasses?' Isabelle leaned in to make a closer inspection of her curved tortoiseshell rims.

'Since I mistook chilli powder for cinnamon in my porridge mate!'

'What?'

'Yeah, that was an interesting bloody sensation I can tell you.' She touched the rims. 'I got these when you were in Sydney. Probably take after Mum; she's blind as a bat.'

'Your mum is an amazing cook Luce. Anyway, sorry for not noticing earlier, my zest for the foundation has rather seized all my available attention.'

'Tell me about it,' laughed Daniel.

'Let's get back on track children,' Hortense said. 'Mission statement anyone?'

They frowned and scratched their heads until Isabelle said, 'How about something along the lines of; created to inspire passion and opportunities for children to reach their full potential through music?'

'It's definitely got something Issy,' said Lucy. 'What you've said covers projects like music therapy, where we can reach traumatised and troubled kids that won't necessarily go on to be performers.'

'Thanks Luce. Well, let's put it down as a suggestion, I'm open to ideas.'

'Issy, have you thought about teaching yourself?' asked Gerry.

'I'd love to Gerry, but I doubt how well it would work practically, given that I can't demonstrate any techniques. But I will do my best to oversee the running of the foundation, and provide a Virtuoso's perspective for my young protégées.'

'And that you will Issy,' Hortense cut in. 'Now you really are playing the music you came here to play.'

'Isabelle I'll try and schedule the radio interview at least a month from now to give you and H time to register the foundation and complete the vital administrative tasks,' said Gerry.

'Great. I've also arranged an appointment to meet with the principle of the Royal Academy of Music to see if they can support us, or at least promote us in some joint marketing or something.'

Saskia came to remove their empty cups and Isabelle looked at her watch.

'Gerry, guys, I don't want to keep you too long, I think we've covered some good ground, so let's be in touch and update each other on our tasks when necessary.'

As they were hugging each other, Isabelle received a text message. She glanced at her mobile and looked up with a smile.

'That was Patrick Hill. My Decree Absolute has come through today, along with the funds. I'm officially divorced.'

'Thank God,' Daniel blurted out.

'Yes. And I can't thank you all enough for your support of me over the last few months and for the depth of your enthusiasm and commitment to my project. It belongs to all of us really. Oh, and there's one last thing. I was trawling the Internet one rainy afternoon and I came across a quote that I'd like to use on our stationary and press releases. You'll be surprised to hear that it's not actually Beethoven.'

Hortense pretended to faint.

'Strewth Issy, you are full of surprises mate,' added Lucy with a hint of sarcasm.

'Don't keep us in suspense,' said Daniel with an air of admonition.

'Well, I think Plato has penned our philosophy perfectly: "I would teach children music, physics and philosophy; but most importantly music, for the patterns in music and all the arts are the keys to learning".'

38

'What's wrong?'

'Have you seen my letter from the Royal Opera House?'

'Are you kidding? I try and steer clear of your paper work Issy.'

Isabelle rummaged through the sheets on her dining room table.

'I left it right here on top of my other letters. If you didn't move it, where can it have gone?'

'Have you looked on the floor, maybe it got whisked off somehow.'

Isabelle couldn't hide her agitation. 'But I know I left it exactly here. I've looked all over the dining room, there's no sign of it.' As she spoke a soft breeze caught the corner of her papers. She turned, and noticed that the window was ajar.

'Dan honey, did you open the window?'

'No, I thought you did, after all, it's been so stuffy and humid.'

'It's like someone's been in the house, and they've taken my Opera House letter.'

'And what would anyone want with that? Is anything else missing?' Daniel gestured towards the remainder of the house.

Isabelle flushed. 'No, I haven't noticed anything else is gone.'

'I mean, if we'd been burgled, surely they would have taken the TV and the valuables rather than just a letter from the Royal Opera House?'

'Oh Dan, I've been so wrapped up in the foundation, I think I must be losing my marbles. And the Opera House. I completely forgot about the Royal Opera House next week. Gerry has just texted me a gentle re-minder. Now I'm in a spin, and I can't find the details. You're right, I sound ludicrous, I must have put it some-where else.' Isabelle slumped onto a dining chair, and with her elbows resting on the table she buried her face into her hands.

'I suppose reprimanding you for worrying is out of the question?'

'You can give all the advice you feel is necessary, but that doesn't mean it's going to be listened to. Not be-cause I'm malicious, just panicked.'

'Yes, but if you know what's good for you you'll lis-ten! It's not that important in the big scheme of things, but look at it like this; it would certainly provide a good opportunity for you to promote the foundation. It fits in perfectly with the ideals that you are planning to talk about, no?'

Isabelle raised her head. 'You're right as usual Dan. Doesn't it get boring being a smart arse?'

'All I'm saying is it isn't worth getting your knickers in a twist over. If you want to get your knickers in a twist, I'll do the deed.' The corner of his mouth twitched.

'Remember how devastating you were at the Met?' A smile crept over his face.

'I mean not just devastatingly beautiful to look at, but you had everyone's attention in the palm of your hand. If you have just a quarter of the charisma you possessed that night, it'll be a runaway success at the Opera House.'

Isabelle had no reply as she leaned into his firm chest to kiss him. They fell into each other's arms and Daniel threw her onto the sofa.

Recovered from their earlier lovemaking, Isabelle sat on the sofa with her pad and pencil making notes for her speech. Daniel had departed for London and her own CD was playing softly in the background. As she was deep in concentration her landline rang. She paused, not wanting to hear the now familiar silence on the end of the line, but lifted the receiver to find Lily's soft voice was speaking.

'Belle, hi it's me. How are you?'

'Hi Lily. I'm glad you called, I've missed you.'

'Dad told me about your visit, the miscarriage and about Sebastian. I'm really sorry. God knows you've been through the mill.'

'It's okay, thanks. I'm getting there. Everything okay with you guys? How's Maia?'

'We're fine. Maia is growing up fast, and her speech is coming on in leaps and bounds. She's still using your colouring set and often asks after Aunty Belle. There is one thing bothering me though. I think Paul might be doing some insider trading. He made a really big deal recently and I feel uneasy about it.'

'Have you asked him about it?'

'Not directly, just a few comments here and there, you know, just hints like, "wow, you made more money in the Pacific Pines deal than any other I can remember" but he's been evasive. He's not a dishonest person, but maybe his desire to provide for his family has gotten out of control.'

'Maybe he's just a bloody good trader and you should stop worrying, like everyone keeps telling me. Try not to think the worst. Anyway, sometimes honest people deceive others and the ones they love with good intentions, or they just can't help themselves. Dan and I fell in love when he was still with Maria, and I know it doesn't sit easy with him. Personally I didn't care for her, but what we did was wrong.'

'Are you very loved up?'

Isabelle sighed. 'Only slightly, completely and totally punch drunk on him. I owe you some gratitude sis, thanks for believing in us enough to give Dan H's number.'

'It was the least I could do Belle.'

'I've got some other news that hopefully Dad hasn't stolen my thunder on anyway.'

'I'm all ears,' said Lily.

'Thanks to a girl called Miranda. I've been inspired to set up a foundation for musically talented and under-privileged kids.'

'Wow, Belle, that's fantastic news. Things are moving in the right direction for you now. This will be your legacy...'

'Has Maia shown any musical ability?'

'She has actually. She loves to sing and plonk the piano keys, so I'm taking her to a toddler's music session once a week in Manhattan. Perhaps she takes after her auntie.'

'Or her grandmother,' Isabelle suggested.

'Apart from your playing, I always knew you would find a way to use your love of music to open people's hearts, and especially children's hearts. I'm so proud of you sis.'

'Thanks Lily, that means a lot to me. I'm getting a lot of help and support from the gang, but I can't doubt myself when you support me too. It's like the confusion and fog that clouded my thoughts after the accident has dissipated, and for the first time I'm getting a glimpse of what it feels like to live free of fear, except, there have been a few... incidents lately.'

'What sort of incidents Belle? You never mentioned anything before. Is everything okay?'

'It's probably nothing. I didn't want to worry anyone with my neuroses, but I can't shake off the feeling that there's a shadow hanging over me.'

'Oh my God Belle, tell me what's been happening.' Lily's tone was urgent.

'It started with a phone call. I got the first one the morning after my housewarming. At first I thought it was a wrong number, but then it started to happen more regularly. I'd pick up the phone and after a few minutes of silence I'd hear a click and the line would go dead. Shortly after I moved in I got a card through my letterbox; it wasn't hand written and it said that I wasn't alone. There was no signature. I thought maybe one of the others had done it as a joke, but now I think someone is trying to scare me.'

Lily gasped, and asked, 'Has anything else happened?'

'Yes, the other day after our gathering to discuss the foundation I had to get home on my own as Daniel had another meeting to attend in the city. I was on my way back from Gerry's office walking towards the tube, when I had the feeling that I was being followed.'

'Shit Belle! This is serious. You're not being neurotic; you've every right to be worried. Do you think it could be a deranged fan?'

'I don't know, but I had the sense someone was following a little way behind me. Every time I turned round all I saw were complete strangers, but there seemed to be the outline of a man with his back to me that looked vaguely disturbing. He was too far away for me to make out his features, and then he stepped into a shop.'

'I take it you didn't approach him?'

'No…I was too scared. Plus I thought I'd look an idiot if it turned out to be someone completely innocent and I accused them of being a weirdo.'

'Belle, you've got to tell the police.'

'Tell them what? That I've had a few crank phone calls to my new property, a typed note and the vague notion that I was being followed?'

'Well, at least say something to Daniel. How can he protect you if he doesn't know what's been happening?'

'I can look after myself,' said Isabelle firmly.

'But that didn't work out too well for you before did it?'

Isabelle faltered. She cast a glance over her stumps and fell silent.

'I'm sorry Belle; that was insensitive of me. I didn't mean it like that. I'm just concerned about you.'

'It's okay, I guess you're right. I just know he'll make a fuss, and I don't want any commotion before the Royal Opera House event. I'll get that out of the way and then I'll tell him everything, otherwise he might try and talk me out of going, or insist that he come along as my body guard.'

'Would that be such a bad thing?'

'Yes, because it will take my focus off my speech if I'm feeling paranoid.'

'Okay. I'll be checking-up on you. I hope it goes well, let's catch up next week,' and she was gone.

The short train ride to Marylebone passed quickly, and soon Isabelle found herself spilling out on to the platform with the hordes of other commuters. Looking at their grey faces, grey suits and crumpled newspapers, she felt pity for their seemingly meaningless daily routines. Pondering the commuters' lives had taken her mind off the task in hand, but as she sat on the tube listening to its familiar rumble and lurching with it as it jolted in and out of the stations, she began to look over her notes to calm her growing nerves.

It felt strange to be travelling to a music venue without her violin. She had nothing to carry, no stares, no negotiating the turnstiles with a bulky case. She was swept along among the throngs of tourists eager to sample Covent Garden.

Standing in Bow Street before the Opera House, she took a moment to appreciate its splendour. Six tall pillars fronted the gleaming pale building, giving it its iconic neo classical appearance. The new adjoining glass atrium that housed the Paul Hamlyn Hall provided a more modern but nonetheless spectacular feature. Isabelle had been surprised to read that over the centuries it had been burned down twice and survived two world wars, but the rebuilding and refurbishment had cemented it as a world class venue with an interesting history. Isabelle had always loved going there, and although she had never performed within its walls, she had seen a few operas and ballets on its hallowed stage. She took a picture with her mobile and sent it to Bill and Lily with a message;

Doing my big speech today! I remember you telling us that Mum performed here as Carmen before we were born!

Isabelle walked through the marble foyer and into the plush red carpeted lobby area, past the box office, towards the west wall and ascended the grand staircase. She climbed the twenty two low rise marble steps also covered in a wide strip of the patterned crimson carpet, held in place by brass bars running the width of the carpet strip. In the middle of the stairs spaced evenly apart stood five decorated brass bar balusters, supporting a mahogany rail that curved round each end of the stairway. There were also wooden hand rails along each side wall, which were covered in large cream coloured panels. As she reached the spacious first half-landing she noticed two large oil paintings on the west wall, separated by three small red wall lamps casting a warm glow, festooned by moulded flowers shaped in garlands above each gilt frame. Directly before her was the modern entrance leading to the Paul Hamlyn Hall, where shafts of light cascaded onto the landing through the wide glass panel above the double doors. She ran her palm over the wooden hand rail of the second, shorter flight of north facing stairs, which had an ornate gilt ironwork railing beneath, running the entire length of the left side of the stairs to where it curved left above the lower stairway. Above her hung a hefty brass Victorian style light illuminating the soaring space from the ceiling to the landing. Its electric candles were enclosed in a single glass case and were blazing. Facing her was the entrance to the Crush Room and hanging on either side were two further large baroque oil paintings. When she reached the first floor landing gallery she turned right through the double glass doors that led to the Conservatory. Long panelled windows adorned by venetian blinds ran the length of the narrow bar, and arched at each end. The distant ceiling curved over them, and palm plants were dotted at each end of the room adding the finishing touch of its colonial décor. Small tables and red velvet covered chairs were spread along the windows, as well as standing tables. Isabelle stood and sipped her tea, watching pedestrians go about their business below her in Bow Street through the slats of the blinds. She then closed her eyes briefly to prepare herself mentally for the task ahead. As she swallowed her last mouthful of warm liquid, she passed back through the glass doors onto the first floor landing again, heading right into the Crush Room. According to Gerry's schedule they were due to take their seats for their sit down meal at 2pm, and then Isabelle along with two other speakers would have ten minutes each to speak afterwards, and the whole fund-raising event was to be finished off with a live performance from the Opera Babes.

She stood in the doorway; taking in the 19th century setting as guests slowly meandered to their seats, apparently equally taken with the lavish décor of the room. Isabelle straightened her sleeveless pale grey sequined waistcoat over her dark grey suit trousers, and removed her jacket as she encountered the warm air in the room. Her heels were sore from rubbing on the back of her three-inch high black stilettos, which she only wore on special occasions. As she came further into the room, she counted ten round tables that were spaced across the sumptuous red carpet, and as Isabelle eyed the long room she couldn't help but be impressed by its Victorian grandeur. The high ceiling, the gilt embellishments on the walls and the two heavily adorned crystal chandeliers gave a feeling of opulence, whilst the 17th century artwork added a historic ambience. A high mirror was placed on the far wall, and a covered baby grand piano sat beneath it.

Once they were all seated the waiting staff worked efficiently and soon she was tucking in to a smoked salmon starter. On one side of her sat a young Asian pianist named Clarence, who it turned out hailed from the Philippines. On the other perched a rotund and middle aged record company producer the others referred to as "Mitch". His grey hair covered the side of his head, leaving a bald patch on top, and his pointy, ruddy features and long front teeth gave him the likeness of a rodent.

He wore an expensive suit, which stretched a little too tightly across his rounded gut.

The conversation on her table was lively. Clarence seemed to warm to her, realising that they both could avoid any awkward questions by sticking together. After the main course had been served, he relaxed and began to tell her his story.

'So Clarence, tell me how old are you, and how long have you been playing?'

'Ma'am, I'm sixteen, and I started playing piano when I was four. It's my first visit to London. I got awarded a scholarship to the Royal Academy, but have not been in the UK for long.'

'Congratulations Clarence. That must be very exciting for you. I studied at the Royal Academy myself when I was younger' Isabelle smiled. 'Did you learn to play in the Philippines?'

'Yes, in my home city of Manila. My mother wanted me to learn, but my teacher said she could not teach a boy with so much potential and do him justice. My father comes from America, he was in the Navy and we moved to California.'

'That must have been quite a culture shock for you at first?'

'Kind of. But I was young. Mother tells me I adapted quickly.'

'If you don't mind me asking, why the move to London? You would have been able to get in to the Juilliard School for example?'

Clarence frowned. 'My parents only wanted the best for me. This is where they wanted me to attend.'

'I'm sure you and your parents won't be disappointed Clarence. Really good luck with your studies. I'd love to hear you perform someday.'

'Thank you Ma'am,' Clarence said.

'What other pursuits do you enjoy?'

'Well I like to play chess. I enjoy the strategy.'

'Something tells me you are good at that too.' Isabelle studied his reaction.

'I'm not bad, but I'm not in the same league as Kasparov. I was a member of a local chess club back home. It's where my parents find me when I'm not practising, which is most of the day.'

'Good for you Clarence. I know us musicians have to put the hours in, but it does us good to relax. It can be detrimental to our development as artists if we become too isolated.'

He nodded in agreement. 'The search for perfection can be an intense pursuit sometimes,' said Isabelle.

A ripple of applause sounded throughout the room. The director of the Opera House had walked up to the podium and was smiling out at them. Someone was tapping a glass, and then silence settled.

'Ladies and gentlemen, I trust you have enjoyed a superb meal courtesy of the Royal Opera House kitchens.' The guests clapped lightly.

'As you are aware, the purpose of today's gathering is to highlight our growing concern with the standard of the musical education our young people have access to in schools across the UK, and of course the lack of opportunities for children in poverty.' All eyes were now trained on him.

'Our primary goal is to successfully lobby the government on the importance of music and other related creative subjects, not only for the enrichment of our youth, but to ensure that future generations of musicians, composers and artists can continue the rich tradition we have in our country. In addition to this, we will be working with inner city schools to support their musical syllabus. I will also ask you all to dig deep into your pockets as there will be a fundraising session at the end of the evening, an opportunity to support our charity "Music for Life". Without your valuable donations we cannot be as effective in bringing to bear pressure on the government to hasten change in the education system.'

He turned directly to the Culture Secretary who seemed to have been deliberately seated as close to the podium as possible. The director waited for the claps to die down before speaking again.

'It seems that with dwindling resources in our schools, music teachers are under increasing pressure. Sadly, the arts are usually where the first cuts are made. I know that many of you in the music and arts industry feel that it's unacceptable for our children to miss out on this opportunity because of the government failings.'

There were murmurs and nods as the room concurred with his statements.

'So it is with much gratitude and excitement that I want to introduce you to our first speaker, a young lady who has come from a family with a strong musical heritage and who has been celebrated as an international star, and one of our best loved home grown violin virtuosos.'

Isabelle could see confusion on some of the guests glowing faces.

'Please give a warm welcome to Isabelle Bryant!'

She felt her legs carry her towards the front of the room. Her pounding heart had all but drowned out the applause. As she inched nearer to the podium she pictured Miranda's innocent face, and her inspiration stirred deep with her. That same feeling she had experienced when walking out on stage with her Nagyvary tucked under der arm, was now pervading her body once again.

With nervous pleasantries out the way, she took a deep breath.

'Music is simply sound, and sound can be described as resonant air. It holds no mystique when described in those terms. Yet this resonant air can affect our health, our mental state, our emotions, our creativity and our memories. It is sublimely subjective. Studies into what physicists call "sympathetic resonance" show the remarkable impact that the vibrations of classical music have on the cells of our bodies. I like to think of it as a kind of cosmic concert.

'While on the subject of literal meanings, the dictionary's definition of the word virtuoso is "extremely skilled" and when related to a person being used as a noun, it refers to an outstanding skill at something, especially at playing an instrument or performing. In other words, it can be summed up as artistic excellence.'

She swept along the attentive faces now watching her.

'I was fortunate to have had the support, the ability and the environment to attain this distinction; to become a virtuoso. I worked hard, but my dedication had a price. Without going into all the gory details, some of you will know that eight months ago I suffered an accident that proved fatal to my soloist's career. You need your fingers intact to play the violin. I tried to eschew my predicament, but I only healed when I faced it.'

Isabelle noticed some members of the audience straining to catch sight of her disfigured hand as it lay inert on the side of the podium.

'But this speech isn't about me, it's about the youngsters. We owe it to them to give them the same opportunities that I had, and indeed many of my contemporaries, and many of you in this room have benefited from. This mission, more than anything else, has come about through my own personal struggles, and has given me a new passion to pursue in the same way I approached my playing.'

A soft applause gave her a moment to take a sip of water. 'Artistic excellence is mainly achieved through nurturing talent and the right education and support. I urge you to give generously to "Music for Life", as it's a great way of making ourselves heard. You, the people in this room can collectively have a profound influence on the future of music in our society. Jamie Oliver did it with school dinners, and we can do it with school music!'

Isabelle sensed she had achieved a good rapport with the audience, and her confidence grew as she continued.

'With this in mind I have recently set up my own music foundation which will be making its very first donation to this charity. I have arranged for a percentage of the royalties from my albums to be paid into the BMS Music Foundation to benefit as many children as possible.'

The red light on the podium flashed its time warning at her.

'We can all be virtuosos in some area of our lives, and for me, if it's no longer going to be as a violinist, I'd like to think that I can give something back to the one thing that has provided me with so much success and happiness over the years. We all need someone to champion us, so let us all be virtuoso supporters for those that need our help. I'd like to conclude that your generosity will provide the inestimable gift of meaning through music to all our students.'

A warm sensation flowed over her as the audience stood to applaud her, and rather more calmly she walked back to her seat.

The next speaker was a music teacher from an inner city secondary school, citing the difficulties he faced providing a musical education and keeping the school orchestra going. It was depressing listening. The last speaker was a young cellist from the Royal Opera House's own orchestra, mainly giving thanks to the charity *Music for Life* that had made it possible for her to progress her cello studies and ultimately join the orchestra she was with now. It was proof of results and just the right note after the teacher's desperate plea. Her speech made Isabelle reflect on Sebastian for a while, and her thoughts drifted to him as the Opera Babes' pure voices carried them away with The *Flower Duet* from Lakme, an aria that had been immortalised in the British Airways adverts that she remembered from her youth.

Afterwards, Mitch's chubby fingers forced his business card into her hand.

'We're always on the lookout for talent.' He smiled, revealing stained teeth. 'Feel free to point any talented youngsters that come out of your foundation our way, we'll sign them and make sure they get a good deal.'

'Thank you,' replied Isabelle as she forced herself to smile at him. 'I trust your firm is also willing to make a donation to such worthy causes?'

His eyes fell to her chest and Isabelle became uneasy.

'Most certainly, Isabelle.'

Royal Opera House staff had been laying envelopes in front of each guest, a form to complete along with a payment section for a donation. Isabelle grabbed her envelope and left Mitch staring after her. She decided to have a wander around the building and evoke some of her childhood memories. She looked at her watch; it was almost 6pm. Guests were already arriving for a performance of Mozart's Magic Flute, due to start at 7pm.

The atrium was now thronging with diners and enthusiastic opera goers, and aiming to find a more peaceful environment she wandered back along to the Conservatory, which was now full of smartly dressed couples and small groups, seemingly engrossed in their private conversations. Standing alone at the bar Isabelle felt a sudden pang for Daniel and began fumbling in her handbag for her phone.

As she was rummaging her elbow took a strong nudge, and she spun round to see who had almost bowled her over. A pungent smell hit her senses before she recognised the person, and instantly it made her want to wretch. A slurred voice muttered an almost inaudible, 'S'cuse me,' as it dawned on her that a very inebriated Howard had almost fallen over her.

She froze to the spot. A dizzy sensation came over. She could feel panic rising.

His bloodshot eyes widened. 'Isabelle! What a pleas, pleasant s-s-surprise,' he slurred again with a hint of sarcasm.

'Howard... What are you doing here?' His ruddy complexion and his muddy blue bloodshot eyes instantly awakened her fear. His glasses only seemed to magnify the crazy look in his eyes. Although smartly dressed he had an air of dishevelment about him, with his pale brown hair in disarray, and his slightly crumpled white shirt was unbuttoned one slot too many.

'What does it look like? I'm enjoying myself!' He proudly swung a glass of whiskey in front of her face. Isabelle stood mute, and as he grabbed her upper arm she almost fainted from the fumes.

'What are you doing here my lovely eh? N-not performing I s-s'pose?' Isabelle recoiled sharply.

'I see your contrite sentiments from our last conversation have gone out the window. It seems the old Howard is back?'

Howard's eyes fixed on her confused and horrified expression. His speech seemed to slow even more and took on a sinister tone. 'He never l-l-left.'

She felt her body begin to shake. With all the control and calmness she could muster Isabelle said, 'It's none of your business what I do with my life Howard. You know, once a loser, always a loser.'

'Once a tart always a t-tart I say!'

Howard seemed oblivious to other people as he hurled his insults at her. Isabelle felt her cheeks burning. Her vision came to rest on the top of a letter poking out of his jacket breast pocket. She recognised the printed heading as belonging to the Royal Opera House. She strained to see the writing, but her concentration was interrupted by Howard's malevolent voice.

'Perhaps you were flirting among the s-s-serious classical artists I've seen c-coming and going today.'

A few of the guests in their vicinity were now staring at them, startled by Howard's spiteful tone and his retarded speech. She stepped past Howard and strode towards the landing, aware of him stumbling after her, voice raised.

'I haven't finished with you yet, you f-f-f-fucking whore!' His eyes were boring into her with pure venom. Isabelle quickly descended the small stairway, and with Howard still on her heels she took a deep breath and turned to face him. Her anger flared uncontrollably.

'How dare you!' She went to slap his face but he caught her arm and twisted her elbow up behind her back. Isabelle yelped under his force.

'Howard what do you want?' Tears had welled up and she strained her neck to see if anyone was close by who could help her. It seemed in a heartbeat opera go-ers had taken their seats and the area had cleared.

'I want you to admit what a s-slut you are, that you never had any talent and to s-say s-s-sorry for spoiling my career. You selfish little bitch!'

'Howard, if you don't let go of my arm I'm going to scream and you'll be arrested for assault!'

'You didn't need to s-sleep around. It was all in the way you dressed and f-f-flirted. Mother warned me you were a h-harlot. I've lost everything because of you!'

'And I suppose I lost nothing! Being your scape-goat is the least of my worries.' Pain shot up her limb as he tightened his grip and pulled her arm even higher behind her back. Her un-zipped handbag slid off her other shoulder, and a moment later her keys and other objects spilled onto the carpet.

'Ever heard of pride go-eth before a f-f-fall my dear?' He pushed her closer to the edge of the grand staircase. Her left hand shot forwards towards the west wall, in an attempt to balance herself as Howard continued to tighten his grip on her bent right arm and at the same time he pushed his right hip into the central balustrade at the top of the mini-landing. She longed for someone to walk through the door way from the Paul Hamlyn Hall behind them and free her from his clutches.

In a moment of sheer panic Isabelle blurted out, 'Is this how you treated Lily before you raped her? Do you know what the payback is for rape Howard? How many other women have you abused?'

'I don't knowing any f-fucking Lily! All I know is I didn't finish you off p-p-properly last time. Now I'm going to t-teach you a lesson once and for all!'

'You don't deserve to have a daughter you animal!' She slapped her hand over her mouth the moment she uttered the words.

Howard held her still, apparently thrown off guard. 'What? What daughter? Liar! You were always were good at d-diverting attention to g-get out of t-telling the truth! Apologise slut!' His eyes blazed with sinister intentions.

'Yes that's right Howard, I'm a liar, perish the thought! You're an insecure and inadequate human being, and the only way you know to annihilate your feelings of frustration and self-loathing is to drown yourself with drink and take it out on women! Your perfect mother has made you a monster Howard!' She yelled back at him. 'You'll get nothing but defiance from me Howard. You've caused enough damage. You can shove your apology where the sun doesn't shine!'

Howard's sanguine complexion deepened to a light shade of purple and his eyes took on that familiar apoplectic stare that she had often tried to shut out of her memory.

A presence above them had captured his attention and looking up he growled, 'Another bitch to t-torment. I'll be able to k-k-kill two birds with one stone.'

Isabelle couldn't turn towards the first floor landing as Howard had her pinned to him and facing the west wall. Sweat had formed on her forehead and her heart was racing as her adrenaline seemed to go into overdrive. In a split second she was aware of other voices, and of the light streaming in behind them from the Paul Hamlyn Hall. She winced as he seemed to renew his grip, and saw her tan handbag laying on the top step, her keys and some make-up strewn along the carpet. The stairs stretched away before her and she could hear movement in the lobby. She glanced at her mutilated hand and tried to shut out the images flashing back into her mind of that fateful night, before succumbing to an overwhelming dizzy sensation in her head. She opened her mouth ready to call out.

With his window of opportunity rapidly closing, Howard pushed her roughly away.

'Vengeance is mine whore!'

Isabelle flew forwards, but her momentum was too great for her to steady herself or alter her trajectory. As she floundered her high heels gave way beneath her and she felt a searing, jagged pain shoot through her ankle as it twisted over to one side. She leant over to clutch it, feeling her whole body contort and twist as she teetered momentarily before toppling over the edge of the top step. She reached out to grab the hand rail but missed.

No sound came out as she fell. Her vision spanned the stairway like a speeding kaleidoscope. She saw Howard step back, then the glint of the chandelier, the swiftly approaching red carpet, the brass balustrades, followed by another sharp pain, this time in her knee and ribs as she crashed down the stairs, smashing her head on one of the four solid feet forming the base of the last balustrade, before rolling like a rag doll onto the exposed marble floor at the foot of the stairs.

Blackness engulfed her.

'Issy? Oh my God Issy. Are you okay?'

Isabelle opened her eyes but they wouldn't focus and she could taste blood. She winced as she tried to bend her waist and sit up. Her muscles felt like jelly and pain seemed to consume her. She kept as still as she could to minimise the intense aching that was pervading her body.

A warm hand was on her forehead, rubbing her hair gently.

'H? Is that really you?'

'I'm here, keep still.'

'My head feels like it's been clamped in a vice and bashed with a hammer,' Isabelle murmured. 'I was too feeble to stop him.'

Hortense lowered her face so that her ear was only inches from Isabelle's mouth.

'H, thank God it's you. Howard...he was drunk...'

'Shush, save your strength. The police and the ambulance are on their way. I just finished my meal in the restaurant overlooking the atrium. I was hoping to surprise you after your charity event. I came searching for you and that's when I saw him assaulting you from across the landing. I'm only sorry I couldn't get to you before he shoved you down the stairs. Howard Miller is not going to escape the wrath of Hortense this time!'

39

Caroline Hess, her interviewer, had made Isabelle feel at ease instantly. She was a short and well-built woman in her forties, with a boyish crop of highlighted mousy brown hair and bright hazel eyes. Isabelle stared at her attractive oval face and perfectly applied makeup with admiration.

'Ready?' Caroline gave her a warm smile.

'As ready as I'll ever be,' replied Isabelle. 'So much has happened in my life since my last radio interview, but this time it feels different somehow. I'm actually looking forward to our chat!'

'That's great. Yes, although we'll be on air in a few moments it should just feel like we're having a private conversation rather than broadcasting.'

Isabelle nodded and then Caroline was introducing her to her listeners. With her usual pleasantries out of the way, she dived into her first question.

'Isabelle, a year ago you suffered a second traumatic incident at the hands of your ex-husband and former conductor Howard Miller. Can you tell us how it has affected you, since he was also implicated in the tragic end to your playing career?'

'It's not something I like to dwell on Caroline, but suffice to say thankfully I only sustained minor injuries compared to the accident that maimed my left hand. I had minor concussion, bruises and a cracked rib. It was more the shock of being in that kind of situation again that affected me. I realised on reflection afterwards that Howard is a tortured soul, and he was completely not himself when he was under the influence of alcohol. I'm not excusing his behaviour, but I am saying that he needs help, and as far as I'm aware the judge who ordered his incarceration specified attendance at Alcoholics Anonymous at the end of his sentence. Even with his privileged background, he was incapable of love. He led a hollow existence so he turned to booze to solve his problems.

'It came to light during the trial that the reason he was there that day was because he had been stalking me. In the weeks leading up to the Royal Opera House encounter I had been getting strange phone calls, creepy correspondence, and he hired a private detective to follow me. He had even broken into my house and taken a document pertaining to my engagement at the Opera House, which is how he knew I was going to be there on that particular day. At first he tried to make out he'd gone for an interview for the assistant conductor position with the Royal Opera House Orchestra, but it turned out he'd already been told point blank that he would probably never work again in this industry, after he maimed me the winter before at our home in Sussex.'

'Sounds like too many people knew about his despicable behaviour towards you, and the alcoholism. But how did you recover from such a cruel action when you had forgiven him and didn't press charges for his first assault on you?' Interjected Caroline.

'Initially I thought he had made some efforts to get cleaned up, but he obviously failed in that too. Instead, he fell spectacularly off the wagon and blamed me for his downfall. In his twisted mind I was the reason he had fallen from grace, and ultimately destroyed his career. I was ignorant of his desire for revenge and his plotting of my demise until it was too late.' Isabelle's voice was matter of fact.

'I don't think of myself as being the victim here, I'm just trying to work out what it was that attracted that set of circumstances to me. Perhaps someone up there was giving me the opportunity to finally rid myself of him. Anyhow as you know, we had an altercation and he tried to finish me off by pushing me down the stairs. I knew I had to deal with it better than I did when my fingers were lost...'

Isabelle paused. 'Since then I've lost a good friend and fellow musician to Malaria, so I keep reminding myself that life's too short for recriminations, condemnation and regret. I need to keep my energy strong so that I don't become depressed again. After I had a chance to analyse what happened I put it down to synchronicity.'

'Can you explain that a little further Isabelle?'

'I'll do my best. The way I understand it, the theory that was proposed by the late Carl Jung, is that a group of seemingly unrelated events can happen to you, and you might be forgiven for thinking that they are co-incidences. But his theory says that in fact they are connected by an unseen force that is organised and that is behind everything.'

'Fate dressed up in different clothes?' Asked Caroline.

'It's a little heavy I know, but I now understand I had to take responsibility for being in the position of marrying him in the first place. Amazingly, out of that situation arose so many other wonderful connections and opportunities that have enriched my life. I think it's healthy to look upon one's trials as a kind of evolution. I don't harbour any bitter thoughts of revenge - that would be futile. I need to focus on the things I want to achieve still.'

'It's remarkably forgiving of you, and in the spirit of forgiveness you have chosen a wonderful piece of contemporary choral music by Karl Jenkins called Sanctus from his album *The Armed Man, A mass For Peace.* We'll be back with you after this heavenly interlude.'

Caroline squeezed her hand as the music started to air.

'Well done, and thanks for coming on the show, I know it can't be easy for you to re-live these ordeals, even if he is behind bars now.'

'That's okay. I appreciate you helping me to promote my foundation, plus it's kinda therapeutic.'

'Well, you'll certainly get the sympathy vote with the listeners,' she said, fiddling with some dials. Isabelle lost herself in the majestic choral music. 'The euphony of human voices definitely reaches parts of the soul that speech can't.'

Soon they were back on air.

'So Isabelle, tell us about your latest project and what inspired you to undertake it?'

'Well, first of all I couldn't have done anything without the help of my Agent, Gerry Goldberg, and many of my friends and associates who have contributed in so many ways. I really owe the idea to a young girl named Miranda who I met when I was in Australia. She really nailed it for me. I knew I always wanted to give something back to society, but initially I didn't know how to, as I was struggling with my own grief over the loss of my fingers.'

Caroline nodded.

'I mentioned earlier that a very close friend of mine passed away recently – Sebastian Cortez-Smith, who was the lead cellist at the LPO and whom I miss very much. Seb was a great musician and we studied together at the Royal Academy for a while, as we were both starting out on our careers. The foundation I have created is the Bryant, Miranda, Smith Foundation, or BMS for short.

Our aim is to provide funds for musical tuition to talented or troubled underprivileged children of school age; offering them meaning through music.'

'As I understand it you have set up the foundation as a charity using the royalties from your very last Album, *The Virtuoso,* and also with donations from other individuals and institutions?'

"That's right. I'm so very grateful to all our donors for helping make this venture possible. We've also established a website for the BMS Foundation where people can donate online, and it will be updated regularly with our progress on various projects, although specific children's details will not be divulged for obvious reasons.'

'Can you tell us what sort of projects will be catered for at the foundation?'

'Basically, it will be any situation where we can positively impact the lives of young people. It could be for example; a talented musician whose parents' can't afford tuition to take them to the next level of performance. It could be a group of autistic children that benefit from music therapy, purely to help them communicate, to enjoy the music and aid with their self-expression. I'm passionate about finding new talent, and eventually we hope to open our own centre for advanced tuition and mentoring for serious musicians. Predominantly it will be stringed instruments; the violin, viola and cello, and the piano. Hopefully in the future, also some wind instruments like the flute, clarinet and oboe. A lot depends on funding and the teaching skills available to us. Like any new venture, we will have to start small and grow according to demand.'

'Well, I can say that we've already had some emails, broadly saying that more successful musicians should exhibit such philanthropic tendencies. The public seem to respect the move and wish you the utmost success.'

'That's great. I really do appreciate everyone's support. The more money we can raise the better it will be for the children.'

'I've read in a previous article that you wrote for *High Notes* magazine that Beethoven was your musical hero. Who else can you attribute your own personal success as a virtuoso to?'

'I owe so much to my parents. My mother was a professional soprano, so we were exposed to a lot of classical music at a young age, and it was her that suggested I have violin lessons. In fact, my mother was almost pathological about my practice, and Dad was a music teacher and so he helped me. After my mother died, my father went back to his native Australia where he still teaches today. He loves the kids. What I respected about them was that they didn't push my brother and sister into a career in music when it wasn't what they really wanted. They knew I loved music and the violin especially, and they gave me more than enough encouragement, and that's what I'd like to offer to young hopefuls who don't have the benefit of a supportive family unit, or maybe they do but their finances won't enable them to learn beyond what tuition they may receive in school.'

'We'll talk some more shortly with my guest Isabelle Bryant, best known for her skill with the violin, and more recently a regular featured writer for *High Notes* magazine and founder of the BMS music foundation. But right now I'm going to play a piece taken from Isabelle's last album, *The Virtuoso*, and it's the first movement of the hauntingly beautiful Sibelius Violin Concerto in D Major, which she told me earlier she loved to play. We hope you enjoy this marvellous recording of Isabelle Bryant playing Sibelius.'

As soon as the soulful palette of the Nagyvary sang out with the familiar notes Isabelle found herself welling up.

'You okay?'

Isabelle nodded. 'I'll be fine. Don't worry you won't have to abandon the interview.'

'I can't imagine how emotional it must be for you to hear yourself playing.'

'It gets easier as time goes by, but occasionally I get a little choked up, even now. I still miss playing very much.'

'Will you be okay to talk about it?'

'It'll do me good, I'm sure.'

Every note flashed before her eyes as she listened in silence to the rest of the movement. Caroline's voice lifted Isabelle from the depths of her memory.

'That was pure magic Isabelle, you must be very proud that you were able to light up people's lives with such a talent.'

'Thank you.'

'Isabelle, can you tell us something about the violin that you played for the last album, and what happened to it after your accident?'

'It would be my pleasure Caroline. I have very fond memories of that violin. It was made by the Hungarian born professor Joseph Nagyvary, a biochemist who had studied Stradivarius violins down to the molecular level. Any musician will tell you that it's vital to have a close bond with your instrument. As the violin was on loan to me, part of the contract was that if I was no longer using it, for whatever reason; that it had to be returned. At the time it was excruciating to let it go, but honestly it's better for it to be with someone who can play it, and make its tones heard.'

'How did he get Nagyvary violins to sound like a priceless Stradivarius? I understand that there was some controversy over the claims?'

'I suppose you could say it's at the cutting edge of science and art. Each note is played many times into a computer based signal analyser, which provides a fingerprint of the sound. The violin is re-worked until the fingerprint resembles those of the priceless Stradivarius and Guarnerius violins. It means modern violins that are the fraction of the cost of a Stradivarius are available to musicians, and ostensibly cannot be differentiated in their sound quality from that of the great master. In fact, his violins have already been collectively dubbed Nagyvarius. There have been public experiments between the Leonardo Da Vinci Strad and a Nagyvary made in 2003, and the results conclusively favoured the tone of the Nagyvary.'

'So his unique understanding of the materials and the chemicals that went into the wood and varnish of a Stradivarius have enabled him to use modern technology as a way of replicating that quality?'

'That's right. His passion for the instrument is wonderful. I believe his first formal violin lesson was on a violin that Einstein had owned. Although the centuries old Cremona made violins are irreplaceable, thanks to him we now have a comparable modern instrument. There's a very interesting article in Scientific American with him, and he talks about how Stradivarius violins project a strong tone in the higher frequencies, and in a concert hall environment it becomes even more sonorous. Also their low, dark components add texture to the overall palette.

'I'm so grateful that Dr. Nagyvary managed to escape from an oppressive communist regime in Hungary in 1956, otherwise we would not have the benefit of these amazing instruments.'

Caroline looked up sharply, and appeared to be in deep concentration as she listened intently to instructions coming through her headphones. Isabelle wondered if she had said anything out of place.

Caroline smiled at her as she spoke into the microphones.

'Thank you for that wonderful insight into modern and antique violins Isabelle. And now, we interrupt the show for a special caller to talk to Isabelle Bryant.'

She shot an alarmed glance at Caroline. For what seemed like eons all she could hear was her heart beating in her ears. Then the line clicked indicating that the caller was on-air. She could hear Caroline's voice again.

'Hello and welcome to the Caroline Hess Interview. Please state your name and question for my guest today; the virtuoso Isabelle Bryant.'

The gap between voices lasted for an eternity.

'Hello Caroline, my name is Daniel Carter. I'm the director of the European publications of Hudson Publishing Inc., one of which is *High Notes* magazine in the UK.'

Her familiar parched mouth sensation had returned.

'Isabelle, I know you must be a little confused right now, but I want the whole world to know how much I love you. But before I ask you what I came on the show to ask you, I want to read you a letter. It's not penned by me I'm afraid, but I'm totally aligned with its sentiments and intentions, and I hope you'll appreciate the use of this *particular* author. Of course we are different people, and it's a different zeitgeist, but nevertheless- you are my immortal beloved.'

His last two words indicated what was coming. Isabelle's jaw dropped.

He cleared his throat and began to read:

'*Good morning, on July 7. Though still in bed, my thoughts go out to you, my Immortal Beloved, now and then joyfully, then sadly, waiting to learn whether or not fate will hear us - I can live only wholly with you or not at all - Yes, I am resolved to wander so long away from you until I can fly to your arms and say that I am really at home with you, and can send my soul enwrapped in you into the land of spirits - Yes, unhappily it must be so - You will be the more contained since you know my fidelity to you.*

'No one else can ever possess my heart - never - never - Oh God, why must one be parted from one whom one so loves. And yet my life in V is now a wretched life - Your love makes me at once the happiest and the unhappiest of men - At my age I need a steady, quiet life – can that be so in our connection? My angel, I have just been told that the mail coach goes every day - therefore I must close at once so that you may receive the letter at once - Be calm, only by a calm consideration of our existence can we achieve our purpose to live together - Be calm - love me - today - yesterday - what tearful longings for you - you - you - my life - my all - farewell. Oh continue to love me – never misjudge the most faithful heart of your beloved.

Ever thine, ever mine, ever ours.'

The silence was palpable.

'Isabelle Bryant, will you make me the happiest of men, and marry me?'

As she studied Isabelle's stunned expression, Caroline swallowed hard.

'Forgive me Daniel, I am at a loss for words, this is the last thing I was expecting!'

'I know it's not a conventional approach, but that was never my style, and I don't think it's yours either Isabelle.'

'Well… I'm going to be conventional now, and simply say, yes!' A few seconds passed without reply.

'Dan honey, are you still there?'

'Yes, I'm still here, just coming back down from the ceiling! I'm so happy words can't really express my feelings. I love you sweetheart. See you later for some serious celebrations!'

'Thank you Daniel, and thank you Isabelle. We are all very honoured to have been party to such a moving and poetic proposal of marriage. It seems only fitting to end the show with a romantic piece composed by Beethoven, played many times by my guest today; a remarkable violinist turned public speaker, and more recently a fundraiser and campaigner through her foundation for bringing music into the lives of both talented and troubled children in the UK, Isabelle Bryant. Here is his ever popular violin Romance in F Major.'

Isabelle removed her headphones, barely able to take in what had just transpired.

'Thank you Caroline, it must have been hard not to give away what you knew was coming.'

'It's my pleasure Isabelle. That ranks as one of the most wonderful interviews I've ever done. Best of luck to both of you!'

Isabelle felt like she was walking on air as she left the studio.

Her mobile bleeped bringing her momentarily out of her euphoria. Gerry's words stared at her from the screen;

CONGRATULATIONS! That's my girl!
G x

THE END

20737950R00268

Printed in Great Britain
by Amazon